The Rag Tree

A Novel of Ireland

ISBN: 1-4392-2831-0

EAN13: 9781439228319

Visit www.booksurge.com to order additional copies.

The Rag Tree

A Novel of Ireland

D. P. Costello

BookSurge Publishing
Charleston, South Carolina

Danny Costello is a second generation Irish-American with roots in Counties Galway and Kerry. He has visited Ireland forty times since 1978. Educated by the Jesuits in Washington, D.C., he has been part of the capital city's vibrant Irish music scene for going on thirty years. *The Rag Tree* is his first novel.

To learn more about *The Rag Tree* and other writings and music of author D. P. Costello visit **www.theragtree.com**

More Praise for *The Rag Tree*

"*The Rag Tree* lights up the page like a cinematic gem... a lilt and a rhythm enveloping each word... The novel brims with mysticism... an unlikely hero's journey... non-stop intrigue." —Chiquita Mullins Lee, playwright, *Pierce to the Soul,* author, *Rainbow Season.*

"*The Rag Tree* is a novel that weds the New Ireland with the faeries, banshees and talking crows. The marriage thrives because the writing is gorgeous and the characters – musicians, politicians, IRA informants and a lethal priest – are absolutely believable." — Denis Collins, author of *Nora's Army*

"A magical imagining of old Ireland meeting the new Ireland. Costello's vivid language in his first book, *The Rag Tree* is enough to make you believe in pookas; that is, if you don't already." — Dan Barry, author of *Pull Me Up: A Memoir*

"The latest in that enchanting line of Irish myth-spinners, D.P. Costello offers a terrific tale of politics, loyalty, tradition, betrayal, love and hard choices. When you turn the last page of The Rag Tree, you'll want to pack your bags immediately and hop on the next flight into Shannon." —Jack O'Connell, author of *The Resurrectionist*

Even a newspaperman, if you entice him
into a cemetery at midnight,
will believe in phantoms, for everyone is a visionary,
if you scratch him deep enough.
But the Celt is a visionary without scratching.

W. B. Yeats

From the introduction of
Fairy and Folktales of the Irish Peasantry — 1888

The Roads of Ireland

There are no straight roads
In Ireland.
They weave, twist,
Hump, dive, turn, writhe,
And dance;
And even when they vow
To run direct before you,
They've got doubling back
In mind.

Ahhhhhhhhh...

They're the true map
Of the Irish soul.

Séamas Ó Flannagáin

For My Mother and Father

The Characters

Mattie Joe Treacy: the Rag Man

Bab Treacy, the Faery Woman of Bamford Cross: Mattie Joe's mother

Biddie Tynan: Bab's best friend and next door neighbor

Cait McGrath: Expatriate Irishwoman, journalist

Kevin O'Felan: Special Detective Unit, Garda Síochána, head of the Rag Man investigation

Peter Doyle: Special Detective Unit, O'Felan's partner

Skinny Farrell: Surveillance expert with the Special Detective Unit

Brigadier General Bartley Drummond: Commander-in-Chief of British Forces in Ulster

Captain Anthony Greenwell: British soldier, Drummond's attaché

Finbar Lawlor: Psychologist who works in an advisory capacity for the Special Detective Unit

Silvia Hickey: Detective Inspector, Scotland Yard

Rev. Brendan Sheils: Catholic priest

Donal Mór O'Toole: Imprisoned IRA leader

Desmond O'Hanrahan: Irish Taoiseach (Prime Minister)

Mariead O'Hanrahan: The Taoiseach's wife

Cathal Slattery: Business tycoon

Mick Mulvihill: Folksinger

Brian: Pooka (a faery spirit most often taking the form of an animal)

The Blackbird—A shadowy figure

At a time not so very long ago

Prologue

… but above all, he was a soldier for Ireland.

Father Brendan Sheils was a few minutes early for the evening meeting, so he used the moment to open his breviary and reflect upon its opening prayer. He was standing outside the appointed meeting place, a whitewashed country pub near Monaghan town called Tíg Tommy's. His shoulder pressed against a lamppost and the black prayer book sat opened atop his colossal belly, like a bird alighting on a black boulder. Indeed, prayer and fine food were his favorite diversions. This evening he feared he wouldn't find much joy in either, though. His appointment, a teenager eighteen years of age, had sounded in a bad way over the phone.

Anymore, it seemed that every phone call was from someone in trouble. Teenagers especially were prone to problems that not so long ago belonged to the rest of the world, but not in quiet and holy Ireland. Unwanted pregnancies and substance addictions were so commonplace now that, deep down, Father Brendan wished that the trouble facing tonight's youth would be so minor. He had reason to fear otherwise. A man in Father Brendan's position heard things others did not, after all.

The man of God closed his black prayer book and took interest in a darkening sky moving over Monaghan's solemn blue-green hills, like a charcoal brush scraping over velvet. Murmuring a little prayer that the young man he was to meet might beat the rain, he decided to pass the remaining wait by reading a copy of the *Irish Independent* that he had intended to savor later along with a rack of lamb and a glass of fine red wine. Thinking of how he'd particularly been looking forward to the column written by the syndicated American journalist, Thomas F.X. Hennessy, he contemplated the need for a second glass of wine, at least. A wind kicked up and blew apart the newspaper's pages, so instead of reading Hennessy, his eyes fixed on a report about the recent IRA escape from the Maze Prison in Belfast. One dead. (Not including a poor cat that had the misfortune of being caught in some sort of crossfire in a Lisburn flat.) One wounded and captured. Four on the run. Names of the escapees had not been released. Father Brendan searched the small article for any hint of other news, but found none. Irish newspapers anymore were all about reporting on the booming economy. The old troubles in the north were treated just like that—old troubles.

Hennessy columns were causing quite a stir in Ireland. Twice a week, the American offered deft, thousand-word opinions on Irish politics and man-on-the-street attitudes, as Ireland moved toward a national referendum that could sever the country from its history for the sake of money— lots and lots of money. Many a family meal in Ireland was being ruined by the factions lining up for and against what Hennessy had to say about the Eire Nua or "New Ireland" referendum. He unfolded the newspaper to page two and gave Hennessy an initial overview—as sort of a starter— since he still was hoping Hennessy would join him for the rack of lamb.

Today, the American journalist was probing the referendum's basic issue: that a "Yes" vote enabled Ireland to move away from its historical position of military neutrality and reap huge American dollars as a result. The U.S. military had secretly coveted Ireland's airstrips and harbors for its western European air and naval outposts. A "Yes" vote meant the Yanks no longer would have to squabble with the irascible French every time they wanted to fly their war-planes into the Middle East. The truth of it was, the diehard Irish nationalists were the most vocal in opposition to the referendum. For them, even the hint of stepping away from neutrality was tantamount to abandoning the Six Counties in the north. An Ireland open to Yank military would also be open to the Brits, and this, from an Irish nationalist point of view, was an intolerable position altogether. The diehard Protestant Loyalist, on the other hand, found the issue to be a conundrum. Whereas he believed it only fair and just that the Irish pull their full weight within the European Union, he was against anything that led to a stronger Ireland, since, in his mind, it spelled ultimate doom for Protestant Ulster.

Unable to contain his appetite for the national debate, Father Brendan was just settling in to a second read of Hennessy's column when, from behind the bar, there came the sound of a car crunching over loose chippings. He moved with a soft waddle to the bar window and pressed his nose flat above the G in the Guinness sign. A skinny lad moved hesitantly through the bar's rear door. He'd grown tall, like an arrow, since Father Brendan had last seen him.

Tíg Tommy's was long, narrow, and dim. A small huddle of men clung to pints of black porter and stared at a mammoth flat screen television hanging from a wood paneled ceiling, which had turned the color of port wine with age. The drinkers were too mesmerized by the replay of an English soccer match to notice a man of God, much less greet him. Alas, there was no luster on the clergy in Ireland anymore, Father Brendan thought. His appointment sat at a low round table near the other end of the bar. Out of the dusk, his wet blue eyes shone in Father Brendan's direction.

Malachy McKee was tall and copper-topped, the image of his father twenty-five years and forty pounds ago. A smile flashed across his freckled face. The smile was a family tic. Father Brendan knew all the McKees, going back to the grandfather, to grin spontaneously, even when there was absolutely no reason to smile. This young McKee even drank large bottles of ale, just like his father.

Father Brendan placed his breviary atop the low round table. "God, but you're looking well," he said, grabbing and shaking a freckled arm that felt more like a piece of kindling he might be tossing into a fire. Just below the elbow was a tattoo of a green Phoenix rising out of red and gold flames. The inscription below read, *"From the ashes of '69 rose the Provisionals."* It occurred to Father Brendan that the boy hadn't yet been born in 1969.

They made small talk in very low voices. The whispering voice, Father Brendan knew, was far more desperate than even cries and shouts. Mostly, the boy kept his lips to the bottle, emptying it so swiftly that it was obvious he was not a stranger to drink. He'd bare his soul soon, Father Brendan thought. It was in his family's nature.

"I have to leave Ireland," Malachy McKee blurted in a restrained whisper. His lips then sank instantly back into the bottle, as if his utterance had exhausted him. Father Brendan said nothing. Instead, he placed a hand on the boy's heaving shoulder and waited. "I hadn't a choice, Father," Malachy McKee continued. "The RUC said that they could put me away for thirty years. Annie, too. That's the worst of it. That's why—"A single teardrop escaped from the dam building in his blue eyes and rolled freely over a pronounced cheekbone. "It's why I hadn't a choice."

Father Brendan understood what the boy was saying. The Royal Ulster Constabulary had caught him and this Annie—must be the girlfriend—involved in republican activities. Malachy would have been forced to play ball and provide information to the security forces, or risk sending himself and the girlfriend to prison for IRA related crimes. Why a dozen men from Malachy's Derry neighborhood had been sent to prison in the last year no longer seemed a mystery. "Have you spoken to your father?" Father Brendan asked.

The boy's jaw twitched. "He won't speak to me. My mother either. I'm dead to both of them. They never liked Annie, anyway. But I have to leave Ireland, now. Will you help me, Father? Please?"

Father Brendan slowly and softly took Malachy McKee's thin hand off the bottle and placed it on top the breviary on his lap. "It would do me no good to lecture on the evils of dealing with the hard men, or that lads like you are just the fuel that keeps Ireland's sorrow burning. But yes, I will help you. Just as Simon became Peter and Saul became Paul, you, Malachy, must repent for your sins and become a new man."

Father Brendan ordered two more drinks and spoke of a priest friend teaching at a university in Seville, Spain, where

Malachy could work for his room and board, as well as get a university education. Safe passage would be arranged for him—and Annie, too—but it would take a day or two. "Until then, you'll have to stay with me at the rectory. Speak to no one, including Annie." The teenager listened and acknowledged Father Brendan's wisdom, including the advice that they remained in Tíg Tommy's until they could slip away to the rectory under the cover of darkness. With a rising mood, they passed another hour; Father Brendan continued to buy the drinks. Occasionally, he'd ask Malachy questions about his involvement with the RUC. "Have they mentioned anything to you about someone called The Rag Man?" he said.

The blue eyes, now dry and eager, opened wider. "In fact they have," Malachy said. "Just the other day, my handler— that's the RUC man squeezing me—he asked me about a Rag Man, as if I should know. But I know fuck-all—Sorry for the language, Father."

They left Tíg Tommy's in a downpour beating against the windscreen so fiercely that Father Brendan pulled over on a quiet stretch of road where the hedgerows had grown together to form a thick canopy. The rain dripped slowly through the tangle of branches in thick, single drops, reminding Father Brendan of teardrops. "I've new wiper blades in the boot," he told Malachy. "Perhaps they could be of some use. But I'm all thumbs with mechanical things."

The slim teenager was eager to help. He was more than a tad tipsy with drink, too. Twice he fumbled the keys to the boot. Father Brendan reached for the flash lamp he kept stowed beneath the driver's seat and brought it and his breviary out into the rain. He planned to ask the boy if he needed light, but Malachy was drunk enough so as not to be aware of anyone standing behind him. With the breviary tucked in the crook of an arm as one might carry a football, Father Brendan's other hand raised the flash lamp over his head. He then brought it down onto the boy's skull with the full weight of his vast bulk behind it.

Malachy McKee was so very light that Father Brendan had little difficulty using just the one arm to drag him into a hawthorne ditch while still clutching onto the breviary. There was a chance the boy was dead already. Opening the black prayer book to where pages had been carved away, he removed a revolver that lay in the hollow. From the boot of the car, he pulled a plastic trash bag and three short lengths of rope that he used to tie the boy's hands and feet. He used the last strand to secure the trash bag around Malachy McKee's head. Again, it was no trouble at all lifting such a rawboned body into a kneeling position. Father Brendan placed the barrel of the revolver on the lump on the boy's skull. The pounding rain muffled the revolver's retort. Droplets splattered in a slow but steady beat against the black plastic trash bag, and Father Brendan reflected on how few tears would be shed for a dead informer. He then twined rosary beads around Malachy McKee's limp fingers and whispered, "Lord, for your faithful people life is changed, not ended."

Father Brendan was a man of God, but above all, he was a soldier for Ireland.

Part I

The Escape

I

...neighbors referred to them as two peas in a pod.

Four days after the escape

Biddie Tynan stood in a soft morning mist with her nose stuck to the keyhole of the red kitchen door belonging to the farmhouse of Bab Treacy, her neighbor and best friend, for all their sixty-seven years. Capturing the warm aroma of fresh baked rhubarb tart, she knew instantly that she'd won last night's argument. Rhubarb tart was Biddie's favorite sweet. It was as close to an apology as she'd ever get from the mule-headed likes of Barbara Concepta Marie Treacy. Snuggling her nose against the keyhole, Biddie savored the sweet and sour scent of victory.

That Biddie and Bab had quarreled was hardly unusual. Best friends were bound to disagree now and again, especially two widows like themselves, who had spent their whole lives doing what the other was doing.

1

In fact, ever since they'd been able to crawl, neighbors referred to them as two peas in a pod. Biddie dearly liked being two peas in a pod with Bab, though for many years, it seemed as if she was the lesser of the two peas. Bab had always been taller, prettier, smarter, the first married (although they had both married lads named Tim), and the only one of them to bear a child. (Bab had even beaten out Biddie in miscarriages, four to two.) For the longest time, it bothered Biddie greatly to be the barren one. But with each passing day, Bab's son, Mattie Joe, grew into the divil himself, and Biddie long ago stopped considering herself the lesser of the two peas.

Last evening's row had been over utter nonsense, in Biddie's opinion. Who cared if there were faeries living beneath the scrawny blackthorn, known as the Rag Tree, growing upon a small knoll at the edge of the Treacy farm? Not Biddie, and she had said as much to her superstitious old fool of a best friend, too. Anyway, she'd won. The rhubarb tart was proof of that.

The long and short of the Rag Tree of Bamford Cross story was, if someone were to tie a scrap of cloth to the tree and make a worthy wish, that wish would come true, if and when the rag fell to the ground. Down through the years, people were after claiming cures for all classes of ills and diseases as well as changes in personal fortunes, all on account of the Rag Tree. Biddie figured that half of these claims were bunk, and the other half were due to good Catholics having their prayers answered. For her money, Biddie would rather put her chances with a good Padre Pio relic.

Throughout the parish, Bab Treacy was known as "the Faery Woman of Bamford Cross" because she knew all there was to know about the old spirits and even older legends.

To hear Bab tell it, she was the "guardian" of the Rag Tree, so entrusted by the Daoine Maithe themselves to keep away all trespassers. Daoine Maithe, meaning Good Folk, was the proper Irish term for the faeries. Bab said the words "faeries" and "little people" were disrespectful terms. Little people, good people, it mattered not a tuppence to Biddie. She pulled her nose from the red door's keyhole just long enough to peer over at the tree with its strange collection of rags that reminded her of Joseph's coat of many colors, torn to shreds and hung out to dry. She'd half a mind to hang a wishing rag herself, if it would help Bab to cease believing in such mindless superstition. It would be one less source of contention between them.

In Biddie's view, it didn't take much to be deemed a trespasser at the faeries' Rag Tree. She'd seen Bab chase away old men with canes, on account she didn't trust the look of the dog that followed them.

Why just last evening Biddie *herself* had been declared a trespasser, and she hadn't even gone near the blasted tree. She very carefully rubbed a finger over the wound on her neck where Bab had smacked her with a spatula. It still stung to the touch. She couldn't be too angry with her best friend, though. Bab was always a bit more irritable when Mattie Joe was away, and the lousy drunken creature had been gone now for a fortnight, no doubt boozing it up and chasing loose women. But loneliness didn't suit some people, and arguing with them when they were in such a state was to take one's own chances. So, in a way, Biddie only had herself to blame for getting smacked with the spatula. Taking a final, satisfying whiff of the rhubarb tart, she stepped through the red door. "Fine day," she said.

Bab stood hunched at the cooker, frying eggs. "It's raining," she said, not bothering to turn and offer a "hello."

Bab was wearing her familiar blue, flowered housedress. Unlike Biddie, her best friend had never taken to the styles of the day; you'd sooner see the Pope in a pair of jeans than you would catch Bab wearing a bit of denim. A blue ribbon tied back Bab's chestnut hair, which somehow had defied turning grey. Biddie herself had turned to the bottle years before. She now was a Summer Sunset blonde.

"Mind you don't make that egg too runny," Biddie cautioned. Then she hastily added, "Please," when she saw Bab gripping down on the lethal spatula.

Bab said nothing, rather she let the clang of the spatula against the fry pan announce her mood. Biddie shouldn't have had to tell Bab how to cook her egg at all; but going back nearly a year now, Bab had taken to cooking the eggs a bit runny, as she used to do for her husband. Sometimes Bab would put a piece of black pudding on Biddie's plate, too. It was Bab's Tim who had liked the black pudding, not Biddie, though she'd swallow it just to keep the peace. She didn't like eating someone else's eggs, though.

The *Irish Independent* lay on the table next to Biddie's cup of tea. "Oh, Bab! Did ye read Hennessy this morning, no? He says that the Taoiseach is giving away free tickets over the Internet to the Rock 'n Nua concert. Would you believe that there's going to be a rock concert just up the road at Kilkenny Castle?"

Bab switched her attention from the fry pan to the sausages warming on the cooker, as if she hadn't heard a word Biddie had just said.

Biddie shook the wrinkles from the newspaper and read, "The O'Hanrahan government hopes its spectacular Rock 'n Nua concert music will be the magnet that brings together tens of thousands of Irish young people in support of the Eire Nua. By no coincidence, the concert is scheduled just one week prior to the initiative vote, now only three weeks away."

Bab stood over the table holding the still steaming teakettle. Her face, beet red from a lifetime of working the farm in harsh Irish winters, held proud and square, like one of Ireland's castles. "We won't be able to go to any concert, Biddie Tynan. We'll be home calming the cows. The rock music would deafen a bat. Heat up your tea?"

Biddie held up her cup. "Bats are already deaf," she said.

Bab shot her a hard look. "Are you starting with me already, Biddie Tynan? Bats are blind, not deaf."

The dust of last night's row still clung to Bab. Then again, Bab had not poured the tea over Biddie's hands, nor had she flipped over the table—sure signs that Biddie and her best friend were well along the path to reconciliation. Wasn't the rhubarb tart cooling on the windowsill, after all?

"C'mon, Bab. We're not too old to go to any concert. Why Hennessy says here that Mick Mulvihill himself is coming out of retirement, just for this one night. You were mad for Mick Mulvihill once, remember?" Bab dropped a plate of fried eggs, rashers, sausages, and beans onto the table with a clatter.

"I remember more about Mick Mulvihill than I want to admit," she said, wringing her hands hard inside an apron already dotted with smudges of the morning's earlier wringings. "I remember in the '60s Mick Mulvihill singing songs for the working man. In the '70s, he sang to free the oppressed peoples in the North. In the '80s, he sang for the hunger strikers. But divil the song about the troubles or the workingman or the republican movement you've heard from him since. Now he's after singing for Eire Nua. I tell you this, Biddie Tynan," Bab drew her hands out of her apron, and up into the air went the condescending index finger that Biddie detested. Bab's voice trembled at the edge of fever pitch. "Mick Mulvihill has always been and always will be on the front end of any down wind. I wouldn't walk as far as your farmhouse to hear the likes of Mick Mulvihill sing one of his protest songs, because by the time I got back to my own house, he'd be singing a song for the other side—if that's where the money was."

Her proclamation over, Bab sat down to a breakfast of grilled tomatoes and mushrooms—to lower her cholesterol, she claimed, though Biddie suspected high blood pressure, too. How else could one account for such an ill temper?

"But Bab, Mick Mulvihill hasn't been singing about anything, let alone the republican movement. He's after having been in alcohol and drug rehabilitation for the better part of two years. Besides, he's a legend, so. And you used to love his songs."

Bab had moved to the sink where she began banging around the pots and pans as she scrubbed. "What else does Hennessy have to say?" Bab asked, with the barest hint of a civil tone.

"Well, he goes on a bit about the escape from the Maze and the aftermath. The death toll is up to two, what with that poor detective being shot in Dublin yesterday. That's not counting the dead cat found in Lisburn, of course. The papers are suggesting there is some connection."

"Don't waste my time on the sidebar stories; I'm after asking what Hennessy has to say. Could you not stick to the point?"

Biddie hid her face behind the newspaper and heaved a heavy sigh. "Hennessy says that the captured IRA man named Liam Riordon is now sitting naked in Portlaoise gaol.

He says Riordon is a symbol for the republican movement in the New Ireland."

"Naked IRA men? I thought they gave up on that sort of caper years ago."

"Well, apparently this Riordon fellow thought he'd give the prison nudity thing another go, on account of the Eire Nua referendum. I'll skim Hennessy, so. 'Riordon... fighting for a nebulous dream of an even more nebulous freedom... sits isolated—just as Ireland... a small nation haunted by its past... sits alone and hopes that other nations will come and invest in her economical freedom... '" Biddie folded up the newspaper. "You're right as rain, Bab. I don't think the IRA should have that man on protest when Ireland is trying to promote Eire Nua to foreign investors. It's a harmful distraction, altogether."

"What are you talking about, Biddie Tynan? The oppressed people of the north can't afford to miss the opportunity to gain notoriety for their struggle while the whole world has its eye on Ireland. Riordon is well within his rights to protest. I support him."

"Well, come to think of it, I can see the wisdom in what you're saying, Bab. I support Riordon being naked, too."

"I said I support his right to protest, not his deviant behavior of going naked."

"Oh, the IRA is full of deviants. You know I've always said that, Bab. What with this cavorting with the likes of Libyans and Russians. Deviants. That's what they are, sure. I've no time for the likes of them."

Bab spoke as she scrubbed away at the breakfast dishes. "Oh, so it's the Russians and the Libyans that make the freedom fighters deviants, is it? Well, did they call the men of 1916 deviants for cavorting with Germans? And what about the Yanks? People have no trouble at all with taking

7

guns and money from the Yanks. Sure, what's the difference where the bullet comes from? It's where the bullet ends up; that's the only thing that matters."

The old creeping feeling of being the lesser of the two peas was coursing on Biddie's bones, and there didn't seem to be any escape from the pod this time. "Well, I've always been for the freedom fighters of the north, just not ones that go around protesting naked. You know that to be true, don't you, Bab?" she said, her voice becoming embarrassingly desperate. "And I suppose a gun from the Russians is no worse than a gun from Libya or America. Sure, a gun is a gun. That's what I've always said. Yes, a gun is a gun is a gun."

Just when Biddie thought she needed a miracle to save her rhubarb tart from the contrary Bab, she got one, but not before getting an awful fright, too. Bab turned from the sink wielding her weapon of choice.

"Trespasser!" Bab barked. "Outside at the Rag Tree." She then shoved the spatula into Biddie's shaking hands. "Chase her off before she upsets the Daoine Maithe and brings bad luck on my house."

Biddie wanted to say that it was more than a little late to keep bad luck away from the Treacy farmhouse, but she didn't dare. She took the spatula and moved outside into the soft rain, wondering why it was that she always did what bossy Bab Treacy told her to do. In her view, the Good Folk weren't good at all. The wee shites caused nothing but hassle. "Shoo. Go away," she called, waving the spatula at a pretty red-haired woman holding a camera and examining the Rag Tree. The bossy Bab hovered just inside the kitchen door grousing about how the Daoine Maithe didn't like redheads. Nor did they like to have their picture taken. Biddie wondered what the Daoine Maithe did like.

The pretty redhead turned and pointed her camera toward Biddie. "Are you the Faery Woman of Bamford Cross? I'd like to take your picture."

Oh no, you don't want a pic— Before Biddie could finish her thought, Bab had snatched the spatula from her hand and charged the Rag Tree wielding her weapon like Teddy Roosevelt charging up San Juan Hill. She struck across the redheaded woman's arm. Blood swelled over a white blouse.

"You cursed woman!" the redheaded woman cried, racing through the corn and away from the pursuing Bab, who now screamed chastisements at her for having bled over the Daoine Maithe.

Once Biddie was safe inside her kitchen, she considered how the redhead had called Bab a cursed old woman. Biddie wondered if the woman had said it out of anger, or did she really know about the curse of the O'Neills of Bamford Cross? This troubled Biddie down to the very last bite of the rhubarb tart.

෧ඌ

Bab Treacy couldn't catch up with the redhaired trespasser, and Biddie had gone home—which was all well and good, because who needed a so-called best friend who hadn't the backbone of a snail? She tried walking the anger out of her head instead. Swallows sprayed out of the thicket of yellow gorse and violet rhododendron, at the crunch of her determined step. It wasn't until she'd gone fully two hundred yards—all the way to Biddie's lane—that she realized she wasn't wearing a jumper to shield her from the soft day, which clung to her skin like tiny wet kisses.

Passing beneath a cluster of trees nearby the old yellow pump, where all the families in Bamford Cross used to come for their water in the days before indoor plumbing, she found her feet beginning to drag as if they'd minds of their own. Before she could reach the old meeting spot, her feet veered off onto a cow path, so she could avoid seeing the neighbors' sideward glances or hear their patronizing, "Oh hellos." There was nothing she hated worse than being treated as an object of pity by people who couldn't wait until she was out of earshot before they started their gossiping. "Isn't that the Faery Woman of Bamford Cross?" they'd say, or, "Oh, there goes poor John O'Neill's daughter. Isn't it terrible about the curse of the O'Neills?" And because people always took pleasure in hearing about someone else's troubles, they would listen for the millionth time to the story of a cantankerous priest placing a curse on the O'Neills, on account of their believing more in the faery folk than in the Catholic Church. For three generations the eldest son would not survive the father, that's what the old priest had said.

Bab ended her walk atop the humpbacked bridge in the village of Bennettsbridge, where she looked below into swirling waters that long ago had swallowed her uncle and brother. If the curse were true, then Bab's Mattie Joe was next in line to go. But the people along the lane didn't know what they were talking about, she thought. There was no curse of the O'Neills. Her dead husband was proof of that.

2

She'd had reason to leave Ireland angry.

Five days after the escape

Cait McGrath lifted the glass coffeepot to her lips and gulped until she had the courage to squint at the shining red digits on the clock next to her bed. She felt absolutely ill. Her head throbbed from last night's overindulgence of alcohol and she'd a pain in her right arm that puzzled her, until the caffeine kicked in and she remembered the Faery Woman of Bamford Cross whacking her with a spatula. The old woman was crazy, and so was Cait for thinking she could come back to Ireland and find that things had changed.

Certainly the damp Irish weather hadn't changed. She'd gone to sleep wearing only a maroon Boston College sweatshirt, and the moment she stepped out of bed the morning chill swept up her long legs. She countered the cold by pressing the hot coffee pot against her cheek.

Coffee, as far as Cait was concerned, was just one of a multitude of things that made life in America preferable to the cloistered one she'd left behind in Ireland. The Irish loved their tea. Tea in the morning. Tea in the afternoon. Tea when you're sick in bed. Tea—tea—bloody, stinking tea. To her way of thinking, her dislike for tea was proof positive that she did not belong in this soggy old country. She'd made it a point to bring with her to Ireland a supply of her special blend of French roast and Colombian coffees. Her job assignment was scheduled to last a month. She hoped to God her coffee supply lasted as long.

In the States, she'd learned a lot about herself and life in general. In the States, there were opportunities galore, even for women, which was a major advancement over her life in Ireland. Most of her Irish girlfriends were on their first pregnancy when she'd left and by now were probably on their third or fourth. She wasn't going to bother to call in on them to find out. Like Ireland itself, the old friends were part of Cait's thankfully buried past. She trudged to the kitchen and poured the remaining coffee into a thermos.

When she'd left Ireland, she'd been twenty-three years old, sexually repressed, guilt-ridden, and unemployed. The States became her liberation. In the States, she found work immediately. In the States, a woman could have sex without losing her dignity. In Ireland, she'd be sentenced to Hell or, worse yet, become the talk of the neighborhood. Cait could no longer belong to a country that believed a woman's primary occupation was to make babies, yet would condemn her for all eternity for enjoying the job. Yes, she could think of a multitude of good reasons for her leaving Ireland, good coffee and guilt-free sex were two of them. Though unfortunately for the last few months she'd been getting by on just the coffee.

She grabbed a bottle of vodka from atop the fridge and poured a stream into the thermos to make a morning cocktail she called a Muddy Mary. The first taste was weak. She added more vodka. After a few more nips, the morning cocktail pleasantly swept the dullness from her head.

She'd been in Ireland a week now and there had been some noticeable advances for women. The growing computer industry was providing Irish women employment opportunities heretofore unheard of. Contraception was now legalized, as was divorce. A woman was President. Maybe Eire was a little *nua*, she thought. But then again, so was she. Brand *nua*. Cait was an American now, citizen and all. After another gulp of the Muddy Mary, she turned on the lights.

The small flat in Kilkenny City was all she needed for her brief stay: bedroom, bathroom, kitchen, and a small eating area. Rows of books and compact discs—mostly classical, a little light rock—filled the three tiers of cinderblock and plank bookshelves. Her computer rested on the round kitchen table. Wires like spilled black spaghetti covered the carpet. Work consumed most of her time.

Work. She checked the clock beside the brass bed. It was nearly five o'clock in the morning. She was going to be late.

She traded the Boston College sweatshirt for a blue Georgetown University one. With the help of a few deep breaths, she then squeezed into black Irish-size-fourteen jeans—the States had liberated her hips, too, unfortunately. She'd left Ireland a long and lean size ten. In fact, the mirror told her that, while she still had some head-turning days in front of her, her time as the fairest in the land definitely had passed. Crow's feet were beginning to spread from her blue eyes. And the bosom that for so long had defied Newton's Law was, like the rest of her, heavier and in need of some toning. She'd have to begin an exercise regimen soon, or else rid the home of mirrors, she thought.

Placing the thermos into a black gym bag, along with a laptop computer and a CD player, she walked into a cool, violet morning. She stepped briskly past the illuminated Kilkenny Castle, directly across the road from her flat, and through the small city, which, in the dark and quiet, unmasked its medieval charm. Cait liked working in the dark, when Kilkenny's secrets were whispered. Ribbons of yellow sunlight, wrapping over the silhouettes of the rolling hills east of the city, told her that she still had an hour of pleasant dimness left.

She came upon an old ruin called Lacken Abbey, where she took the winding stairs two at time, until she came to a bench looking over the ancient stone walls at the grey and swiftly rushing River Nore. In an order that had become ritual, she pulled from the gym bag her thermos, her laptop computer, CD player, and a cigar. The splendor of Mozart swam through her head. She puffed on the cigar until the sweet smoke channeled her away to a cubby desk at *The Washington Post*, where a beefy man with alert eyes and a cigar hanging from his lips beat on a computer keyboard with his two index fingers. Cait took a long quaff of Muddy Mary, wiped her lips with the back of her hand, and called out to her muse, "Talk to me Thomas Hennessy," she said, and she began typing an essay that began: *THOMAS F.X. HENNESSY, Washington Post Syndicate.*

An hour later, she gave the keyboard a final, satisfying poke. Cait saved the document, then in the rising dawn, walked back to her flat where she emailed the document to Thomas F.X. Hennessy—the real one. Snuggling back into bed filled with a sense of pleasing vindication, she pondered how this New Ireland would respond if only they knew that the Hennessy they adored was really a daughter who the old Ireland had cast away five years ago.

3

*"It will do you no good to be wishing for boiled spuds,
once you've mashed them.*

The night before the escape

Mattie Joe Treacy pushed the bill of his blue prison
warder's cap sideward and pressed his bearded face flush
against the gate lock bars. D-Wing was beginning its
nightly singsong. The prisoners' muffled voices leaked
through inch-high gaps at the bases of thick steel doors,
just a few meters from where he was standing. It was a
traditional Irish melody and, because the inmates sung in
Irish, Mattie Joe was the only prison officer able to translate
the IRA secrets hidden within the songs. The British
government paid him well for his service.

The songs were slow, sad longings for either freedom
or girlfriends—boring stuff that couldn't keep Mattie Joe's

mind from drifting. One thought that snuck into his head was something his friend, Brian, had told him years ago. "It will do you no good to be wishing for boiled spuds, once you've mashed them. Just eat them the way they are, or else starve on your wishes." Brian was a great one for giving advice. Some of it was good. It was Brian who had told him to grow his hair out and wear a gold stud earring. "A prison warder tends to live longer if, at the end of the day, he blends in with the environment." Mattie Joe recalled his friend's advice as he swept long and itchy copper locks off his face. The pinch of the gold stud earring annoyed the hell out of him.

He'd been working for a fortnight now as a Gaelic interpreter—long enough for him to learn that, these days, nothing much was happening with the Provisional Irish Republican Army. So far, he hadn't heard a single secret being sung. To the British, Mattie Joe was nothing more than a high-priced whore. The prisoners, if they learned his true identity, would consider him the worst of all traitors. Gaelic interpreting in a British prison didn't offer many employee benefits. The trick was to get your money and get out, before you were killed. Spuds, boiled and mashed, again crossed his mind.

His eyes inched along a mental tight rope, stretching from D-Wing's twenty-five cellblocks, past the black iron gate lock, and down a dim corridor to a lounge area called the Circle. There, three other warders sat passing the night playing cards. The inmates' song echoed along the corridor. The last chorus slipped away without any secrets passed, leaving in its wake the silent prison nothingness that clung to a body. Mattie Joe's time had come. There would be no unmashing of spuds now. Clearing his throat, he sang in

Irish. *"Sceoileadh me soar thu. Amárach. Amárach,"* which, in English, means, "I will set you free. Tomorrow. Tomorrow."

His song faded into the silent nothingness. At last, the hush broke when one of the prisoners broke into what sounded to be a dangerous choking fit. "Medical situation!" Mattie Joe cried. "Cellblock twenty-five!"

4

He didn't know if they were angels or divils...

The night before the escape

Donal Mór O'Toole hadn't liked the idea of doing it on the beach, but he wasn't about to argue the point. He lay tangled inside the skinny woman's sleek thighs on a bed of cold sand; while a high sea chewed up the strand so fast he feared he just might drown before getting the job done. One watery mountain shocked him so badly that his mickey almost went slack.

She was a bit small chested, but nevertheless round and firm in all the parts that mattered at the moment. And moments were something that Donal Mór did not have many of. The woman was a little too patient for his liking. Even when the sea spray left her looking like a blonde Medusa, there was not a hint of panic in her to start the job. Slowly she moved on top of him and, with her smooth, round arse rolling softly over his starving loins, she swayed in the yellow glow of a full moon. The sea's sighs and roars begged Donal Mór to hurry. At last the young one put her wet mouth into his ear and sang in Irish, "*Sceoileadh me soar thu...Sceoileadh me soar thu.*"

Donal Mór had heard that air before, but he wouldn't bother to place a song to it now. He looked into glistening cat-like eyes and smiled. "Set me free," he said. "Oh God, set me free now."

She was still singing when the sea devoured them. Wave after wave pounded at Donal Mór. One moment he was sinking into the black depths, the next he was gasping for air and bouncing like a ball on top of the waves. He bounced right into his skinny woman. She was treading water like a natural born seal and wearing a smile to beat the band. "*Sceoileadh me soar thu*," she sang. "*Amárach. Amárach.*" She did whirly flips and other things that gave Donal Mór a few ideas, should they make it back to the beach alive. With what he figured to be his last precious breath, Donal Mór made an Act of Contrition, confessing for the first time to having blown up that British convoy. He still did not consider it a sin, but he thought it best to cover his arse, just in case. The truth be known, he was far sorrier for having let himself be talked out of the back seat of his car and onto the beach.

His senses fading, Donal Mór heard the faint cries of distant voices. He didn't know if they were angels or divils, but he could tell they were angry with him all the same.

"Turn the shaggin' Provo bastard on his stomach before he chokes."

"Filthy Fenian scum. He's only getting what he deserves for smoking himself to death. He's a lifer anyway. Letting the murdering scum die would be doing him a favor."

"Who is this man? Why isn't he in hospital?"

"His name is O'Toole. He's called Donal Mór, or Big Dan. He's the D-Wing Officer Commanding of the Provisional IRA. Try squeezing his chest. Stubborn bastard has cancer, but he refuses medical attention. Fears truth serums will be put into the painkilling drugs. C'mon, Dan, cough it up. Don't die on my shift."

"Big Dan? Jasus, he hasn't arse enough to hold up his own trousers. Try hitting him between the shoulder blades. That might shake something loose."

Sometime about the fifth or sixth whack to the back, Donal Mór realized that he was no longer drowning in a dream, but choking to death in his prison cell. The Brits called the place The Maze. IRA men like Donal Mór would forever call the wretched prison by its original name, Long Kesh. The shouts and curses of the screws trying to free the phlegm from his lungs replaced the roar of the waves.

Orange light from the corridor swept into his cell through the open door, illuminating Donal Mór's three blue uniformed assailants. There was a stubby, biscuit-faced bloke, a tall cunt of a die-hard Orangeman, and the third looked like bleedin' Wolfman with big brown Bambi eyes. The others called this last one "Tíghe." Donal Mór didn't have a clue who Tíghe was, but he was the one squeezing the living hell out of his chest.

Tall Cunt stood by the door, grinning. "Oh, Dan is a big man, alright. He knows where all the guns and bombs are. Don't you, Dan? Clever security move by the IRA, or so they thought. Each time an arms dump was moved, the location would be communicated here to Dan, because he was the loyal Provo hero. He was their prison god. Only Dan knew where the weapons were. Now the IRA wants to negotiate peace, only they can't because Danny Boy won't tell anyone where the guns are. Because he's a hardliner and wants the war to continue. Can't blow up bars and department stores if you give away the bombs, can ye, Big Dan? Real big Dan. I hope you fucking hack yourself to death, you scum."

After three coughs, Donal Mór spit a gutful of phlegm all over the front of Tall Cunt's blue prison warder's uniform. "A blow for Ireland," Donal Mór grunted, then fell back onto a mattress lying on the concrete floor. He closed his eyes and hoped to God that he could get back to the beach before his skinny woman put on her clothes. He hoped to feel the warm, pleasant arousal bringing life back to his decaying body. But it was of no use. The skinny woman was gone.

"Provo bastard," Tall Cunt screeched. "I hope your new fucking Ireland lets all you Fenian scum rot right the fuck away in here. New Ireland—New Ireland—New Ireland…" the screw spat the words out as if ridding himself of spoiled food. Donal Mór simply smiled, showing as many teeth missing as were not. He couldn't let the enemy know just how terribly those two words—New Ireland—stung.

When he'd entered Long Kesh prison camp for the first time, he'd been sixteen and little more than a stone and bottle thrower fighting for an Ireland united, Gaelic, and free. By age twenty-five, he was an IRA hero and back inside the prison walls. Now he was fifty and his life was measured by all that was lost. He'd lost his wife and child. He'd lost his freedom. His hair had gone white, what was left of it. Half his teeth were gone, too. And in just a few weeks time, when the people in the Republic of Ireland punched the Eire Nua referendum ballot, he'd lose his dream of a united Ireland. When the day came that all hope for an Ireland free of the British was dead, he hoped he'd be the same.

The two older prison warders left Bambi Eyes to watch over Donal Mór. When the beardy-faced screw tried to wipe the spittle from his stubbled chin, Donal Mór shoved his hands away. "You're prostituting our language!" he said. Seeing the traitor in the flesh reminded Donal Mór of just how ill he was. His hands and arms were just twigs. Otherwise, he'd ring the divil's neck.

Bambi Eyes was a finger's width one side or the other of six feet tall, with hair the color of a carrot. He wore a gold stud in one ear and the whiskers piled up on his cocksure face made it difficult to place an exact age on him, though his step was youthful and athletic. Donal Mór doubted Tíghe was the man's real name.

Bambi Eyes pulled out two baby whiskeys from his trousers. "Y' know what we need is about a ten-day piss-up." He tossed one of the miniature bottles to Donal Mór. "Cheers," he said. "Have you a fag?"

Against arguments from his mind and throat, Donal Mór ignored the miniature bottle—Bushmills Black—on account it was the traitor's whiskey. Bambi Eyes shrugged and set one of the bottles onto the concrete floor. "It's yours, if you want it," he said, only he was looking away as if speaking to someone else. It was then that Donal Mór noticed a field mouse crouching by the door. In twenty-five years inside, he'd never seen a rodent before.

But the sad truth was, Donal Mór was so sick he couldn't trust anymore what he did see and what he didn't. The pain in his chest was so severe that he suffered lapses in concentration. When Bambi Eyes started darting about the cell, Donal Mór felt in the throes of another mental lapse. He'd been unable to prevent the swift moving screw from swiping the Saint Columbanus medal from around his neck and use it to tap against the steel pipes running against

23

the ceiling of the cell. A chill invaded Donal Mór's bones. How was it that Bambi Eyes knew the prisoners' code? It took the prisoners themselves months to become fluent at it, but the screw, who'd been at Long Kesh a fortnight at very most, had very adeptly tapped out a request for cigarettes.

Moments later, three cigarettes came sliding beneath Donal Mór's cell door, aboard a brass cross and chain medal, which was tied to a piece of thread taken from a towel. Some of the prisoners preferred the lightness of the brass crosses. They maintained that the flat surface made it easier for the messages to slip through the inch-high gap at the base of the cell doors. Donal Mór, himself, was a staunch Columbanus man. Had been so for twenty-five years. The oval medal had the bit of weight to it; you could get the good grip on it before you flipped it beneath the cell door. Bambi Eyes flipped one cigarette onto Donal Mór's lap and, before lighting up himself, set another on the floor. For the mouse?

Again moving in a blur, Bambi Eyes reached below the mattress and removed the disposable butane cigarette lighter Donal Mór kept hidden in a small puncture in the foam rubber. He lit his own cigarette and held out the flame for Donal Mór. "Did you hear the latest about the Eire Nua referendum?" he asked. "The clergy are against it because a 'Yes' vote will do away with Saturday evening Masses. Seems the priests in Dublin are having a difficult time anymore finding babysitters," he chuckled, adding, "I thought you'd like that one." The crazy screw was talking to the mouse, not to Donal Mór.

For several minutes Bambi Eyes smoked, drank, laughed, and talked to himself. Donal Mór decided the screw was a total eegit, or maybe even mad. Either way, he was begging to be killed. Donal Mór could see to that. He smoked a cigarette down to a nub. "Who are you?" he said. It was a command, not a question.

Bambi Eyes blew out a stream of smoke, then dropped and snuffed out the smoldering fag with his foot. The brown eyes shrank into small, angry slits. Moving two steps back toward the open doorway, he took a small piece of tweed from his trousers pocket and flipped it at Donal Mór's bedside. It was brown tweed about eight inches in length and half as wide. "*Sceoileadh me soar thu. Amárach,*" Bambi Eyes said.

"When tomorrow?" Donal Mór asked.

"Exercise period. Five men go out. Liam Riordon has to be one of them. You're free to come, if you want."

"The rules for escape plans are clear. All plans for escape first must be brought to me, the Officer Commanding."

"The rules have changed, Dan. The IRA Army Council isn't even speaking to you these days. And they're not about to until you tell them where the arms depots are." Bambi Eyes stooped and picked up the second miniature bottle of whiskey off the concrete floor. It was empty. "*Amárach,*" he said, walking out.

It was true that Donal Mór wasn't on the best of terms with the Army Council. His repeated requests for a face-to-face meeting to discuss Eire Nua, conditions for peace, and the location of the arms depots had gone unanswered. He considered the possibility that Bambi Eyes was a British agent, since it was not at all out of the realm of possibilities that the Brits would engineer a Provo escape, only then to kill him. They'd love to see him dead before he chose to reveal the arms depots with the Army Council. Considering all the ramifications of an escape was confusing and mentally tiring for a sick man, yet one thought pierced through all the rationalizations and contradictions—freedom. Donal Mór had a chance to be free!

Once all the screws were gone, the radiator pipe crackled with questions for Donal Mór. Tap-tapping: *Who were the screws in his cell? What was all the screaming and cursing about?* Ping tap tap tippity: *Had Donal Mór hit one of them?* Tap tippity tippity ping pong tap pong: He was full of conflicted emotions at the moment and listened to the incessant coded chatter, as long as he could bear it, before rapping his Columbanus on the pipe. *Shut up!* he told them.

From the tiny hole in his mattress, Donal Mór removed the pen cartridge and a slip of paper. He wrote a brief message and wrapped it in a thumb-sized piece of plastic cling film. Unfastening his belt, his trousers slid off his bony frame. By bending forward, he allowed his rectal passage to fully open. He shoved the message wrapped in cling film up his arse. Thirty minutes passed before a call went up in the cellblock. "There's a bear in the air." A screw was patrolling. Hearing the footsteps outside the door, Donal Mór called, "Guard."

"What do you want, Dan?"

"See the doctor," Donal Mór said.

5

He was speaking to the ghosts of Milltown.

The night before the escape

Brigadier General Bartley Drummond sat inside the Royal Ulster Constabulary station on Belfast's Falls Road, alone in a room lit only by the luminence cast by six security television monitors. It was past 0300 hours and Bartley felt at ease staring at the monitors and sipping smoky-sweet Drambouie from a Waterford tumbler. He narrowed his gaze on the screen showing a lamp-lit view of the Falls Road and Milltown Cemetery in the background. Milltown was where the nationalists buried their dead. Silhouettes of stone Celtic crosses spotted the reflection of Bartley's lean face, jutting chin, and prematurely white hair. He was mildly surprised at the twisted grin that he wore, courtesy of the Drambouie. He didn't feel that drunk.

"Where oh where have your heroes gone?" he whispered, his breath fogging a Celtic cross. He was speaking to the ghosts of Milltown.

A flash of movement from one of the television screens momentarily startled him. He then recognized the image of his military attaché, Captain Anthony Greenwell, just before he entered the station via a rear door. Smiling, he poured Drambouie into his glass and another besides. Tony would be bringing significant news.

Bartley pulled the fidgeting mass of muscle through the door by the sleeve of his airborne bomber jacket and handed him a glass. Tony, a tremendously devoted attaché, removed his beret and rocked from one black booted foot to the other like a kid holding his pee. "We heard from the Blackbird," he said. "There's going to be an IRA escape attempt. He didn't say which prison. I'm guessing the Maze."

Bartley clinked glasses with his attaché. The truth be known, he was less interested in news of an escape attempt than he was excited by being contacted by the Blackbird, an informant who was privy to the most sensitive of IRA matters. None of Bartley's predecessors had ever been able to garner such a highly placed informant. He also wondered if any members of parliament had equal access to such vital information. The government squires were his competition in the race in settling the Irish issue once and for all. In Bartley's view, politics started wars; it did not finish them.

"Did you speak to the Blackbird personally?"

Tony shook his head. "I received the phone message, recorded, giving me the Blackbird's verification code. I followed instructions by going to the appointed phone—in Ballymurphy no less. There, I am in the bowels of a nationalist neighborhood waiting for a phone to ring. Christ!

I was behind the sofa, I was. Anyway, the Blackbird calls and says, 'Prison escape. The Rag Man.' Then he hangs up. The Rag Man is the one who led the Brixton escape a year ago."

Bartley nodded. The Rag Man had infiltrated the Brixton Prison laundry. He left with an IRA man named Liam Riordon, since recaptured and interned now in the Maze. Investigators found a swatch of tweed attached to a note reading, "Understand the haunting." The Brixton Prison warder, whom the Rag Man had overpowered and stuffed into a laundry bin, remembered hearing a song sung in Irish. Only the lousy blackguard couldn't remember the tune.

Tony still looked as if he had to pee. Perhaps he should have poured him a double, Bartley thought. "Something else, Captain?"

"I'm afraid we've lost another informant, code name Rabbit. He was found near the border. Garbage bag over his head. Face blown off—just like the others. That's three we've lost in the last month."

"Not to worry," Bartley said. "Actually, by eliminating their informers, the Provos are ridding us of some loose ends. Rabbit," he said, grabbing the Drambouie bottle and refilling his glass. "Eighteen-year-old explosives courier for the Provos. He helped us close down the bomb making in Newry."

Tony Greenwell swallowed hard and nodded. "That's the one. He was caught by the RUC in the back seat of a car having a jump with his girlfriend. Poor little republican bastard. We had him by the balls—literally."

Bartley shook his head with disbelief. He rolled the burning alcohol over his tongue as he considered Ireland's pathetic young Catholics. Here was a boy who turned informer against the IRA because he was too afraid of his priest or mother knowing he was having sex. He shook his head again. "Young, scared, dead. Wars are won and lost on boys like Rabbit," he said. "If we're not careful, the politicians will steal this war from us, Tony. If that happens, we will never end this thing. Ever."

The hour and booze finally were taking their toll on Brigadier General Bartley Drummond. The room started a slow clockwise spin. He started seeing two of Tony. It was past time even to call it a night and sleep off the booze, but he couldn't resist telling Tony one more time his prescription for defeating the Irish.

"You know where the politicians have gone wrong, Tony? They have never seen beyond what we used to call The Paddy Factor, that the IRA was an ill-disciplined band of hooligans who would ultimately be victims of their own bungling. Year after year passed, and who were the real bunglers, heh? Us, that's who. This position that the violence in Ulster was a direct result of the existence of the Irish Republican Army, and if it were not for them there would be no need for the Protestant paramilitaries or even the British Army itself was—is—utter nonsense. It's politician-speak."

The Drambouie had lost its flavour. The alcohol poured straight into the mushy pool in his brain. He was enjoying hearing himself talk. "Whatever IRA bungling that had occurred during those early months soon disappeared. The old neighborhood brigades, battalions, and companies, which fell rife with informants, were replaced by a leaner and deadlier cellular structure where information was shared only on a need-to-know basis. Thus, the IRA," Drummond pulled at an imaginary shade, "became an invisible army. So what have I done?"

"Built an invisible army to combat them," Tony Greenwell offered.

"Not to combat them, to *defeat* them," Drummond corrected. "You must understand your enemy in order to defeat them. Unlike we English, there's nothing pedigree about the Irish. They're a bubble-and-squeak race of Norsemen, Celts, and Normans, within whom centuries of wretched poverty has created an inherent resourcefulness. How do you defeat an army that draws its life's blood from dead heroes? They're like those old Japanese cinema monsters that grew two heads for every one you cut off. The only way to win is to render the beast helpless, then kill it entirely." He couldn't help but smile at his own words. "And I will 'kill it entirely', and I will do it with an Army of Five."

∽

Captain Tony Greenwell listened to his commanding officer rant about Irish ghosts and an Army of Five until the booze finally dropped him gently onto the floor. In a few moments, Drummond was snoring loudly.

Tony slumped into a corner. Though proud to sit by and protect his commanding officer, his mind drifted and he began reflecting on how he nearly allowed this opportunity to slip away six months ago. He'd had a good offer with a London import-export firm. The pay would have been excellent and the travel opportunities far exceeded this hardly exotic Belfast boondoggle. But then came the first of many phone calls from the Blackbird, and Tony realized that he was exactly where he was supposed to be at this moment in time—especially since the Blackbird was paying him fifty thousand quid for his services, a bit of information Tony saw no reason to share with his commanding officer. As the great man passed out before him roared like an engine stuck in neutral, Tony thought of how Moses had needed help holding up his arms so God would look favorably on the Chosen people during battle. He wondered did Moses ever pass out in a drunken heap? It was then that he noticed the military dog tags entwined round Drummond's flaccid fingers. Tony nosed over to read the name on the dog tags: Pvt. Thomas R. Durrow. The dog tags were but a minor curiosity to Tony, until Drummond awoke and rummaged frantically through his pockets like a man in search of missing keys. Tony took note of how Drummond's bloodshot eyes bulged when he found the dog tags inside his own hand.

6

A large raven was smacking his beak against the pane.

The day of the escape

Mattie Joe Treacy returned to a one-room apartment in Lisburn, after midnight, to find a note from the landlady taped to the door:

Dear Mr. Tíghe,
Remember to collect the mail. Remember to feed Fluffy before going to the prison in the morning. Remember the house rules: NO smoking. NO alcohol. NO loud music. I'll return from my wee holiday with my sister in two days.
Regards,
Louise Taylor

Mattie Joe booted away the black and white cat brushing between his ankles. He was tired of taking orders from Louise. He was tired of being "Mr. Tíghe."

"The rules just changed, Louise," he muttered, entering a drab room consisting of a sink and a single bed he'd left unmade. Lighting a cigarette, he pulled a half-empty bottle of Bushmills Black from beneath the mattress and took two hard swallows. A black boombox shared space with a lamp, on a nightstand crusted with water-ring scars. He poked at the boombox, inciting the Rolling Stones to rattle the second story window looking out to an Ulster summer sky, changing from black to lavender. Holding the whiskey bottle like a microphone, Mattie Joe screamed along with Mick Jagger, "Please allow me to introduce myself, I'm a man of wealth and taste..."

He sang until the bothersome Fluffy returned to twine around his ankles. Sweeping a hand beneath the pillow, he found the handgun equipped with a silencer. "Pleased to meet you. Hope you guess my na-a-ame!" he said, pulling the trigger. The cat scurried away minus the tip of an ear. Mattie Joe turned the bottle back to his lips.

The whiskey soon restored him, and he set about the big job of readying himself for the escape. First order of business was to cut off his long hair and shave the bushy beard that had itched him for months. He then dyed his close-cropped hair a nut brown not too different from his natural color. The sheared strands of copper hair he left strewn across the hard wood floor. Neither did he bother wiping away his fingerprints. Finally, using a bar of soap, he scribbled a message on the mirror.

He replaced the Rolling Stones with another cassette, but did not switch on the boombox. Just as he was about to switch off the reading lamp next to his bed, there came a rapping at the window. A large raven was smacking his beak against the pane.

"You're just what I need," Mattie Joe said, opening the window. "You can come in, but for the love of God keep it quiet. I've a big day ahead of me." He flopped back on the bed.

The bird fluttered round the small room once, then alighted on the bedpost and began singing. *"I was born in a crossfire hurricaaannne! What happened to the Rolling Stones? Turn on that black box and open the bottle. Ye are going to be blamed for shooting that cat, y' know. You better hope it doesn't die,"* the bird added.

"Hello, Brian," Mattie Joe said, wearily. Brian was a pooka, a spirit from the faery world with whom Mattie Joe was all too familiar. The Treacys had a close relationship with all classes of faeries, going back donkey years. Leprechauns, clurichauns, even the terrible banshee, all were known well by Mattie Joe and his relations, especially on his mother's side. A pooka was a special faery in that it took on the shapes of animals. Sometimes Brian was a horse, other times he was a dog or some class of bird. Most times, like tonight, the pooka came as a raven, because ravens were supposedly creatures of great wisdom, and Brian had a high opinion of himself. At the moment, Mattie Joe wasn't in the mood for the pooka's wisdom, good or otherwise.

"Talk to me in the morning, when you're not so snookered, Brian. That was a snoot-full of whiskey you drank at the prison. I don't think mice hold their whiskey too well."

"Snookered is it? That's the black calling the pot a kettle. I mean the pot calling a black—Oh, never mind. Have ye made sure ye have the proper number of rags? Last time ye hadn't enough, remember? That's probably why the plan did not work. Are ye sure ye have enough of the rags? Jasus, what would you do without me? Are ye going to share that bottle, or no?"

Mattie Joe poured whiskey into an ashtray. "For your information, I do have enough rags. One for the bin lorry man. One for the bin lorry itself. And one for when I get to Dublin. So, you see I'm well able to do things without your interfering." He set the ashtray on the floor before the waiting raven. "Now go ahead and drown yourself and leave me be to get a few hours sleep," he said.

The raven pecked at the ashtray. Its black throat swelled into a small bubble with each sup of whiskey. *"Did I ever tell ye the story of Icarus, boyo? And the lesson in it?"*

"You did. He was an old fool who kept pushing a big rock up a hill, only to have it roll back down on him. The eegit didn't know when to give up."

"No, that was Sisyphus. That's another story, but one worth telling again. Icarus was a young man who wanted to fly so badly that he was given wings of wax and—"

"And he flew too close to the sun," Mattie Joe interrupted. "I remember. What's your point, Brian?"

"The point is, I don't like this crowd yer after running around with. Yer getting too close to the sun. I can see it coming."

Mattie Joe rolled over and buried his head in the pillow. "I'll be all right. I'm always all right. What I need is a decent night's sleep. Now, leave me be."

"Leave ye be? I wish to God I could leave ye be. Why don't you look at the mirror and tell me again that ye don't need me."

Mattie Joe wanted to sleep in the worst way, but he knew better than to disregard Brian. He was a contentious old pooka when he was on the drink, but he did always have Mattie Joe's interests at heart. Mattie Joe once again pulled himself out of bed and, going to the sink, turned on the hot water. It took a full minute for the mirror to steam over. "Oh, for fuck's sake," Mattie Joe grumbled. The message on the mirror read, *Understand the hunting.*

He took the soap and scrawled the lower case form of the letter A, then drew an arrow placing it front of the letter U. If only the police could understand the haunting, it would surely ease Mattie Joe's pain.

༄

Mattie Joe had only a couple of hours sleep before dressing again in his prison warder blues. Going outside, he squatted low inside a line of park cars, when at the stroke of 5:00 a.m., the bin lorry man stepped out of a brown duplex and sniffed at the musty morning. Reaching thick arms over a barrel chest, the bin lorry man ritually pulled on Wellington boots, zipped up olive coveralls, then wiped the morning dew from his black-rimmed eyeglasses. Finally, he snapped off a salute toward the flag of the Red Hand of Ulster fluttering over the door. Mattie Joe appreciated his target's commitment to routine. It would make his job easier.

The bin lorry man marched in quick, stumpy strides that smacked clump-clump against the rain-glistened street. He was whistling a merry tune, called "The Olde Orange Flute," and was completely unaware of Mattie Joe stepping behind him.

"Damp day," Mattie Joe said.

The bin lorry man spun around, startled. "My God, man. You stole the breath out of me." He wore dentures, which, apparently, the sudden fright had loosened. Behind the black-framed glass, his eyes settled on Mattie Joe's blue prison warder uniform. "It is indeed a pleasure to make the acquaintance of a fellow Ulster civil servant," he said, extending a hand.

Mattie Joe whistled and shook off the sting of the strong grip. "You've a mighty grip, sir. Actually, I was wondering if you might be headed near the prison, and would you mind giving me a lift? I'm a bit late this morning. By the way, I'm Billy Tíghe."

"Mind? How could I mind taking to work a man who risks his life to keep safe the God-fearing Ulster Protestants? Mind? It is my honor and duty, sir. I am in fact going to the prison," he said, snapping off another salute. "Tíghe, odd name for a warder, isn't it?" he asked. Tíghe was a Catholic name. The bin lorry man had good reason to question it.

"Actually, I'm William Patrick Tíghe," Mattie Joe lied. "My father's the Catholic, my mother the Anglican. I'm the only eegit reared in Keady town with an orange head and green arse, which was fine enough for my parents. They've retired to Australia," Mattie Joe joked.

"Well, at least your brains are the right color." The bin lorry man was not joking.

Mattie Joe walked astride the bin lorry man, producing a duet of clumping feet with a marching beat. He began singing "The Olde Orange Flute" so as to show a bit of Protestant allegiance. "And blow as he might he made a great noise, but the song that he played was the Protestant boys—"

The bin lorry man joined in. "Toora loo, Toora lay, its six miles from Bangor to Dunamanway—"

"Tis dangerous this Eire Nua business, no?" Mattie Joe asked.

The bin lorry man snorted. "There is no denying anymore the treacherous intentions of the British government. London is going with the money. They're selling out the loyal Protestants to the Dublin papists, with all their false promises of peace. And after all we Protestants have done by playing the orange card and keeping the politicians in Parliament. *New Ireland*." The mere words made him grind his teeth, which again loosened his dentures. He gave them another push with his thumb.

"You know how this happened to me?" the bin lorry man said, pointing to the false teeth. "Little scum Catholic, terrorists-in-the-making, threw a rock over the peace wall and knocked out my real teeth. Little scum bastards."

They climbed aboard a blue bin lorry, the cab of which looked like a businessman's desk. Glued to the dustless dash was a small, framed picture of what figured to be the bin lorry man's family: a teenage daughter, a son about ten years of age, and an attractive bleached-blonde wife. He explained how Thursday was typically a light day for garbage and how, with fifteen years of working for Ulster garbage collection, he only serviced the plush routes anymore. "No homes with dogs. No pickups near the fucking Peace Wall. I've only two clients, both respectable. The new supermarket by the river and the Maze. She's my jewel."

Yet, when they arrived at the supermarket car park, the sight of strewn garbage caused the bin lorry man's round shoulders to drop in disappointment. "Gypsies," he grumbled. "They scavenge the place, then leave it a mess." The bin lorry man began his work by searching through the debris, as someone might looking for a lost set of keys, then stooped to inspect a dented can of tomatoes. He put the tomatoes inside the bin lorry on the driver's seat, announcing, "I probably save three hundred pound a year in food because of people's waste." He picked up and admired a pair of nearly new Wellingtons. "I can't believe it. Ten and a half. My very size." When the bin lorry man sat down on the car park to try on his claim, Mattie Joe approached from behind and put a gun to his ear.

"Hand over the keys to the yoke and don't turn around," Mattie Joe said.

The bin lorry man thrust two quivering hands over his head. "My God, it's come to this. Ye murdering cowards have descended to commandeering bin lorries. What, are there no mothers wheeling prams left to hijack? You'll have to shoot me before I give up my keys. No Surrender!"

Mattie Joe pressed the gun further into the blue vein pulsing on the frightened man's neck. He could tell it hurt because tears pooled in the bin lorry man's eyes. He then pressed a white putty against his target's forehead. "Oh, shooting ye would be too easy," Mattie Joe whispered into the man's ear. "You know what that stuff on your forehead is? Plastic explosive. Enough to blow up ye and this fucking Protestant supermarket to tiny bits. A dropped melon would be easier to put back together than your fat head."

Even though it was a cool morning, the bin lorry man sweated profusely and his thick body shook, which was probably the cause for his front teeth popping out yet again. Watching the dentures roll away made Mattie Joe want to laugh, until it occurred to him that the bin lorry man might become so frightened that he'd shit himself, which would be disastrous. Mattie Joe needed the man's pants.

"Phwuckf ooph," the bin lorry man said, still trying to sound brave, though that was hard to do without his upper teeth. The tears that had been welling in eyes now flooded down his chubby face and fogged his glasses.

"We're blowing up the supermarket because it doesn't employ Roman Catholics. And in a socialist democracy, if the Catholics don't work, then nobody will work. Now hand over the keys, or they'll find your brains minced in with the bangers and black pudding."

Mattie Joe forced the bin lorry man to strip down until he wore nothing but the foggy eyeglasses. He then handcuffed the sobbing man to his own lorry and let him watch as he slipped the olive coveralls over top his blue prison warder's uniform. He used cotton balls in his cheeks to fatten his face.

"Not bad, heh? Could fool your mother," Mattie Joe said, finally putting on the black-rimmed glasses. After gagging the bin lorry man with one of the three tweed rags, he held out a small timing device and placed his thumb atop the red button as he slowly backed away. The bin lorry man's eyes rolled backward until they were glassy white, like two tiny billiard balls. His knees buckled and he slumped to the ground. Mattie Joe leaned over the unconscious man. "Well, you were easy," he said. After stuffing the bin lorry man into the lorry's garbage hold, Mattie Joe drove toward the Maze, whistling "The Olde Orange Flute" the whole way.

7

Des continued to back-slap the Irish Americans...

The day of the escape

Taoiseach Desmond O'Hanrahan stood as the United States Marine Corp Band played the Irish and American national anthems, letting his eyes wander around the glitzy Washington, D.C., ballroom. This was his fifth dinner in as many days; San Francisco, Chicago, Boston, and New York had come before. And as had been the case in those cities, the ballroom was chockablock with four hundred black ties and gowns, and no empty seats. Congressmen and senators, union men and businessmen, women sparkling in their jewelry—this was Irish-America's top shelf. They had come so Des could inspire their wallets to open for his New Ireland. And open they would in a big way, he thought, once he played his ace.

While a week on the Yank steak and potato circuit had left Des disinterested in food, his wife, Mairead, had an unquenchable appetite for America, especially for Washington's pageantry. The twinkle in her blue eyes had not faded since early that morning, when she received a peck on the cheek from the handsome U.S. President. The President had been very good to Ireland and was publicly on board for Des's Eire Nua. But in private session, he had asked that Des placate America's romantic Irish nationalists. Some of the President's key Democratic congressman and senators desperately depended on that Irish vote. And Des was keenly aware that these self-same politicians were the key links to passing a congressional bill designed to steer funds for job creation along the Ireland-Ulster border. Throwing a few bones to achieve such a noble end for Ireland would not be a problem. Des's coalition government was built on the mountain of bones he had thrown around Ireland. The President would get his, too.

After a desperately sweet dessert of Irish trifle that Des only picked at, the Master of Ceremonies, a curly grey-haired lawyer named Shaw, started telling jokes. There were some Shaws from Des's hometown of Mullingar. Those Shaws liked to talk, too.

"...He was born in 1946 in Mullingar, County Westmeath. Educated at University College, Dublin. His life in public service began when, at age twenty-three, he became one of the youngest members of Ireland's Dail... Known affectionately throughout Europe as Des the Decent...a man who epitomizes progress...leader whose courageous foresight and dedication has brought unity and prosperity to Ireland...Ladies and gentleman. Proud Irish-Americans, it is my distinct honor to present to you Desmond O'Hanrahan, Taoiseach of Ireland."

Des made a show of having to reach up for the microphone and pull it down to meet his modest height of five-foot eight. It got the laugh he wanted. "I'm reminded of the time when Bing Crosby's horse won the Irish Darby," he said. "There was the great crooner himself accepting the trophy and singing 'When Irish Eyes Are Smiling.' Just then, a man from the back of the crowd says, 'We can hear you, Bing, but we can't see you. Could you stand on your wallet?' Don't laugh," Des added. "It's your wallets I'm after standing on!"

After the laughter subsided, Des offered a reflective pause, then slipped bifocals over his pug nose. "Friends of Ireland, let me say that Irish eyes are indeed smiling, perhaps as never before. Smiling because for the first time in centuries Ireland is united. United in its desire for peace. United in its quest for a stable economy, which will allow Irish children to remain in their homeland, to one day see their own sons and daughters born in Ireland.

"For centuries our small nation of saints and scholars has endowed the world with Ireland's greatest resource— her people. In every corner of the globe there are Irish men and women enriching their adopted countries. All of you here in this room tonight are testimony to Irish character and Irish achievement in this most prosperous of nations, the United States of America.

"In particular, I want to thank the thirty-three members of your House of Representatives, who have endorsed the resolution for the Irish-American agenda for the White House Conference on Trade and Investment. This agenda seeks to put the United States in negotiations with the Republic of Ireland, the United Kingdom, and the European Union, as well as international financial institutions. The purpose of which is to establish an Ireland Development

Bank that will provide economic development and job creation in Ireland's border regions."

Des continued to back-slap the Irish Americans, saying that for each of them there was an Irish person of spirit and determination who set out to build a life in a new world. That done, he could get on with the business of Eire Nua.

"The historic Eire Nua referendum is now only weeks away and, simply stated, ratification is all but assured. The Irish people, through the agencies they support, trade unions, independent merchants, farming bodies, have all embraced the wisdom of Eire Nua. Additionally, the fervent and united effort of the Irish House and Seanad in bringing about Eire Nua itself has been nothing short of historic. Labor, the Progressive Democrats, Fine Gael and Fianna Fail, all say 'Yes' to an initiative that can only bring greater prosperity to Ireland. Indeed, the Irish people are saying, 'Yes,' to peace. 'Yes,' to prosperity. 'Yes,' to being a nation that is fully ready to assume its responsibility to the defense of Europe, by being compliant with the NATO nations."

This was the mildest of references Des dared make about abandoning Ireland's status as a neutral nation. It did not serve his purposes to dwell on what could be a controversial issue, so he moved on quickly to throwing the President's bone.

"The next few weeks will be reflective ones in Ireland, especially in the north, where Irish people will be celebrating their distinct and separate traditions. I have personally spoken to the British Prime Minister, reminding him that it is more important than ever that his government be cognizant of, and respectful to, all cultures of the island. To do otherwise is to say that the nationalist and unionist cannot differentiate between peaceful demonstrations and acts of terrorism. The Irish government knows the nationalist community, too, wants peace. Peace with dignity. Peace with hope. Peace with pride and equal representation. This, too, is part of the backbone of Eire Nua. Because it is the firm belief of this Irish government that, once peace reigns north and south of the border, once the nationalist community is given the rights of equal representation that have for so long been manipulated away from them, then north and south will move to be physically united as they are today, becoming united in spirit. It is our sincere hope that, in the coming weeks, the nationalist community will embrace Eire Nua, which through collateral efforts of all peoples involved—nationalist and unionist, Irish and British—will make possible one Ireland for all cultures."

Des took a breath as the hard faces joined another interruption of applause, thankfully. Now, he would introduce his ace.

His ace sat on the far right of the dais, his lean face and deep-set eyes showing no emotion. It was the very same face Des had known since first grade, when he and the ace sat across the room from one another in the Mullingar parish school. A sudden unease crept over Des.

"It seems as if Cathal Slattery has always been giving me something," Des said. "He was always the one in school with the right answer when you needed it. He was always the one on the parish hurling team, passing the ball over, so his short little pal could have a chance at a goal ball. And when it came time for the parish dance, he was the one with the pretty cousin." Desmond extended a hand toward Mairead. There was laughter, then applause. "But tonight, my dear friends of Ireland, Cathal Slattery, CEO of Bounty-Co., the world's largest manufacturer of food products, is giving a most wonderful gift to Ireland—a food processing factory, which will employ seven hundred persons. The

American equivalent would be in the tens of thousands—a whole city." Des raised his voice above the excited crowd. "This will bring millions of pounds to the Irish economy, making it possible for generations of Irish children to stay home in Ireland. Ladies and Gentleman, this is what Eire Nua is all about!"

The audience stood and cheered the ace. Cathal Slattery barely broke a grin, as he slowly hobbled to the podium, showing off the stiffness of his hurling career-ending knee injury as if it were a badge. Des embraced his boyhood chum. Together they waved to the adoring audience, which seemed as if it would never stop applauding. The business mogul raised Des' arm as a show of triumph, then leaned down, appearing to give Des a peck on the cheek. "Phoenix Park Hotel. 2:00 a.m., Penthouse Suite," he whispered. "Don't be late."

Cathal Slattery's Bounty-Co. was known as the world's major breadbasket. Nearly every government in the world was doing business with Bounty-Co. Des had heard one story that had his grade school chum playing umpire between the Canadians, Russians, and the United States. Russia needed grain and didn't want to beg for it. Canada had grain to sell, but didn't want to upset the U.S. The U.S. had a grain embargo against the Soviet Union over some human rights violations in Afghanistan. To Slattery, the answer was simple: he sold the grain to the Canadians, who sold it to a Mexican company, who sold it to the Russians at a handsome profit—for Canada, Mexico and, of course, Bounty-Co. Des smiled whimsically. Once upon a time, he had worried that his boyhood friend coveted his political position. But Ireland turned out to be far too small a playground for Cathal Slattery.

Des had to knock several times before the hotel door opened. A stunning blonde in a black string dress brushed passed him without a word. "Evening, Slats," said Des, thinking that using the old parish nickname was a good way to reinforce their childhood friendship.

"Evening, Piggy," Slats said.

Des changed his mind about parish nicknames. He felt the heat rising in his cheeks. He dismissed his aids to the hotel bar with a terse wave of his hand.

Slats moved to a wet bar, behind which was a window looking out to the Capitol building. The hurling hero's gimp seemed far less pronounced without an audience. He filled two Waterford tumblers with Bushmills, straight up. "You were a big hit tonight, Piggy. How many Silicon Valley companies in Ireland now, five?" he said.

"Thanks to you. Bounty-Co. coming to Ireland is the biggest coup yet for Eire Nua. The Irish people owe you a debt of gratitude. We've eight Silicone companies," he added. "You know about Intel, of course?"

Slats nodded. "Ireland's greatest resource—a young, highly educated, English-speaking population with no work. Ireland is very cost effective for technology enterprise."

"And for the production of cereals and dairy products, thanks to Bounty-Co. We've a large workforce ready for employment in areas other than computers."

Slats did not respond to Des's overture. He gazed out the window, toward the Capitol building, and changed the subject. "Piggy, I asked you to drop by because I'm interested in what you think about the New York State Board of Education approving the institution of the "Famine curriculum" into its schools. Imagine, the Irish holocaust as part of its world history studies— interesting, no? I mean, after all these years, young Americans will finally come to know that, in the 1840s, the British government systematically allowed two million Irish to starve to death. They will know that the British also forced the emigration of two million more, many of those dying aboard the coffin ships. Perhaps now more people will come to know how the seeds for the Troubles in the north were planted. I think that's a good thing, don't you, Piggy? Oh, and by the way, how are our Irish schools addressing this issue, now? Any change? Or do we still refer to a regrettable agricultural misfortune—then quickly turn the page to World War One, while sweeping British culpability under the rug?" Slats turned away from the window. His eyes shot accusingly at Des.

Des stiffened. He knew there would be a price to pay for the Bounty-Co. factory. And the price was small enough if all he had to do was endure Slattery's baiting. It was nothing new. Being called "Piggy" was starting to get to him, though.

"Amazing at how quickly a nation's history can be rewritten, isn't it, Piggy? Actually, it's more like amputating history."

"Putting history into relevant perspective is my way of looking at it," said Des, adding some starch to his tone. "Being pragmatic, rather than shackled by a timeworn idealism. Would you really want this generation to march around the schoolyard singing about Kevin Barry swinging from the gallows, like we did? God, it's a wonder any of us are the full shilling, what with the hatred and fear that was spoon-fed us. The bottom line in education is to prepare our children to be the business leaders in a world marketplace. You, more than anyone, should understand that. Perpetuating the memories of the sins against us will do nothing for Ireland's future. Ireland has finally turned that page, Slats."

Slats turned a weak grin. "Pragmatists fear losing the body. Idealists fear losing the soul. It's the soul of Ireland that's at risk, Piggy. For goddsakes, the country is becoming fuckin' Paddyland. Planet Ireland. Every castle and historic site has a ticket booth and fence thrown around it. Where's the giant mouse with the green ears? He can't be long away, is he, Piggy?"

Des didn't have a chance to respond to this latest barb. Slats turned his eyes to the ceiling and continued speaking.

"Tell me, Piggy—you've given this thought, I'm sure—what steps are being taken to ensure that Eire Nua does not completely shatter the nationalists, hmmm? And this is a business question, not a historical one. Eire Nua leaves them no dignity. The suspension of constitutional claims to the north is tantamount to a public flogging of the nationalists' ideals, in full view of the world. They're now in a position where they *must* oppose the abandonment of neutrality, compliancy—whatever the hell you want to call it. People don't like to be backed into the corner, Piggy, which is exactly what you're doing to the nationalists. Bringing a sudden end to their war puts scores of IRA men out of work. Once their payroll dries up, they could become desperate. They could blow things up, like my factory for instance. Then I might have to set up expansion of my European operations in, say, Latvia? Or the Czech Republic? What would that do for further investments in Ireland, hmmm? And what, my dear friend, would a 1970s gun running scandal, suddenly unearthed, do to the political career of Piggy the superstar Taoiseach?"

Des put a hand on back of a cushioned chair to steady himself. Slats sneered like a dog that ate sheep.

"Ah, the glorious past," Slats exulted. "I suppose it would be nice to be able to rid ourselves of past doings—ones we would like to forget—ones that we could never explain away, no matter how noble our intentions."

Des took a large gulp of the Bushmills to fuel the fire welling inside. "For fuck's sake, Slats, the nationalists should realize that pumping investments into border regions is a far quicker way to get the British out of Ireland. Once your factory is built on our side of the border, and northern Protestants are coming to *our* country for work, attitudes will change. But so help me God, Slats, if you expose the gun running you'll go down with me. Those were different times in the '70s. We took action. Both of us."

"Different times, Mr. Taoiseach? Or do we just look at things differently as time passes? And do you really think the world leaders, all of whom have benefited from my companies, will care a damn if I was involved in gunrunning during a highly volatile era? Or that the Irish people would turn their backs on their greatest hurling hero?" Slats chuckled. "It's funny how life tosses you little twists. In the '70s you gave the rocket launchers to Donal Mór O'Toole. Now you want them back, only he won't give them to you. Ironic, no?"

"You've set me up, Slats. Eire Nua can fly—is flying—without your bloody factory. But now that you're in the game, it would be devastating if you pulled out. Every CEO in the world will wonder why. I'll lose some of the companies already on board. What is this really all about? What do you want from me?"

Slats buried his face in his glass, drained it, and emerged grinning. "I'm afraid you have to leave now, Piggy. The press is waiting for your statement."

"Statement? On what?"

"The escape, of course. Five men escaped from the Maze an hour ago. Your friend Dan O'Toole is among them. It was good seeing you again, Piggy."

∾

Donal Mór O'Toole could scarcely breathe while the bin lorry commandeered by the Rag Man rumbled away from the Maze, and it wasn't due to the stench of the garbage or the cancer in his chest. He was free! True, being buried inside a mountain of refuse had not been his image of freedom, but he was beyond the wall. He really was beyond the wall!

The bin lorry rolled to a bumpy halt. The hydraulic door groaned, and the four with him scrambled through a sliver of daylight, leaving Donal Mór to pull himself through the garbage. He was still inside the bin lorry when he heard the crack of gunfire. Falling to a ground covered in pine needles, he found himself inside a forest. One of the five, Liam Riordon, was clutching a bloody wound in his left leg. A naked man was lying face down on the ground, dead. The Rag Man was gone.

∾

It had been three days since the escape from Belfast's Maze Prison and Mattie Joe Treacy was in no special hurry to get out of Dublin's Heuston Station, even though the 8:15 a.m. train he was on was crawling in at 8:45. Wearing sunglasses and a pink Rock 'n Nua baseball cap pulled low over his head, he stepped from the train, observing the irritable businessmen dodging around a young itinerant boy sitting cross-legged on a frayed blanket. No more than eight years of age, he squawked out a verse of Molly Malone, while holding out a grimy hand to all who passed. As Mattie Joe moved toward him, the young gypsy raised the volume of his crackling voice, "Alive alive Oh! Alive alive Oh!" Mattie Joe handed him a ten-pound note. "Take this and run like hell," he said. The boy did as he was told and a man wearing a blue pinstriped immediately gave chase. No longer did Mattie Joe have to wonder whether or not he was being followed.

8

"It's not a rebel song, at least not in the modern way..."

Three days after the escape

Kevin O'Felan, Garda Síochána Detective Inspector, shuffled his feet around the four spent cigarette butts he'd dropped while waiting the arrival of the Rag Man on the 8:15 from Dundalk into Dublin's Heuston Station. His wristwatch said it was 7:45. Lighting his last cigarette, he snorted a ball of white smoke, and then cursed his tardy partner, Peter Doyle. Big Peter wasn't much of a morning person.

Kevin and Peter Doyle were detective inspectors assigned to the International Cooperation Unit (ICU) of the Garda Síochána. Their present mission was to swiftly and silently apprehend the Rag Man. As head of the operation, Kevin would direct matters in a way that prioritized *silently* over *swiftly*. The O'Hanrahan government wanted no public distractions from the current warm and fuzzy political climate—spell that B-I-G -M-O-N-E-Y—which it had so carefully nurtured.

As the cigarette smoldered to a nub, he considered, yet again, going off the smokes, but yet again concluded that it wasn't a good time. He couldn't risk blowing up like an even bigger balloon than he already was. His eldest, Siobhán, was getting married later that summer, and she'd pleaded that he look fit for wedding photographs. So, for the past month, he'd been jogging until his knees begged his feet to stop, dieted on carrot sticks and cabbage dipped in Bovril, and still he could not lose the paunch around his middle—the curse of the little man. (He was 5 feet 8 3/4 inches tall, which left him a quarter inch shy of Garda Síochána height requirements. Only for a family connection was he accepted onto the force.)

He'd been a bit edgy of late, too. On top of going broke with the wedding, there was the matter of his sudden and curious transfer to the ICU. Kevin had no interest in international affairs and had said so to the deputy commissioner of operations. "I'm forty-seven years of age. I'm an old dog who doesn't need any new tricks. If it's all the same, I'd prefer to finish my three years to retirement sniffing around the home turf," he'd pleaded, in vain. The truth was, Kevin was far more worried about being stuffed behind a desk in ICU than he was about having to travel. He'd a bad knee that he'd kept hidden from the doctors. When the inflammation was at its worse, his right knee crackled like rice cereal. The cigarettes were not good for his heart, though the jogging was—except that was bad for the knees—albeit good for the waistline, as were the cigarettes. The waistline, not the heart, was the battlefront at the moment, and just thinking about it sent hunger pains searing through his belly.

He hid his face behind the morning *Irish Independent* and surveyed Heuston Station's long concrete platform. A grimy itinerant boy was busy preparing for the day's begging by smoothing out his phony homeless blanket across the platform, utterly unaware that standing above him was one of the three detectives (besides Kevin) assigned to the Rag Man detail. That detective, dressed in a blue pinstripe suit and wearing wire-rimmed eyeglasses, was playing the part of a businessman. A second detective was on the train with the Rag Man. The third was Kevin's tardy partner, Peter Doyle. For a brief time, they had worked together in Kevin's old crowd, the Special Detective Unit. Life was simpler in the SDU. You could lock up your perpetrator without an ounce of worry that it might affect the likes of Interpol, Scotland Yard, or the FBI. Kevin was missing the simple old days as he tried reaching Peter Doyle over his mobile phone. *"The mobile phone you have dialed is turned off or beyond the service area. Please try again later."* Kevin, his face still hidden inside the *Independent* shoved the small phone back into his trench coat. "Bleedin' blackguard," he muttered.

"Bleedin' blackguard reporting for duty," a deep, throaty voice whispered. Turning on his heels, Kevin found himself nose to necktie with Peter Doyle. His partner's bloodshot eyes jumped out at him like brake lamps on a white car. He shoved a file folder into the big man's paws and waited while drawing heavily on the last threads of smoke. "You look like you were up all night with the divil himself," Kevin said.

Peter Doyle wore a blue suit beneath a beige trench coat, like Kevin's, though his suit was probably five sizes larger. Standing well over six feet with muscles on top of muscles, his thick moustache dipped to the edges of his smooth jaw, and his coal black hair dangled down his neck. Both moustache and hair were in conflict with Garda Síochána dress code regulations. But Peter's rich daddy was a major backer of Taoiseach Desmond O'Hanrahan. And Peter Doyle had an Oxford degree in criminal law. At only twenty-nine years of age, the well educated, rich, and handsome Prince Peter was rumored to be on the short list to become a deputy minister of Anglo-Irish Security Affairs, once the Eire Nua referendum passed. Kevin long ago accepted that not all the rules applied for golden boys like Peter Doyle.

Doyle yawned and rubbed black stubble on his jaw. "It wasn't the divil I was with at'all, but a rare bird named Aoife. Or was it Naobh? Minor detail. Anyway, she was a real Mullingar heifer, this one—beef to the heels." The big man turned a dastardly grin and pantomimed doing a dirty sex thing with his hips. "And very religious, too. She was after crying 'Oh God, Oh God,' all night."

Kevin tapped a finger on the file his partner had already rolled into a small baton. "It's for our eyes only. Hush-hush stuff, altogether. Straight from the Puzzle Palace."

Puzzle Palace was the nickname for the Garda Headquarters located on Hartford Court, Dublin. The reason the Rag Man file was for his and Doyle's eyes only was because the government wanted no public forum for terrorists on the advent of the Eire Nua referendum, lest the foreign investors in the New Ireland get nervous and take their money to some emerging third world nation. When it came to Eire Nua, Britain was in bed totally with the Irish government. The security forces of the two countries were working together as never before, though Kevin wished the Brits would tighten up on their end. Somehow the Rag Man had managed to slip the whole lot of British security in the north: the Special Branch, the RUC, *and* the Army.

Regardless, the Rag Man was trapped on the train. The way Kevin had it figured, he and Doyle should have the Rag Man in custody by dinnertime. Why was he always thinking about food? His gut felt like a football with the air being squeezed out of it.

Doyle flipped through the inch-thick file for maybe thirty seconds, then said, "Alright, so. Dan O'Toole, the dying rebel himself, and four other Provos scarper from the Maze and are on the run. And our perpetrator gets his jollies by tying a rag somewhere around the scene of the crime. Maybe it's cheaper than sending out the laundry. So, what else? You're the profiler. Summarize this bloody book for me."

Kevin, annoyed at Oxford boy's flippancy, tossed away the butt. He briefly explained how the Rag Man, who was obviously adept at disguise, had infiltrated the Maze as a Gaelic interpreter and had engineered the escape using a commandeered bin lorry. "The Rag Man crossed the border by boat last night at Carlingford Lough," Kevin continued. "He was immediately marked by Detective Inspector John Farrell from Security and Intelligence."

"Skinny John? The gangly, weasel-faced bloke? Jasus, this is important. Skinny's our best surveillance man. Who was it that the Raggity Sam killed anyway?"

"Rag Man. He killed the bin lorry driver, and if you had been here in time to read the bloody file you'd know that. And Skinny Farrell is little more than a peeping Tom with a shield, if you ask me."

"Yeah, well, he's still damned good at what he does. I've seen some of his hobby work. He can get his camera so close he'd give you an eight by ten of a finger caressing a nipple, clear as a bell. Go on about the bin lorry man, the poor old divil. Gone to the big trash dumpster in the sky, so."

Kevin began to draw on a cigarette that wasn't there. "The Rag Man bought a Dublin bound ticket—non-return. Farrell believes he's marking a small time IRA courier. Your man down there thinks the same." Kevin nodded toward the detective in the blue pinstriped suit, then handed Doyle a train ticket. "Once we have the Rag Man completely alone, we'll lift him and turn him quietly over to British authorities in Ulster, as if he had never entered the Twenty-six Counties. Eire Nua proceeds without distraction."

The file included a photograph of the piece of tweed. Kevin explained that a swatch of one of the rags had been provided by the RUC for the Garda Síochána to analyze.

"Forensics matches the murder weapon with a bullet found in the wall of a Lisburn flat that the Rag Man let. A piece of a cat's ear found in the wall, as well." Kevin held up a copy of the *Irish Independent*. "The funeral is in today's paper."

"The cat's?"

"No, the bin lorry man's. The Rag Man killed him. Shot him in the back, so. The bullet came from the same gun that killed the—" Kevin didn't want to say it. He slapped the newspaper into Peter's chest.

"The cat? I can't believe he shot a cat. That's not normal. Christ, anyone could shoot a man. I've done that. But a cat?"

Kevin watched a smirk flee the big man's face the moment he focused on the newspaper. Spread across the front page was a photograph meant to turn hearts and stomachs against terrorism. The photograph showed the graveside agony of the bin lorry man's family. The photographer had manipulated his depth of field so that wife, daughter, and son stood alone in sharp focus against a fuzzy background of graveside mourners. The wife's face was as emotionless as a white marble statue. There was no thoughtful depth to her eyes. No tears. She looked directly into the camera lens like someone waiting for a traffic light to change. The face of her teenage daughter, however, was awash in tears; black rivers of running mascara coursed around cheeks and lips pinched in anguish. Closest to the camera was the boy. He appeared to be ten years of age, maybe. His necktie hung so crooked that it looked like the first time he had tied it himself. The photographer seemed to be saying that the boy now would have to do a lot of things for the first time.

"So, your wounded man caught crossing the border the other day was, indeed, one of the escapees?" Doyle said, his eyes tracing down the newspaper. "And he's now baring it all in the name of Ireland's freedom. At this stage of the game, I suppose all the IRA has to give up are the clothes on their backs. Do we have a bead on the murderer?"

"There were fingerprints found all over the Rag Man's flat—no matches yet—and a message on the mirror written in soap. It said, "'Understand the haunting.' A cassette tape was found in a boom box with only one song on it. One of the warders from the Maze thinks he heard the Rag Man singing the same song—in Irish—during a prisoner singsong, the night before the escape. He couldn't translate the Irish, of course, but the melody of the song was the 'Last Rose of Summer,' the same song that's on the cassette."

Doyle's face screwed into a knot around his big moustache. "Last Roses?"

"'The Last Rose of Summer.' It's one of Moore's melodies."

"Who?"

"Tom Moore. You've heard his songs millions of times, you just don't realize it. 'Oft in the Still Night,' 'Believe Me if All those Endearing Young Charms,' and..." Kevin raised his voice as this was his trump, "'The Minstrel Boy.'" He'd a horrible singing voice, but Kevin offered a bit of a verse. "The minstrel boy to the wars has gone. In the ranks of death you will find him—You know it, sure."

"Ah, a rebel song. Figures as much," Doyle said, nodding.

"It's not a rebel song, at least not in the modern way. It's a historical song about pride and sacrifice and courage, the values upon which Ireland was founded."

"A rebel song is a rebel song. We can't expect the Irish people to differentiate between generations. Singing about war and death is very harmful. Just think about the number of lads killed because some yahoo gets his blood up after listening to the likes of those rebel songs. The singer is as guilty as the gunman, I'd say. We've all been raised with the background music of war. It's got to stop. Besides, I don't know any of those old songs from your day, Kevin. I'm into the *new* Ireland. New songs. It's time to break away from the shackles of the past."

Doyle, delighted by his own wit, laid a sledgehammer-sized hand on Kevin's shoulder. "Face it, Kevin. All that matters now is Eire Nua. Last roses. Endearing charming minstrel boys. They're part of an Ireland that's all but gone, now. And good riddance, I say."

"We haven't time to debate Eire Nua now. The train is nearly here," Kevin said. Truth was, he didn't want to get into political sparring with a man whose arse was nearly sitting in a deputy minister's seat.

Doyle's mobile phone rang. "Oh hello, Skinny. Minding our Rag Man, no? Where are you, anyway? You're late."

Detective John Farrell was on the phone. Kevin tried to be patient while Doyle kept mumbling, "I see," and "Is that so?" This went for minutes before Doyle finally said, "Yes.

Yes, she has a sister. Now you mind our boyo there, and I'll see you when I see you. Right. Thanks a million. Bye." He shut his mobile and turned to Kevin. "Delayed a half hour," Doyle said, mumbling on about missing his breakfast, as he pulled a cherry tart dripping with frosting out of his trench coat pocket. Kevin's stomach growled.

Doyle spoke with his mouth full. "The train is held up in Drogheda. Ragged Sam is wearing sunglasses and a pink Rock'n Nua baseball cap and a black Rock'n Nua T-shirt. You know the ones with the electric guitar made out of the map of Ireland?"

Doyle licked his fingers then continued, "So, where were we? Oh yes. Endearing charming minstrel boys—Don't tell me you're not going to vote for Eire Nua, Kevin?"

"Undecided."

"One of the three-percenters, are we now? It's the neutrality issue, isn't it? What is it Hennessy says here this morning?" Doyle flipped the newspaper open to the inside fold. "Giving up neutrality is equivalent to using a piece of the house to keep the fire going. Pretty soon you have a nice fire but no house. Eventually you won't even have the fire." He folded the newspaper under an arm. "Insightful man, that Hennessy," he added.

"Blabbering Yank," Kevin grumbled. "Should mind the problems in his country."

"Still hung up on that eight hundred years of English tyranny thing, aren't ye? Face it Kevin, Ireland needs the English. Only for them we'd be killing ourselves."

Kevin bit his lip as Doyle went on and on about how Ireland had grown out of its isolation, prospered as a member of the European Union, and was addressing economic matters now with, "A global view." Doyle continued, "Foreign journalists, like Thomas Hennessy, offer objective observations. We have to be open minded, Kevin. To move ahead we have to be willing to let go of some of the old ways. Besides, when hasn't it been good business for Ireland to play ball with the Yanks?"

"I don't care much about a global view. I care about Ireland. The country's changing too fast. Condom dispensaries in every loo. My God! What's happened to our faith? Why does a new Ireland have to mean sweeping away the old Ireland? And another thing, why is Ireland's past always described as having shackles? If you ask me, Eire Nua and its global view have a few shackles of its own. The Germans have nearly bought up the west of Ireland. And you can't get a bloody tee time—if you could afford one—because the Japanese and Americans have invaded the links. I say give Ireland back to the Irish, before it becomes a fire sale altogether. Everyone's grabbing for the last few pieces of a nation once proud to be known as Irish. Have you heard what they're after talking about now? A common currency for the all of Europe? No more pounds and pence. We'll all be spending Euros or Peans, whatever. God, I hope I don't see the day."

A phone call from John Farrell mercifully interrupted the conversation. The train was on its way. Kevin dropped all the talk about Eire Nua because, in his view, neither he nor Doyle was in the proper frame of mind to take on a murdering terrorist. That needed to change immediately.

"Have you never heard again from that girl?" Kevin asked. "What was her name? Kathleen? Eileen? Maura? It was Maura."

The question had wiped clean the smirk from Doyle's face. His eyes clouded over. "Kitty," he said, reluctantly.

"Maureen. Kitty. Minor detail. Have you not heard from her since? I thought she would be the one."

Doyle's eyes narrowed. He rolled his big shoulders, as if he were getting ready for a fistfight, then opened his trench coat for a last peek at his uzi. Kevin now felt secure.

The train pulled into Heuston Station. John Farrell phoned and said, "This is it. Follow the bloke in the pink baseball cap and sunglasses. He's getting off." Kevin watched the Rag Man step casually from the train, then walk over and give a handout to a tinker boy singing Molly Malone. When the itinerant took off running, Kevin's man wearing the pinstriped suit, a young detective named Paddy Burke, instinctively gave chase. It was poor instinct. The Rag Man now knew that he was being marked.

But if the Rag Man did know he was being followed, it hardly concerned him. He sauntered along the River Liffey with a tourist's dawdling curiosity, making it easy for Kevin O'Felan and his team to follow the tall man's bobbing pink baseball cap. At the moment there were a million people in Dublin's city center, pushing their way to work, and one as cheery and carefree as a sweepstakes winner. When the Rag Man moved back across the O'Connell Street Bridge and began a shopping spree on Grafton Street, Kevin ordered the tail tightened. While the other detectives moved into position at the front and rear doors of shops, Kevin kept watch from the other side of Grafton Street. Peering through the human parade filling Dublin's favorite shopping district, he stuck a hand into a pocket, again searching for a cigarette that wasn't there.

Kevin likened profiling suspects to painting by numbers. Each characteristic was like one of those little spaces allotted for a different color. A color could be predominant and appear several times, or it could be subtle shadings, which nevertheless completed the picture of the perpetrator. It was a utilitarian, yet effective, process that suited Kevin. He didn't like to rush things. Short cuts only led to mistakes. The paint-by-numbers system was something he kept private from the other detectives, lest they accuse him of being crazy. The only person he'd shared his system with was his wife, Mary, and she'd long ago decided he was crazy. Mary often wondered aloud why he could paint such complex pictures in his head, but was all thumbs at painting anything at home.

His early picture of the Rag Man assumed some basic brush strokes. The standard IRA operative was a male from the north of Ireland, twenty-two to thirty years of age, with no university degree and either unemployed or underemployed. Almost always, there was a family history of republican activity. Kevin considered some of these colors. The age range was consistent with the standard profile. But that was not the case with the employment history. In both the Maze and Brixton escapes, the Rag Man had driven large vehicles with comfort and skill enough to pass through prison security. The Rag Man could be employed driving sixteen-wheelers, or he might be a farmer adept at managing heavy equipment. The Rag Man's exact occupation amounted to subtle shading that Kevin would consider later. At the moment, the most important color was the one that showed that the Rag Man did not kill for the money.

Stalking a murderer along Grafton proved to be tougher duty than anticipated, since every time the Rag Man stopped to shop, Kevin seemed to be stationed outside the front door of a restaurant. Standing in the doorway of an Indian restaurant was particularly torturous, since the aroma of peppery hot, curried lamb immediately seduced his neglected belly and sent his mind drifting away from the world of counter-terrorism and into a bowl of steaming white rice and a glass of chardonnay. Fortunately, the Rag Man, now lumbering along with several shopping bags, settled in for lunch at a trendy establishment on Harry Street called Bruxelles' International Cafe Bar and Lounge. Kevin whispered into the wireless, directing the detective detail, including Paddy Burke who'd returned after being outrun by the tinker boy, to hold their positions. "Let the Rag Man have his meal. We'll lift him as he leaves. Quietly," he added. He then moved to take up his own position across the street at McDaid's Bar when he walked into a man who looked like a walking tree stump. It was Finbar Lawlor, a professional friend. He smelled of port wine.

"I was praying for an excuse to have another, and now God has sent him to me," Finbar said, a smile peeking out from behind his full and ragged grey beard. "And aren't you looking svelte these days, Kevin. Dieting are we?" He grabbed Kevin by the shirtsleeve and pulled him into the small barroom, fronted by tall cathedral windows.

Kevin had met Finbar Lawlor, a professor of psychology at Trinity College, when first he joined the Detective Gardai ten years back and needed a psychological profile for a murder suspect. Finbar always had been forthcoming with insight and information, especially when their meetings were held over a long meal. The professor's assessments of criminal behavior had been so helpful to Kevin that Lawlor had become a sort of good luck crutch for him, not to mention the rainbow of colors he'd provided Kevin's paint-by-numbers pictures. The relationship had mutual benefits. Lawlor was paid for his services, of course, but he also knew that Kevin had family connections that could help reinstate him as a practicing psychologist. (He'd lost his license on account of the drink.) Kevin had made a call or two on Finbar's behalf, but so far nothing had come of it. He thought it indeed fortuitous, if not downright providential, to meet Finbar now, since the Rag Man affair had come up too suddenly for him to seek advice earlier. Lawlor, who had Puzzle Palace security clearance, helped Kevin fill in the shades of grey.

Lawlor ordered a port wine. Kevin asked for a diet coke old style—no ice—paid for the drinks, and then motioned the professor over to a small round table by one of the cathedral windows. There he could keep an eye on the front door of Bruxelles' International Cafe Bar and Lounge. Peter Doyle, who was marking the Rag Man from inside the restaurant, would make the call to move.

"I need some information on obsessive-compulsive behavior. You cover that sort of thing in your classes, Finbar?"

"Oh, I would, indeed. What sort of compulsion does our quarry have? Sex? Please God, I hope it's something dicey."

"Just your basic everyday obsessive-compulsive behavior," Kevin said. "Only it has something to do with rags and maybe roses."

Finbar pulled the glass of port out of his beard. "An obsession, is it? Or fetish? Is it roses and rags, or rags and roses? And may I ask how either relates to your suspect?"

"At this point you may not. Hopefully, I can tell you before the day is out, maybe even before the hour is out." Kevin glanced again over at the café bar across the street. "Anyway, you're on the clock. Give me what you know about rose and rag obsessions." The professor would understand that much of his job was to read between the lines of what Kevin could and could not divulge at the moment.

"A pseudonym?" Lawlor asked.

"I didn't tell you that," Kevin said, meaning "Yes."

Finbar nodded, closed his eyes, and rubbed his scabrous beard, as if doing so would summon the dark spirits. He opened his eyes and spoke in a hushed tone, like a priest on the other side of the confessional screen.

"Now I know the use of pseudonyms has become cliché in this time of spy films and such, but given that we are speaking of an obsessive-compulsive individual, one would be wise to look seriously at what it is he is offering through his pseudonym. Think of it not as a clue, but more of a window through which he is offering others a view of his soul."

Kevin wasn't thinking about clues. He was thinking colors.

"Now, we must remember that the use of pseudonyms for clandestine purposes is very Irish. In fact, you might say we invented the practice. One is reminded of the patriot, Robert Emmett, who went by the name of 'the Drake.' He was hung, drawn, and quartered. In more recent times, Bobby Sands was both, 'the Lark,' and for his writings, he went by 'Marcella.' He died on hunger strike in 1981, of course."

Kevin nodded. "Hardly adverts for the use of pseudonyms," Kevin said, not intending to be humorous. The studious Finbar did not take it so. His dark eyes stared blankly out from behind folds of pink flesh and the spray of grey hair, as if letting the meaning of Kevin's comment soak into his huge vat of knowledge.

"Indeed," the professor muttered to himself before continuing. "Yet, even Emmett, who died nearly two centuries ago, was following a tradition adopting a pseudonym which began long before. During Penal Times, when England's colonizing was taking a firm grip on Ireland, it was unlawful for Irishmen to attend Mass, to speak their native tongue, in short to do anything to obstruct our colonization. So, the people began to speak in allegory and attached pseudonyms to persons and places that could be endangered. I'm aware you know most of this, but it's important to place everything in context."

"I understand." Kevin kept his eyes trained across the street. If the Rag Man was eating light, Doyle could call to move at any moment.

Finbar continued. "We Irish, with our intrinsic gift of language, transformed this necessity of using pseudonyms into a poetic legacy. There are from this tradition many names for Ireland herself, Dear Dark Head, Kathleen ni Houlihan, and Róisín, which you know of course, Kevin, is Irish for rose. So, if the pseudonym has something to do with the rose, we could be referring to a symbol for Ireland herself. Perhaps your man is connected to nationalist endeavors. Is that a help?"

"Not at all. You're after singing to the choir, though I admit it's a song I don't tire of hearing. As a nation, we'd do well to pay more attention to our history. What about rags?" Kevin asked.

"So our pseudonym has something to do with rags? Would it be, say, Billy the Rag? Or perhaps something even as trite as Rag Man?"

"I didn't say that," said Kevin, again meaning "Yes."

Finbar paused, raised his glass to the light, and inspected the dark wine. Kevin was watching maroon droplets clinging to the grey moustache when his mobile phone rang. He suspected a call from the Puzzle Palace, or Mary.

It was Mary.

"Are you busy?" she asked.

"I am," Kevin said. "Deadly so. I could leave at any moment."

"Well then, I'll only be a moment."

"Is this about the guest list? And whether my second cousin should come or not? I say, 'No.' It would make a mockery of the wedding and draw attention from Siobhán. It's her day, not his."

"Why can't the two of you just be friends?"

"We are friends. We have to be. Our wives get along."

"Very funny. Besides, I'm not calling about the guest list. The caterer for the wedding is here for the taste testing and I need your help. I can't decide on the starter. Our choices are egg mayonnaise, or potato soup with leeks—"

"I vote the potato soup. Now I've really got to go."

Finbar held up his empty glass and gave Kevin a sad-eyed look. Kevin handed him a fiver from his wallet, then turned again to keep a look out the window.

"But, Sweetheart, potato soup is so boring and so...Irish. And we said we wanted Siobhán's wedding to be special, didn't we?"

"Yes, we did. So let's serve the soup cold and call it vichyssoise. And this is a hell of a thing to be talking about to a man that has to eat bloody spinach leaves and an apple to fit into a suit he can't afford. Now can I go?"

"Wait. There is another choice—a little over budget. But let me finish before you say, 'No.'"

"How much over budget?"

"Giant prawns, marinated in lime juice, chili, and ginger, barbecued on a skewer with pineapple and roasted peppers. Doesn't that sound fun?"

"How much over budget?"

"They're eight pounds."

"A person? Jasus, Mary. Why can't we just go with the potatoes? Irish people eat potatoes. Barbecued, skewered, scalloped, I don't give a damn. I want potatoes. And why

71

all of a sudden does Ireland have to prove how un-Irish it is? We had potato soup at our wedding. Do you remember that, Mary? Mary? Ah, Jasus."

Kevin returned the phone to an inside pocket, just as Finbar returned from the bar with a new glass of port pressed to his beard. "A hassle in the castle?" Finbar asked.

"Bleedin' wedding. It's sending me to the poorhouse—and divorce court. Go on about the rags, please."

"Well, I've given you the guts on pseudonyms, but how this information applies to whomever you are marking—and I assume we're speaking about whomever it is you're watching across the street—is interesting, indeed. I mean it's not your usual ultra machismo pseudonyms, such as the Eagle, or the Fox, or the Jackal. Perhaps your man's pseudonym is somehow related to a personal haunting."

Kevin turned away from the window and stared at the hoot owl. "Kevin?" Finbar said. "The twitch in your eye suggests I have hit upon something. No?"

"It's just hunger pains, Professor. Give me the ninety second course on hauntings."

"Oh my, there are volumes and volumes on psychoanalysis of haunted persons. But boiled down, the characteristic common to all haunted persons is a sense of being incomplete. Understand that in everyone's life there are significant persons and events that transport us from one life stage to another—stepping stones, if you will. Parents, first loves, schooling, athletics, first dances, any or all of these could be significant vehicles that are important components in our personal maturation. Each relationship and experience in some way 'transports' us to the next stage in life. Now, in the case of a haunted person, one of his or her transporters failed in some way to function properly. Think of it as some sort of mechanical function gone awry.

The normal process of personality development has been interrupted."

"So the haunted person seeks some sort of reconciliation with the past?"

"No. The emotionally healthy person would reconcile with his past and move on. In other words, 'he deals with it.' That's normal. The haunted person is a slave to his tortured soul. Only a total reckoning will appease him. And then only for a time. The illness must be treated, not the symptom. Kevin, I must say that the potential for violence among severely haunted persons is very high."

Peter Doyle broke in over the wireless. "We're losing him, Kevin. Move!"

Kevin reached inside his coat to the weapon strapped to his breast. He tapped it five quick times—once each for his three kids, once for Mary, and once to St. Christopher to intercede on behalf of his safety. He was moving across Harry Street with his weapon raised when he heard the crack of gunfire coming from inside Bruxelles'. Doyle now was shouting over the wireless, "Man down! Man down!" A man in a pink baseball hat and black Rock 'n Nua T-shirt rushed out of the restaurant, followed by another. And then several others. Kevin saw as many as eight more men all looking very much like the Rag Man running off in every direction. In the middle of the hysteria and being pushed away down Harry Street, like a man being swept to sea, was Detective John "Skinny" Farrell. The Rag Man had disappeared.

Inside Bruxelles', Kevin saw Peter Doyle's broad back trembling. A plump priest knelt on the floor. Stretched across the floor was a pair of legs dressed in pinstriped trousers. "His name was Paddy Burke, Father," Doyle said when the priest asked. The big man then turned to Kevin.

He spoke through a trembling lower lip. He was shot from behind, Kevin. We never saw it happen. The Rag Man started handing out free Rock 'n Nua gear, and before we knew it, there were a dozen of him in here."

Finbar Lawlor arrived holding the Rag Man's shopping bag. "I think you two will want to look at this," the psychologist said, pulling a newspaper from the bag. On the cover of the *Irish Independent* the face had been cut out of the photograph of the bin lorry man's son. In its place were the pen scrawled words: Understand the haunting.

Finbar Lawlor spoke. "Gentlemen, the man responsible might very well indeed be carrying out a terrorist agenda, but I am very sure that the messages he leaves are personal. Psychologically, he's suffering. He wants you to find him."

Kevin knelt down with the priest alongside young Paddy Burke. Blood spilling from exit wounds in the detective's chest and head flowed over the tile floor like a deep red river. Kevin added a new color to his picture: the Rag Man murdered at close range. He then looked up and surveyed the room of strewn chairs and overturned tables. "Where's Skinny?" he asked.

∾

Father Brendan Sheils, having boarded the Dublin train bound for Belfast, took a seat four rows back from a man he recognized as having been inside Bruxelles during the mahem. He contemplated the sweat running down the man's chiseled jaw, and how the blood drying on the sleeves of his own black clerical jacket had so quickly lost its color. He reflected, too, on all the suffering in the world and on his own small role in trying to deliver Ireland from its bondage. Then he prayed for the soul of the dead detective.

9

Bab Treacy awoke wondering what was causing the faery winds to blow so hard and angry.

Cait McGrath allowed a gloriously cool breeze to sweep the long auburn curls from her eyes as she sat on the old winding stairs of the Lacken Abbey ruin, gazing out on the moonlit River Nore. The waters babbled merrily. Nips of vodka kept her warm. Her computer screen was full of words. She was putting the finishing touches on her bizarre encounter with the mad woman at the Rag Tree, when the wind turned suddenly angry. It twisted out of the grey dim of dawn and lifted a shower of water out of the river that looked to Cait like a waterfall in reverse. She leaped off the bench, sending her computer rolling over the riverbank like a ball that had just been kicked. "Shite! Oh, Goddamnit," Cait moaned. Her computer slipped into the dark, swirling water.

∾

Taoiseach Desmond O'Hanrahan and his wife Mairead were on the plane home to Ireland when the cabin began suddenly shuddering. Des waited for the turbulence to subside, nudged Mairead to make sure she was sleeping, then slipped off to a corner of their private cabin and picked up the phone.

"...You heard me. Not a word about the Rag Man to the press. The nation must not know about him, understand? I want this terrorist brought down immediately, quietly, and by whatever means necessary."

As Des tiptoed back to his seat, another sudden turbulence rocked the airplane, sending him crashing face-first against the cabin wall. Dazed, he felt the warm flow of blood gushing from his nose as if it were a faucet. The wind had broken his nose.

∾

Donal Mór O'Toole awoke to a howling wind that brought him out of a dream where he was flying in the wind like that Witch of the West in *The Wizard of Oz*. Only it was soldiers and a bin lorry flying past him instead of Auntie Em. He was aware that he was sleeping in a room with an orange light flickering beneath a picture of the Sacred Heart of Jesus. The wind was blowing outside like a hurricane.

"My God in heaven, he's awake." Donal Mór heard the woman's voice, but was too weak to open his eyes to see who it was. "He's out of his coma. Dan is out of his coma, please God. Can you hear us, Dan?" the woman asked.

Donal Mór felt himself slipping away again. He used his ounce of strength to ask about the only thing that mattered to him. "Am I in Belfast?" he asked.

"Aye, Dan. God save you, you're home."

The wind continued to howl. Donal Mór didn't think he had the strength, but he could feel a smile lifting his hollow cheeks and soaring on the wind. He was home.

∽

Brigadier General Bartley Drummond sipped his cherished Drambouie as he stared at the video monitor images of Milltown. A high wind had kicked whipped debris across the familiar silhouettes of stone Celtic crosses. He leaned close to the screen. "How are you keeping?" he whispered. He was speaking to the ghosts of Milltown. "Don't forget our date. It's coming soon. Very, very soon."

∽

Tony Greenwell, having sat through another evening of his commanding officer's drinking and ranting, opened a window in hopes that the sudden wind might pour through and sober the Brigadier General. It didn't. While Drummond's gray head wobbled, Tony picked up the papers that the wind had scattered across the room. He was all set to place the papers atop Drummond's desk when he caught sight of the words "Army of Five" followed by only four names: Olivier, Hill, Ranger, and Chubby. Tony wouldn't venture a guess as to who belonged to the strange names, but he was certain that the fifth man in the Army of Five had to be the Brigadier General, himself. Another gust then swept into the room, grabbing the Army of Five out of his hand.

∽

Detective Peter Doyle listened to the wind ripping through Dublin. The gusts banged hard against the bedroom windowpane above where he lay with a silky woman, whose name he had already forgotten. A long leg wrapped itself around his naked body. "Hold me," she cooed. And he did so, but only as an investment. The more the wind pounded the house, the more his one-nighter snuggled into him. The more she purred into his ear, the more he thought about the old girlfriend. He wished the wind would stop its fuggin' blowing.

∽

Detective Kevin O'Felan wrapped a pillow around his ears, trying to block out the taunting sound of the wind. It was like a song skipping on a record player, over and over and over and over. He hadn't slept a wink. Why was the wind not bothering anyone else in the house?

The sad truth was Kevin wouldn't have slept even without an ornery wind blowing. Every time he shut his eyes, he saw the newspaper with the face ripped off the boy at the funeral. Only in his mind's eye, the hole in the newspaper was filled with the frozen face of the young detective, Paddy Burke. Into his ears the wind sang over and over, "Understand the haunting. Understand the haunting. Understand..."

Mercifully, his mobile phone rang. It was the Puzzle Palace. There were new developments. Peter Doyle would remain in Ireland to continue the hunt for the Rag Man. Kevin, as head of the International Cooperation Unit investigation, was to fly to London in the morning and meet with Scotland Yard, alone.

∽

Mattie Joe Treacy, a dinner of booze spilling out of him, crawled on all fours to the top of the small knoll and looked up at the Rag Tree. "I'm so sorry," he moaned. Hundreds of swatches of cloth in various stages of decay hung from the Rag Tree, all unfurling like tiny flags before an angry wind. Yet even among the tangle of windblown rags, he easily found his own clutching to a branch as steadfast as the first day he'd tied it there fifteen years ago. A cold gust bent the Rag Tree sideward. Mattie Joe lay shivering atop the faery rath, too full of drink and self-pity to move away. He then heard the sound of a piper playing a slow air so sorrowfully that tears like droplets of ice rolled from his eyes.

"How dare ye come here looking for sympathy, Mattie Joe Treacy. Ye didn't even bother to come home until ye were drunk. Understand the haunting, ye say. Well, try as ye might, boyo, ye will never be able to drown it with drink." A shrill voice rose above the sorrowful pipes. A blackbird pecked its beak into Mattie Joe's ribs. It was Brian. Between the pooka ranting and the faery piper's sorrowful song, he felt like a fist was grabbing and squeezing the last drops of hope and dignity from his troubled heart. When his suffering became so terrible he could no longer stand it, Mattie Joe wept and grabbed onto the trunk of the Rag Tree, which was no bigger around than a strong man's wrists, and squeezed until the jagged bark cut into his palms. His blood and tears spilled over the faery rath.

～

Bab Treacy awoke wondering what was causing the faery winds to blow so hard and angry. The moon was full and the stars burned bright. There was no telling what harm could come when the blood was stirring hot inside the Daoine Maithe. After a moment's contemplation, she realized the awful truth.

She raced through the house without stopping to put on her robe or slippers, or bothering to turn on a light.

She went to the parlor and grabbed the long plank of wood she kept hidden beneath the sofa for just such emergencies. It was all she could do to not curse the Daoine Maithe aloud. There trapped atop the small knoll, just as she feared, was her Mattie Joe. His eyes were frozen in a horrific stare that made Bab shiver right down to her bare feet. Singing, he sounded more like a mad dog howling at the moon. Setting the plank of wood down onto the faery rath, she moved across the board, being careful not to have as much as a toe touch the soil, lest the Daoine Maithe bring her to a very sad end. The plank was very old and splintery. Bab wished now that she had taken the time to put on her shoes.

She moved toward her poor, suffering son, now mad with drink and the curse of the Daoine Maithe, which, she knew, was why he drank so in the first place. Mattie Joe's head fell and nestled against her breast. His arms flopped around her shoulders. Big as he was, he felt no different to her than he did as an infant. For all his sins and graces, he was her Mattie Joe, and no one was going to take him away from her. When they reached the kitchen door, her son's mad eyes glared at her and sang. "'Tis the last rose of summer, left blooming all alone..."

Inside, Bab brought Mattie Joe tea with a dash of milk. Nothing like a cup of strong tea to mend the body, she told herself. "Hush up that singing," she said, then poured the cure into him. Outside, the faery wind kept blowing. Bab again wondered what it was that had angered the Daoine Maithe so, and what other poor souls they were haunting on this strange night.

∽

Detective John "Skinny" Farrell protected himself from the strong wind by ducking behind the hawthorne ditch across the road from the Rag Man's farm home. The terrorist, whose moonlit silhouette swayed in the wind, appeared to be either drunk or on drugs. First, he cried, then, he laughed. By the time a strong-built woman, who appeared to be the mother, lifted him off the ground, the Rag Man was mumbling to himself incoherently. Once Skinny was certain that no one was coming back out of the house, he used a mobile phone to dial the Blackbird's beeper number. Half an hour passed before his mobile rang.

"This is the Blackbird. Talk to me." The voice was deep and dark.

"I've got him marked," Skinny said. "He lives on a farm off the Kells Road between Kilkenny and a village called Bamford Cross. So when do I get the fifty thousand quid? And how are you going to keep all this from the Puzzle Palace?"

"Drive to Carlow. You'll see a black Mercedes parked by the castle. The keys are behind the right front wheel. Throw the keys into the river and lock yourself inside the boot. The Gardai will receive an anonymous tip. They'll let you out. You will request a leave of absence from Security and Intelligence. It will be granted, of course. Then you return to Kilkenny and mark the Rag Man. That's when you'll get your money. In the meantime, you mark the Rag Man and note any contacts he makes, understood?"

The Blackbird's voice remained very cold. Skinny wanted to be angry with the man, but at the moment he was too frightened. It was hard to be angry and scared at the same time. And he didn't like at all the thought of being locked in the boot of a car.

"I don't think the boot of the car is very believable. If the Rag Man had kidnapped me, why wouldn't he just kill me like he did the others?" Skinny asked.

"That can be arranged."

"The boot of the car is fine," Skinny said, quickly. "But I understood I was supposed to mark the Rag Man, then get paid the rest of my fifty thousand quid. Now you're after stretching things on me. I don't even know who you are. What's stopping me from keeping my ten thousand quid advance and quitting you right now?"

"You already gave the reason," said the Blackbird, his tone still flat. "You don't know who I am. But I know who you are. And you just can't walk back into Garda headquarters, can you? The rest of your money will come when I say. Now, anything else strange?"

Skinny was sorry now he was involved in the whole Rag Man mess. Of all the lawmen who took bribes, why did the Blackbird have to pick him?

"Yes, there is something strange," Skinny said, now especially eager to please the Blackbird. "There's a tree growing on a knoll beside his house. Damnedest thing you ever saw. It's got all these little rags tied to its branches. There must be hundreds of them."

Part II

Rock 'n Nua

10

In his view, the concert should be called "Mick Nua."

Mick Mulvihill stood alone in the Kilkenny Castle banquet hall, staring out of a high arching window while gently plucking the strings of the worn guitar he called "Deirdre." The chiming strings echoed throughout the hall, which was as cavernous as a church full of empty pews. Mick contemplated the long afternoon shadows stretching over fairway-like grounds, then inspected the construction crew sawing and hammering across a stage as wide as the staid stone edifice itself. In his mind, he fast-forwarded a fortnight hence and saw himself standing triumphantly in the center of the stage, the blinding yellow spotlights swallowing him as he and Deirdre rocked out for the thousands of fans sprawled over the castle's lawn.

Two years back, not a soul would have imagined Mick Mulvihill being welcomed back on any stage, let alone to the site of the biggest rock concert in Ireland's history.

The image of himself, fat, boozy eyed, and being helped off stage at Lisdoonvarna, still pained him. *The Sunday World* had screamed, "Mulvihill Rocked." Now in a fortnight's time his new—or was it nua—slimmed-down image would be beamed via satellite throughout Europe. Rock 'n Nua be damned. In his view, the concert should be called "Mick Nua."

His fingers danced over Deirdre's metallic strings in happy expectation of the comeback concert. He began thumping out a bass-driven beat and singing in a soulful voice that in his heyday was described as honey oozing from a jar.

"Nua—thump thump—Eire Nua—thump thump—let the voices of our people sing at last. Nua—thump thump—Eire Nua—thump thump—'tis the victory we won for the sufferings of our past..."

The song was the O'Hanrahan government's Eire Nua anthem, written especially for Mick on the occasion of the Rock 'n Nua Concert. In his view, the song was merely Eire Nua happy-crap, but once he and Deirdre fused some life into the lyrics and amended a few of the chord changes, the government would have the hit single they wanted.

The irony of him singing for the government greatly amused Mick. He'd guzzled away his first fortune, made by singing protest anthems against their sins. Now he was starting on his second fortune by singing songs supporting the very same government. His fingers soon grew bored with pimping the government's song. Instead, he slipped into the comfort of bending mean bluesy notes that never lied about Mick's moods. Showbiz and politics made strange bedfellows, he thought. A bent string moaned in agreement.

A sudden clacking of hard sole shoes over the polished wood floor echoed off the stone walls, distracting Mick. Turning, he saw a dandy man, dressed predominantly in black and stepping toward him with an outstretched hand. It was Shay Butler, a Dublin theatre man who had managed Mick, until his substance abuse relapse. Butler had an animated personality that Mick wasn't sure was due to his hanging around too much with the theater crowd, or if he was gay, or both. Mick would have hated Butler, if it weren't for the fact that the chubby little puff was about to pour fifty thousand quid into his empty pockets.

Butler approached with his arms spread like the wings of a penguin in flight. "God, is it the same Michael Mulvihill or no? You're the picture of health, man. How much weight have you lost? Two stone?" He folded his arms over his chest and shook his head with a look of utter disbelief. He offered his hand.

"And then some," Mick said, ignoring the offer of a handshake. "But it didn't happen over night. Of course, how would you know that? You've been a stranger for these past two years."

"Michael. Michael. Michael." Butler held out his hands palm up like a street beggar. "What did I promise you? Once you put your life together, I'd be the first back in your corner. And here I am. And here you are. Together again, and putting on the biggest concert in the history of Ireland. You know very well that it was I who told the government that there was only one man to sing their Eire Nua song. It's going to be fabulous." He showed all teeth when he said, "fabulous."

"Their fabulous song sucks. I've miles of work to do on it before it's even half presentable. And why, if I'm supposed to be the big headliner, am I not going on last?"

Butler now folded his hands with the polished fingernails against his thick, pouting lips. "Michael. Michael. Michael. You know poor Van still suffers from acute stage fright. Even with dark glasses on, he insists that the sun be fully down so he can't see the audience. Surely you can find it in your heart to let the poor little man go on last. Besides, *when* you play is not important. You're the headliner. You're the one everyone's asking to sing a duet with. Bono, Mary, Elvis— By the way, how rude of me. How are you, Deirdre dear?" he said in a baby-talk voice. He leaned forward and kissed the old guitar where a billion or more strums had scrubbed a valley in the instrument's pale finish.

Mick was of a mind to wipe the spot where Butler had planted his slobbery lips on Deirdre, but he thought better of it. He didn't have his fifty thousand quid just yet. Deirdre would just have to put up with a bit of slobbering. "So you give me Sinéad," Mick grunted.

"I had to, Michael. Taoiseach's orders. And you have to admit that it's tremendously symbolic from the government's point of view, given your respective activist pasts. Sinéad and—I mean *you* and Sinéad singing together epitomizes the healing that has brought together all generations of Irishmen and Irishwomen. By the way, have you seen this castle when it's backlit by a golden setting sun? At nine at night it stands silhouetted like faeryland magic. Oh, Michael. This concert is going to be fabulous, indeed. Fabulous."

Mick wasn't buying Shay Butler's huckstering. He turned his back on his former manager and again looked out the window at the stage—his stage.

"Aye. And won't it be just fucking fabulous seeing the government's two most public agitators standing side by side to sing a shitty song that'll make millions for Eire Nua." Mick spun around and glared at the incessantly grinning manager. Butler had always reminded Mick of a light bulb that never switched off. "I'm telling you now, Shay, you can tell Her Baldness that she's singing in my key or not at all. And as for the fat little mole with the sun glasses, you can tell him that I'm going to cure his stage fright, because the audience will be after leaving once I'm done singing—which is not until I'm damned good and ready. Am I clear?"

Shay Butler kept grinning. Mick didn't know which had the greater luster, the producer's pearly teeth or his polished fingernails.

"About the key, Michael. Have you made up your mind on that yet? It's not for Sinéad," Shay Butler added quickly. "It's for the Flamenco rhythm section."

"The wha'?"

"The Flamenco Rhythm section. And the German Oompah horn players. I was going to tell you, honest. But remember, Michael, this concert is being seen throughout Europe, Australia, parts of the States. It's imperative that we don't come off as being *too Irish*, you know what I mean? Rock 'n Nua is more of a *global* event, really. As a matter of fact, do you know what the newspapers are calling your return to the stage? The British Isles equivalent of Dylan's appearance at the Concert for Bangladesh. Isn't that big stuff, heh, Michael?"

"Yeah, and that American whore of a writer Thomas Hennessy called me a what? A sunshine patriot?" Mick scoffed at the words. "Who was it who sung the Birmingham Six out of prison? And Nicky Kelly? And the Guilford Four? And who put the last words of the hunger strikers' to music, while government goons breathed blood down my back if I didn't shut up? Sunshine patriot? Call me a drunk, a junkie, I couldn't give a damn. But a sunshine patriot?"

Shay Butler placed his polished fingernails on Mick's shoulders.

"Michael. Michael. Michael. The only thing that shines on you is the star over your head. You're a star again, Michael. Thanks to Eire Nua."

II

Clumpity clack, the beat of hooves
While Erin, grey-faced, slumbers late
A horse and cart, black cloaked courses
On Lacken's beam rides the Faery Host,
Moonstruck.
Horse and driver and I make three
Raven eyes fly forth upon me
And clutch me to its tangle
Twisted within an ancient smile,
Beguiled.
Fantasy pulls my heart
Fear shackles my feet
I turn to ponder days gone by
Clumpity clack sounds its hooves,
Away.

Cait McGrath sat cross-legged on her abbey ruin perch, nipping at the dregs of her Muddy Mary thermos while returning the vacant stare of an alabaster moonbeam.

Between sips, she snorted cigar smoke streams into the mist-heavy, predawn air. Her new computer's screen was as blank as the moonbeam. If inspiration was on its way, it had better come soon, she thought. She hadn't many sips left.

The writing had been hard going ever since a strange windstorm had sent her trusted laptop tumbling into the River Nore a few days ago. Gone with the computer were all her stock lists of metaphors and similes, pages and pages of fabricated dialog from fabricated characters and, worst of all, her muse's whispers of an Ireland brimming with irony. All gone. *Gone with the bloody fucking wind* gone. With her deadline for her next Hennessy column looming that evening, her writing was dead in the water—literally and figuratively. She blamed it all on her having visited that damned Rag Tree.

Cait was bribing her muse with a final quaff from the Muddy Mary jug when a gravel-crunching hum broke the stillness. A quarter mile down river, the silhouette of a horse and cart rumbled across John's Bridge. Like a fleeting dream, the horse and cart were gone in an instant, but not before Cait heard her muse whisper, "Aisling."

Aisling, a Gaelic word meaning vision or dream, was a popular art form hundreds of years back when poets wandered Ireland's byways, picking up meals and coins for reciting poems foretelling of Ireland's freedom. Energized by a sudden epiphany, Cait flipped the cigar into the river and attacked the computer's keyboard. She would depict the driver of the horse and cart as being Kathleen ni Houlian herself, come in form of a dark and sorrowful beauty, now wandering lost amid the glitter and tinsel of Eire Nua. She banged her ideas onto the keyboard as swiftly as they entered her head.

But after half an hour, Kathleen ni Houlihan was stuck in a horse and cart whose wheels would not turn. Cait's fingers, now idle and thoughtless, had scratched out a fifteen-line poem and little else. Nearby, a lorry was coming to a brake-whining stop. The rising sun first flickered against the black rocks jutting out of the river. Ireland had woken. And Cait's muse slipped off to snooze. Disheartened, she looked at her computer screen and the sad story of her pathetic longings:

Picnic on the Nore. A bottle of wine chilling in the river. Strawberries dipped in chocolate. Nestling against the rock-hard thighs of a brown-eyed, handsome man.

As much as she wanted to blame her writer's block on the Rag Tree and that crazy Faery Woman of Bamford Cross, she knew that her real problem was that that her body ached for the distraction of a man. Nothing serious. Just someone to play with. She shook her empty thermos. The Muddy Marys were just no cure for the type of draught she was experiencing.

Back in her flat, she was greeted by an email she'd been dreading. Thomas Hennessy was expecting a new column, today. Cait lied and wrote back that she was tying up some loose ends on a story and that the column would be sent that evening, Irish time. But instead of working, she took a nap she didn't need with the hopes it might clear her mind. She awoke to the clumpity clack of hooves outside her window.

There, rising out of the small dip in the road, a horse and cart came rattling near. Clutching the reins was a woman with dark hair flowing out from under a red hood. *"Follow the vision,"* Cait's muse whispered. Jumping into her hired blue Renault, she followed from a distance, in hopes that the mysterious woman guiding the horse and cart was leading her on to some sort of festival or fair. Five miles down a twisting road, she brought the car to a halt atop a humped-back bridge, coursing into the riverside village of Bennettsbridge. Clogging the bridge and stopping traffic was a throng of people moving over the bridge. As disappointed as Cait was watching the horse and cart being swallowed into the crowd, she became even more perturbed upon learning that all the fuss had to do with nothing more than a lousy local hurling match.

In Cait's view, the only good in a sporting match was the opportunity it provided for admiring scantily clad men. Since her car was hopelessly blocked in, she hadn't a choice but to make the best of things by scouting out some firm thighs.

Navigating a sideline thick with spectators, she eavesdropped on conversations with faint hopes of capturing the inspiration for her Hennessy column. But the talk proved to be sports drivel about some lad named "Big Heff." "Mighty Heffernan." "Kilkenny's greatest hurler ever." Some worn, old hurler was not the story Cait was looking for. What she needed was something with real spark. Something that would leap out of that green cow pasture like an angry monster and bite the arse of Eire Nua. What she needed was for her aisling to reappear.

The match was about to start and Cait nestled next to three women. One of them, a dumpy woman wearing a green and gold jumper, proved to be the wife of Kilkenny's greatest hurling player ever. The woman whined, "My poor Brian has awful knees," and, "Don't I have to give him cold compresses for two hours after every match," and, "'Tis a nice thing that a man of Brian's stature entertains on the club level, don't ye think?"

Mrs. Heffernan's two friends were closer to Cait's age. One was a petite blonde, dressed in red leather, and the other a moon-faced girl with pretty brown eyes. They both waved as an ox of a man in a green and gold uniform of the James Stephens Club trotted toward them. His arms were the size of Cait's legs. The front half of his head was bald, and he was grey from there on. His ears stuck out from the sides of his big head like tea saucers standing on their sides. Nasty scars twisting over both his knees reminded her of country road maps.

"Good luck, Sugar beet," the dumpy Mrs. Heffernan said, rubbing noses with the sporting legend.

Sugar beet? Cait thought the man looked more like a large sack of potatoes, which was fine, since Mrs. Heffernan looked like a small sack of potatoes.

Though Cait knew nothing of hurling, it didn't take a genius to recognize that the large sack of potatoes with the shredded knees was single-handedly destroying anyone wearing the maroon and black uniform of the Bennettsbridge club. Seemingly every few moments, the giant Heffernan would extend a huge paw into the air, snatch the ball, then smack it with his hurley stick. The ball either went into the goal or over the bar. Everyone cheered. This happened over and over again. The only thing keeping the match from being unbearably boring was one Bennettsbridge player, who Cait found distractingly handsome. She inched closer to the pitch each time he ran near.

It was halftime when Mrs. Heffernan and her friends took a sudden interest in her. The leather-clad blonde spoke first.

"You're very quiet, Miss. You must be a Bennettsbridge supporter. Is your man playing for them, so? Don't worry, they'll do better next week, against the likes of Clara."

Cait examined the women wearing patronizing smiles and decided that she did not like any of them. "Yes, as a matter of fact, my boyfriend does play for Bennettsbridge," she lied.

Just then, the Bennettsbridge hurlers ran back out on the pitch led by the distracting fellow with short-cropped hair and the most gorgeous brown eyes Cait had ever seen on a man. His rippled thighs would be worth a week of daydreams, maybe more, Cait thought. (She was a leg and eyes girl; she couldn't lie about that.) "That's him," she said, not caring a damn if she was caught in a lie. "Isn't he gorgeous?"

While Mrs. Heffernan and the moon-faced woman inspected Cait as if she was a mannequin in a dress shop, Miss Red Leather crossed her arms and swung her head away.

"So, your Mattie Joe Treacy's latest and greatest?" said the one with straight brown hair, reaching to hold the leathered one's hand. "Do I hear a hint of an American accent?" she added.

Being called an American pleased Cait immensely. So did the women's furtive glances as she removed her jumper, showing off a figure far curvier than those of her three new adversaries. "Why in America there are shopping malls that would fit the whole of Kilkenny inside, and then some. You really should think about coming out," she said, knowing how the Irish detested haughty Americans.

When the match resumed, Mrs. Heffernan and her two friends had lost all interest in hurling. All three held Cait with laser beam stares while she focused on her handsome new "boyfriend." Miss Red Leather's mascara-caked eyes kept sizing up Cait's chest. *Read 'em and weep, Honey. Thirty-four B.* Cait thought about saying.

When a high ball came sailing Brian Heffernan's way, Cait's new *boyfriend* snatched the ball and knocked the big ox to the muddy pitch in the process. For the first time, the Bennettsbridge supporters cheered their own club and Cait's lad with eyes like balls of brown fire. "Fair play to ye, Matthew," Cait cried, joining in. From the corner of an eye, she saw the faces of three aghast women rolling their eyes. Hurling suddenly did not seem so boring anymore.

"Matthew is planning to come to the States at the end of the summer," Cait told the three. "I work for an American university in Washington, DC. Matthew is going to enroll in the undergraduate business administration program." It was hard not to laugh aloud when the mouths of the three women dropped like trap doors and hung open, until all the flies in Ireland could have landed on their tongues.

Miss Red Leather had had enough. "Matthew my arse. Mattie Joe Treacy couldn't pass his leaving cert let alone go to an American university. He's a drunk and a whoring skunk, and you're very welcome to him!"

"Well, I have to admit those brown eyes do melt the britches right off a girl, don't you think? And those legs— My gawd! Muddied or no, you wouldn't be a woman if you didn't want a rub against those thighs." The little erotic groan Cait added for spite was just enough to send Miss Red Leather away in tears, wrapped in the consoling arms of the woman with the moon face and straight chestnut brown hair. "I hope it wasn't something I said," Cait said to Mrs. Heffernan.

Mrs. Heffernan pushed the sleeves of her green and gold jumper above knobby elbows. She glared at Cait. "Feck off. Your man is a pig, and I see he found himself a suitable match."

Cait couldn't care less what the dumpy Missus Heffernan called her, but she'd be damned if she'd allow anyone to insult her new boyfriend. "Well, we'll see whose pig wins the day," Cait snapped, "my handsome one, or that waddling hog you call a husband."

∾

Detective Skinny Farrell's job of spying on the Rag Man had brought him to a hurling match in the riverside village of Bennettsbridge, where the only excitement thus far had been provided by two female supporters screaming and scratching at one another. The battling women put on a good show, but Skinny eventually turned his full attention to the match, because there wasn't much he enjoyed more than the ol' clash of the ash and the soaring flight of the small ball. Hurling played properly was something to be treasured, even more so than watching two women ripping at one another.

Watching a hurling match on a Sunday afternoon didn't much seem like work, but then where was the rule that said work couldn't be fun? The truth of the matter was he hadn't raised a sweat since he'd been freed from the boot of the car in Carlow, just as the Blackbird had promised. And because he had suffered such a "psychological trauma," he was immediately granted a fortnight's administrative leave from the Criminal Investigation Unit, again just as the Blackbird had promised him. Now he was collecting the Blackbird's money for tailing the Rag Man, which, so far, had been nothing more than one big pub crawl. The toughest part of the job was dealing with the sore head in the morning, though that didn't last long, either, since the Rag Man was a great one for having a bit of the hair of the dog by lunchtime. When this whole Rag Man caper was finished, Skinny thought he just might have to go on holidays, to get some rest.

The Rag Man was a brilliant hurler, murdering and terrorizing aside. Not only was he speedy, he was a tricky divil, too. When a high arching ball, that by all rights belonged to Brian Heffernan, came hurtling down not far from where Skinny stood, the Rag Man plucked the ball right out of the big man's hand like a kid snapping an apple off a tree. He then raced down the pitch and blistered a ball that the poor divil of a goalkeeper merely waved at in self-defense. Skinny might have seen the equal to the Rag Man's solo run, but none better. 'Twas a pity though that such a top class sportsman had resorted to a life of crime.

As the second half wore on, the Rag Man's swiftness began sapping away at the hurling hero's strength. The Bennettsbridge crowd, who had been cheering Heffernan, began exhorting Mattie Joe Treacy. And as Skinny's luck would have it, the two great hurlers were stationed close enough for him to hear them taunting one another.

"What's wrong, old Heff?" the Rag Man asked. "Was that your old woman I seen in the scrap over there? B'Jas' I'm grateful it's not her I'm after marking. That one could do damage, I'd say."

And so it went throughout the second half; the two best hurlers on the field tormented and cursed one another. At one point, the tiring Heffernan shot an elbow into the Rag Man's nose, causing blood to flow like water from a faucet. Skinny had no tolerance for dirty play and was now solidly supporting Mattie Joe. He was glad when the Rag Man, his face splattered with blood, spit on Heffernan's spikes. When Bennettsbridge evened the score, Skinny was so excited that he forgot himself and cried out, "Fair play to the Rag Man!" Luckily, everyone else was screaming, too. Seemingly, no one had heard him.

Heffernan began puffing like an old tractor. The Rag Man's right hand was swollen nearly to the size of the ball itself. His lower lip bled freely, as did his swollen nose. His ribs had been so tenderized by Heffernan's hurley that any time the ball was away, he bent over at the waist and held his sides. How the man continued, Skinny hadn't a clue.

The ball floated Heffernan's way. The Rag Man was bent at the waist and leaning on his hurley for support, like a man on a crutch. "He's spent," Skinny muttered and those near him nodded in agreement. A reenergized Heffernan pivoted and lowered his shoulder. He seemed intent on ramming his way to the goal right through the Rag Man. But the nimble footed Rag Man suddenly danced out of harm's way like Fred-fucking-Astaire, himself. With nothing to ram his huge body against, Heffernan stumbled and fell face down into the turf and mud. The Bennettsbridge women openly cursed the fallen giant. The Bennettsbridge men, their eyes popping and neck veins bulging, cried for Mattie Joe Treacy to "Fight fire with fire." The Rag Man cleared away the loose ball. The full-forward put the ball over the bar. Car horns blared. Bennettsbridge was ahead by a point!

The clouds that had been gathering throughout the afternoon now formed a charcoal blanket spreading low over the pitch. Wind blustered against reddening faces and billowed coattails. Every few seconds, clashing hurleys cracked in a desperate battle for the ball. The match was nearly over and Skinny was so nervous that he could barely breathe. The Rag Man spit up blood as he straddled Heffernan's hip. What might just be the last played ball of the match sailed lazily toward the two hurling warriors.

Heffernan reached high for the ball. The Rag Man slipped his hurley inside Heffernan's opened palm and the ball rolled down into his waiting hand. The Bennettsbridge supporters cheered and tumbled over one another as a whistle blew and the match was won.

But Skinny, as his job demanded, never took his eyes off Mattie Joe Treacy. He saw how the rage began to boil over the Rag Man's wounded face, and how, with the ball in hand, he turned and faced the lumbering Heffernan. It happened so fast that Skinny never actually saw the ball come off the Rag Man's hurley. The hurling legend fell straight back as though struck by a truck. Then, taking a running start, the Rag Man slammed the ball with all his strength into the unconscious Heffernan's groin. At that moment, Skinny saw the monster living inside the Rag Man coming out and wondered, *Did I sell myself too cheaply to the Blackbird?*

As the jubilant Bennettsbridge supporters carried their new hero into the village pub, Skinny detoured down a small lane, twisting along the river to an old abandoned grain mill. There he found a woman dressed in a red cloak, waiting for him next to an old horse and cart, just as the Blackbird had said she would. He handed her three, hundred pound notes. "What am I supposed to do again?" the woman asked, tucking the money inside the pocket of the low rider blue jeans she wore beneath the cloak.

"You're supposed to make up an old aisling vision poem, and spook the bejasus out of the pretty redhead who was in the cat fight," Skinny said.

∽

Cait McGrath found herself feeling surprisingly united with the Bennettsbridge supporters, not a few of whom congratulated her for giving Mrs. Heffernan what she'd long had coming to her.

Friendly locals welcomed her into the Bridge Bar, a snug village pub that long ago had been someone's family sitting room and parlor. The wood floors and paneling had probably been blonde when the place was first built, but a century of being lathed in smoke and whiskey had turned them to wizened brunettes. This was your grandfather's local. This was where men came after long days in the fields, wearing the same dusty jackets and ties day after day. And day after day, they'd come and hang for hours over the rims of their mistress glasses, the smoke from their cigarettes and pipes speaking nearly as loud as their whispering voices. Today, the Bridge Bar roared hosannas for two heroes: Cait McGrath the Bitch Slayer and Mattie Joe Treacy the Giant Slayer, the latter of whom Cait saw had been dumped into a corner while pint after pint of beer was being poured over his battered body. Some of it went down his throat, too.

A shaft of light from a new afternoon sun snuck through the opened bar door, interrupting the celebration. Awash in the yellow rays stood a stern man with red knobs of quivering flesh high on his square and firmly set jaw. The Bridge Bar fell quiet. Cait heard whispers that the man was an official of the Gaelic Athletic Association. A path was cleared, and the stern man found his way to where Cait's handsome but bloodied hurler sat on the floor, grinning like a schoolboy who had just farted in class.

"Mattie Joe Treacy," the G.A.A. man announced, "for your deliberate and malicious attack on Brian Heffernan, you are from this moment forward barred from the Gaelic Athletic Association. Don't trouble yourself with an appeal. You have disgraced the sport of hurling, the good people of Kilkenny, and your father's people, in this fine village of Bennettsbridge."

Glasses moving swiftly from lips to tabletops sounded like hail balls hitting a window. Cait watched horrified as one by one, the very men who only an hour before had given Matthew a hero's ride through the village, disowned him. For his part, Matthew was nearly blind with bruises and drink and did not seem to care. He continued sucking down the beer as he winked to a couple of the lads nearby, even as they turned their faces from him. A low buzz coursed the barroom: Brian Heffernan was in hospital, in shock.

Soon, everyone had left the Bridge Bar and, just that quickly, Cait had won her pair of hard thighs and brown eyes—battered as they were. Crouching on the floor next to the semi-comatose boy, she placed a cold compress made from a bar towel and ice against his swollen cheekbones. As the heat poured off his flesh, Cait felt the loneliness seeping out of hers.

She was half-carrying and half-dragging her wobbling Matthew Treacy to her car when a woman wrapped in a red, hooded cloak rode up in horse and cart. It was Cait's vision woman returned.

The hooded woman looked nervous. She cleared her throat twice before speaking haltingly. "Umm...Lo though I am weary from wandering, alas you have brought me... umm brought to me, my lost son, the brave warrior prince, who will save the soul of Erin—Oh for chrissakes, is he alright?"

Matthew had slipped from Cait's hold and was curled into a ball on the pavement. He let out a loud belch.

"He'll be fine. Just help me get him into my car," Cait said.

Back in the flat on Father Bennett Lane, Cait eagerly addressed her computer without the support of vodka, cigars, or classical music. Her fingers danced over the keyboard, waltzing with a glorious lie about how the Rag Tree symbolized the last stand of Ireland's old ways before being swept away in a tidal wave of Eire Nua. With a final victorious punch of her forefinger against the keyboard, she sent off her column, "The Rag Tree," as an email to Tom Hennessy. She then contemplated the sweetest, most soothing sound she'd heard in weeks: a man snoring in her bed. She couldn't wait until her warrior prince of Erin sobered.

∾

Tom Hennessy read over an email about the Rag Tree in Ireland, growing along the side of a winding road. Taking a long drag from his cigar, he then blew out a cloud of sheer relief. Outside the window of his paradise hideaway, turquoise waves slid across alabaster sand, stopping just short of a green ribbon of palm trees. Life could be no better, he thought. He had his computer, his cigars, his booze, his island heaven and, with the arrival of Cait McGrath's email, money. A lot of money.

He made a phone call to a pager, then dialed in his number when he heard the beep. While waiting for the return call, he fixed himself a celebratory drink: four fingers of Mount Gay rum over crushed ice, with as many wedges of lime and a splash of tonic.

The phone rang. "You called," the Blackbird said. His voice was its usual flat monotone.

"The Rag Tree has been delivered, finally. Not bad either, if I say so. One of the best columns I've never written." Tom could not help giggling. The rum was going straight to his

head. He didn't give a damn if the Blackbird didn't have a
sense of humor.

"Alright so. And you'll make sure the column appears
the morning of the Rock 'n Nua concert, of course?"

"And first you'll make sure the rest of the fifty G's show
up in my account, of course?"

There was silence, then, "Has there been problem with
payment thus far?"

"No. No, I guess there hasn't," Tom said. He became
aware of the ice rattling against the side of his glass. He
gulped the rum. "You did say the woman would stay
unharmed, though? Right? Hello...?"

12

...both were higher-ups who were "in the know"...

Donal Mór O'Toole lay on a bed in the safe house, slipping in and out of consciousness, too weak to greet most of his friends, too disinterested to speak to his enemies. Last night, over the dregs of a rain dripping through the gutter, he'd heard the whispers that his end was near. A tube for oxygen was shoved up his nose. The call had gone out for the priest.

He'd been fully conscious most of the morning. His makeshift infirmary was someone's parlor. Searching the room, his eyes landed on a tinfoil flame spinning orange and gold beneath a picture of the Sacred Heart of Jesus hanging over a silent, green marble fireplace. Given his choice, he would have chosen the warmth of a turf fire over the Son of Man's faux flame. Even with the oxygen tube, it was difficult trying to fill his lungs with enough air; it was like trying to blow up a new balloon, only it hurt. His mind tended to dwell on a singular thought for long stretches, and for some reason a lyric was now stuck in his head: *"I've fought all my life for freedom, but I'd give my life just one day to be free."* He fixed his gaze on the twisting flame. Rain gurgled down the gutter. The tinfoil flame spun round and round. Was this it? His one day to be free?

He heard the scuffling of feet outside the parlor door and immediately shut his eyes. If he didn't like the person who had come to see him, he'd just play dead. Some old blackguards would be visiting, just so they could claim they had seen the great Donal Mór on his deathbed. He didn't like the idea of being a status symbol for those who'd let the republican movement rot in his absence.

Two pair of feet scraped through the door, slowly.

"Hello, Donal. It's me. Tadgh Dougherty. I'm here with Father Brendan Sheils."

Donal Mór played dead. It wasn't that he didn't like these two, but both were higher-ups who were "in the know" when it came to IRA operations. Eavesdropping on their conversation could yield some news of the republican movement. He sneaked a peek at Tadgh Dougherty, a comrade from his border battalion days. Drink and hard weather had turned his craggy face beet red. Dougherty was a republican hardliner, like himself.

The tea came and the door was shut. His visitors intended to stay awhile. Donal Mór eagerly listened for news of the republican movement.

"Father Brendan, I don't see an end to our hard times now," Dougherty said, his tone downcast. "Remember back in the '70s when we could detonate thirty bombs a day? Now we can't even gather the wires and batteries to make a bomb without someone touting on us. How can we have any credibility as a military organization by decommissioning our weapons, when we can't even find them ourselves? Everything is trapped inside Donal's head. And he could be brain dead already. This is very bad."

"Will our day in court tomorrow not help us?" Brendan Sheils asked.

Donal Mór sneaked another peek. Brendan was filling himself with food—he'd always been fond of his ham and cabbage. Dougherty, ever the pessimist, shook his head in resignation.

"We can only hope our legal maneuvering can buy us time to carry off one successful bombing mission, at the very least. It's absolutely essential that we be able to assert ourselves now, before Eire Nua flushes us down the drain for another generation, maybe forever."

In contrast to Dougherty, Brendan was ever the optimist, especially when his mouth was full. "We're not done yet," he said, licking the cake crumbs from his lips.

Our day in court. Legal maneuvering. Donal Mór was eager for the pair to expound, but they drifted off in moribund nostalgia about him and how things might have been different had he not been in prison these past twenty-five years.

Donal Mór was all too familiar with the tragedy of the last ceasefire. Only a year before, the Provisionals entered into secret talks with the British government to discuss terms for peace and recognition of Sinn Fein as the legal political voice for nationalists. It seemed like a very good idea at the time, since the Brits had refused to hold talks for over twenty years. When word of the talks leaked, it had been a republican propaganda heyday. He'd seen the tabloids smuggled into the prison: "Whitehall and IRA Hold Pillow Talks." Parliament went bleeding berserk. Heads rolled. Sinn Fein sought talks that were "political, open, and vigorous." But Britain bent to the pressure from the Orangemen of Ulster, whose votes desperately were needed for the ruling party to remain in power. The Prime Minister demanded a decommissioning of arms before talking openly with Sinn Fein. Such a move was tantamount to an IRA surrender. Talks stopped. So did the ceasefire.

"What's your read on this escape?" Dougherty asked. The volume of his voice dropped a notch. "Do we have *any* clue who is responsible? I'll tell you the whole situation makes me nervous."

The last comment answered one of Donal Mór's questions. His escape had not been IRA Army Council approved. The bastards *were* going to let him die in prison. He peeked again. Brendan appeared to be choosing his words carefully.

"The escape from the Maze is still a puzzle. Maybe an escape led by renegades. Maybe a British counterplot. One theory is that a prison mole was in danger of being exposed, so the escape was a way for the Brits to justify clamping down on the prisoners. But why would they ever want to put *him* back on the street?"

Donal Mór kept his eyes shut. He knew Brendan was talking about him. The priest continued, "Yet, the current net effect of the escape seems positive. Fundraising in the States got a real shot in the arm. Liam Riordon, now being incarcerated in a Republic of Ireland prison, gives us a social justice issue that should help pull media attention away from Eire Nua for at least a couple of minutes—and you know how difficult that has been. Enthusiasm among nationalists grows each day our remaining three lads stay on the run. Tadgh, you said it yourself. We need a major public relations victory, in a big way. I think we have one coming soon in the form of a funeral."

"Aye. I've thought of that. His funeral will bring out the old crowd, surely. And our day in court tomorrow will help too, of course."

The dripping rain became louder, the voices softer. Donal Mór felt himself slipping away. The last thing he heard was Tadgh asking, "What was her name?" Brendan answered, "Angeline."

He remembered her little arms being barely long enough to surround one of his legs. In the wee hours of the morning, she would clutch onto him like the press of tiny pillows. "Daddy, I'm scared," she'd whisper, and he'd pull her closer and murmur, "Sshh, Daddy's here. Daddy's here." They could hear the clanging from the street below. The Belfast women were beating trash bin lids against the pavement, warning that the Brits were moving through. "Daddy's here." Lightly, he'd draw his fingers through her silky black curls until his wee girl fell back to sleep.

She'd been only five when he'd left their home in the Andytown section of Belfast for good. *"Daddy's here."* The words haunted him still. Daddy hadn't been there in a long, long time. How many more nights did she cry out when he was not there? Was she crying out for him when her young life was snuffed out by British soldiers? Rebels didn't make very good dads.

The image of his wife had not endured with him through the long years, as had their child's. Bridgid had faded from his memory somewhat, though her desperate cries still seared to the core of his memory.

"I did not marry a man; I married a cause! You love no one, only Ireland. What has Ireland done for us, Donal? She's taken my brother and your father. I can't give any more away. I have to live. Even if it's for a day, *I have to live.* There is no life left for us in Ireland. Please! Come with us!"

He woke up, feeling the rub of the holy oil on his forehead. Brendan was mumbling prayers over him. His thoughts were still back with his wife and daughter.

He'd let them go because, like many young men, he'd not yet been beaten enough by life to ever doubt that his dreams would come true. He was utterly convinced they'd be a family again, soon, once Ireland had won her freedom. And what if Ireland *were* free? By now, he and Bridgid could be doting grandparents, staring into smiling faces featuring his straight nose and Bridgid's blue eyes.

Brendan Sheils whispered over him. "Through this holy anointment may the Lord in his love and mercy help you with the grace of the Holy Spirit. Amen. May the Lord free you from sin, save you, and raise you up."

Donal Mór opened his eyes and, with all his strength, struggled to a sitting position.

"I'm saved," he rasped.

The look on Brendan's chubby face was nearly worth the price of dying. His eyes popped and his great belly trembled. Donal Mór laughed. He'd always enjoyed taking the mickey out of his brother-in-law.

They embraced. He felt the shock in Brendan's thick fingers as they pulled suddenly away from the brittle bones knobbing on what used to be his shoulders, as if they might break if he held on any longer. Brendan reached into the pocket of his black clerical trousers. He held a scrap of cloth. The small talk was over.

"You were clutching this tweed rag when they found you," the priest said. "Tell me what you know about the Rag Man, Donal. We know you spoke to him. There's a lot riding on this."

Donal Mór slumped back against his pillow. The effort in sitting up had sapped his one ounce of energy. "Tell me about Bridgid and Angeline first. Tell me the story, then I'll tell you everything."

His brother-in-law sighed in resignation. Descending over his tiny eyes packed in pink flesh was the same sad glaze that always came with the telling of the story. "You were on the run," Brendan began, "and there was no way of getting you and the girls out of the country together. So, I was driving the girls to a safe house in the republic."

The girls. After all these years Brendan still referred to his sister and niece as the girls. Donal closed his eyes and let Brendan transport him to the place he'd imagined a million times or more. It was past midnight as Brendan drove the wee rolling backroads to the border.

"You're very quiet tonight, Bridgie," Brendan said. "Talking will take your mind off things."

His baby sister said nothing. She just stared ahead, the flash of headlamps from the occasional oncoming vehicle revealed a face of stone. Suffering in silence was the Irish way. Perhaps the Italians, who, granted looked like right eegits with their wailing and collapsing theatrics were the wiser by giving grief its due. The Irish heart buried grief alive in a cold tomb. Even if the dead were laid to rest in peace, the living never did. With every dark mile he drove, Brendan could see the tomb closing on Bridgie's heart.

"How's the little boss?" he asked, glancing into the rear view mirror. He thought that, maybe, wee Angeline could diminish some of the sorrow of the moment.

His sister turned and looked into the rear seat. "Sleeping," she answered reluctantly.

"You did remember the falsified passports, no?"

This time she did not answer. She slumped down and turned her head to the window. He took that as meaning "yes."

In his role as priest, Brendan had counseled hundreds of persons in distress. The first rule was to listen. Venting anger and fear was a prerequisite to healing. But when the anger and fear were trapped too deeply inside, then he had to be the one to speak first. He prayed that, in time, his words would find a soft spot and penetrate his sister's heart.

"You know it's impossible for him to come with you, Bridgie. It would accomplish nothing, only that we're all caught. Have faith that God will reunite you. Go to Canada and wait for him. The Army Council will see to it that he joins you, soon. Have faith—"

"Roadblock!" Bridgie cried. "Oh Jesus."

A bright light leaped out of the darkness and blinded Brendan, forcing him to stomp on the brakes. Was it the Army or the Royal Ulster Constabulary? It made a difference. Whereas the police could detain you, the British Army had no legal rights to do so.

"RUC. Shit," said Bridgie.

"Look sleepy," Brendan whispered. "Where are the passports?" Bridgie slipped a pair of booklets out of her purse. Golden harps emblazoned the green booklets.

A tall RUC man dressed in blue uniform and black-billed cap strode slowly toward them. He twirled his finger, signaling for Brendan to wind down the window. A second policeman, shorter and squarely built, slowly circled the car. "Late to be traveling," the tall man said. His deep-set eyes searched the inside of the car. He held out his right hand.

"Could you not tone down that light? You see the child is sleeping. I'm taking my sister and niece home," Brendan added, impatiently. A priest had license to be moderately indignant. He placed the passports into the RUC man's waiting hand while watching from the corner of his eye as the second policeman returned to his vehicle. He would be radioing in the license plate number, Brendan knew. He prayed that the car he'd been provided was clean.

The tall RUC man looked doubtfully at the pair of Republic of Ireland passports. "Late to be traveling," he said again. "Why take the small road?"

"The child, she needs to sleep. The headlamps and noise on the main road would wake her. Any chance of dimming that light?" Brendan asked again.

The RUC man returned the passports. "Take it handy on the small roads, Father."

The oppressive spotlight dimmed. Bridgie's face turned the slightest hint of a grin. Brendan heard her sigh. He hoped the darkness masked his growing concern. They'd been allowed past the roadblock too easily.

The back road that was supposed to be their passage to safety was now their enemy. A thin, winding thread tossed amid an undulating countryside was ripe for ambush. Behind which turn were they waiting? Behind which hill? He accelerated through a serpentine curve faster than he should have; the tyres screeched. He strained his eyes, hoping to find the barn that marked the bier, where he would turn and cross the border by way of a newly mowed path through a hayfield. Just around a curve, just beyond the next hill, he prayed he'd find the safe passageway and not doom for Bridgie and Angeline. "They ran the roadblock," the RUC would later testify. "They were traveling with falsified documents and the driver was armed." They would be correct on all accounts. On the seat beside him lay his New Testament, fully loaded.

"Any idea when you'll be coming out?" Bridgie asked, still unaware of their peril.

The possibility that they might never see each other again, up to this point, had been avoided. He had told her that his being a priest would not cover his involvement with the Provisionals forever. He'd come out before the Brits could get him. It was a lie. The Brits would never get him. He was a soldier of Oglaigh na hEireann, the Army of Ireland. He never answered Bridgie's question.

It was a throbbing, thump-thumping sound that alarmed them. Bridgie grabbed his arm, causing the car to swerve. Angeline awoke, crying. Like a giant monster, a helicopter leaped from behind a hill. It showered their car with near-blinding light, then swooped toward them. "Get her down!" Brendan screamed, referring to Angeline. "Down!" The horrible whirling sound disoriented him. He gripped the wheel with all his strength. The helicopter scraped the roof of the car. Angeline and Bridgie both wailed. *Where was the bloody barn?* His driving became jerky, as he tried first to outrun the helicopter, then slowed to look for the barn. *Please, God, let there be protection at that barn*, he prayed. *If only the Provos could just hold off the helicopter long enough for them to reach the border...*

The helicopter soared ahead a hundred metres. It swooped in an upward arch, reversed its direction and hovered twenty metres above the road. It fired a single beam of light at Brendan's windscreen and, in the soft glow that fell on the pasture below, the barn came into view.

Someone had touted. The Brits knew the exact escape route. Brendan, battling the blinding glare, looked into the rear view mirror. Turning back was out of the question. Undoubtedly, there was pursuit from the rear. Their only hope would be to lose the helicopter in a high-speed chase, find a place where the helicopter could not go—like a barn housing a brigade of armed Provos. He stomped on the accelerator. The speedometer topped seventy. Angeline wailed uncontrollably. Bridgie returned to stone. It was as if her soul were already taking leave of her mortal being. The helicopter dropped for the kill. There came from the barn a flash of light racing through the night like a comet. The Provos were providing protection! An instant later, the helicopter was a blazing inferno crashing into the road only twenty metres from Brendan.

Brendan spoke slowly and softly, like someone lulling a child asleep with a bedtime story. Donal Mór, his eyes shut, heaved for air. He knew his brother-in-law was hoping that he would be asleep and therefore not have to finish the story.

"Finish it," Donal said, opening his eyes.

"They both called out for you at the end, Donal. Their final words were your name. To this day, I don't know why God spared me. I was thrown clear of the wreckage."

Donal Mór let his eyes drift slowly closed, mumbling the message that the Army Council could wait for his information. He owed them nothing. He thought about the Rag Man and decided that he wasn't ready yet to surrender the man who'd given him his day to be free. "I'm going to sleep now, Brendan," he said. "When I sleep, Bridgid and Angeline and I are all together again. It won't be long now. It won't be long..."

13

"...the moment London was aware of the problem the Rag Man presented, Dublin was contacted."

Detective Kevin O'Felan found a Scotland Yard car with darkened windows waiting for him on the Heathrow Airport tarmac. An hour later, the car slid off the motorway and onto a hilly ride, which ended with Kevin catching the briefest glimpse of a golden thatch roof, before being pulled inside a whitewashed cottage where he faced two men in dark suits. Outside, the car's tyres spit out the loose chippings as it sped away.

The taller man was fiftyish, with bushy grey sideburns framing a square face, washed in a healthy red glow. He moved with an athletic jaunt toward Kevin. "Roy Atheridge," he said, wrapping Kevin's hand with a firm grip. The other man introduced himself as Graham Potter. He was a bespectacled man with a less confident bearing than the older Atheridge.

The cottage had not been occupied for some time, maybe ever. A film of dust lathed the dishes displayed on an open pine hutch. No lingering smells of cooked food. A silver teapot, three clean white cups with red rims, and a small mountain of shortbread biscuits sat on a silver serving tray on a slate hearth. Kevin lit a cigarette and flipped the match into a glowing coal fire.

"Unseasonably cold, isn't it?" Atheridge said, pouring the tea. "Reminds me of a summer's holiday I once spent as a child. We were on your West Coast. Bantry Bay, I believe. Bloody froze. Haven't been back to the Republic of Ireland since, I'm ashamed to say." The Scotland Yard man chuckled. Kevin chuckled too, though he didn't know why. He did not appreciate the Englishman demeaning the Irish weather, even though he cursed it often enough himself.

"Should have tried our East Coast. Some great beaches there, I'll tell you. Bord Failte has never given the southeast its due," Kevin said.

Atheridge answered through a tight grin. The steel grey eyes bore in. "That's right. I understand that you're a Waterford man."

Kevin filled his lungs with smoke. Atheridge was letting him know that he knew all about him. Why hadn't he been clued about Atheridge or Potter? Because the Puzzle Palace was letting him take the fall for Paddy Burke's murder. Peter Doyle, meanwhile, was being allowed to distance himself from the ICU embarrassment. It wouldn't look good for a deputy minister to have a cop's blood on his hands. Kevin surprised himself by politely waving off the offer of biscuits.

"Tell me, Kevin, your Eire Nua seems to be moving ahead right on target," Atheridge said, speaking over the rim of a teacup. "Who would have predicted that finally moving away from neutrality would be so lucrative? The people of Ireland will come out of this referendum as real jackpot winners."

Kevin flicked the butt into the fire, then fortified himself with the hot tea. That Atheridge cleverly slipped in the word *finally* pricked at Kevin's national pride. The British had long chastised Ireland for its adherence to neutrality in time of war. "Well, according to the EU, Britain stands to cash in on Eire Nua too," Kevin said.

Atheridge cocked his head questioningly. "Do tell, please. Perhaps there's a bob or two in this for Graham and me." Atheridge and Potter exchanged what Kevin read to be condescending grins.

"I doubt it. But your government should get fat for a while. With the naval base being established in Cork, the British government can count on massive reductions in defense spending. And with new jobs in Ireland opening daily, especially in the computer software industry, the airplanes and ferries from Britain are already chockablock with young Irish men and women returning home for work. There's even a considerable number of young French and Germans and Poles moving into Ireland as well, but that's an aside. The advantages to Britain go well beyond the military spending cuts. For one, they rid themselves of the Irish ranks on the dole. And the Irish who were holding jobs in England create vacancies for young Brits, thereby moving them off the dole, and into the ranks of income tax producers. The annual net income, in the form of new taxes and savings on the dole, would be in the several millions pounds." Score one for tiny Ireland, Kevin thought.

Atheridge nodded, his painted grin fading. He sank his lips into his teacup and held them there for several moments before speaking haltingly. "Moving on to the matter at hand, it has been difficult...to keep up with the unfolding events...even with Intelligence giving the situation priority, and London and Dublin working hand in glove...Suffice to say, the moment London was aware of the problem the Rag Man presented, Dublin was contacted."

The coal fire brightened one side of Atheridge's square face. He nodded to Potter, who adjusted his black rimmed glasses more firmly to the bridge of his long nose, and then ceremoniously reached inside a brown leather carrying case resting on the floor beside his chair. When his hand emerged, the mystery of Kevin's meeting with Scotland Yard was answered. Graham Potter handed him a swatch of brown tweed. It was identical in color and texture to those left behind by the Rag Man.

"Fiber tests confirm it to be of the same cut as those swatches found in the Rag Man's flat in Lisburn," Atheridge said. "And in the bin lorry used in the escape from the Maze. And most recently in the Dublin restaurant, where the Rag Man slipped the Garda Síochána."

Kevin looked at the tweed without flinching.

Atheridge continued. "All the swatches come from the same suit coat. The age of the garment is consistent with the wool and tailoring style used in the 1970s by Guillespie's Irish Woolens of Donegal. Also significant is that each swatch comes from a single coat, the left sleeve. The swatches fit together."

Graham Potter handed Kevin a diagram of a suit jacket with the areas of the extracted swatches highlighted in yellow. He held a finger to a yellow spot near the right sleeve as he spoke.

"We believe the Rag Man purposely selected the swatches from the same suit coat so we would be able to determine the size and make of the coat. It's a thirty-eight medium. Whoever originally wore the coat was not a very big man."

Kevin bit his lower lip. Thirty-eight medium was his size.

Graham Potter continued. "This particular swatch was found in the laundry room of Brixton Prison, after an IRA escape in June of last year. At the time, it seemed a minor event. Everyone was recaptured within hours, including the bloke engineering the escape. Or so we thought. We know differently now." Potter continued to explain that the man originally held responsible for the escape had been captured in Belfast and interned at the Maze Prison.

Kevin paused to digest the splatter of questions feeding his brain and then spoke deliberately. "So, the wrong man now sits in the Maze, and once all this becomes public, which could be at anytime, there will be hell to pay. It will be like the Birmingham Six and Guilford Four all over again. The IRA will have the propaganda vehicle it so desperately needs on the eve of the Eire Nua referendum. It's an interesting turn of events, I grant you, but like you yourselves said, this is a British internal matter, no? Why am I here?"

The two Scotland Yard agents had stiffened at Kevin's reference to the Birmingham Six and Guilford Four. In both cases, Irishmen, after years of incarceration, were released from British prisons. The British, while never admitting culpability, passed both cases off as shoddy police work. Most of Ireland believed the cases were frame-ups.

"Were it that easy," Atheridge said, with obvious restraint. "The reality is that the Irish government has very high stakes in this, far more serious than Britain's, really. You see, the man arrested at Port of Belfast is no longer in the Maze. At this very moment, he's in Portlaoise prison hospital in the Republic of Ireland, refusing to wear prison clothes. It gets worse," Atheridge added. Without taking his stony eyes off Kevin's, the Scotland Yard man pulled a *London Times* newspaper from the leather briefcase. The paper was folded open to a back page. Kevin read the report of an IRA informer changing his testimony in court.

"The worst is true, I'm afraid," Atheridge said. "With the informer recanting his testimony, previous cases where his testimony was used to gain convictions will most certainly be subject to review and possible reversal. One of those cases, a bombing in Belfast, involved one Liam Riordon, the very same Liam Riordon who escaped from the Maze in the Rag Man's bin lorry, and he now sits undressed in hospital. Technically speaking, there may no longer be sufficient evidence to sustain his conviction and hold him in custody. But can your government afford to just let Riordon put on his trousers and walk out of prison a free man?"

Kevin sensed the gathering storm. The IRA had cleverly manipulated into their favor the very courtroom that had long been their scourge. He spoke as his eyes scanned the newspaper report for a second time.

"So let me get this straight, Roy, Graham. If justice prevails, Riordon walks out of Portlaoise a free man, to the embarrassment of my country and yours. The IRA wins, probably gaining sympathy for its Eire Nua 'No' campaign in the process." Kevin folded the newspaper.

"And the opportunity for Ireland's sound economic future and a more secure European community could be dashed at the polls. It's all very possible, I'm afraid." For the first time, Atheridge had lost his authoritative air.

Kevin searched for a place to deposit his cigarette butt. "Any clues as to when the IRA will go public with the Riordon situation? Certainly they must know the government has figured out their scheme and is taking measures to combat it."

"The prevailing opinion is that IRA is waiting for Dan O'Toole's funeral," Atheridge answered. "Apparently he's near death with cancer. Here again, justice is being held by the short and curlies. To hunt down and arrest the dying rebel would only inflame the situation. You won't see O'Toole recaptured."

A silence followed. Kevin's mind spun between thoughts of whether the Puzzle Palace was putting him out to pasture or asking that he personally prevent the Rag Man from destroying Eire Nua. The pasture was looking pretty good at the moment. He noticed Atheridge bracing himself with a deep breath.

"Let's just say a political solution to the Anglo-Irish problem does not suit all," Atheridge said. "The Irish troubles contain a wartime economy: police forces, weapons trade, drug trade, soldiers of fortune, even down to the charities established to help children on both sides of the conflict. Lumped together, you're talking about massive amounts of money changing hands around the globe. Eire Nua, as you put it so well, Kevin, is an economic boom for much of Europe, but not so for wartime profiteers. There are the influence peddlers, mongers of factionalism in government and from the pulpit, whose pockets spring leaks the moment peace is assured. Intelligence believes that the Rag Man had highly sophisticated help in engineering these escapes, and that the help is coming from deep inside. But the question is, deep inside *where*? Whoever it is has full knowledge—and access—to the penal and court systems, British military, the IRA itself, and..." he paused and breathed deeply, "We've no idea at the moment how close or far we are from identifying who's involved in what could be a massive conspiracy. Our immediate responsibility is to disrupt the conspiracy's momentum by bringing down the Rag Man."

Outside, car wheels crunched over loose chippings. Kevin looked at his watch. In little more than a quarter of an hour, he'd learned that the line between the good guys and the bad guys was almost indistinguishable. He had just one last question. "I was told that Scotland Yard asked for me specifically. Why am I here instead of looking for the Rag Man in Ireland?"

Atheridge took a deep breath, filling his broad chest. The glint returned to his grey eyes. "Because you have one qualification that no one else does. You have seen the Rag Man. You have watched him eat, walk, talk. Yes, he eluded you, but he's a master of disguise. Hasn't he eluded everyone? And why are you in England? Because, this all started at Brixton Prison a year ago. Even if the Rag Man is at large on your island, the key to finding him might very well be found here on ours."

Kevin nodded as if comprehending, though his head was swimming. They chose me: forty-seven, fat, bad knees, and with a detective's death under my supervision. ME! Why?

Later that night, Kevin was standing inside a phone booth in Piccadilly Circus and reading a phone number he'd scrawled on a napkin. The connection was good. For all the laughter and chat, he could have been standing inside McDaid's's on Dublin's Harry Street.

"My dear, Kevin. B'Jasus, what a pleasanfuckin' surprise," chirped Finbar Lawlor.

The psychologist sounded well into his cups. By nature, his speech was slow and deliberate. In drunkenness, he maintained his deliberateness, but he lost the continental-professorial tone, which only went to show Kevin that you could take the boy out of north Dublin, but not the north Dublin out of the boy.

"Not much time to talk, Finbar. Tell me, what is it that makes a person mistrusting and argumentative?" The phone booth was directly outside a neon-lit Italian restaurant called Elio's. Kevin chose the spot in hopes that the constant foot traffic passing in front of the phone booth would make it impossible for his lips to be read. Scotland Yard undoubtedly was marking his movements.

Finbar burped. "Fuckin' fear, man," he said. "Fear and, or, feelings of inferiority. It's a bit more complicated than dat, of course. Do you have time for me to expound?"

"Not much, but go on."

"What is key to the whole bleedin' 'ting, is the fuckin' source, know what I mean, Kevin? It could start with an abusive authority figure, such as a boss, a priest—and who has abused the poor Irish more den da fuckin'—burp—clergy? Anyone who is perceived as holding da upper hand can be da source of another person's feelings of anxiety and unworthiness. It's a complicated 'ting, dis inferiority complex. It can be passed wit'in a family from generation to generation. For dat madder we Irish as a race suffer from feelings of inferiority."

"The whole country? How's that possible?"

"Very easily, my dear Kevin. Studies have shown dat a race of people under prolonged oppression suffer greatly in terms of self esteem, partly because dey submit demselves — burp—just to cope with their oppressors, and because it serves the oppressors' purpose to create an illiterate peasant class. After generations of such submission and ignorance, a racial identity is formed, some of the manifestations of which are high rates of—burp—alcoholism and abuse of one another. And, Kevin, we both know that the Irish are hardest on their own when it's the fuckin' English, the bloody cause of all our problems, who we should be hardest on. Take a look at da blacks in America and the problems dey have had forging a positive self-image. When dey look in da mirror, they just as well would see an Irishman. D'ere's great fuckin' parallels, man. Only the Irish were enslaved longer den da blacks."

As inebriated as was the messenger, the message itself seemed sound, in Kevin's view. Finbar kept talking.

"Just look at the Yanks, Kevin. Dey all think they're wonderful, do dey not? And why? Because dey have wealth. Dey've won their wars—most of them, anyway. And the rest of the world comes to them begging. Who has come begging to Ireland? No fuckin' one, that's who. Until now. Eire Nua, man. Best 'ting that's happened for us, Kevin. Ireland as a nation can 'tump its chest to da whole fuckin' world, man. I sense we are building a fuller profile of our fugitive murderer," Finbar added. "I assume we're talking about the Rag Man?"

Kevin hung up the phone. Finbar had assumed wrong. Kevin had been talking about himself.

The sweet and pungent aroma of simmering tomato with garlic seeped through the night, snaring Kevin by the gut and dragging him to the restaurant door. He no longer cared a damn about fat grams or a size thirty-six waist tuxedo. God had made him fat and who was he to go against His eternal plan. Within an hour, he had downed a massive feed of Spaghetti Bolognese and a loaf of garlic bread. Beside his pasta rested a newspaper. Anyone would have thought he was engrossed in reading the news. The truth of it was he was staring at a picture of a faceless boy standing at his father's graveside. Three glasses of house red washed down the meal and lifted his spirits, to the point that he decided to call home and argue with Mary about the wedding.

14

...”Sí Beag, Sí Mór,” the small faery hill, the big faery hill,”...

Detective Peter Doyle watched his golf ball shrink into a single white speck, floating down and then nesting in the rim of purple heather that dressed the valley sweeping off Lunaquillia Mountain. Beauty, power, grace: the good golfers possessed them all. Peter considered himself to be a very good golfer.

He'd come home to Doyle Hall, the family estate, tucked inside the pines of the Wicklow Mountains, because Taoiseach Dessie O'Hanrahan had requested a confidential meeting. The isolated estate was as good a spot as any in Ireland to avoid media scrutiny. "Even I can't find the bloody place, and I've been there scores of times," the Taoiseach had confessed with a laugh. Peter suspected that Dessie most likely wanted to discuss the Rag Man, or his appointment to deputy minister, or both. If it were the latter, Peter would play it close to the vest. The words *deputy minister* would never cross his lips.

His tee was at the edge of a garden of purple rhododendron. Nearby in a concrete lily pond, a bead of water arched from the pipes of a bronzed Pan. A cool wind hummed through the mile thick curtain of tall pines, concealing the thousand-acre estate.

He liked coming home to Doyle Hall and did so as often as his father and his new wife were away. She was young and blonde and pretty, and Peter would have fancied a go at her himself, if she wasn't his stepmother and a gold-digging snake charmer who flaunted living inside his inheritance.

According to Peter's mother—God rest her soul—what was now called Doyle Hall had commanded the crest of Keadeen Mountain, unscathed since it was built in the eighteenth century. Its ivy-covered stone walls, gleaming leaded windows, and thirty-five rooms had been spared the republican torches that burned Protestant big houses during the troubles in the 1920s. There was a story in that. His mother was a Blennerhasset, Church of Ireland by birth. Seems that the Lord Blennerhasset at the time of the troubles had smelled the rebel winds on the way and wisely packed off to London. A French family, Catholics, rented the home exclusively for long summer holidays. The IRA spared Blennerhasset Hall, as it was known at the time, on account of the French having aided Ireland during a revolution more than a hundred years before. Eventually, the old Lord Blennerhasset's granddaughter, Annie, hitched herself to a big handsome Irishman named Buddy Doyle. They moved in and rechristened the estate Doyle Hall. Peter was their prince.

Mam was lost to cancer, some five years now. Peter remembered how she would refer to Keadeen Mountain and its larger neighbor, Lunaquillia Mountain as *"Sí Beag,*

Sí Mór," "the small faery hill, the big faery hill," on account
that Keadeen Mountain looked up to Lunaquillia like a
toddler at his Da. Then she would hum to him the soft
melody, "*Si Beag, Si Mór.*" Legend had it that the blind
harpist Turlough O'Carolan had composed the soothing
melody, so as to appease the faeries living inside the two
mountains. Humming the tune aloud sweetened the
memories. In his mind, he traced the lost years since his
mother had gone.

He stroked another ball deep into the heather.

"My God. I'll lose you to the Irish Open with the likes
of that," called a voice from behind.

Peter recognized the voice of Taoiseach Desmond
O'Hanrahan. Keeping his head down, he drove another ball
out toward Lunaquillia. "You might just," Peter quipped,
only then turning to greet the nation's leader, who had to
look up at him the way Keadeen did to Lunaquillia.

"How's things, Dessie? Lost again, were we?" Peter set
the club aside. The Taosieach wore a blue blazer with grey
slacks, which matched the curly mop atop his head. The
evening sun exposed a deepening of facial lines. Time and
pressure of Eire Nua were catching up with Dessie, Peter
thought.

Dessie shook his grey head. "Bloody Glenmalure.
Ireland's Bermuda Triangle, as far as I'm concerned."

Peter turned to a middle-aged servant woman, named
Noabh, who'd shown Dessie to the golf tee. "Noabh, the
Taoiseach would like a single malt. And some smoked
salmon with onions, capers, the lot of it. What about the
lads?" Peter asked, looking up the hill at the two dark suits
standing against the ivy-covered wall.

O'Hanrahan smiled at Noabh, causing the housekeeper
to blush. "Go ahead, Luv. Ask them. Let 'em fight over
whose going to drive back to Dublin. We couldn't get

any more lost." He turned back to Peter. "How's Buddy keeping?"

"A far sight better than you or I at the moment. In the Canaries, strapped at the hip with the fountain of youth."

"Always ahead of the game, your father." Dessie's small brown eyes rolled and he grabbed Peter in a friendly way just below the elbow. "Listen, I want you and Buddy at my side Thursday a week, inside Kilkenny Castle. You're to be my special guests at the pre-show reception for Rock 'n Nua. Unless of course you rather rub shoulders with Mary Black, Sinéad, or Van the Man, himself? Your choice."

"You'd better put me next to Mick Mulvihill. You'll need a strong man to keep the glass out of his hand and the spoon from his nose."

They shared a laugh at the folk singer's expense, and then continued small talk about the G.A.A. results, the brilliant weather, and nothing that really mattered. Naobh brought two Waterford tumblers of the Jamesons single malt and a platter filled with buttered brown bread, smoked salmon garnished with capers, chopped onion, and tomato. The Taoiseach was upbeat and chirpy. He groaned with delight each time he tasted the salmon. Peter enjoyed seeing Dessie in such high spirits. They conversed not as leader of the nation and detective, but as the godfather and godson they were. Dessie and Mairead themselves were childless. And Peter often saw in Dessie's eyes the longing for the son he'd never had.

Dessie, suddenly excited, spoke with crumbs of brown bread spilling from his mouth. "Oh, you'll never guess who Mairead saw while up in Donegal. Your old bird." He swallowed hard. "You know...Kitty?"

Dessie's eyes danced merrily, as if he had just given Peter a wonderful gift. He'd given a gift, all right—a cannon ball right to the gut. Peter took a belt of the Jamesons.

The cannon ball didn't wash away. He managed a heavy smile.

"Anyway, there was Mairead meeting with a women's social concerns group in Donegal," Dessie continued, "and who does she spy at the rear of the parish hall but your woman, Kitty. 'Looking beautiful as ever,' says Mairead. And no rings," he added, cocking his head.

"She's not my woman anymore. Ancient history."

"Well, according to Mairead, history has a chance of repeating itself, if you had a mind for it. Apparently, Kitty made a point of coming up to Mairead after the meeting. And if it matters at all, Kitty was the one who mentioned you first. Mairead made a point of telling me that. She thought you'd want to know."

If it mattered at all to him? His heart flew truer than any golf shot he'd ever hit. His ears rang with "...Kitty was the one who mentioned you first...*who mentioned you first*!"

Peter bowed graciously. "Make sure you thank Mairead for me. She's always been looking after the affairs of my heart. Tell her the next time I'm up in Donegal town, I'll look up Kitty," Peter said, fishing for more information.

"Not Donegal town. Ardara, on the coast near Killybegs. In the mountains."

Peter ate and drank without tasting a thing. *Kitty! Asking about him!* Maybe she was finally coming around. He'd always thought she would. The only surprise was that it had taken this long.

Once all the salmon was finished and the small talk done, he and Dessie retreated to a bench alongside the bronze Pan. The treetops became silhouettes stabbing into a purple sky. They sat. Dessie brushed the crumbs from his suit jacket. His face grew stern, as if momentarily lost in an unpleasant thought. He now looked more like the nation's leader than an old family friend. Peter, fortified by the news of Kitty, was ready for the test.

"I appreciate you taking time away from the investigation to meet with me," Dessie began.

Peter shrugged. "At your service. With Paddy Burke being slaughtered, the cloak is off the hunt. Every guard and detective is putting in extra hours. They want this man very badly. Borders are sealed shut. Same with airports and sea links. We have the fingerprints. Witnesses. Divil the chance the Rag Man has gotten away. It's only a matter of time now."

Dessie sipped the whiskey and nodded thoughtfully. Peter suspected the Taoiseach was still climbing the hill toward whatever it was he came to talk about. "Your partner?" Dessie said.

Peter took a deep breath and held it, as a way of showing he intended to choose his words carefully. It would be considered unprofessional to criticize one's partner. He needed to demonstrate loyalty in the face of adversity.

"In England at the moment, as I'm sure you're aware. Spoke to him yesterday. He brought me up to speed on the Brixton situation. Says he's suspicious of Scotland Yard's motives." Peter chuckled. "You know my partner. The spirit of Eire Nua has yet to capture him fully. He's still hanging on to the eight hundred years of bondage thing."

Peter noted that his godfather did not share the joke, so he added quickly, "If there's something to be found, though, Kevin will find it, surely. There's none better than he in the Detective Units, myself included. We all should be as determined as that man."

Peter anticipated Dessie following up with more questions about Kevin. Had he slowed down? Should he be put to a desk? Would a younger, fitter man have been able to prevent Paddy Burke's slaughter? But Dessie passed.

He was in the middle of a long pause, the prelude to the true purpose of his visit.

"Peter, I wanted to tell you personally that, as soon as I return to Dublin this evening, I'm going to allow full disclosure about the Rag Man to the press, the murders of the bin lorry man and Detective Paddy Burke. With Kevin in England, I'll need you as the head of the investigation to support me on this. It could be unpopular with the security personnel. I need you standing beside me before the cameras."

It wasn't Peter's place to question the nation's leader—out loud. Full disclosure of the Rag Man gave a platform to the IRA. Full disclosure of a killer on the loose would spread fear throughout the nation. Full disclosure put a chink in the previously unblemished armor of Eire Nua—at precisely the worse time. Peter showed no reaction. Friendship aside, Dessie was going to have to explain himself. Besides, Peter did not want to appear as though he'd roll over too easily for anyone. Deputy Ministers did not do that sort of thing, did they?

Pain creased Dessie's face as he spoke to the Wicklow Mountains. "Believe me, I've reflected deeply on this. The Irish people deserve honesty. If for one moment they thought I was withholding information about a killer on the loose for political reasons, placing them and their families in danger, Eire Nua and all the gains we've made would be lost. And deservedly so," he added. "With the developments in the north. With Liam Riordon's prisoner status now in question..." His voice faded with worry.

"You hardly need worry about Eire Nua. There's nary a blip on the public opinion radar. Holding firm at eighty-seven percent. *Cén scael* on Riordon?" Peter asked, purposely using the Irish to impress Dessie.

Dessie shook his head in frustration. "The story is, until charges in the north are officially dropped, we've no choice but to abide by the agreement and proceed with extradition. Mind you, we're buying some time by claiming his wounds are preventing his travel. The capture of the Rag Man would give us the opportunity to quietly return Riordon to the Maze while public sentiment is behind the security measures. 'Til then, we have to be careful not to give the appearance of appeasing the British too quickly. The Prime Minister understands," he added.

A silence followed, broken by Dessie. He seemed increasingly agitated. "Trust," said the Taoiseach, more to himself than Peter. "I just have to *trust* that people realize the Rag Man is a flare-up of the troubles only. He will be captured and dealt with according to the law. That's the way the New Ireland works. The era of silence is over. I have faith in the Irish people." He turned to Peter. "I'm making your job tougher, I know."

"I was hired to do a tough job. Are we naming names?"

"Everyone we know. Rag Man. Liam Riordon. Dan O'Toole. The dead bin lorry driver, the lot. It will sicken the Irish people. They will reject once and for all the men of violence."

"What about your man Cathal Slattery, the Bounty-Co. chap?"

"What about him?" Dessie asked, surprised. His tone was defensive.

"He's long been a major financial backer of the IRA. He's forced his Famine Studies on our universities at a time when we as a nation need to look forward, not behind. He's long been a master at throwing his money at two bickering parties, just to keep the political status quo. You've worked too hard, Dessie, bringing this country into the twenty-first century. Don't let your trust of an old friend blind you.

Where the hell was he in Ireland's time of need, before you turned the economy around? Divil the penny he was throwing to the border people then. The Puzzle Palace has a file on Slattery as thick as your arm."

These were tough words for the Taoiseach to chew on. Peter raised his glass to his lips, but never backed off Dessie's stare. Again, he was making a point to be his own man, which he would continue to be for several more moments, before vowing his unconditional support and loyalty. The truth of it was that Peter believed Dessie wanted to do too much, for too many people, too fast. He shouldn't be accepting gifts from the likes of Bounty-Co., no matter that Slattery was his wife's cousin.

"I'm aware of the suspicions," Dessie said, his tone tinged with anger. "I'm also aware that there has never been a single allegation of impropriety proven against Cathal Slattery. Further, I'm aware that bringing nearly a thousand jobs to the border region, serving people on both sides of the political divide, is the best recipe for lasting peace on this island. I appreciate your concern, and any further information that might demand greater caution on my part. Now, will you stand beside me?"

"I will, of course."

The professional airs of Taoiseach and detective dissolved with a handshake and refilled glasses. Peter was sure he'd passed the test.

Later that night, after standing stoically in front of the television cameras in Dublin, Peter drove his Mercedes swiftly through the midlands. On the radio, a grave-voiced Taoiseach was warning the nation that an IRA terrorist calling himself the Rag Man was on the loose. Peter switched the radio off and hummed "*Sí Beag Sí Mór*" all the way to Donegal.

15

Love is pleasing
And Love is teasing
Love is pleasure when first it's new
But when love grows older
Love grows colder
And fades away like the morning dew
-Traditional

Mattie Joe Treacy tiptoed through the family farmhouse, hoping not to be seen or heard by his mother. Mam caught up with him coming out of the loo, though she lingered only long enough to reinforce the fact that she was not speaking to him, on account that he was dating a red-haired woman. The truth of it was, Mattie Joe was pleased his mother was letting him alone. Cait, at that very moment, was waiting for him in the milking parlor. If Mam were to show herself, Mattie Joe would be stuck between two women with sour dispositions. In his view, his mother's disapproval had a lot less to do with the color of his girlfriend's hair than it did

139

with her curving body. He was fairly sure that the Daoine Maithe didn't have any rules against fine looking women.

At last, Mam huffed and took off for Biddie Tynan's and their Thursday night potluck dinner. No sooner had she left, than did Mattie Joe have to deal with another old curmudgeon. Brian winged into the milking shed and perch himself atop a brown and white freshen.

The pooka sang cheerily, *"Love is teasing love is pleasing love is a pleasure when first it's new. When love grows older, sure love grows colder, and fades away like the morning dew...Oh, Matthew. Oh, Matt,"* Brian mocked. *"You're not a Mattie Joe at all. You cook too good to be a Mattie Joe. Alright, listen to me now,"* the pooka sternly warned. *"This relationship has gone on long enough. Mind my words, boyo, there's many the woman who has wrecked a good plan. It's time to cut this bird loose."*

Mattie Joe slapped a cow on its hindquarters, sending the beast lumbering out of the milking parlor. The next cow in line moved forward instinctively. Mattie Joe made the Sign of the Cross, lest the faeries turn the milk sour. He affixed the steel milking mechanism onto the cow's udders. The beast gave a little kick, then settled. New milk coursed upward through clear plastic tubing and swirled into a massive steel holding tank.

"I'm doing alright so far, am I not? Besides, she makes a good cover, so. And can't we talk about this later?" Mattie Joe had had a great day with Cait. They'd gone on a picnic and he'd rather think about how pretty Cait looked when she smiled than deal with the pesky pooka. He had wanted to tell Cait that he thought she was pretty, but she'd made it clear that she did not want a serious relationship. Mattie Joe used to be of the same mind. Now, he wasn't so sure.

Brian hopped onto the next cow in line. *"I'd say she makes a great cover. That's all you've been doing lately, having her bones covering yours. Too much of that business affects the brain. I can see already that ye are not thinking clearly."*

"That's not what I meant. What I mean to say is that it's not good for me to be walking about alone right now. You blend in more when you're a couple. So my thinking is fine. Besides, she's part of the plan."

"Plan? Divil the plan ye have ever made without me. How long do ye think ye can keep this charade going? Ye can't open a newspaper or turn on the radio without hearing the news of the Rag Man. Soon this place will be crawling with guards, then where will ye and your plan be?"

The next cow showered the floor with urine and dung. Mattie Joe gave the concrete floor a quick hosing down. "I'll be so deep in Connemara that only the goats will find me. I've hired a bungalow on the side of a mountain, miles from any village. The people out there are very stubborn about only speaking Irish, so if anyone was to stumble upon us, Cait won't have a clue what they're talking about. She's no Irish to speak of. As far as she's concerned it's a lover's holiday."

"Well, which is it? A plan or a lover's holiday? By the looks of ye, I'd say it's the latter. And why Connemara, for Jas' sake? There's nothing for me to do out there. I'll be damned if I'm flying all the way out to there to hover over bloody rocks and lakes and hills, while ye are on your lover's holiday. You're taking a dog along this time. At least that way I can chase some sheep."

The conversation was going nowhere in Mattie Joe's view. He tried ignoring Brian.

"And tell me please, when did ye start up with all this Yes Yes Daddy classical music? Where's the Rolling Stones? Ye and I always listen to the Rolling Stones...I can't get no, dum dum dum, satisfaction." Brian flapped his wings so vigorously that he nearly took a tumble.

"Easy there, Mr. Jagger, before you're after hurting yourself. Besides, the man's name is Yo Yo Ma. And Cait doesn't like the Rolling Stones or any hard rock stuff. It's not bad, really, the classical music. You get used to it after a while. Very soothing. And as far as you flying to Connemara, save your wings. I wasn't planning on you coming."

"Oh, so Cait doesn't like the hard rock stuff. Cait likes soothing classical music. Cait gets to go to Connemara. Now I understand. It's all about pleasing this bird, Cait. Ye have found yourself a redhead and a new plan. Well, what about me? What about the plan we've been working on since ye were ten years of age? Proving that the curse is true. Finding your father, remember that plan?"

"I remember that your job is to protect me until we prove that the curse is true and my father is found. It's been donkey years and we haven't proven fuckall. Now why don't you just get lost and leave me be? I can handle things."

"Fuckall, is it? Get lost, so? Here ye are dodging bullets and bombs from the likes of British soldiers, Orangemen, IRA men, the whole lot of the Garda Síochána detective force, all without getting as much as a scratch, and that's not proving fuckall? I'll give ye the night to think about that one, boyo. I'm of a mind to do just what ye say and get lost. Then we'll see how much protection that redhead is. Mind my words, a red-haired woman is bound to bring bad luck on ye, and it's already started."

Mattie Joe chuckled as Brian flew out of the milking parlor. The pooka was starting to sound a lot like his mother. He'll come back, Mattie Joe thought. Brian always came back.

∽

Cait McGrath awoke to the sizzle of frying rashers and the warmth of a morning sun piercing the drawn window shade. She saw yesterday's clothes marking a scrambled trail across the floor, from the door to the bed. Her blue jeans and bra lay five feet inside the door. Her green jumper hadn't even made it that far. And where her underwear was anyone's guess. A smile crept over her face. She was back in the race and riding at full gallop.

Her racehorse was moving about her kitchen, preparing her cup of coffee, just the way she'd taught him. His faded jeans clung to him like a layer of blue paint.

Since dragging Matthew Treacy home on Sunday, she'd enjoyed five days of pampering. Except for the couple of hours at dawn and dusk when he left to milk the cows—and she'd hustle through her Hennessy assignment—she'd had the handsome hurling hero all to herself. In the mornings, she'd be back snug under the piled blankets by the time Matt brought her breakfast in bed. He was so sweet to her that she was no longer counting the days until she could return to America. Now Rock 'n Nua, which marked the end of her work assignment, was a week off. If things with Matthew stayed as hot as they were at the moment, she actually would be sorry to leave Ireland. Not in a million years would Cait have predicted that.

Nor in a million years would she ever have imagined that living for the pleasures of the moment could have such a calming effect on her whole being. She'd been raised to believe that self-denial built strong character and that pleasure and sin were the right and left hands of the devil. It was a philosophy well suited for priests and poor Catholic families, to keep them from coveting more than they had. Yet here she was, making good money and, for once in her life, satisfying her every physical and emotional need. Maybe the real secret to happiness was for your right hand to know what the left hand was doing.

Hearing the clang of knives and forks, she again peeked over the covers to see Matthew setting two places at the table where he'd already placed a glass brimming with fresh pink roses. She also saw a shaggy, black and white dog sniffing at Matthew's heels. A dog in her flat was no surprise, unfortunately. She'd never met a man so attracted to animals as Matthew Treacy, and vice versa. Then again, she'd never dated a farmer before. From the moment she'd met Matthew, some class of creature was hanging around him. Most times, it was that damned black raven. The ugly scavenger had a particular habit for rapping at the window every time Matthew entered her bed.

As she lay dozing, she reflected on the last few whirlwind days and considered that her little fling with Matthew wasn't any sort of moral collapse, but rather hard-earned back pay for years lost forever to an imposter called abstinence. Her thirtieth birthday was only weeks away. Was she to waste her gift of youth waiting for a knight in shining armor who might never come? Matthew stood over the eggs with spatula in hand. The muscles in his upper back rippled through his white T-shirt. A life spent working the farm had made him strong and kept him lean. That he was utterly untamed bothered Cait not in the least. Having a romp with the town bad boy was far preferable than thinking that she was sleeping with Farmer Brown or, worse still, Doctor Doolittle. Besides, it was her little fling and she could think of it in any terms she wished.

The mingling aromas of smoky rashers and the pungent black pudding and mushrooms began tugging harder. When the toast popped up, Cait did the same from the bed, covering herself with a sheet. On her way to the dresser, her toes discovered her missing underwear, and she was reminded how she used to only dream about days like yesterday.

Yesterday, Matthew had returned from the morning milking wearing blue jeans rolled up to the top of cowhide boots and his usual white T-shirt. Around his waist, he'd tied the arms of a black leather jacket. A picnic basket in his left hand was heavy enough to make him lean that way. He wouldn't say what was in the basket or where they were going. "Wear walking shoes," he said, flashing a mischievous grin that deepened the dimples. Cait could let her eyes sip on him all day long.

The countryside was alive with blazing, golden gorse and scarlet fuchsia spilling from the hedgerows. Roller coaster roads twisted through sun-drenched vales of lush, green farmland and climbed into the foothills of the Blackstairs Mountains, where pine-filtered air filled Cait's lungs like gulps of cool water. To her utter delight, Matthew slipped into the compact disc player a new release of the cellist Yo Yo Ma, her favorite. The cello's deep, soothing voice lifted her until she could feel herself floating over Ireland as if in a parachute. When she descended, she found herself in a hidden glen at a village called Inistoige, where the sense of timelessness was palpable. Quaint shops trimmed a tree-lined village green. In her mind's eye, she saw the nimble Gene Kelly sweeping hand-in-hand across the Inistoige green with the beautiful, black-haired Cyd Charisse. *Brigadoon* was her all time favorite film.

Only she didn't get to stay in lovely Inistoige for long. Instead, they trudged along a riverbank of mud and rushes, seemingly halfway back to Kilkenny before Matthew finally stopped where there wasn't two feet to stand on between the river and a steep grassy bank. "Here we are," he said, pointing to the middle of the river. "Our table is waiting."

Grabbing her by the hand, he began skipping nimbly over scattered stones in a wild circuitous route until he guided her onto a flat stone the size of an automobile. From the picnic basket, he took an oilcloth and spread it across the rock with all the style of a seasoned waiter. Out from the basket he brought his Mam's finest crockery and tumblers, and a bottle of white wine. It was all very dreamlike. It was as if Cait really were in an Irish Brigadoon. Then an awful thought shattered the dream. Obviously, she wasn't the first Cyd Charrisse Matthew Joseph Treacy had brought out to the rock for a meal and who knew what else! (Of course, she knew what *what else* was, since she'd been enjoying *what else* for the past five days.)

She reminded herself that she really didn't care what Matthew had done, or would do, with his women, all of whom were very pretty, no doubt. Caring wasn't part of the terms she'd set for the affair. Still, she was quite certain the wild boy had entertained scores of young lovelies on that romantic river. The way he'd danced over the rocks, as if he were walking on water, was proof of that. Yet, after some consideration, she came to the satisfying conclusion that, had her time in Ireland not been so short, she absolutely would have made Matthew take her to the rock first, before she'd given him the chance to do *what else* with her. Knowing this made her feel much better. She now could enjoy the picnic.

The wine was crisp and light, the perfect complement to the picnic tea of finger-sized cucumber and onion sandwiches made with fresh baked brown bread and creamy butter and a good cold chicken.

For her dessert, Cait savored deep pools of chocolate rimmed with long black lashes that she'd love to brush with mascara, just to see how long she could make them, and how they would taste brushed against her wine lips. Sometimes as he spoke, the brown moons would shift away in mid-sentence to some hidden place that harbored his secrets. She wondered if his hidden place was somewhere where he was not considered the village rogue? Or was it someplace where a burning desire, known only to himself, drew him to its flame? When she stared at him for too long, her chest began to ache and she could feel herself actually free-falling into his eyes. It was a wonderful feeling, this falling. Falling without worry. Falling safely inside deep pools of chocolate.

When the day gave way to a late afternoon shower, they pulled their bodies together beneath the oilcloth. The rain pattered with a soothing drone. A stirring heat moved from Matthew's cheek into hers. His thigh slid slowly up and down alongside hers. She wanted his kiss. She held her breath as Matthew skipped over the kiss and reached directly for the zipper on her jumper. He slowly pulled the zipper up to her neckline. "You'll catch cold," he said.

The zipper went up. *Up!* Matthew folded her in close. His eyes drifted down river to that hidden place, only this time a little nudge against her shoulder told her he was taking her along. Oh, that this moment could be saved in a box and taken out on a rainy day, she thought, warming her cold cheek against his face. She realized, of course, that it *was* a rainy day, and the small act of a zipper moving five inches up instead of ten inches down just might have been the most intimate—and torturous—moment she'd ever experienced.

Matthew extended an arm toward the charcoal sky. "Ah, there it is. I was hoping it would come," he said. "Now wait…wait. Here comes another. It's forming over top the first one. See it?" His face sparkled with a childish delight as he pointed ahead to where the river vanished into a hilly gap and two rainbows connected the mountains like bridges hanging in the heavens.

Matthew tightened his arm around her shoulder. "You're only the second person I've ever been here with. I was hoping to have a rainbow to give you," he said. His gaze remained fixated on ribbons of red and yellow and arching across the violet sky. "Have you ever thought how only the joining of seeming opposites—rain and sunshine—produces nature's most beautiful face? It's a union seemingly so rare, yet rainbows happen every day. They come without warning and fade softly away, too soon gone. If you really want to see a rainbow, you have to stare straight ahead into it, until the colors seep past your eyes and deep into you head. Your mind's eye will see that rainbow forever. I can still remember the first rainbow I saw here. There was more red in that rainbow."

"Do you remember who you gave those colors to?" Cait now more than ever wished she had been the first to get one of Matthew's Inistoige rainbows.

"Oh, I didn't give that rainbow to anyone. Someone gave it to me: my father. He and I came here once. I haven't been back since."

They left in a gentle drizzle and Cait looked back on the tiny hamlet held in the palm of the mountains, watching the rainbows arching peacefully, seeping away into the reborn sun. She then considered the man who had given them to her. *A union seemingly so rare...rainbows happen everyday...*

But all that had been yesterday. Cait now looked into her bedroom mirror as she pulled the brush through her long auburn curls. Thinking back now on Thursday evening, she supposed there were a few times that she'd broken the terms she'd imposed for the affair. Today, she'd be more careful. For one thing, she was going back on the vodka and staying away from the wine. She knew how to control vodka. Too much wine always made her a bit crazy.

Giving her long curls a last toss, she moved eagerly to her breakfast. "Good morn—" She stopped short. The shaggy sheep dog was sitting at the table, lapping eggs from a plate. *Her eggs.* It snatched up her rashers and black pudding, too. She then saw the suitcase sitting on the floor alongside Matthew.

"Join us? Better hurry," Matthew chirped. "Our friend here is powerfully hungry."

The suitcase chased Cait's hunger and replaced it with a sinking feeling. "Going somewhere?" she asked.

"Going on holidays. The city is stifled with tourists coming in for Rock 'n Nua. I'm thinking Connemara, where the stone walls kiss the sea and sky. I was hoping that you'd come along."

"But what about the cows? And your mother?"

"The cows will be taken care of. And my mother and I are not speaking, remember? It's just as easy not speaking from Connemara as it is here. In fact, it's easier. C'mon, will you not go with me? We'll come back for the concert, sure."

Would she go? How could she not go? All her inner peace, all her newfound joy and carefree life were packed inside that suitcase and heading off to Connemara. Of course, she agreed to go. Only then did she realize that she was still falling.

The dog followed Matthew to the door, yapping furiously. Matt spoke to the dog the way he did to all animals, as if they really understood what he was saying. "No, you're not coming to Connemara and that's the last time I'm telling you. Now get lost."

∽

Father Brendan Sheils, standing behind a telephone pole, watched the young couple drive off from the flat on

Father Bennett Lane, a yappy dog chasing after them. He then waited for three quarters of an hour before jimmying open the lock to the woman's home. His two feet had not passed the threshold before he sensed her presence.

If someone didn't know the occupant, there wasn't much about the flat's décor—a computer, stereo and not much else—to make a comment on the person one way or another. However, Father Brendan knew her to be a woman of concealed passions, and that the computer and stereo said plenty about her. She had always hidden herself behind words and music, and the memories she was trying to obliterate. Checking the refrigerator, he noted a half-finished bottle of white wine. In the trash bin were two empty vodka bottles. His heart began to sink slowly. He had intended to log into her computer to read her latest compositions, but he made the mistake of first strolling into her bedroom, where the essence of her invaded him. The fragrant shampoo in the bathroom. The subtle scent of perfume near the dresser drawers. It was the smell of her body from the unmade bed that caused a film of tears to glaze his eyes. He missed her terribly.

Later, when he had recovered his emotions, he phoned Belfast. "She's here," he said.

∾

Tom Hennessy read for the third time the garbage Cait had just emailed him. Oh, with enough editing he could make it passable, but it wasn't like Cait to do such sloppy work. This concerned him. Staring blankly out at a turquoise bay, he considered how he was simultaneously tiring of rum and his novel. The sunshine paradise was dulling his brain. Then he thought about the money and how the Blackbird had warned him that if he set foot in

Ireland, the payments would stop. Losing thousands of easy dollars was suddenly less disturbing than the very real possibility that had he had allowed the Blackbird to put Cait McGrath in a situation far more dangerous than he'd originally been led to believe. Seated at his computer, he searched the Internet for the cheapest fare to Ireland.

16

She reminded Kevin of an African night...

Detective Kevin O'Felan couldn't put a finger on the exact year he'd transitioned into middle age, except that it had been around the time that his belt buckle had seemingly skipped ahead three holes at a time instead of one. And that one day he was twisting Siobhán's pigtails, and seemingly the next, he was preparing to give her away to another man. Maybe middle age officially starts when you find yourself wearing odd socks, because you haven't been able to find your eyeglasses, he thought. To some degree, he supposed he was prepared for his body to start breaking down, but he'd always thought the compensation for physical deterioration would be the attainment of some advanced wisdom. But anymore, he was feeling like a man operating a few steps behind an ever-changing world.

At the moment, the changing world around him was a grey and depressed West Indian section of London.

He was riding in the back seat of another Scotland Yard courtesy car, this time heading to Brixton Prison, the site of the Rag Man's first prison escape a year ago. A street sign read Jebb Avenue. Reggae music boomed from open tenement windows. In his hands, he held a background file on the Brixton Prison escape provided by Scotland Yard. He was flipping through the pages describing how the old Victorian prison was beset by overcrowding, understaffing, racial tensions, and an epidemic of prisoners with drug and alcohol dependencies, when the car slowed in front of a gated stone fortress, dotted with smokestacks.

At Brixton's main gate, an official-looking fellow stood waving. He had a salt and pepper mustache—mostly salt—that compensated for his shaved head. He would be John Sommerville, Brixton's fourth prison governor in as many years.

Alongside Sommerville stood a pencil-thin black woman in her upper twenties. She reminded Kevin of an African night, she was that dark and sleek. True, he'd never been to Africa, or even seen a picture of it at night, but that's what she reminded him of just the same. She wore a black leather jacket that, at her narrow hips, melted into a black skirt, which covered only a modest portion of the longest and darkest legs he'd ever seen. She wore her hair in taut island-style braids that cascaded into dangling strands around her long neck. Kevin rethought his image of her and decided she was more like a black swan. He'd seen loads of swans, though maybe not any black ones.

The pretty black swan opened the door and slid in to the back seat next to him. At the same time, the gentleman pushed in from the other side. He shook Kevin's hand vigorously.

"Detective O'Felan? John Sommerville, prison governor," he said with a nervous chuckle. For all the prison governor's lack of formality, he might have introduced himself as John the baker, or John the chimney sweep. He looked past Kevin to the young black woman. "Oh, and I'm very sorry. Forgive me, please. I've forgotten your name already."

"Sylvia Hickey. New Scotland Yard. I'm your partner." She gave Kevin a creamy soft handshake. In Kevin's view, Detective Hickey was there less to be his partner in finding the Rag Man than to be Scotland Yard's watchdog. Her job was to keep an eye on him. Undoubtedly, Hickey would claim she was there to provide assistance in any way she could. Truth was, she was there to learn whatever he learned. Kevin decided whatever he told Sylvia was something he wanted Scotland Yard to hear and nothing else.

"It was nice of Scotland Yard to send you along, Detective Hickey. I'm sure I'll need all the help I can get," Kevin said.

"We'll be working together for a while and in some very close surroundings. Best to lose the professional airs from the start, Kevin. Get used to calling me Sylvia," she said, seizing him with paisley-shaped eyes. Her deep, silky voice suited her dark sleekness. Kevin wondered why he was always being paired with the aggressive young ones, thinking how Peter Doyle fit the same mold. At least Sylvia Hickey was nicer to look at.

By all appearances, Brixton was the open book that the Scotland Yard lads Roy Atheridge and Graham Potter had promised. Prison Governor Sommerville himself gave a personal tour through the old stone fortress. After half an hour of smiling and chortling and describing with enthusiasm his plans to reform Brixton, Sommerville made an offer of lunch. Kevin politely declined. He was eager to continue the investigation.

"I'd rather keep at it and meet with the guard who was on duty at the time of the escape. Walcott, I believe.

Dennis Walcott? I was told he'd be available," Kevin said, and then suddenly remembered his manners. "Unless, of course, Detective Hickey, I mean, Sylvia, would rather stop for a meal?"

Sylvia shook her head. "I'll eat later," she said. By the looks of her, Kevin knew she wouldn't be eating much.

Sommerville had been leading the way down a long, lower-level corridor, toward the prison laundry facility. He winced at the mention of the prison guard. "I, uh, was going to get to that issue, really," he stammered. "It seems Mister Walcott is not as available as we had hoped. We don't know where he is, really. I was caught totally unaware, I assure you." Sommerville looked to Sylvia Hickey for support. Her response could not be heard above the rumbling noise coming from behind the door at the end of the corridor. Kevin cupped his ears with his hands.

"I said, Scotland Yard is aware of the situation. We'll have access to Walcott the moment he's located. It shouldn't be long," she said.

So here it was at last, Kevin thought. Poor, naïve little Paddy was being given the run-around by the British brass. He had expected as much. Only the deceit was showing its face even quicker than he'd expected.

The prison governor chuckled nervously, a habit Kevin was quickly tiring of.

"You see, Dennis did the proper thing and resigned his duties after the escape. And to be quite honest, it was time. Prison work is no place for such a bright young man. He went on to university, I'm told. His leaving did, however, give us the opportunity to hire a person of color for the prison staff. Diversity of staff is an issue I'm working hard to address. At any rate, Dennis seems to have gone missing. This is very bad, I know."

Kevin asked to see the missing prison guard's work record. Dennis Walcott had been one of only two people to directly encounter the Rag Man the day of the escape. The other was the laundry lorry driver whose identity the Rag Man assumed. Only he was beaten within an inch of his life and still had no recollection of the event; he was no help to the investigation. From there, the file became very thin: the Rag Man arrives at the laundry facility, overpowers Dennis Walcott, and leaves with three inmates of Irish extraction. If the Rag Man left an obvious trail, as he had in Lisburn, it had gone undiscovered. Instead, British authorities had believed Liam Riordon to be the Rag Man and had chased him all the way to the Port of Belfast. Now a year later, Kevin was trying to find the pieces that never made it into the file.

The machinery rumbled and hissed. Billows of steam rolled along a concrete ceiling. Kevin quickly counted ten men in brown prison bodysuits and two prison guards, one black and one white, holding automatic weapons perpendicular to their waists. The guards stood watch by a closed cargo bay. The faces of the inmates, all white men, blushed red in the heat. They worked with heads bowed over steam presses and bundles of laundry, but the corners of their eyes were locked on Sylvia Hickey.

Sommerville made a sweeping motion with his hand. "We do all the laundry for the prison, as well as for some other government agencies. That's what gets shipped out." He pointed across the steamy room at the bay door. "Work lasts from 7:00 a.m. to 7:00 p.m., with shift work during noon tea. That's when the Rag Man struck. They escaped through the cargo dock."

Moving quietly away from Sommerville and the Scotland Yard detective, Kevin slipped his way between industrial washing machines and dryers the size of small huts. Stopping beneath a ceiling vent, he looked up, grunted, and then moved on to the cargo bay doors. Kevin took one quick look on the outside of the bay door onto a narrow alleyway, between two red brick buildings.

The noise and heat began to stifle Kevin's thinking. He nodded for Sommerville and Sylvia Hickey to follow him back into the corridor. As the laundry door shut, the inmates whistled and jeered. "Don't leave, baby. Bring that fine black ass over here." Kevin stiffened. Sylvia took as much heed of the inmates' taunts as one would notice walking past pigeons in a park.

Sylvia fixed her large almond eyes on Sommerville. "John, wouldn't you agree that the Rag Man obviously had infiltrated the prison laundry well before the escape? How else would he have known when the Irish shift would be working?"

Again, Sommerville appeared edgy. He looked to the corners of the ceiling before speaking. "No one remembers anything happening out of the ordinary." Sommerville began counting the fingers on his left hand. "Main Gate guards, tower guards, certainly Dennis Walcott, they all swear that the man who came that day was the usual lorry driver. He had all the proper identification credentials. But we know that to not be the case, don't we?"

Sommerville filled his chest with air. Even though the escape had not occurred under his watch, he seemed to accept the fact that he was the man who had to apologize for a multitude of errors. "He bound and gagged the poor chap—that would be Dennis Walcott—and hid him in a bin of dirty clothes. A tweed rag was left tied to the laundry bin. On the side of the bin was scrawled, 'Understand the haunting.'"

Kevin excused himself and reentered the laundry facility. He began a second tour of the room, conscious that Sommerville and Detective Hickey were observing him through the window. Placing a hand on a canvas laundry bin, he pushed it back and forth on its wheels a dozen times, then went to his knees to inspect the construction of the wheels. Kevin wasn't sure himself why he was moving the bin back and forth, though he liked the way Sommerville watched open-mouthed from behind the glass.

"Well, I guess that's about it, then," Kevin said, pushing the door open with one hand while extending the other toward a surprised Sommerville. The abrupt ending was a ploy. In the next few moments, Sommerville would reveal much about himself, Kevin knew.

"That's it? Are you sure there's no other way we can be of help? Of course, you still need to see Dennis' work record. Won't you?"

"Yes, I'll need that work sheet. I'd like to study it a bit. But, no, I don't think there's anything else for me here without Walcott. Sylvia?"

She shook her head, sending her braids dancing over her slender shoulders. No doubt she was waiting for him to make his next move. He vowed to make it a long wait.

A prison guard came down the hallway holding what Kevin assumed to be Walcott's work file. He handed it to Sommerville, who transferred it to Kevin, saying, "There is one thing that you won't find in the file. Maybe I'm grasping at straws, but Dennis once told me that the Rag Man has a habit of mumbling to himself constantly, as if talking to an invisible third party. Is that silly?"

Kevin nodded. "At this point, we don't rule anything as being silly. Thanks for letting us know. Good day."

Kevin's ploy had produced the results he'd hoped for. Had Sommerville readily accepted the quick ending to the meeting, then he might be withholding information. Had he been overly forthcoming with additional information, then his story was likely to be bogus and an attempt to divert the investigation. John Sommerville was a truthful man, Kevin concluded. He'd added a new color to his picture of the Rag Man.

Back in the rear seat of a Scotland Yard car, Kevin tried painting his picture while sneaking glances at the distractingly pretty Sylvia Hickey. It was during his fourth peek that Sylvia turned and arrested him with almond eyes. "I don't know what the attire is for working undercover in Dublin, but if the two of us are going to pass as a couple, you're going to have to get out of that blue suit and into something a little more fashionable." The instant she finished speaking, her full, glossed lips again retreated to a flat, expressionless line. For the moment, the picture of the Rag Man went blank.

When they were not far from Piccadilly Circus, Sylvia announced that she was now hungry and by happy coincidence directed the driver to Elio's, the same Italian restaurant Kevin had dined at the night before. And though he felt as if he could eat a whole cow no problem, he decided to forego beef and pasta and have a bit of fish.

A hostess walked them toward a private corner.

"Actually, could we sit over here?" Sylvia asked, stopping at precisely the table where Kevin had sat alone the previous night. Then she added, "Bring us two plates of your Spaghetti Bolognese and a bottle of the house red. My friend here is partial to it," she added. Finally, Sylvia Hickey's face bore some expression. It wasn't a pleasant one.

"The heels add three inches. The braids take three hours. I wouldn't have thought that a hairdo, shoes, and some black leather would keep an ICU detective from recognizing the server who had brought him his meal only hours before. And unless you want me to walk out now, you'll tell me what you know about the Rag Man. And you can start with the newspaper with the torn photograph."

17

It wasn't that he'd lost interest in peeping...

Detective Skinny Farrell didn't know where Mattie Joe and his woman were headed when they suddenly drove away from Kilkenny, but as good luck would have it, they drove west all the way to Connemara in the County Galway. It had been years since Skinny had come out to Ireland's rocky wilderness and witnessed the naked beauty of looking glass lakes and the endless stone walls that stitched together sea and sky. Connemara, with its big sky and sea-scented breezes, offered a relaxing change. In fact, Skinny hoped that the couple would settle here on the wild and rocky shores for a good few days—as long as he was back in Kilkenny for Rock 'n Nua. He didn't want to miss that!

In Skinny's view, it was wise of Mattie Joe to come to the remote Gaeltacht region, where people preferred to speak the native Irish language and it would be easier to shield Cait McGrath from the breaking news about the Rag Man and his double murders. Of course, Mattie Joe probably had already figured as much. It's probably why he came to Connemara in the first place, Skinny thought.

The Rag Man and his long legged beauty settled into a cuddly thatched cottage, resting snug and white on a rocky slope of the crystal Casla Bay. Though secluded, their cottage was close enough to the village of Carraroe for the sound of fiddles and accordions to sweep over the still bay. Skinny loved the diddly diddly of the toe-tapping jigs and reels and the boom-ratta-tat-boom of the sheep-skinned drum called a bohdran. As a boy, he wanted to be a musician. But one Christmas Santa had brought him a Polaroid camera and he'd been mad about photography ever since. Only for that camera he might have become a piper, or a fiddler.

He took accommodation at a bed and breakfast on the opposite shore and within acceptable binocular distance of the lovers' retreat. The bed and breakfast came with a small dock and rowboat. Skinny took to fishing daily in Casla Bay. The fish didn't bite, but he caught all the close-up views of Mattie Joe and Cait he wanted. Someone less familiar with the pair might claim there was nothing much worth watching. But Skinny and his camera had peeped at enough couples to know the difference between lovers and a couple of goats in heat. Even Mattie Joe and Cait might not have been aware of it yet, but their relationship was moving on to a new level. Skinny was sure of it.

A professional voyeur noticed things about lovers that they didn't notice about themselves, such as how after time, foreplay became more conversation and cuddling than a tango of biceps and boobs. After they'd been in Connemara for three days, it still had been all talk and cuddle and no tango. They hadn't even made it out of their underwear yet—except for when Cait took a shower. Skinny couldn't be sure about Mattie Joe, since he didn't bother spying on him in the loo. Mattie Joe and Cait probably didn't even realize that, despite the fact that they'd groped and probed every inch of each other, they hadn't held hands until they started taking strolls around the shore and into the purple heather hills of Connemara. It all was a fair bit more exercise than Skinny was used to and, unfortunately, the overdose of fresh air didn't seem to tire the happy couple as much as it did him. He stayed up late, night after night, watching the pair sitting by the turf fire, just talking and laughing. One night they were up so late, and Skinny sitting in the row boat so long, that he actually caught a fish.

Dinner everyday was a home-cooked meal prepared by Mattie Joe. Each evening as Cait curled up in a chair with a glass of wine and a book, Mattie Joe would work away in the kitchen, with a glass of wine. Skinny wasn't normally a big eater himself, but the pleasant aromas of simmering country cooking sweeping over the bay made him so hungry that he began packing a sandwich for his fishing trips. One night, the couple feasted on bacon and cabbage. On another, they had Irish stew with a dessert of rhubarb tart. On the evening Mattie Joe fixed colcannon, Skinny thought he would die if didn't get a taste of the buttery potato concoction. His own mother had cooked the best colcannon, and by the smell of it, Skinny wondered if the Rag Man had stolen her recipe.

He used the same medium-sized head of cabbage cut into fours and washed in salt and water. Then between four or five outer leaves he put in layers of chopped cabbage, parsnips, onions, and potatoes. He seasoned the lot of it with salt and pepper. For thirty minutes, Skinny stared through the binoculars in agonizing ecstasy as the aroma of the simmering colcannon wafted over the bay. He couldn't bear watching Mattie Joe adding the smothering butter. Instead, Skinny rowed ashore and drove to the hotel in Carraroe, where he had a big feed of roasted leg of lamb with mint jelly. The lamb was fine, though the whole while he was dreaming of Mattie Joe's colcannon.

Once the fire in his belly had been put out, Skinny returned to spying on the two lovers. He knew that someone new to the surveillance business probably would have found it boring duty. As was often the case with people who truly cared for one another, they were in no rush to get down to the business of the bedroom. Skinny rather enjoyed waiting through the long gazes into one another's dewy eyes, though. On the night when they slowly pulled the clothes off one another in the soft light of full moon and candles, Skinny put his binoculars down and rowed to shore. It wasn't that he'd lost interest in peeping. He just didn't feel right anymore about looking in on Mattie Joe and Cait. Besides, the Blackbird had called earlier that day and was pulling him off the job. Skinny had found the balance of his fifty thousand pounds wrapped in a bundle below a seat in the rowboat.

18

"...And the raven was—is—the Celtic god of war..."

The Detective Kevin O'Felan stood before a bathroom mirror not knowing whether to laugh or cry. He was dressed in undercover attire that, though a bit far fetched, at least didn't make him look like the tired old detective he was.

Going undercover had been Sylvia's suggestion. Even though London hosted every nationality and class of freak, a forty-seven-year-old white man walking alongside an ebony beauty queen screamed, "Police," to anyone who had reason to be cautious.

Once upon a time, when he was young and full of spit, undercover work had been fun. He remembered how on his first assignment he'd dressed up in an embroidered Turkish dashiki, bellbottom trousers, and platform shoes, which he especially liked. With a guitar strung over his shoulder, he'd buskered up and down Dublin's Grafton Street, singing over and over the first verse to "The House of the Rising

Sun." The plan was for him to meet hippies who might offer him drugs. He'd met plenty of hippies, alright, but none offered him drugs. Most of them just wanted to play his "axe." Some of the hippies produced harmonicas and asked if he wanted "to jam the blues." Kevin didn't know how to jam the blues. He only knew how to play "There is a house in New Orleans, they call the Rising Sun. It's been the ruin of many a poor boy, and God I know I'm one..." He'd soon lost that job to a fellow detective named Willie Troy. Troy played saxophone—which Kevin came to learn was also an "axe." Willie Troy could jam the blues on his axe, and within days, he had uncovered a Dublin marijuana ring.

Sylvia had taken it upon herself to pick out Kevin's "blending outfit." In Kevin's view, she'd had a little too much fun doing so. He found himself wearing a hip-length black leather jacket and a gold stud earring. When it came to his hair, Sylvia ordered it cut tight and dyed platinum blonde. Closing his eyes, he dropped a gold chain over his head, knowing that Mary and the kids would laugh themselves sick if they saw him now. By some miracle or God's infinite mercy, he hoped when he opened his eyes that he wouldn't look like a complete eegit altogether.

God's mercy came in the form of a phone call. It was probably Mary or, with some luck, Finbar Lawlor. Kevin could use the chat. Without thinking, he opened his eyes and caught the image of himself in the mirror. Not bad, he thought. He definitely looked years younger. And better still, he was able to slip two fingers between his trousers and belly. He picked up the phone with a smile on his face. It was Sylvia. His smile faded. The matter of his withholding the torn newspaper as evidence was still a wedge between them.

"We've got Walcott," she whispered. "A yellow taxi is waiting for you. It's Scotland Yard," she added.

A soft rain painted a glossy sheen over London's streets. Kevin sat in the back seat of the yellow taxi as it inched through heavy traffic toward Piccadilly Circus. The tourist season was on; London was wall-to-wall people. While still a block away, Kevin easily spotted Sylvia Hickey waiting beneath an umbrella on a crowded sidewalk. Wearing a sky-blue denim jacket over a cherry red T-shirt, she looked like a United Colors of Benetton advert come to life. Behind her, children flurried toward an office building with a glittering neon sign announcing "Segaworld," a video game arcade. Sylvia opened the taxi door. Her lipstick matched the color of her T-shirt. Droplets of rain clung to her long ebony braids. She pulled him close and pressed soft lips to his ear. Her breath was warm and sweet. "Remember, we're a couple," she cooed. "Our spotters have Walcott on the third floor."

In a single day, Sylvia had transformed from cop with an attitude to gushy, wide-eyed party girl. Kevin liked the party girl. She was a lot nicer. More than ever, though, he knew he was working with a real pro. Locking arms, they sauntered into Segaworld.

On the third floor of what seemed to Kevin to be a carnival built inside a three-story shaft of showering light, a man dressed in jeans and blue pullover jumper stepped away from a virtual skiing game. Sylvia simultaneously pulled Kevin toward the vacated game. Just opposite to the left, a burly man a few years shy thirty threw punches at a virtuosity game called "Fight of the Century." On his right forearm was a tattoo of a black and white striped tiger in full sprint. It was Walcott. The former prison warder snorted as he snapped off an impressive left jab that sprung back and forth from his shoulder as if on a taut spring. Kevin pulled his shield from inside the black leather jacket. "Irish International Cooperation Unit working with New Scotland Yard. We have to talk, Mister Walcott."

The would-be prize fighter nodded. "No problem. Should we go to the office? It's not as noisy."

Office? A quick sideward glance from Sylvia told Kevin she was as surprised as he.

Walcott led the way up the elevator to a large, swank office featuring photographs of boxing immortals and floor-to-ceiling windows looking out on Piccadilly Circus. Toweling sweat from his brow, the boxer sank into a burgundy leather chair.

"I've been here for two months now and I go a few rounds a day on that game for the aerobic workout. I've lost half a stone," he said. He grabbed a handful of belly. "I don't mean to sound cheeky, but what took you guys so long? You're here to talk about the Rag Man, right?"

Sylvia leaned forward over the desktop. "We were told we'd find you at Brixton. No one there seemed to know where you were."

"Rubbish. Someone's not doing his work. I signed my resignation papers and went back to school for business management. But after a month of listening to lectures on business theory, I decided, why not just go work and get paid for learning. What took you so long?" he asked again.

"Can you give us your take on the Brixton escape?" Kevin asked. "It says in the file that the Rag Man overpowered you? You're a pretty big man. And handy with your mitts."

Walcott shrugged. "What can I say? He was quick as a cat. One moment he's packing the laundry into the bin, the next he's packing me in it. Then he's out the cargo bay with the three Irish lads jumping into the lorry. Don't forget he had a gun. Mine," he added.

The conversation derailed as Walcott made a point to explain how he'd come into the good fortune of an administrative job at Segaworld. He'd been a video game junkie for years and had a good sense for what made games popular or not. "After spending most of my paycheck playing these games, now I get paid to do the same thing. Not bad, heh? The Japanese companies even send representatives to talk to me."

Something was wrong. Kevin didn't trust overwilling witnesses. Most times they were lying. He could feel the old mistrust monster growing inside of him.

"That's it? He took your gun and stuffed you in the laundry bin? There must be other reasons, or why else would you be waiting to be questioned? I can think of some," Kevin said quickly, purposely not allowing Walcott a chance to respond. "Why did a hardened IRA man, who's killed before, not kill you? How is it that you identified Liam Riordon in a lineup as being your assailant? Liam Riordon is a slender man who couldn't lift your right leg, let alone put you in the laundry bin."

Walcott grinned and pointed to a photograph on the wall showing a sneering Muhammad Ali standing over a fallen Sonny Liston. "What can I say? One day you're the champ and the next you're the chump. It doesn't make sense, does it? My not being killed, I'm talking about. As for identifying, or misidentifying, Riordon, let's just say that when a gun is stuck in a bloke's nose, one is not apt to be admiring the gunman's grooming, heh? At the time, I couldn't be sure that Liam Riordon was not the man. That is the Rag Man's MO, right? Disguises? But if I may, I'd suggest that we're straying from the two most important aspects of this case. The first is the fact that the Rag Man talks to someone named Brian."

Sylvia interrupted. "But you told Prison Governor Sommerville that the Rag Man talks to himself."

"Yeah, I told the prison governor that the Rag Man talks to himself. But I had to cover myself a bit, too, y' know? Truth is, he yaps under his breath to this 'Brian.' I definitely heard him say, 'Shut up' and 'I can do this on my own.' To me, he sounded more like a teenager protesting to his parents." Walcott shook his head as if still trying to comprehend the incident. "I open the cargo bay, right? And this black raven flies into the laundry, right? I thought it was an accident. The bird could have been attracted to the warmth of the laundry, right? But that raven was never more than five feet from the Rag Man. It was as if some invisible strand attached them. I'm telling you that the Rag Man was talking to the bird. Swear to God."

"Hold on. I thought you said he was talking to someone named Brian?" Kevin said.

Walcott paused again. He twisted the ends of the towel into knots. His eyes rolled toward the ceiling. Kevin sensed that the former prison warder wished he was back at the video games, bashing heads. Walcott spoke to the ceiling.

"I'm a Celtic history buff. It's a hobby of mine. That's why I know that the Celtic name for Brian is Bran. And Bran is the Celtic name for Raven. And the raven was— is—the Celtic god of war. My take on it is that the Rag Man is not IRA at all, but a man fighting a *personal* war, and this Brian, or Bran, is some form of pooka. In the Rag Man's mind he is, anyway," Walcott added. He then offered a mini-lecture on Celtic faeries, the upshot of which was that a pooka was a faery that took the form of an animal.

Kevin listened, knowing that he was learning more about Walcott than he was about faeries. "You were transferred to Brixton from Dartmoor Prison supposedly to help the new governor bring some experience and stability to the prison. You don't think that was the reason for your transfer, do you, Dennis?" Kevin asked. Walcott pursed his lips and slowly shook his head. "Nor was it a coincidence that the Rag Man struck at the Brixton laundry while you were on guard?"

Walcott, his lips now twisted in a little smirk, shrugged again. "You're on to the second important key to this case— me. I was transferred because I had stumbled across a cover-up at Dartmoor Prison. Fifteen years ago, people died there. The prison officials didn't want to hear about it, but the *Sunday World* did. They printed my story. The next day, I find myself transferred to Brixton."

Kevin quickly did the math. The Rag Man's age was put somewhere between twenty-five and thirty. Fifteen years ago, he could have been ten years of age—just like the boy whose face was missing from the newspaper photograph. Finbar Lawlor could be correct. They *were* looking for a little boy. Only the little boy had grown into an angry man with murderous intent.

Dennis Walcott eagerly offered his conspiracy theory. There had been a fire at the prison. It was thought that everyone had safely escaped. Only an older guard named Bernard Tolleson rushes back into the prison and saves some forgotten inmates. Tolleson himself was badly burned. He received a commendation from the Queen and a cushy retirement at a place called Surrey Hall. That's the story Dennis knew.

"So the cover-up?" Kevin asked.

"It has to do with some graves being accidentally dug up at the Dartmoor cemetery and the Special Powers Act," Dennis added. "Under the Act, suspects could be held up to a fortnight with no charges being filed. A man could be in prison, and for all the world to know, he might've disappeared. Lots of Irish held under the Special Powers Act."

Kevin nodded. He was well aware of the England's Special Powers Act and the harsh employment of it in an attempt to subdue the IRA.

"Anyway, the prison cemetery is for inmates who finish their days incarcerated and with no families to claim their remains. So I'm on my dinner break, watching as some poor bugger's grave is being dug and bang! Damned if the blokes didn't hit on an old coffin. It wasn't supposed to be there, right? Or else why were the blokes digging there in the first place? Anyway, they call over to me and we lift the coffin out of the ground. First thing I notice is that this coffin—simple pine box, not varnished or anything—is not all that old, y' know? So I take a good look at it. A real good look. I look to see the kind of wood, the contours of the cuts, the lot. Then one of the blokes says, 'Let's open 'er.' Well, I'll tell you the thought of doing that sent shivers up my spine, but not as much as when I saw what was inside: the remains of *two* men." Walcott let the image of two decomposed humans hang in silence.

"Now I'm no coroner," he continued, "but I visited one and described the conditions of the bodies. This man told me that, based on what I told him, these men burned to death, probably about fifteen years ago. But I've another card up my sleeve. I'm saving it, y' know? It has to do with the casket. These yokes were made by the inmates themselves right there in the prison, right? And I see this etching on the casket saying, 'Best of luck beyond the wall—Cue.' So

I do a bit more digging around and find out that it was customary that the inmates like to sign their handiwork. And guess what I find out? That there was a fellow who went by the name of Cue, on account he was some sort of billiards shark, who made these coffins. What's more, Cue was incarcerated at Dartmoor eighteen years ago and died there in a fight thirteen years ago."

"So the coffin had to be made somewhere between thirteen and eighteen years ago. Maybe it was fifteen years," Sylvia said, doing the math.

Walcott continued. "So, this thing is plaguing me, right? So, I do some library digging of old newspapers and learn that fifteen years ago, just a few days prior to the fire, a bomb was found in a railway station. The IRA was suspected. Two men were arrested under the Special Powers Act. I say it was those two blokes in the unmarked grave. That's what I tell the *Sunday World*."

Kevin nodded. "So you think that the Rag Man striking at Brixton during your shift is no coincidence?"

"Only if it's also a coincidence that it happens on a day when I'm a replacement for a bloke who calls in sick. Only if it's also a coincidence that three Jamaican inmates land in hospital with a sudden flu and their all replacements happen to be Irish. No, I don't think it's a coincidence. My take is this: The Rag Man saw the article in the *Sunday World* and came looking for those two fellows we dug up in the unmarked prison grave. And his only way to find the dead buggers was to start with finding me. I guarantee you that bit of tweed he left behind has something to do with those dead men. The Rag Man might be IRA. He might not be. But his mission is personal. I'm sure of it."

At the very least, Walcott had introduced new colors for Kevin to consider for his picture of the Rag Man. He and Sylvia shook hands with Walcott, promising to keep in touch. "By the way, what university was it that you left to come here?" Kevin asked. "They lost a good student, I'd say. You might think of going back."

The question caught Dennis Walcott off guard. After a pause, he answered, "What? And leave all this? It was Kings College. Business school."

Outside, blue streaks cracked an otherwise charcoal sky. The sun would be out within the hour. Kevin and Sylvia stood on the sidewalk as children poured past them into Segaworld like water spilling around a couple of rocks. Sylvia held his hand, reminding Kevin that they were still "blending." "Lunch?" she asked.

"That would be grand. But someplace quiet. My ears are still ringing from those video games."

"I agree. Our place? It's close."

Kevin chuckled privately. Elio's was just around the corner. It quickly had become "their place." His relationship with Sylvia was definitely on the upswing. "Why not?" he said. "No fat grams in a bowl of pasta, no?"

Sylvia surprised him by loosening her long fingers from his, then slipping them between his pants and shirt and pulling until there was an inch gap between trousers and belly. "And negate all this hard work? I've noticed a difference in just the few days. Cut back on the carbohydrates and you'll look just like David Beckham in no time." She ran a hand through his new platinum blonde hair. "I'm recommending the Caesar salad. And stop blushing. You'll blow our cover."

"I always blush before Caesar salad. The anticipation, y' know?"

Sylvia smiled. "Do you like to talk during salad?"

"I do. I'm a right chatterbox, so. We could talk about whether Walcott is leading us to the Rag Man or just leading us astray. He's lying about university, I'm sure of it. You're kidding about me looking like Beckham, aren't you?"

"I'll get back to you on that one. After we talk some more about that torn newspaper."

It would have to be a big salad, Kevin thought.

For the next hour, Kevin and Sylvia impersonated ebony and ivory lovers by holding hands across the red and white checked tablecloth, leaning close until their lips were inches apart. Kevin again apologized for withholding the torn newspaper from her and, grinning sheepishly, confessed to liking the feel of the new leather jacket. Sylvia responded with a furtive wink and one of her moonbeam smiles. Kevin had noticed how she knew just how to posture herself in a way that was just ever so shy of being suggestive, though definitely alluring. He also noticed how her silky fingers twining over and around his were sending signals to other regions of his body. It made having to munch on soggy lettuce while Sylvia enjoyed saucy fettuccini Alfredo tolerable. And it made the hour drive to find Bernard Tolleson, Dennis Walcott's theoretical hero of the Dartmoor Prison fire rescue, enjoyable.

Sylvia drove a sleek two-seat sports coupe. The first quarter of an hour was spent crawling through London traffic and agreeing that Dennis Walcott had been overly eager to help. Sylvia acknowledged having close ties with the London West Indian community who, with one visit to friends incarcerated at Brixton, could garner all they needed to know about the former prison guard. "Walcott could be a red herring meant to throw the Rag Man investigation off kilter," Sylvia said.

Kevin held a cigarette out the passenger window, adding to the London smog. "The question then becomes, who's selling the red herring? Whoever wants to keep the guerilla war black markets open? Or someone larger? Very likely, it's someone who wants a major eruption of the troubles in the north of Ireland, so foreign companies would start pulling their operations out of the Republic of Ireland. The resulting financial upheaval would be larger by far than the collapse of any black market. We're talking major money. Major power. Eire Nua could tumble like a house of cards. The devastating effects would be felt throughout the EU."

They'd reached the motorway and Sylvia stomped on the accelerator. "Dominoes," she said. "The whole case will fall like dominoes. I imagine each case as patterns of information. Push the wrong piece of information and nothing happens. Push the right piece and the whole thing tumbles down sequentially. Dominoes. So, today we push on Dennis Walcott and see where it takes us."

Kevin enjoyed the cool air blowing across his newly cropped head. "That's a very chancy process," he said. "You can be after pushing the wrong thing time after time. No, I think a case is like painting a picture by numbers. Each bit of information is a new color to be added. Brush stroke by brush stroke and number by number, the big picture comes into view."

Sylvia gave him *that* smile. "You choose the first domino, Kevin. Walcott? Or the torn newspaper photo?"

"Walcott. The paint is still wet on him. Besides, they're not mutually exclusive. Think about it. The Rag Man left that newspaper to guide us along. Isn't that his game? Strategically doling out information in hopes that we'd follow? If Dennis Walcott is correct and the Rag Man wanted us to find him, then the logical course of action is to give a brush stroke to everything connected to Walcott. That's why we're headed to see Bernard Tolleson. The Rag

Man is leading us to Surrey Hall. You see in a paint-by-numbers painting, you start with one number and you color that one entirely."

Sylvia twisted her cherry red lips into a knot, and then allowed them to dissolve into a wry grin. "That's too easy. We agreed Walcott could be a red herring. You are sharing everything, aren't you?" Her tone bordered on accusation.

"I am—I mean—I was. Oh, it's just something Dennis Walcott said that made me curious and I've been chewing on it ever since. It was that bit about the Rag Man's motives being personal and not political. That's the second time I've been told that."

"By whom? Following your method, Walcott and this other person should be linked—the same number, color, whatever. Start brushing, painter boy."

Kevin was explaining his relationship with a psychologist friend who assisted his criminal profiling when suddenly his tongue locked up inside his jaw. In his mind's eye, he was falling through a long black tunnel. Cold, clammy sweat came oozing from his pores. He landed hard on the cold floor of Bruxelles' Café, his hands dripping with dark red blood, flowing like an open faucet out of young Paddy Burke's head. From a place far, far away Sylvia's voice echoed, *"Are you alright...alright...alright..."* The words drummed against his brain as his mind's eye found fat Finbar Lawlor waddling toward him with a newspaper in his hand. It was the tears flowing cold on Kevin's cheeks that brought him back to the moment. Once again, the investigation was back to the newspaper with the torn photograph.

Sylvia's fingers made a quick dance over the mobile phone saddled on the dashboard. "Colin? Sylvia Hickey, here. Fine. You? Yes, I do need something. I need to see any photos taken at the funeral of the Belfast bin lorry man.

Talk to Roy Atheridge. He'll understand why." Sylvia ended the call. "I'm afraid we'll have to assume that newspaper is compromised evidence. And I do feel badly now for thinking that you were withholding evidence from me. You've probably been withholding it from yourself without realizing it. I'm beginning to wonder if there isn't more than just a little boy's photograph torn out of that paper."

There was a long period of silence between them. Kevin took several deep breaths. Sylvia produced a tissue seemingly out of nowhere. He wiped his eyes and then exhaled heavily one last time. She drove with one hand and caressed his with the other. It was no game this time. Sylvia offered kind words that washed over Kevin with little soothing effect. "Why me?" he thought. No matter what explanation was offered, or how much he tried to detach his personal feelings from the Rag Man investigation, he always returned to the same question: "Why me?"

They passed through a gated entrance announcing Surrey Hall and Sylvia guided the sports coupe slowly past a tea garden of roses and boxwood hedges. Kevin was now feeling better for having blown off a little steam. Maybe he was just a little teapot short and stout, after all, he thought.

Surrey Hall was a stately, stone and stucco Tudor. Kevin grabbed hold of a burnished lion's head doorknocker. "England certainly treats their heroes well," he said. "Back home in Ireland, you might get a slap on the back and your named shouted from the pulpit."

A blonde woman, who looked to be a few years shy of forty, welcomed them. She had a wide smile and lively, green eyes. She wore a red scarf around her neck, white blouse, and a forest green skirt that touched the top of her ankles. Kevin wondered was she Tolleson's daughter, but when the refined woman remarked that "Bernie" would be thrilled to have company, he then wondered if the rich old man hadn't robbed the cradle. Introducing herself as Constance Bradshaw, she led them along a marble corridor. Kevin could see his reflection in the high-gloss stone floor. "Your first time to Surrey Hall?" Constance Bradshaw asked, opening a door.

Kevin exchanged a telling glance with Sylvia: Dennis Walcott *was* a red herring. Surrey Hall was a nursing care facility.

The woman spoke as she stepped along a corridor lined with old men in wheelchairs as hastily as someone avoiding oncoming traffic. "Surrey Hall is among the finest elder care nursing facilities in all the UK. It was deeded to the government by a man who stipulated in his will that it be used for the care of those who dedicated their lives to the service of the Queen. Bernie certainly qualifies, now doesn't he?" She turned and smiled again. "My position is head of the volunteer services. And I must confess that Bernie is one of my favorites. A lovely man. And a true hero." She nodded in agreement with her own comment.

The smells of disinfectant and soiled underclothes seeped throughout the harshly bright corridor. Kevin counted a dozen elderly men sitting in wheelchairs with feeding trays pressed beneath wrinkled faces holding eyes searching toward heaven. Kevin's thoughts had already moved past how the fire hero might help them solve the riddle of the Rag Man, to wondering who was behind leading Sylvia and him into the dead end.

The head of volunteer services strode into a sunlit recreation room where the old ones seemed to be in far better condition. If Bernard Tolleson were among this group, maybe he'd be of some help after all, Kevin thought.

On one side of the square room, a perky young woman played piano and sang very slowly and loudly to a group of old women. "All I want is a room somewhere, far away from the cold night air," she sang. Constance Bradshaw waved a finger in tempo with the piano player, then smiled at the old woman who'd named the tune. "Right, Sheila," said Constance Bradshaw. "It's from *My Fair Lady*. Now tell me everything you can remember about *My Fair Lady*. No, Rita. That was Mary Poppins who flew with an umbrella."

Constance Bradshaw extended a long right arm toward the piano player and singers. "This is our music therapy class, and," switching to her left arm, added, "the men like to watch sports, of course." On the other side of the room, six old lads stared blankly at a cricket match showing on television.

They moved outside to the lovely tea garden they'd passed upon their arrival. "Which newspaper did you say you are from?" Constance Bradshaw asked. "The interest in Bernie never seems to diminish. He's a real hero."

Kevin shook his head. "No newspaper. I'm with the International Cooperation Unit of the Irish Garda Síochána, working in alliance with New Scotland Yard. We're hoping Bernard Tolleson might be able to shed some light on a particular case."

Constance Bradshaw shook her head, sending her dyed blonde hair scrubbing over her shoulders. "Oh, I'm afraid that's not possible. The privacy of the occupants is highly guarded. These people have served their country with dignity and—"

Sylvia pushed her silver shield inches in front of the indignant woman's lightly powdered nose. "Then they'll be happy to serve their country again. It would be far less hassle if you just let us talk to Bernard Tolleson."

On an iron bench tucked amid the rose bushes sat a small man with slumping shoulders. A shovel lay propped on the bench beside him. A blue jumper hung nearby from a low branch of a shade tree. Constance Bradshaw put a hand on the old man's shoulder and spoke as if addressing a small child, "Taking a break, are we, Bernie? There are some people here to see you. Bernie likes to keep the garden clear of weeds. Don't you, Bernie?"

The old man turned slowly. One look at his mutilated face and lost eyes told Kevin that he and Sylvia had, indeed, reached a dead end. (He couldn't help but thinking that they had pushed the wrong domino and couldn't wait to say as much to Sylvia.) The right side of Tolleson's face was a disfigurement of molten lumps and craters of pink flesh, common among severe burn victims. Thin strands of white hair sprayed stubbornly from an otherwise bald head. The burnt side of his mouth lay dead. On the other, unspoken thoughts trembled on his lips like drops of water clinging stubbornly on a leaf, only to dry away before falling. Kevin struggled to imagine this shrunken man as ever having shoulders and arms thick enough to carry grown men out of a burning building.

Constance Bradshaw, obviously sensing that her case had been made, now spoke softly. "You can see that Bernie suffered hideous burns while saving others in the prison..." She finished her sentence by silently mouthing the word *fire*. "It was months before he was able to speak. He suffered shock, dreadful amnesia, and now the poor creature is in the advanced stages of Alzheimer's disease. I'm afraid he's of little use to your *investigation*." She wrapped an arm around Tolleson's thin shoulders. "Where's your wrap, Bernie? Oh goodness," she said, retrieving the jumper from the tree branch. "Hasn't he given enough for his country?" she said with a tone of finality.

Kevin nodded. "Just two more questions of you, Miss Bradshaw. Why did you assume we were newspaper people and not friends or family? And what is music therapy?"

"Well, you're obviously not family," Bradshaw said, looking first at Sylvia, then Kevin. "Bernie has no family. The only people who ever come to see him are newspaper people. Regarding the second question, music therapy is used to help Alzheimer's victims recall events in their lives through association with music. Music can be a key, if you will, to unlock those memories."

"Does Mister Tolleson participate in music therapy?" Kevin asked.

Bradshaw shook her head *no*. "His condition has gone way beyond anything music theory could help, I'm afraid. His injuries in the..." She again mouthed the word *fire* and continued, "took away any music he had in him."

"Does he ever speak about the fire?" Sylvia asked.

"Fire!" Tolleson cried. His eyes came alive and darted around the garden as if he was looking for something. "Fire! Fire! Fire!" Tolleson's wailing voice could be heard long after an intensely angry Constance Bradshaw abruptly ended the visit by leading the hysterical old man back inside Surrey Hall.

"You did that on purpose," Kevin said, climbing into Sylvia's car.

Sylvia smiled *that* smile.

19

"So fare thee well my own true love.
When I return united we will be.
It's not the leaving of Des the Dacent that grie-eves me
But Mairead when I think of thee..."

Mick Mulvihill gave Deirdre a few snappy strums, then with a wink acknowledged the giddy applause of the Taoiseach's party full of black ties and long gowns. Desmond O'Hanrahan embraced him. The Missus, still a looker at fifty-plus, planted a peck on his cheek. Then with his chin held high, he and Deirdre moved slowly past the guests and began their descent through Kilkenny Castle's dark and winding stairway. Mick had insisted that the route from the banquet hall to the Rock 'n Nua stage was to be kept dark and off limits to everyone. Maybe it seemed eccentric, but to Mick it was deadly essential that he and Deirdre make the last leg of their comeback odyssey alone—just as they had been for two stolen years. Besides, he'd wanted to use the brief solitude to focus his thoughts on the performance, and to take a belt of the wine he'd poured into the plastic Irish spring water bottle. California chardonnay. Great stuff altogether.

In the belly of the castle, he heard the cheers of a hundred thousand people echoing eerily against the great stone walls. Were these ghosts from past performances come to welcome him home? Or to haunt him as they had during the stolen years? Where were the screaming hundred thousand when he and Deirdre were all alone?

When the gigs had abruptly ended with no offers forthcoming, Mick wondered how he could survive without the applause. Even when the cocaine was dragging him down, he'd had the applause to hang on to. For a good year or more into his rehab, all he could think of was working his way back to the applause. Then the epiphany came: he and Deirdre were beggars. They were addicted to applause, not cocaine. Sure, the drugs weren't healthy, but hadn't he proven he was in control by going immediately cold turkey in rehab and staying clean for two years? Not hearing the applause was another matter entirely. For more than a year, his body shivered for just the slightest taste of it.

From age fifteen, when he and Deirdre begged for a living by buskering on Dublin's teeming streets, he'd measured his life by the approval of others. Once he became a star, his appetite for applause grew. He fed himself on the raucous roars of crowds that included the entire Irish Diaspora. From Melbourne to New York and Cricklewood to Stuttgart, he and Deirdre were adored. Sometimes he had wondered if he and Deirdre had become expat performers would he ever have started shoving the white shit up his nose? Pleasing the audience at home was hardest, like bobbing for apples in the dark, trying to figure out what they wanted to hear. The rebel songs of the '70s gave way to disco. In the '80s, it was he who'd brought the calypso beat to traditional Irish music and was soon copied by everyone. To be hip in today's music scene, a performer first had to prove how "un-Irish" he was. Witness all the bands that had played the Rock 'n Nua thus far tonight, he thought. But soon, Mick and Deirdre would turn the tables on everyone. They weren't beggars any longer.

Ahead, the open door to the stage let in a brilliant shaft of light that drew a yellow line on the old stone walls. Standing in the light were the big name performers pushing in at the doorway like a crowd of trick-or-treaters, trying to get the first glimpse of Mick and Deirdre. These were people used to being first in line. He decided to make them wait. He stopped short of the light, took a long suck of the Chardonnay, and felt a bolt of energy sear through his body. He moved Deirdre onto his chest. "We made it, girl. We made it back," he said. Then he and Deirdre strode onto the stage to thunderous applause.

∽

The best surveillance detective in Ireland, perhaps in all of Europe, sat perched inside the leafy cloak of a massive tree with a bird's eye view of the Rock 'n Nua concert. Even though the Blackbird had paid him and taken him off the case, Skinny Farrell wasn't about to walk off the job on the biggest night of Irish entertainment ever. He was so near the concert stage that he could feel the boom of the bass drum pulsating against his Adam's apple.

He used the binoculars to view Des O'Hanrahan and the beautiful people gazing out the Kilkenny Castle windows. Cathal Slattery stood at the Taoiseach's shoulder. Hovering over both was the Herculean Peter Doyle, Skinny's mate with the Garda Síochána. Doyle's presence was a clear signal that the noose was tightening around Mattie Joe Treacy.

From his perch, Skinny easily spotted Cait McGrath standing alone and fidgeting near the castle gate. Every few moments the beautiful woman with the flowing red hair would give a worried glance at her wristwatch. Skinny had peeped on hundreds of women, professionally and otherwise, and in time grew tired of even the best of them. But Cait McGrath was different. Her pure ice complexion, perfect white teeth, and eyes like blue moons unsettled Skinny every time he saw her. He'd seen her so many times now in the flesh that his mind's eye could peel the blue jeans right off her. This was another thing he was going to miss about the Rag Man case: not seeing Cait McGrath in the buff on a daily basis. He consoled himself by reasoning that at least he'd have his photographs to remember her by.

A loud roar erupted and Skinny turned his attention to the image of Des O'Hanrahan raising a glass on the massive television screen at the rear of the stage. The Irish people with a long and heartfelt ovation were giving credit where credit was due. Skinny, too, out of respect for the nation's great and kind-hearted leader cheered himself hoarse. He then resumed peeping on Cait, because, although Des O'Hanrahan was a wise man with important things to say, he didn't have a full bosom slowly rising and falling within full and easy view. Yet, as much as her lovely pair pleased him, a deeper instinct pulled his eyes to Cait McGrath's hand as it purposefully pushed a pen over a note pad. In Skinny's view, becoming a top class surveillance man couldn't be earned or learned. Rather, you had to be born with an appetite for discovery so insatiable that it would never dull, even during the tedium of a long investigation. Skinny smelled the scent of discovery in the ink from Cait McGrath's pen. He trained his lens squarely on her notepad.

Setting

- violet sky illuminates castle in enchanted glow

- thousands of Irishmen and women—mostly kids—near delirious with drink and rock and roll. This is the biggest party in Ireland's history

- Where is Matthew?

Des

- despite the cheery smile frozen on his ruddy face, heavy bags under Des O's eyes show the strain of Eire Nua. One senses he'll be glad when it's all over.

- says Eire Nua is not moving away from the past, but building upon it...history is in the making, a new Irish history....massive applause from a suddenly attentive and obedient crowd.

- jobs jobs jobs. Des O's hammers this theme. No mention yet of EU military compliancy or naval base in Cork

- Ireland's national security no longer a worry—will this be the only reference to dropping neutrality?

- Where is Matthew???? Could I possibly stay in Ireland? Live on a farm? Am I in love?????????

Skinny laughed and said aloud, "Of course you're in love, woman. And hadn't I been the first to realize it?"

Cait, her beauty now creased by worry, added another heading to her list. She wrote and underlined _Hennessy_. By the way her pen hand hovered undecidedly over the paper, Skinny sensed that whatever secret there was to Cait McGrath would be answered with what she wrote next.

- must finish column and email by 11:00

- tell Hennessy he can write articles himself. I'm quitting.

She scratched a line through the last entry and wrote beside it: _Get paid, and then quit._

In his career as a detective, Skinny had helped solve many a mystery, but the hidden treasure he'd just uncovered would have to rank among the very top: Cait McGrath was a ghost writer for Thomas Hennessy. Yet, even as one piece of the mystery unraveled, another presented itself. A young woman had just approached Cait McGrath, handed her a note, and then walked away. With his camera lens placing his right eye so close to Cait McGrath's hand that he could see the wrinkles on her knuckles, he watched as she slid a scrap of paper over her notes. It read, *Meet me at Lacken Abbey in one hour.*

When Mick Mulvihill came out on stage, Skinny decided to leave Rock 'n Nua on a high note. Using nightfall as his cover, he slipped across the river, where he staked himself in another tree, this one protruding into an old abbey ruin.

∾

Cait McGrath huddled against an old stone wall surrounding the plush grounds of Kilkenny Castle, shifting her attention between drafting a Hennessy column and searching the black arched gate for Matthew. He should have passed through more than an hour ago. During their time together in Connemara, she'd grown accustomed to his boyish grin and eyes of sweet chocolate. Now without him, she felt a hole growing at her side. She wanted it filled.

And yet, even this newfound aching brought with it a sense of joy. Because for the first time in years, her life was being defined by what she wanted to keep, rather than what she wanted to throw away. She'd tried to throw away Ireland. She'd tried to throw away her whole past. And in the process, the only thing she'd truly thrown away was herself. Only because of a chance encounter with a wild boy farmer, who'd put the tingle back into her bones, had she rediscovered pieces of herself that she hadn't even realized had been lost. Most of all, she'd discovered that she had the capacity to love.

She endured the wait and the aching hollowness of Matthew's absence by taking notes for her final Hennessy column. The Taoiseach appeared on a mammoth video screen hanging suspended against the castle walls. Crystal glass in hand, he toasted the Irish people and the nation's bright future. When Mick Mulvihill, the famous folk singer, arrived on stage to even louder cheers than were afforded the nation's leader, Cait considered it no more a distraction than the person who'd just bumped against her.

"Excuse me, Mam? A man asked me to give you this." A teenage girl with a silver stud in the side of her nose handed Cait a note, then slipped away. One look at the piece of paper and the crowds vanished. The music turned off. An initial shock dissolved into a feeling of resignation. Cait rubbed a finger wistfully over the drawn image of a bird taking flight from a heart. He'd found her.

Mick Mulvihill began screaming into the microphone. "Cueness! I said. I've a phone call for Jasus' sake." The big screen showed Mulvihill holding a silver-colored mobile phone against his ear, and the night of explosive noise became one of looming silence. "Now, you've got to speak up and tell me again who this is." He held the mobile phone against a microphone.

A voice, muffled but utterly familiar, said, "I am the Rag Man."

All through their affair, Cait had thought that it was she who had been using Mattie Joe. She had been so horribly wrong that she began to run, to the only place she could go—into her past.

20

The song rose from her toes and the years slipped away.

Though the television screen showed the largest crowd of happy people Bab Treacy had ever seen gathered anywhere, let alone almost in her own backyard, she had absolutely no desire to be part of it. She sat snug in the old parlor love seat, with her cheek turned toward a low smoldering fire. A blanket of bobbing heads and waving arms spread over the television screen. Biddie Tynan owned two of those arms, but only half a head, as far as Bab was concerned. If Biddie showed her face for breakfast tomorrow with a sore head, she'd not get an ounce of sympathy from Bab. The crowd on the television were raising a ruckus, but not so loud that she couldn't hear the kitchen chime of spoon against glass. Mattie Joe was stirring sugar into the Irish coffee.

A mother didn't need a big advertisement to recognize a special moment with her child. A soft glance. A lingering at your side for an instant longer than normal. A spoon tinkling against the glass in the kitchen. Her spat with Mattie Joe was over. So sure was she that tonight was a night to cherish forever, that she placed herself on the left-hand side of the old parlor love seat.

She'd moved to the right-hand side after her husband died because it was a small comfort of sorts to rest on Tim's side of the love seat. At first, she could even smell the sweet scent of the soap he'd used, when washing up after the evening milking, and the pungent pipe tobacco she'd never liked but had always tolerated. In the cushions she could feel the contours that his compact and powerful body had dug over the years. The old love seat had been there during the waking of her mother and father. Through her four miscarriages. Through those happy early years with Mattie Joe bouncing on his knee. Sitting on Tim's side of the love seat was like having his arms still wrapped around her, in a way. It was the smell of him that faded first. Then gradually the contours of the cushions became her own, and her Tim was fully gone. There hadn't been the time much to mourn him, though. She'd always been too busy trying to rebuild the wreckage that had become Mattie Joe.

What was once a bright and happy child slipped away into a world of silence, anger, and divilment. Oh, the neighbors were supportive at first, until their senses of duty were fulfilled and they tired of cooking meals that went to feeding the chickens more than her or Mattie Joe. But divil the neighbor that raised a hand to help her as the years passed and Mattie Joe did poorly in school, and got into scrap after scrap. It seemed then that a fortnight didn't pass when the gardai weren't again driving up her lane. It only became worse once he was old enough to take a drink. Where were the neighbors then? Standing in their doorways wagging their fingers, that's where. Or whispering behind her back that all her troubles were on account of the curse of the O'Neills.

In Bab's view, it was all the talk of a curse that caused Mattie Joe's trouble. There was no curse. Some of the more kind-hearted neighbors suggested that Mattie Joe's problems stemmed from the fact that Tim's body had come back from England burned beyond recognition—a gas explosion at the work site, the parish priest had told her, though she'd always felt he was hiding the truth from her. Mattie Joe never got his final farewell. But, even this, Mattie Joe would have gotten over in time, had it not been for all the talk of the blasted curse. In Bab's view, the neighbors were the ones who never let poor Tim rest in peace.

Mattie Joe arrived holding two Irish coffees. The long-stemmed glass was hot against her lips. Her heart fluttered as Mattie Joe lay his hand upon hers and his lips turned with his father's easy grin. For a fleeting instant, she saw her Tim. He was back on his side of the love seat, putting an arm around her and watching the television.

It was one of life's wondrous mysteries how a mother knew so well what was in her child's heart, but never really knew what going on inside his head. The moment you think he's going to hell in a hand basket, he surprises you with a kindness that draws the blinders of love over your eyes, and you clutch to that glimmer of hope that feeds your starving heart. Raising Mattie Joe alone had been like being tied to a tether and dragged over the hill and dale of emotions. How many times she had thought of letting go of that rope. Letting go and freeing herself of the anger, the depression, the sleepless nights. But she never did let go. She hung on with every ounce of strength her heart could muster—even against the doctor's suggestions. The doctors knew only of the stress that weakened her; they never saw the smile that healed her.

If there was any sadness in the evening at all, it was that Bab knew she no longer had sole claim on her son's easy grin and twinkling eyes. She now shared them with the redhead. (She knew the woman's name was Cait, but she was not yet ready to grant her that much recognition.) But even at that, who was it that Mattie Joe had chosen to be with on this night of nights? With this last thought came a darting hope that maybe Mattie Joe and the redhead had had a falling out. Bab's heart again fluttered. Then she decided that such a wish was being too greedy. Besides, if she were to be granted one wish at that moment, it would be that all the neighbors and all the people in the parish could peek through her window and see the goodness in Mattie Joe. That would be her first wish. Getting rid of the redhead was second.

On the television, the Taoiseach looked haggard. His message was old news. Jobs. Prosperity. Yank warships in Cork Harbor to beat away the Hun. Bab wouldn't waste her thinking time tonight on the likes of Eire Nua. Still, there was one part of the concert she hoped to stay awake for. The television roared with the sound of people cheering. Mattie Joe threw a playful hug around her with his left arm. "Here comes your boyfriend," he said. Mick Mulvihill appeared on the screen.

She couldn't deny that Mick Mulvihill looked to be a cut of his old self. The heavy jowls were gone. Most of the belly, too. The '70s heartthrob, gone to seed via the booze and the feedbag, was back in form. When he sang, his voice reached the high notes without a crack or a warble. And while the divil was in his blue eyes, Bab knew it was the look of redemption that shone from Mick's face this night.

She was sipping her Irish coffee and sighing for days now gone, when a vision of her Tim suddenly visited again.

He passed in front of the telly wearing a grin. In an instant he was gone. It was wonderful to see Tim again, but at the moment, she was occupied with Mick Mulvihill. She'd think more about Tim, later. He'd been gone fifteen years; he could wait on her another hour or so.

Mick Mulvihill, panting and sweating like a racehorse, held up for all to see a plastic bottle of mineral water as proof he was off the drink. The cheering again was long and loud.

"Your boyfriend is on the water now," Mattie Joe teased.

"You'd do well going on the water yourself. Fix me a half one," she said, handing Mattie Joe her empty glass.

Mick sang "Whiskey in the Jar" and "Paddy on the Railway." He did his bit for the local crowd when he sang "The Rose of Mooncoin," and the Kilkenny people made their presence known by bellowing the county song. Then when Mick gave the guitar two quick strums, Bab felt Tim pulling her by the hand. She blinked and realized the hand belonged to Mattie Joe. She knew the sound of that strum, a special snap of notes played together in such a way that only Mick and she knew what song was coming before any one else in the world. She began singing with Mick right on cue. "I dreamed I saw Joe Hill last night, alive as you and me. Said I but Joe, you're ten years gone, I never died said he. I never died said he…" The song rose from her toes and the years slipped away. She and Mick Mulvihill matched, soaring note for soaring note. She wished the neighbors could peek through her window now and see her singing as once she had sung so many years before. "…I never died, said he. I never died, said he."

She fell back into the chair, out of breath. She had not felt so simultaneously exhausted and happy since…well, since times long gone, *and Tim Treacy wipe that dirty grin off your face!* For a moment, she'd swore that Tim had moved in next to her on the love seat. The big meal, drink, and all the excitement were making her dreamy. Mick Mulvihill was singing her lullabies. She'd close her eyes for just a moment, she'd thought. Mattie Joe would wake her when he came in with her Irish coffee.

"...never died, said he. Never died, said he..."

When she awoke, her eyes were shut and her head fogged. It was if Tim had been sitting right there on the love seat with her. When her head cleared, she thought it odd that Mick Mulvihill was singing Joe Hill a second time. "...never died..." When her eyes focused on the television, she saw a very queer thing: Mick Mulvihill was not singing at all. Rather, he was holding a mobile phone against the microphone. She recognized all too well the voice on the other end.

"A priest put a curse on my mother's family. I know my father never died. Never died..."

21

Mairead's eyes once again soaked in her splendid reception.

Ninety minutes into the reception, Mairead O'Hanrahan felt her hostess smile beginning to wear heavy on her jaw. She'd puckered enough for one night, and was now ready for the limousine ride to Dublin. The prospect of listening to her husband speak was far less enticing than the glass or two of port she planned to enjoy during the long trip home. (It was a personal rule to never drink at official functions, though she really wanted a drop at the moment.) What she really craved was just a moment's peace to savor her crowning achievement as Ireland's First Lady. Retreating quietly to a wall, she treated herself to what she promised would be her last self-indulgent gaze around the Rock 'n Nua reception.

Kilkenny Castle—her choice—was medieval elegance freshly scrubbed. Large enough to handle a politically inclusive guest list, it nevertheless was sufficiently contained, so that the affair kept an air of being ever so slightly beyond elite. Mairead loved the vaulted ceiling, the wide plank wood floors, and the flying arches adorned with the colorful, intertwining Celtic design. Initially, she'd considered the plan to refrain from electric lights as taking the historical accuracy business too far. But now, seeing the soft glow of the sun and moon mystically hanging in the same dusky violet sky, and the candlelight's warm radiance, she felt the connectivity of past and present. Dessie, in his toast to the nation, would laud Ireland's ancient culture and similar romantic cow shite. Mairead just liked the view.

Truth was, Dessie was the only real glitch in the evening, in Mairead's view. Neither the twinkle in his blue eyes, nor his bellowing laughter that intermittently roared through the room, fooled her. She knew Dessie. He was more of a chuckler than a bellower. But bellow he would for a pig farmer, if there was a campaign contribution in it. She knew, too, that those knobs of flesh the size of golf balls she saw quivering on his jaw meant he was very worried about something. Those knobs of flesh had been quivering for weeks now.

That she hadn't a clue as to what was troubling Dessie disturbed her more than any perceived problem. The polls showed the "Yes" vote running so far ahead for the Eire Nua referendum that only complete disaster could prevent its passage. Yet, Dessie still grumbled about the "No" vote forces and the trouble they could cause him. He was even more of a grumbler than he was a chuckler, and he especially grumbled about Hennessy, the American journalist. "He's a pot stirrer," he'd say, stabbing his fork into his rashers. As best as Mairead could see, there was no pot to stir, though that didn't stop Dessie from jumping out of bed early just to read Hennessy's column and commence his grumbling a half-hour earlier in the day. Eire Nua was supposed to be a joyous time. Dessie was taking away all the fun. The other day he'd terrified her by muttering something about "our life after office," as if it were actually on the horizon. Mairead's eyes once again soaked in her splendid reception. Eire Nua had been a long, hard race. She'd be damned if she were going to give up her victory lap.

Her eyes sifted the crowded room, moving quickly past the grossly underdressed Mick Mulvihill and that ratty old guitar of his, until at last she found the most compelling man in the castle. One look at his gleaming white hair and Mairead again agreed with the decision to use candlelight. His face glowed with a red athletic burn. Mairead felt her skin blush with the same combination of desire and familial pride that had confused her for decades. Looks, brains, and money—lots of money—here was the whole man, she thought. Here also was her first cousin. Cathal Slattery cast a devilish wink and began moving her way.

Wrapped around his black tuxedo were the porcelain arms of a raven-haired beauty wearing a black lace dress, which was more lace than dress, in Mairead's view. She was twenty-five years younger than Mairead, if a day. This one was Welsh. An actress, guests whispered. Weren't they all? Mairead mused. She'd a moon white complexion and depending on one's preference for body parts, you could stare all day at her majestic cheekbones or all of the buttery flesh blossoming forth from the tiny bit of a dress. She had Bond Girl written all over her, which she would be, if Cathal wanted it to happen. Yet, Mairead knew that the pretty woman meant no more to Cathal than the chair from which he had just risen. Mairead could tell everything about Cathal, what was in his mind and in his heart.

The raven beauty might share Cathal's bed that night, but she'd never be on the receiving end of his waiting eyes. Those belonged to Mairead.

"Jessica Williams, this is the Queen of Ireland, Mairead O'Hanrahan. Mairead *Slattery* O'Hanrahan," said Cathal. The pride in his voice was not gratuitous.

Mairead nodded and grinned gratefully as the young beauty delivered her lines, a string of rehearsed compliments about the reception and Eire Nua. "My grandmother was an O'Mara from Tipperary," the actress said, as if Mairead would actually care.

After a sufficiently polite period, Cathal's date excused herself to the ladies room. Perhaps it was the exclusive family chat that had chased her, though Mairead doubted it. The actress undoubtedly saw the firelight in Cathal's eyes and knew she was no longer the leading lady. Heads, both male and female, turned and followed Jessica Williams' slow parade across the banquet hall.

"She may be your loveliest yet, Cathal. Twenty-seven?" Mairead asked.

"You know me, always looking to improve. She's twenty-four. I think."

"Hmmff. Cradle robber. University trained, no doubt?"

"We haven't discussed education yet, but she's trained well I assure you."

"Please tell me that chest is manufactured."

Though no question was off limits between Mairead and her first cousin, she'd nevertheless caught Cathal off-guard with this one. His delay in responding told her that Jessica Williams' body was God-given. Where do these girls come from? She wondered. Mairead changed the subject. "I saw you speaking to Dessie. Seemed serious."

Cathal offered a dismissive shrug of the shoulders. "When was speaking to Dessie ever not serious? I shared some disturbing news. My timing might not have been the best, but I swear the sun sets its alarm by his worrying."

Bashing Dessie was not off limits either. A hand to her mouth stifled a burst of laughter. Cathal always knew how to disarm her. Only for their common blood could they get away with looking at one another the way they did.

It would always be unresolved whether Dessie became Taoiseach on his own merits, or because the country knew that his wife's cousin was a billionaire who could solve the nation's economic problems. Mairead liked the complicity. She'd never had to play the role of subordinate. Indeed, she *was* the Queen of Ireland. But only for her bloodline, she could have been more. She could have been a Bond Girl.

Jessica Williams returned. Mairead's husband lifted his glass, signaling her that it was time to stand by his side for the televised toast to Eire Nua. Mairead felt as if her glass of port had been taken away after the smallest sip.

22

"I leave behind a rag, a small strip of cloth..."

"Hello, Mick? This is the Rag Man calling."

Mattie Joe, having left his mother dozing in the parlor, drove the few miles to Cait McGrath's flat, where he now spoke to the great Mick Mulvihill via mobile phone. A script had been provided with numbers assigned against all the questions, so there would be no confusion in his discussion with the great folksinger. "I'm calling to set matters straight on a couple of issues," Mattie Joe said.

"I'd say you have a fair few issues alright, Rag Man. At least two, anyway. The bin lorry man and the poor devil of a detective. You killed them both," Mulvihill said.

Mattie Joe scanned over the script. The part about killing two people was question number four. Mulvilhill was supposed to ask him if he was a member of the IRA Then he was supposed to ask Mattie Joe if his phone call was part of some "No" campaign stunt.

"Listen, Mick. Issue number one is that the people of Ireland need to know that I didn't kill those two poor lads. Issue number two is that Liam Riordon is in Portlaoise gaol under false charges. He was initially imprisoned in the Maze for leading an escape from Brixton Prison in London. He had no part in that escape. It was me who did that."

"It was *I*. You're the subject in the sentence, not the object."

Mattie Joe examined the script and it said "me." He was only reading what he was given. "At any rate, Mick, I cannot let an innocent man take the blame. And, in case you're wondering, I'm not a member of the IRA, nor does this phone call have anything to do with the 'No' campaign."

"I don't remember asking if you were IRA or a 'No' campaigner."

"No, you did not. But in case you were planning on asking, I thought I'd save you the bother."

"It's no bother at all. So, why don't you let me ask the questions? This is my show you're after busting in on, Rag Man. Alright, so. Let's go back to issue number three, your motives issue."

There was no issue number three on the script. There were only two issues, both of which Mattie Joe already had addressed. But Mulvilhill was sounding a bit confused, so Mattie Joe figured he hadn't a choice but to follow the guitar man's lead.

"My motives are purely personal. I'm on a quest and have been on a quest for the better part of fifteen years, ever since I was ten years of age. I've meant to harm no one and regret deeply that innocent people have lost their lives in the process. If given the opportunity to prove my innocence, I can do just that."

As he spoke, Mattie Joe felt a surging exhilaration. It occurred to him that the words he had just spoken had been imprisoned inside him for the past fifteen years, and now that they'd escaped, he felt a tremendous weight leave with them. He felt like dancing on air.

Mulvihill continued. "How do I know you're the full shilling, Rag Man? You might be just another fan wanting to talk to the great Mick Mulvihill. Have you any proof that you're the Rag Man? And what class of eegit name is Rag Man a 'tall."

Mattie Joe did not need the script to tell his life's story. He began with explaining each escape in detail, including dates, times, and persons involved. He told about leaving the notes reading "Understand the haunting," then he began to explain about the rags.

"I leave behind a rag, a small strip of cloth, to let the authorities know it was me who was there."

"It was *I*, you're the subject here again. You need a bit of extra schooling, Rag Man."

"Perhaps, but if the police have to go through the ranks of all those who didn't get their leaving cert, I'm safe for donkey years, now aren't I?"

Mattie Joe could hear the laughter through the walls of Cait McGrath's flat. "Anyway, Mick, the strips of tweed all come from the same piece of clothing, left hand sleeve, shoulder, elbow, and cuff. The. authorities would have— should have—caught on to this fact by now. And that's the whole point, Mick, I've been after leading the authorities, but they just can't keep up."

"But what is this quest of yours all about, Rag Man?"

"It's about a curse put on my family by a priest generations back. There was an argument on account of my family following the old ways and believing in the faery folk. Anyway, the old bugger of a parish priest became quite angry with my great-great grandfather and said from that day on, as long as there were people in the family who gave credence to the faeries, the oldest son would not survive the father. And for three generations, that curse has come to pass, until me...I?"

"No, you got the right of it, it would be *until me*. But, Rag Man, you're after leaving me with an ass'n cart full of questions. Shouldn't you be happy about this, I mean you're alive."

"That's the very point, Mick. I *am* alive. So my father must be alive too. He went off to England fifteen years ago and hasn't returned since. A coffin arrived home with the remains beyond recognition, but it couldn't be my father because of the very fact that I'm still alive, the eldest son."

A long silence followed. Mattie Joe watched the television as Mick Mulvihill unconsciously stroked his guitar. He seemed to be carefully pondering his next words.

"We'll let go of the faery business, for the moment. Am I to guess that what you're trying to do is lead the police along in hopes that they'll solve the mystery? You're like a moth heading for the flame, Rag Man. I hate to throw water on your dreams, but your father has been gone for donkey years. Is there even a hint that he's alive?"

"The answer to that, Mick, is the Rag Tree at Bamford Cross. It's on the Kells Road not three miles from where you're sitting. The faery folk live beneath the tree. If you tie an old rag to the tree and make a wish, then the faeries could grant that wish. They leave a sign by having your rag fall to the ground. There's been marriages mended, cancer cured, money found, you name it, and the Rag Tree has done it. People can learn all they want about the Rag

Tree in tomorrow's *Independent*. I've told my whole story to Hennessy."

"I'm no fan of Hennessy," Mulvihill growled. "I'm due a retraction from him."

"I'll see to it that you get that retraction, Mick. Now, before I go, could I make a request? Would you sing 'The Last Rose of Summer'? It's my father's party piece."

Mattie Joe set down the activated mobile phone on a chair and left the flat. Outside, he stared up at a clear star-filled Kilkenny sky that he might never see again. His father's favorite song echoed in the night.

∽

Detective Peter Doyle considered how Mick Mulvihill's lonesome voice resounding in the clear Kilkenny night was sending a chill through a banquet room full of embarrassed guests. At first, the powdered-faced ladies supported their friend, Mairead O'Hanrahan, by echoing her admonishment of Mick Mulvihill. But the wily performer's song was slow and sweet—like a haunting funeral dirge that crawls beneath the skin. One by one, the guests turned their eyes away from the bewildering scene beyond the windows. Glasses still full of champagne began quickly gathering upon white-clothed tabletops.

Peter had known the feisty Mairead O'Hanrahan his entire life and knew how each discarded glass was tearing away at her. No bloody way would she tolerate the theft of her party of parties without a fight. Before it was all over, she'd take her piece of hide out of Mick Mulvihill and others besides. "Pull that disgraceful gypsy off *my* stage," she demanded. She ordered guests to "Not waste the expensive champagne," while pushing glasses back at anyone who was empty-handed. She then turned on her husband.

"I warned you that Mick Mulvihill would make fools of us. I *warned* you," she said, her voice quivering.

If Mulvihill were to sing for another five minutes, Mairead might just have a coronary, Peter thought. She was that red with rage.

The Taoiseach, on the other hand, stood snow-faced and motionless by the window, reminding Peter of a man facing a firing squad without a blindfold. Peter couldn't decide who at the moment was more deadly to poor Dessie's dignity, the cocksure Mulvihill singing with a dangerously infectious passion, or the screeching wife. Meanwhile, Peter's father seemingly was trying to save the day by personally rescuing each glass of the discarded champagne. The old man's blue eyes bugged pleadingly at Peter. "Do something to fix this," Buddy Doyle said.

Moving to the Taoiseach's side, Peter heard his godfather attempt to bring some order to the banquet hall. Dessie turned to Cathal.

"She hasn't had her glass of port, Slats," Dessie said, quietly. "I'd be most appreciative if you would take care of that." Dessie then returned his stoic gaze upon Mick Mulvihill, whose ostentatious bows moved the audience to laughter, and then applause. It was then that Peter noticed the Taoiseach's hand hovering by a black switch built into the windowsill.

Even from a distance, it looked to Peter that Mick Mulvihill was fully aware of the chaos he was creating inside the banquet hall. The singer looked up at the window and waved. He then began strumming a thumping rhythm on his guitar. "C'mon," he called to the audience, "clap your hands." As incomprehensible as it seemed, the audience totally disregarded Mulvihill's arrogant usurping of the event's purpose and began a rhythmic clapping that echoed off the castle walls, like the sound of storm troopers marching down High Street. The aggressive tempo must have been some form of cue, because onto the stage hustled a band of Spanish mariachi guitar players, followed by a group of German horn players. Both musical groups wore traditional dress native to their respective nations. The bald woman singer named Sinéad was hovering in the wings when she was felled by a passing tuba. There would be no duet tonight, Peter thought.

"Ready muchachos," Mulvihill quipped. "How 'bout you, oompah lads?"

"This is it, the Eire Nua song," Dessie said, speaking more to himself than anyone in particular. Turning to Peter, he said, "This song will salvage the evening. The audience will love it. Van will come on and the evening will be salvaged," he said again. Some color began creeping back into Dessie's face.

*Thump...Thump...*Mulvihill spoke as he continued beating an infectious rhythm on his guitar.

"This song is dedicated to anyone who has ever wished for something, anyone who's ever prayed for a miracle, anyone who's suffered in the name of a cause thought lost by everyone but themselves. It is a song about the spirit sustained through darkness and exile, a spirit that knows salvation only comes from belief in a higher being, not from capitulation to fear. It is a song dedicated to the spirit of all the people of Ireland, especially generations now gone, who sustained themselves on hope and faith, by guile and courage, in the face of all indignities that can be bestowed upon man—a spirit that through eight centuries has time and again withstood the attempted theft of the soul of its nationhood, its religion, language, and customs by the hands of an imperial and tyrannical power. Tonight, we celebrate the deliverance of Ireland from its years of struggle. The world is watching the Irish spirit manifest in economic strength and a cultural richness that is known throughout the four corners of the world, brought there by the legions of Irish men and Irish women forced to leave their native land. Tonight, each of us must look deep within to where the soul of Ireland resides and ask ourselves, 'Do I nourish my Irish soul? Do I take my Irish soul for granted? Am I willing to give it up for the dollar, or the punt? How dear my Irish soul? Is it for sale?'

"Tonight, the soul of Ireland has spoken to us from depths of a mind surrendered to a dream and a heart consumed with hope. The soul of Ireland says an innocent man sits naked and alone in an Irish jail. Are we to turn over yet one more innocent Irishman to hands that have long enslaved us?"

The mariachis strummed their guitars furiously. The German horn players added a pulsating force. With his guitar sounding like a thumping heartbeat, Mulvihill began singing.

"There's a place I know, where magic grows. Down a lonesome road, where Druids strode." Mulvihill roared, "Rag Tree…"

Peter pulled his wireless from inside his black tuxedo. "This is Doyle. I'm taking orders directly from the Taoiseach." Peter then wrapped a long arm around the sunken shoulders of his godfather. "Say the word and I'll have Mulvihill removed and the television transmission shut down."

"Yes. Shut it down!" a voice shrieked from across the banquet hall. "Shut it down this instant." It was Mairead. Black mascara tears streamed down her face. Port wine splashed from the glass rolling unsteadily in her hand. A bemused Cathal Slattery shrugged his shoulders as if to say, *"I can't control her."* Mairead pushed away the hand Dessie kept hovering over the black button on the windowsill. "I'll shut the bastard off," she wailed.

Mairead pushed the black button and an explosion shook the castle. Fire rockets filled the sky north of the castle, across the River Nore. Flaming fountains sprayed the night with gold glittered brilliance, and then exploded again into green, white, and orange tongues of fire cascading softly downward.

Boom...

"Rag Tree! You let the dumb man talk."

Boom....

"Rag Tree! You let the lame man walk."

Boom...

"Rag Tree! You let the blind man see."

"What is this?" Mairead screamed. "You never said anything about fireworks to me."

"A surprise," Dessie said. "I wanted to surprise you."

"Well turn them off."

"I can't. It's all computerized to last fifteen minutes. I'm afraid you'll have to wait it out with the rest of us...Dear."

Deciding that the situation had deteriorated enough, Peter addressed the walkie-talkie microphone inside the lapel of his tuxedo. "Doyle here. Take Mulvihill from the stage."

Outside, Peter proceeded hurriedly toward the castle gate, where he stopped to take a bemused look at the soon to be unforgettable concert. The mariachis and German horn players played on as their bandleader was being pulled across the stage, arse first, by police. Mulvihill kept one hand clutched to his guitar while pumping a fist into the air and crying, "Rag Tree." The song echoed through the maze of deserted back streets, where Peter jogged until he came upon Mattie Joe Treacy seated on the bonnet of Peter's silver Mercedes and peacefully gazing skyward at the fireworks.

"Pretty night, no?" Peter said, nodding his head toward a sky bursting with fire. He tossed a set of handcuffs to Mattie Joe. "In case we're stopped," he added.

"Brilliant night," Mattie Joe said, snapping the handcuffs around his own wrists.

෨

Mattie Joe Treacy looked out from the back seat of the big detective's silver Mercedes, as it climbed a mountain road toward a black hole cut in the bottom of an otherwise star strewn sky. The scent of rain-fresh pine grew steadily as the black hole drew nearer. The big detective was quiet, so Mattie Joe let him have his peace.

The past year had been a hard run for both of them. It all began when Mattie Joe had been arrested for being drunk and disorderly, again. Only this time, the guards didn't throw him in a cell. Instead, they put him in a room with Detective Doyle, who threatened him with an extended stint in the nut house for evaluation. Or he could accept the big detective's offer of a deal. It had seemed too good to be true at the time, and, in many ways, it still did.

"There will be no personal contact between us," Doyle had explained. "I'll direct you by phone as to where to go, what to do, what to say, what to wear, how to look, escape routes, the lot. Follow my directions and you'll walk on water, right through this thing. Meanwhile, the Special Detective Unit is conducting a secret operation to find your father. That's the deal."

Infiltrating two, high-security prisons and engineering escapes wasn't exactly walking on water as Detective Doyle had described, but here Mattie Joe was a year later, alive and ready to meet his father. He felt as he had as a small boy on Christmas Eve night—eager to fall asleep and wake up to the promise of a marvelous tomorrow. At least as marvelous as a tomorrow could be for a murder suspect on the run.

The Mercedes' headlamps landed on an ancient round tower. "That's your new home. Someone will be around in a few days to let you out. Best of luck to you," the detective said, freeing the handcuffs from Mattie Joe's wrists. Mattie Joe climbed a wooden ladder toward the portal fifteen feet up the side of the tower when Detective Doyle stopped him by calling him by his name, for the first time.

"Mattie Joe," he said, then paused. It was so dark that Mattie Joe could no longer see the big man, but he heard him shuffling his feet through the bed of pine needles. "I wanted to let you know you've been brilliant." Doyle paused again, then finally asked, "Did you really kill that cat?"

"I did not. I shot at one, but I missed."

෴

Taoiseach Desmond O'Hanrahan trod softly across the Kilkenny Castle banquet hall, trying to minimize the sound of his feet crunching against the shards of broken glass glistening in the candlelight. As his advisors blurted their opinions on how to spin the Rock 'n Nua debacle, Des waved his arms, demanding quiet. "Shoosh," he said, even though the room had already fallen eerily silent. A hollow moment passed, then...

"I told him not to bring that gypsy around here. I *told* him!" Mairead's wails echoed from a winding tunnel stairway. Glass shattered against stone.

Des waited for another crash, but when none came, he assumed Mairead was out of ammunition. Gazing around the banquet hall, it seemed as if the floor was full of rubies. Mairead had broken most of the champagne glasses during her initial party-clearing assault. Sighing, Des turned toward his press secretary, a slightly built man wearing glasses. "What do we have, Sean?"

"We'll answer three questions," the press secretary said. "RTE will be waiting on the right. They'll ask about potential negative effects on the Eire Nua referendum. You tell them that there will be no negative effects, of course. To your left will be the BBC corps. Someone will question the breach in security; how could the Rag Man and Mulvihill pull off such a stunt? They'll try to follow up by questioning the wisdom of having Mulvilhill perform in the first place. Ignore that and turn around."

"For whom?" Des said, nodding. "Who's last?"

"The Americans. CNN. They are still debating their questions. But we can trust the Yanks, of course." The press secretary cast a nervous glance over his shoulder, then added, "They're holding Missus O'Hanrahan at the rear door. If we're going to cover her exit, we've got to move."

"Of course," Des said, exhaling heavily.

He stepped through the castle's huge arching wooden gates and into the wash of blinding lamplight. For a moment, he wondered why he didn't let his irascible wife face the press while he escaped through a back door. He looked ahead at the twenty paces between him and the limousine and wondered if it weren't twenty paces down a gangplank. Looking to his right, he caught the waiting eyes of the RTE journalist. "Michael?" Des pointed a finger toward a thick, middle-aged man.

"Mr. Taoiseach, could you comment on the possibility of negative repercussions for the Eire Nua referendum in the aftermath of what can only be described as a debacle and a major embarrassment to Ireland?"

"No negative repercussions whatsoever. The people of Ireland are committed to building a stronger European alliance. The antics of a folksinger and a man sought for murder and mayhem would hardly dissuade a determined people."

Moving closer to the black limousine, he put a hand to his forehead to shield the light. He looked left and found the female BBC reporter stretching a microphone toward him. "Tell us about the breach in security. How was it possible that Mister Mulvihill and the Rag Man were able to pull off such a stunt?"

Des looked the slender blonde in the eye but kept moving. "Obviously there was a breakdown, but I have no answer for you on that now. I assure you that the appropriate security units are busy looking into that as we speak."

There were other questions shouted at him. "Is Mulvihill under arrest?" "What are the projected lost revenues from the Eire Nua song being mocked?" Des ignored these and, just before slipping into the limousine, turned around and found the sharp-featured CNN reporter wearing a blue suit.

"Mr. Taoiseach, I've information from the Portlaoise Prison that Liam Riordon had escaped custody early this afternoon, yet the information was withheld from the news media. Can you comment as to the accuracy of this report? Did you know about the escape?"

Des felt the heat of the lamps burning his face. He turned his head just enough to see the vehicle carrying Mairead slip off into the night. "I cannot," he said and slumped into the back seat of the limousine.

23

She'd been in Brendan's car for over three hours...

Cait McGrath huddled against the cold ruin of Lacken Abbey, her fingers twining the note that had brought her there. The fireworks exploding around her sent acrid clouds of spent gunpowder sweeping into the ruin. Lumps of limestone tore loose from the ancient walls and she wondered if she'd be choked to death by smoke or buried alive in rubble of stone.

Boom...! A burning tree spilled yellow embers like a swarm of fireflies over her. She could not sweep her hands over her body fast enough to keep the shards of fire from stinging her arms and burning her hair.

Boom...! A large burning branch crashed to the ground and blocked any escape path she might have considered. If the tree followed, it would cremate her. Not wanting her last view of the world to be that of her own burning tomb, she again buried her head inside her hands.

219

Boom…boom…boom…The din of fire rockets halted abruptly, mercifully. Through the clouds of smoke, a black- and silver-studded sky slowly reappeared. A shower of water doused Cait and the burning tree. It was only then that she remembered having seen the fire brigade stationed above on the Dublin Road. Soaked to the skin and shivering from fright, all she could think of now was escaping from the abbey alive. The shower of water had reduced the fiery branch blocking her path to a smoldering log that Cait could easily step over without getting burned. But as she moved to do so, she saw that the branch wore shoes. And eyes like small billiard balls bulged from blackened flesh that melted away from protruding white bone. A telescopic camera dangled from the charred remains of a man's neck.

A hot trickle of whiskey slipped down her throat and she became aware of being in the front passenger seat of a car she couldn't remember climbing into. The whiskey bottle was clutched against her chest. Ahead in the road, an illuminated green road sign announced their proximity to Belfast. She'd been in Brendan's car for over three hours, yet remembered only screaming and warm meaty hands pulling on hers. Another trickle of whiskey chased the last of the explosions from her head, and she could hear the hum of tyres against the road.

Brendan Sheils was even heavier than when she'd left five years before. His neck hung over his Roman collar, like a roll of soft white dough waiting to be flattened. His cherub face sagged with an unfamiliar worry. "Sweetness," he said, noticing that she'd come around. He patted the burns on her arms with a wet cloth. He'd always called her "Sweetness."

She couldn't remember life before Brendan. The story was that he'd taken personal responsibility for her after her parents drowned in a holiday boating accident. There was no extended family. It didn't matter exactly in whose house she ate and slept, she'd always considered herself as living with Brendan. To everyone else, the fat and jolly priest was Father Sheils, or Father Brendan. But he'd have none of that with her. "I'm Brendan to you," he'd say, trying to be stern, which was a joke. Brendan could never be anything but kindness itself. She remembered once as a teenager when she'd been very angry about something and she told Brendan she wished she'd fallen from the boat and drowned with her parents. He'd grabbed her by the wrist and made her promise never to say such an awful thing again. By the time he'd let go of her wrist, he was in tears. Cait never said such a thing again, though she thought about it a lot. She was thinking about that now, as she could taste Mattie Joe's lips on the whiskey bottle.

She was five years of age when she and Brendan had come up with their own secret sign of the two birds flying from the heart. "That's your mother and father flying up to heaven," Brendan said pointing to the birds. And the heart stays on the ground because wherever people may fly off to, to God in heaven or to foreign lands or to wherever, love never leaves home."

The only flying Cait had ever done was away from Ireland and all her problems. Now she was back, making the same mistakes, having to have the same person bail her out. It was as if she'd never left. She took another bittersweet sip of Mattie Joe's lips.

"Brendan," she said, breaking her silence, "back there at the abbey, you called me *Angeline*. Why?"

"No, Sweetness. You didn't hear me right, on account of the fire rockets. I must have said *Angel* or something. All that matters now is that you're safe." He was lying. He kept

221

looking ahead at a black road as if there was something deadly important there, whereas moments before, he'd been swathing her burns with one hand while driving with the other.

"Brendan, I heard you call me *Angeline*."

Before they had traveled another mile, Brendan was sobbing and pulling the car off to the side of the road. Though she hardly thought it possible, the tale he told her made her feel even worse. He told her about a boating accident that never was, about a helicopter crash, and how he was her uncle and loved her more than life itself.

24

When there came a scratching and a knocking on the roof...

Bab Treacy had dozed off after the big meal only to wake up and hear her son speaking on the television. Hearing Mattie Joe's disembodied voice while her head was still thick with sleep was like being inside a bad dream, only she knew that she was awake because there was an awful tingling feeling shooting up and down her arms. By the time Mattie Joe told the world and Mick Mulvihill about the Rag Tree and the curse of the O'Neill's of Bamford Cross, she felt as if there were a hammer banging inside her chest. Her breath grew short. She ran a hand over her forehead and felt a cold, clammy sweat. She would have thrown water over the fireplace coals, but suddenly her legs hadn't the strength to lift her off the love seat.

A noise from outside made Bab wonder if Biddie had come home early. But as the sound grew louder, she recognized a low, moaning howl. Biddie wasn't a moaner or a howler, even when things were very bad for her. She talked her troubles away, like some cackling chicken. It was probably just the wind, Bab thought, hopefully. But when she looked first at the television, then outside her own window at the dusky night, she could see there were no trees bending in any breeze. When there came a scratching and a knocking on the roof, and the moaning grew louder, Bab knew it was not the wind she'd heard. As the thud from inside her chest grew louder, so too did the moaning cries of the banshee.

"'Tis the last rose of summer, left blooming all alone…"

A sweet voice sent a sense of calm seeping into her. The pounding inside her chest abated. The banshee, too, seemed soothed by the crooning voice. The moaning was there, but the scratching and knocking at the roof had ceased. A hand clasped onto Bab's, pulling her from the love seat and onto her feet.

"Thank you, Tim," Bab said.

Her Tim had finally come home. His eyes twinkled as he sang, *"All her lovely companions are faded and gone."*

"You're looking well," she lied. His old stinking pipe was hanging against his unshaven jaw. She wanted to give out to him about tracking dirt into the house, but it was so nice hearing him sing again. "C'mon, will ye, and help me up the stairs. We have to save our son."

"No flower of her kindred. No rose bud is nigh. To reflect back her blushes. Or give sigh for sigh…"

So soft and sweet was Tim's singing and so gentle his touch that Bab felt herself floating on air, just like she had when she and Tim danced their first dance to this very song. She stood at the foot of the bed where a white doily and a china vase full of artificial red roses rested atop a cedar trunk.

She handed the vase to Tim, who dropped it. The vase shattered. She wanted to give out to Tim on account of his clumsiness, but sure if she hadn't cured him of that by now, she never would. The suit coat was at the bottom of the trunk beneath a pile of folded blankets. She inspected the brown tweed thoroughly, holding it off as far as her arms could reach. The left sleeve was missing. "You barely wore it," she said, shaking her head.

"I'll not leave thee, thou lone one! To pine on the stem;
Since the lovely are sleeping, go sleep thou with them..."

Tim's soft serenade and the grip of his hand made the trip down the stairs so very easy. Bab felt no pain at all when she stepped outside and saw the banshee hovering just above the slate roof. The faery spirit was a young woman, completely ice-white with sorrow. She dragged a comb through her long white hair and her mouth was agape with agony, only there was no keening coming forth from her now. Tim's song was keeping her quiet.

"Thus kindly I scatter thy leaves o'er the bed.
Where thy mates of the garden lie scentless and dead..."

Bab gripped Tim's fingers and pulled him toward the Rag Tree atop the faery rath. There, grazing on the rath was the raven she knew to be a pooka. A man and a boy were there, too, their backs turned to Bab. Tim kept on singing.

"So soon may I follow, when friendships decay,
And from love's shining circle thy gems drop away!
When true hearts lie withered, and fond ones are flown,
Oh! who would inhabit this bleak world alone?"

As Tim's song ended, she could feel his fingers slipping away. Then he just floated off into the starry night. Bab didn't know if the old song had a second verse, but if it had, Tim had never bothered to learn it. She wished she could hear a second verse now. In an instant, Tim was gone and Bab was left wondering how the years had passed without her having missed Tim, because now her heart ached for him something terrible and he'd only been gone a few seconds. Again, she felt so very alone. The banshee resumed her awful keening. The pooka was humming *Phil the Fluther's Ball*. The hammer in her chest resumed its pounding.

"With a toot on the flute and a twiddle on the fiddle, hoppin' up and down like a hare on the griddle—Arrah, look who's come to see us, lads," the pooka said. *"Do my eyes deceive me, or is this the Faery Woman of Bamford Cross herself come to the Rag Tree? To what do we owe this great honor, Barbara Concepta Marie O'Neill? We're having a bit of an old singsong. Pity poor Tim couldn't stay. Up down pass around...hadn't we the gaiety at Phil the Fluther's Ball."*

The raven's eyes blazed brighter than the coals in Bab's fireplace. The man and the boy, both wearing caps, sat with their backs to her, their eyes fixated on the Rag Tree. The banshee moaned.

"You know very well why I'm here, Brian. I've come to break the curse. I have to save my son."

"Curse? What curse? Ye always have maintained there was no curse, Barbara. Why do you come to me now?" The moonlight gleaming against the raven's eyes was almost blinding.

"You've been minding him, so."

"Sure, he told me to feck off. He said he didn't need me. Dumped me for the red haired woman with the fleck in her eye, he did. And now, after denying the curse all these years, and waiting until the hand of death is at your throat, ye are asking me to break it? And just how is it that this curse is supposed to be broken?"

"The priest put a curse on the O'Neills of Bamford Cross to last for three successive generations. In each generation, the eldest son would not survive the father, unless—"

"Yes, Barbara? Unless what?"

"Unless a son and a daughter of the same family were to die before their time."

"But Barbara, you're sixty-seven years of age. You've a bad heart. I'd say this is hardly before your time."

"I'll spend the night on the faery rath, Brian. The Daoine Maithe can have my soul. Only save my son, please."

"The Faery Woman of Bamford Cross giving up her soul. There's some attraction in that, I'd admit. Even at your age, Barbara. Sure, I dunno. What say ye, lads?"

The boy and the man turned and faced Bab. They'd fiery eyes like the pooka. "Maurice," Bab gasped. "Frankie..."

To see her brother and uncle in the flesh, when she knew them to be cold in the ground these many years, was both joyous and terrifying. "Oh, Maurice, a piece of me has been missing every day since you've been gone." She reached a hand toward him. Maurice pointed a finger to the Rag Tree. A scrap of cloth broke free on its own and fluttered to the ground.

"That's it," the pooka said, elated. *"The curse of the O'Neill's of Bamford Cross is broken. Barbara Concepta Marie O'Neill Treacy you will spend the night on the rath and your soul will join the souls of the Daoine Maithe for all eternity."*

Just as her Tim had done, Maurice and Frankie floated away into the night leaving Bab all alone. The banshee's wails stabbed into her ears. The white spirit ascended off the slate roof and began floating at a slow descent toward the Rag Tree, finally hovering just a few feet above Bab. With her white arms spread wide, the banshee looked as if she were about to envelop her.

"It's time, Barbara," the raven said.

∽

Biddie Tynan told the cab driver to keep the motor running, then by force of habit she raced around the Treacy farmhouse and entered through the back door. "Bab!" she called, her hand sweeping the wall for the light switch. She should have listened to her best friend, she thought. She never should have gone to Rock 'n Nua. Her place was here, with Bab, the other pea in the pod. "Bab!" She searched the parlor, which was dimly lit by embers in the fireplace and a soft glow from the television, showing the fireworks exploding over Kilkenny Castle. Bab was sitting upright in the love seat, her back to Biddie.

"Jasus, are ye still that upset with me?" Biddie moved around the love seat and faced her best friend. "Bab?" There was no answer. She put a hand on Bab's shoulder and there was no response. "Oh no..." Biddie switched on a lamp and looked into the stone face of her best friend. Bab's eyes were frozen wide open in horror.

25

"...Find me the perfect fool."

When Peter Doyle had agreed to join the Blackbird's cabal, he was told it would be his job to recruit the conspiracy's trigger man. The Blackbird described the traits he was to seek in a candidate capable of wrecking the Eire Nua initiative.

"Look for a man who hopes too much. Who cries too much. Who fights and loves too much. A man who would do anything to realize a dream. Find me the perfect fool."

Police files contained a list of hundreds of men suspected of criminal involvement or republican activity. There were men who fought too much and men who cried too much, but only when he'd found a Kilkenny dairy farmer with holes in the elbows of his jumper and fingertips cigarette stained the same red-brown color as the pint of ale that seldom left his hand, did Peter find the man who loved too much. Sometimes it took seven or eight pints, sometimes only three or four, but the perfect fool nearly always ended the night's drinking with his large melancholy eyes drooping over the rim of his pint glass, as he told anyone who would listen how a family curse was proof that his father was still alive.

Now the town yahoo wore new pressed clothes that fit close against his lean, athletic body. His brown eyes were clear and lucid. His hair was close cropped and neat. Looking into the rear view mirror, Peter thought how the only thing familiar about Mattie Joe Treacy was the cigarette dangling from his lower lip. Seeing, too, the reflection of his own eyes, searching and sad, Peter pondered whether life held any such changes for him .

With headlamps turned off, he guided the Mercedes up the Blackstairs Mountains, a lonely high country where as far as Peter could tell, the only hint of human habitation was that someone had to own all the bloody sheep milling in the road. Switching the headlamps back on, the light washed against the grey ruin of an ecclesiastical round tower, a hundred foot high stack of stone that centuries ago gave Irish monks refuge from the Viking invader and now would serve as safe house for the Rag Man.

He'd tried a few times during the ride to tell the Rag Man all about Kitty, and how the Blackbird had promised to reunite them. But as was always the case when his mind strayed too close to speaking his true feelings, his tongue ceased to function. Now, as Peter found himself cradled in a cocoon of trees, atop a holy mountain with the breadth of God's heavens staring down at him, he heard the gentle whispering of his heart. *"Now, Peter. Who better to make a confession to than the Rag Man, the standard bearer for those who had lost everything but hope?"* Peter tried, but all he managed was to ask Mattie Joe if he had killed a cat.

He'd driven within five miles of Kilkenny when the Blackbird called.

"Expect your partner back from London tomorrow. He must be diverted away from the round tower. Do that and your job is done. Done," the Blackbird insisted. "I've already one detective dead tonight because he did not follow my instructions. The worst can still happen."

Peter wondered who the dead detective was, but instead asked, "Did Kevin find the father?" He wanted to know if the Blackbird kept his promises.

There was a long pause before the Blackbird murmured, "He's working on it. You'll find the authorities swarming around a flat just opposite the castle on Father Bennett Road. You'll find Kitty there. Tonight." *Click.*

Peter found a half dozen detectives working the sparse flat across the road from Kilkenny Castle. Some were cataloging clothes and personal articles, others dusting for prints. One fellow stared into a computer set up on a small white desk beneath a window. Peter, still dressed in a tuxedo, showed his shield to a local detective named Jack Deegan.

"It's a game of *Try and Catch Me,*" Deegan stated. "The mobile phone was purposely left on so we could easily trace Mulvihill's call."

Peter nodded and feigned a preoccupation with the activity inside the flat. Truth was, he was really preoccupied with looking for Kitty. "You've an I.D.?" Peter asked.

"No mystery there," Deegan said, consulting a notepad. "Matthew Joseph Treacy—Mattie Joe—by all accounts a local yahoo. No known republican activity. No sheet on him other than a half dozen trips to the drunk tank. A little over a year ago, he was printed on charges of resisting arrest—again related to overconsumption of drink.

The charges were dropped when he agreed to a psychological evaluation." Deegan handed over a computer printout of Mattie Joe's driver's license.

"Anything there?" Peter asked, though he knew the only thing wrong with Mattie Joe was a longing heart.

"Inconclusive. The psychiatrist's report suggests that the Rag Man's binge drinking and delusions of faery sightings could point to a schizophrenic disorder. Or that the drinking serves to mask an ongoing depressive condition. We found the scrap of tweed cloth tied to the bedpost and the message "Understand the haunting" written with soap on the mirror in the loo. No attempt to wipe down fingerprints either. We've already sent the scans to the Dublin mainframe." Deegan pointed over to a female detective standing in the kitchen alongside the refrigerator. A laptop was cradled in her left arm. "She'll let us know soon if there are any matches," he added.

The Puzzle Palace mainframe had fingerprints on all criminals in Ireland and could be linked to crime fighting organizations worldwide. Peter, though, remained distracted by the slender woman with waving dark hair that stopped halfway down her long neck. She stood with a dignified professionalism—very straight, a bit rigid—and yet the way her blue uniform skirt clung round her hips and ascended to a narrow waist would take any man's mind off his work.

It was Deegan asking questions that pulled Peter back onto the job.

"Where have you been, anyway?" Over where they found Skinny? The poor ol' divil. A fire rocket up the bum. That's going out in a blaze of glory." Deegan shuddered.

So it was Skinny Farrell who had not followed the Blackbird's instructions and had paid for it with his life,

Peter thought. He should have made the connection the moment Skinny had disappeared from the gun battle at Bruxelles' Café in Dublin. Peter found it unsettling to contemplate the extent of the Blackbird's power to infiltrate official institutions such as the detective units and the prison systems, so he decided against it. He'd simply do as he was told: keep Kevin O'Felan away from the round tower and find Kitty.

The female detective had turned her head enough for Peter to admire her gripping blue eyes and long, coal black eyelashes. He'd always liked his women tall. He'd always like them dark haired and blue eyed. Truth was, she looked a lot like a young Kitty, only prettier.

"We're downloading photos from Skinny's camera now," Deegan said, pointing his big chin in the direction of a bespectacled man staring into the computer by the window. "And oh, wait until you see what else we found," he said, and then called across the room. "John, can you put a hold on Skinny's photos and go back to those emails." Deegan wagged his note pad. "We've the makings of a very major conspiracy at work. Look at this."

The computer brought up email correspondences between a Cait and a Tom, all referring to the Hennessy newspaper columns. Deegan shook his big square head in bewilderment of the windfall of evidence. "In all likelihood, the Hennessy articles originated from this computer. Only it appears your man Hennessy didn't write a thing. *The Washington Post* itself will have some big explaining to do. Let's see what Skinny found for us. The poor ol' divil."

"All the prints belong to two people, and we've matches on one," said a deep and silky female voice. Peter turned and held his gaze on red lips and a face as white as winter.

The woman detective walked toward him presenting a piece of paper. She'd long fingers and glossy, manicured nails. And no rings. Deegan introduced her as Detective Tiernan with the Kilkenny Detective Unit. Peter leaned in close to look at the slip of paper, brushing the biceps of his left arm against Detective Tiernan's shoulder. "Who have you found?" he asked.

"The matched prints belong to an Angeline O'Toole. The Puzzle Palace claims she's Dan O'Toole's daughter. She was thought to be dead."

"Before my time," Peter said, shaking his head. Deegan, older than Peter by a couple of decades, explained how during the 70s, when the troubles in the North were at their absolute boiling point, Dan O'Toole's wife and toddler daughter were fleeing Ireland when they were in a crash up with a British Army helicopter. The deaths had sparked rioting across Ulster.

"British policy at the time was to fingerprint the families of suspected IRA members." Deegan added. "That's why we have the fingerprints now. Dead little girls coming back to life. Mick Mulvihill making a bollix of the concert. Major newspapers infiltrated by conspirators. For what? What do they want?"

"We've got pictures," called the man peering at the computer. "Boy, do we have pictures."

The underexposed photos all showed a couple engaged in sex. Peter was not surprised. Skinny Farrell had been little more than a peeping Tom with a badge. It was several frames before Peter recognized Mattie Joe as the man in the saddle.

"That's our couple," Deegan said. "See the dresser drawers with the electric clock on top just to the right of the bed. That's our bedroom here, alright."

"The best prints came from the bed posts and computer keyboard," Detective Tiernan said without the hint of embarrassment. "See, she's holding tight to the bedposts."

"Any aliases?" Peter asked.

Tiernan referred to her notes. "She now goes by Cait McGrath and works as a reporter for *The Washington Post*. She was known as Kitty McGrath when she was arrested for civic disturbance at a republican demonstration in Dublin five years ago. She emigrated to the States after that."

Peter's heart, which had been beating bruises against his chest since talking to the Blackbird, stopped. The Blackbird had fulfilled his promise. He also was shoving a mirror in Peter's face and making him confront the image of a man who'd given away years of his life to self-pity. What Peter realized at that moment was that moving from intense love to loathing was not the heart's leap across a vast chasm, but as simple as stepping across the line between trust and deceit.

The Blackbird had said that the worst could still happen, and as far as Peter was concerned, it just had. It was he who had been the perfect fool. His heart resumed its pounding, only it now pumped hot and fast with an anger coursing through him. It settled him not at all seeing how Kitty had ruined her hair, chunked up to the point where her ass belonged in a rugby scrum, and changed her name. The bitch had stolen his life.

What finally separated him from watching the old girlfriend wrap herself around Mattie Joe was the recognizable deep thud of a body being slammed against an automobile, followed by the inevitable cries of protest. "Turn me loose! Don't you know who I fucking am?" The voice belonged to an American. Moments later, a man with tan skin and wild, angry eyes pushed his way through the door and rushed bull-like toward Detective Tiernan. He managed to call out, "Cait," just once before Peter emptied his fury with a straight right hand that felled the man as if his legs were cut at the knees. A lump the size of a golf ball swelled over the unconscious man's left eye.

Peter was rubbing the sting from his knuckles when his hand was taken from him. "Get him some ice," Detective Tiernan called out, then held him rapt with her ice blue eyes. "You're Peter Doyle," she said. "I've heard about you. I'm Róisín Tiernan."

"Ireland's rose," Peter said, aware of the soothing softness of her palms cupping his injured hand. And he prayed that there could be redemption for a perfect fool.

At Peter's feet, a policeman dug into the fallen man's hip pocket, removing his wallet. "Blessed are the saints! Says here that his name is Thomas F.X. Hennessy."

26

God save Ireland say the heroes...

The Blackbird breathed low into the telephone. "Has he given any indication that he's any closer to finding the Rag Man's father?"

"Not in so many words. But he has settled down emotionally. His speech patterns are more concise, a big improvement from his desperate ramblings before he left for England. He's much more calculated now in what he tells me. It's my sense that he's zeroed in on the profile of the Rag Man. Of course, the big hurdle for him has always been achieving a sense of trust with anyone. He's working with a young black beauty, who, I take it, is as tough as she is pretty. I think our Kevin might be a bit beguiled..."

As the Blackbird abruptly hung up the phone on what was his last call of a very busy night, he wasn't sure if what he was feeling was more a sense of satisfaction, or relief. Certainly he'd sleep better tonight knowing that Special

Detective Doyle had delivered the Rag Man safely inside the round tower. And he very much was looking forward to tomorrow morning and reading the newspaper accounts of his singularly conceived plan to save Ireland from destroying itself with Eire Nua and its inherent greed. Was it vain of him to want to admire his own success?

Not that his plan was proceeding without flaw. The mounting death toll was disturbing. While it might have been noble of him to try to save Ireland by waging a bloodless war, it ultimately had caused him to expand the conspiracy beyond that which he could control. Since Mattie Joe Treacy had killed neither the bin lorry man nor the detective, that meant someone had broken ranks with the plan and was taking matters into his own hands—a rogue. If the Blackbird was to accept sole credit for the genius of his plan, then didn't he have to accept the responsibility for miscalculations of character? He would have to live with the blood on his hands.

His plan was simple, really. It was based on the premise that every man, even the most righteous, had a price for which he would render services otherwise unthinkable. And so far, he hadn't met a price he couldn't afford. The Blackbird was the great Oz. He understood that the world was comprised of Tin Men and Scarecrows, and that in every heart there grew a Rag Tree laden with cloth of hope and desire. So, then, whose heart had he misjudged? Whose heart was so consumed by hate that it contained no hope? Whoever it was, needed to be eliminated. There would be yet more blood.

The problem weighed heavily on him as the need for a good night's sleep began to tug even harder. Despite his weariness, he was determined to take time now to fully reflect on everything that had happened and to make any necessary amendments to his plan. Because tomorrow, when all hell started breaking loose, it would be too late.

He poured himself a Scotch and turned out the lights so he could better savor the solitude. Closing his eyes, he sipped the whiskey and listened intently to the miracle of his own breathing. The alcohol soon dulled his nerves and the rhythm of his breath soothed him, like the sound of waves gently breaking upon an unspoiled shore. He became filled with an awareness of how it was that these tiny puffs of air, one after another after another, and the awesomeness of a hurricane were of the work of the same Maker. And how, ultimately, the breath of life was a far mightier force than the most destructive of storms. A voice in his head whispered, *"Digitus Dei est hic."* The finger of God is here.

Digitus Dei est hic. Indeed, the finger of God was on Ireland. Could there be any other explanation for how this tiny nation had survived famine, invasion and oppression, poverty and the bloodletting of emigration? The finger of God had been on Ireland when Brian Boru defeated the heathen Dane at the Battle of Clontarf on Good Friday morning in the year 1014. The finger of God had been on Ireland when, in 1879, He sent His own mother to appear at Knock County Mayo, bringing spiritual sustenance to an impoverished people who were still ravaged in the wake of the Great Hunger. Surely, he thought, it was the finger of God that had anointed the patriots Theobold Wolfe Tone, Padraig Pearse, James Connolly, Michael Collins, and so many others who became holy martyrs for Ireland's sake. And now the finger of the Great Almighty rested squarely on him. He felt its touch and was not feared by it. Rather it was like fuel being pumped into his spirit, and he knew that God was calling on him to save Ireland. He opened his eyes to the darkness, smiling. He felt at peace. A song entered his head, and he went off to bed humming it over and over again:

God save Ireland say the heroes
God save Ireland say we all
Whether on the scaffold high or the battlefield we die
Sure no matter where for Ireland dear we fall...

Part III
Rag Mania

27

"Give me a few moments," she said.

Detective Kevin O'Felan sat in Sylvia Hickey's sports car, watching in silence as the soft palm of England's countryside rolled past. He was preoccupied by the new colors the poor Alzheimer's afflicted Bernard Tolleson had provided for his picture of the Rag Man and was pretty certain that the contemplative Sylvia was imaging a new line of dominoes. They drove leisurely along a two-lane country road. Kevin broke the quiet by confessing to feeling fatigued. He blamed it on the busy day, the travel, his earlier emotional outburst, and on just plain getting old. "At my age, the air goes out of the balloon after suppertime."

"Nonsense," Sylvia declared. "You've gone too long without a meal, that's all. Your blood sugar level is low. What you need is a pint or two and you'll feel like a new man."

"Ah, the age-old antidote. Do you make house calls, Doctor?"

"I do. But not for tired old men." She shot him a playful glance from the corners of her eyes.

They came upon a whitewashed public house called the Clever Fox Inn. Kevin admired the array of summer flowers spilling out of the boxes set beneath the inn's windows and chuckled upon seeing the red and gold sign hanging over the pub door, featuring a fox sitting on its haunches with a pint in his paw and a wry grin on its face. Depicted in the distance were horsemen and dogs giving chase in the wrong direction. Kevin wondered if the Rag Man was similarly grinning and having a pint while he and Sylvia, like the horsemen, were chasing in futility. Sylvia called into Scotland Yard and was told that the photographs of the bin lorry man's funeral would be faxed shortly to the inn.

They took drinks in a garden while seated on a wooden bench just big enough for them to snuggle hip to hip. Wisps of white smoke curled from the inn's gold thatch roof, then faded off into the descending dusk. Sylvia drank vodka and orange. She made no attempt to keep her long legs from rubbing against his. Kevin drained a pint of John Courage—because he considered English Guinness intolerable—and was well into his second glass when he began to feel better. Sylvia's antidote was taking effect. The doctor was making a pleasing impact, too.

She laughed heartily at his little quips, allowing her head to fall against his shoulder, where she left it a note longer than it seemed necessary. In his day, such touching was a clear signal, but things were different now, he told himself. When Sylvia excused herself to check on the Scotland Yard fax, he watched the sway of her hips.

The sweet fragrance of her hair lingered, like the aroma of a fine meal just taken from a room. Why did everything always remind him of food?

For the first time since leaving Ireland, Kevin did not feel the itch to return—Rock 'n Nua or no Rock 'n Nua. Rag Man or no Rag Man. Wedding or no wedding. Ireland at the moment was a dull blur in the back of his mind, stuffed there by the alcohol sedative and the tranquility of the English vale that was steadily taking him behind a grey curtain of dusk. There in the dark, wearing his leather jacket and sporting platinum hair, it felt good to be a different man, in a different world, a world where touching meant nothing. The different man was younger. He flexed his right leg to work the stiffness out and, for once, the knee didn't crackle like a bowl of Rice Krispies. He sipped his pint. The bitter ale slipped pleasingly over his tongue and stoked his spirit. Oh, but wasn't that the secret to everything, he thought, how to keep the spirit from burning out? The swanlike silhouette of Sylvia Hickey was gliding back toward him, reminding him how life seemed to be slipping steadily by, each year being a little shorter than the one before.

Anymore, it was impossible for him to shield his eyes from Sylvia's loveliness. If he tried not to notice the taut satin sheath of her exposed stomach, then he dare not look down because his eyes might very well get stuck on her long legs wrapped in blue, skin-tight denim. Nor dare he look up at her small, firm breasts with her nipples turning hard in the cool of the night and pushing against her red T-shirt. The only safe place to look was directly in her eyes and become arrested by them.

She'd brought back the photographs, two more drinks and some news.

"Walcott's story checks out about his transfer from Dartmoor Prison to Brixton. The education records are all on the level, too. Even his position at Segaworld is legit."

"Damn, I was certain otherwise. Especially about the job," Kevin sighed. He began scratching out the color from some of the numbers he'd painted onto his big picture.

"Hold on for a moment. Walcott got the position—a *newly created position*—shortly after investing fifty thousand pounds in Segaworld. I know," Sylvia added. "Where does a prison warder come up with that kind of cash? It's going to take a little time to suss that one out."

Kevin exhaled a chestful of wrong answers, then sucked in the new questions. His moment of arousal had been short-lived. He was back on the case.

Sylvia flashed a penlight over the photos. "It's probably best that we look at these out here in private. It's a bit crowded inside." She moved the photographs to Kevin's lap and leaned in close, moving the light slowly over each face. "Recognize anyone?"

Kevin examined each photograph in the area where the boy's face had been torn away. Unlike the newspaper photo, the security photographs were focused on the background faces, not on the grieving family. He slowly scanned each of the dozen photographs, then began flipping back and forth between two of them. He placed a finger on the face of a man in sunglasses standing just off the right ear of the boy.

"This one. His name is Cathal Slattery."

"The billionaire? Why would he be at the funeral of a bin lorry man?"

"Billionaire and legendary Irish hurling hero, and a former friend. I've followed him since I was a kid. To say I was a big fan of his would be a massive understatement.

Sunglasses or no, I'd recognize him. And as for why is he there…where isn't he? The world is his playground. He goes wherever it fancies him at the moment and throws money at it. Throwing fifty thousand quid at a prison warder would be pocket change for Cathal Slattery," he added.

Kevin went on to explain more about Cathal Slattery, the financial ties to foreign governments and his penchant for young actresses. "I'd like to know whom he's talking to," Kevin added, moving his finger over the image of a strongly built man with his hair cut high and tight. He looked to be military, though he was dressed in civilian clothing.

"He does have the distinct look of 'Army' about him," Sylvia agreed. "But we won't find out who he is tonight, will we?" Sylvia sighed.

Kevin peered into a half full pint glass and returned Sylvia's sigh. "Yes, and I suppose we should be getting back to London. Are you alright to drive?"

"No. And neither are you." Sylvia slumped down in the bench and closed her eyes to the moon as a sunbather would at the beach. "We've worked enough today. It seems a shame to rush out of such a nice evening," she said, her eyes still closed. When she reopened them, she fixed her gaze directly on Kevin. Her nose was nearly touching his. "They have rooms here." After a moment's pause she added, "There's a vacancy."

The jitters started in Kevin's shoulders and ran downhill, fast. "Separate rooms, of course," Kevin said.

"Wouldn't that compromise our cover?"

He waited for the telltale body language that customarily punctuated her flirting. Would it be a playful sideward glance from her paisley eyes? Or her wide, soft lips twisted in a wry grin? Or maybe she'd illuminate the night with her moonbeam smile, which usually caused a greater stir in him than her teases, but now would serve to douse the slow building fire inside. Sylvia, though, sat comfortably erect. Her hands folded across the lap of her long, long, blue-jean legs. Her eyes were wide and calm. Her full red lips were poised in a slight, dignified smile. She was offering.

His mind raced ahead to a dark, upstairs room, crisp sheets, and a cool breeze from an open window pouring over him. Sylvia was slender and very, very long. The sweetness from her hair that now hinted like honeysuckle in the breeze would soon envelop him. Sylvia was soft, silky, and so very, very slow. He saw with each passing moment, her black loveliness seeping into the descending darkness, until she was nearly one with the night. She was offering.

She leaned forward and kissed him gently on the neck, settling his jitters but further stoking the fire below. Rising slowly rose from the bench, Sylvia stepped toward the inn. "Give me a few moments," she said. Kevin again watched the syrupy flow of her hips. She froze when his mobile phone rang.

He knew what she was thinking, because he was thinking the same thing: the phone call was about to steal away their night. By her utter stillness, he knew that she was leaving the choice to him. She had offered. The phone kept ringing. He wondered if the call might save him from a mistake his body begged him to make. He placed the phone to his ear.

"Right. This is O'Felan. Jasus, you're not serious. God in heaven I hope that's the case. I understand. Straight away. Thanks a million."

Sylvia walked back to him and took his hand. This time she offered only a resigned grin. "Good news?"

"Yes. I mean, no... I mean, that was Dublin calling. The Rag Man and Mick Mulvihill made a bollix of Rock 'n Nua. But the Rag Man claims he killed neither the bin lorry man nor Paddy Burke. It all has to do with some family curse or another. If it's all true, it means that I—"

"It means you're not responsible for Paddy Burke's death."

If she weren't holding his hand, he might have fallen to the ground, like a feather blowing in the wind. He wanted to dance. *He hadn't killed Paddy Burke after all!* The fire in his loins had vanished. "There's a plane waiting for me at Heathrow," he added. "Sylvia, I—"

She put a finger to his lips, then lightly drew her hand away. Kevin caught it and drew her close and hugged her. He brushed his nose against her ear and whispered words that caused her to bite her lower lip. They parted hands and walked to the car. He'd told her that her offer alone had made him a new man.

A trail of red brake lamps lined the access to Heathrow Airport. Horns blared at an increasing rate. Disgruntled motorists began abandoning their cars and a sick feeling built inside Kevin's gut. This was no ordinary traffic jam. Please God let it be the Arabs, he thought. Reaching in a pocket for a cigarette, he remembered having smoked his last. Searching among the folks in the road, he saw cigarette smoke drifting through the headlamps a dozen yards away.

"I need to bum an old cancer stick," he said, moving to get out of the car. Sylvia stopped him by seizing his wrist.

"Better let me go," she said.

He got the news while Sylvia was gone. The traffic jam was not due to the Arabs. Two men stood right outside his window. They were not happy lads.

"Dirty fucking Irish. A mortar attack on the airport runway. Bloody cowards," said the one.

"The mortar didn't even detonate," the other said, shaking his head. "The incompetent idiots."

"Would you expect anything else from Paddies?"

Sylvia returned, handing Kevin a cigarette. "The airport is closed. The bomb squad will be hours removing the mortar shell."

"IRA?" Kevin asked.

Sylvia nodded. "Yeah. I called Scotland Yard. It seems as though the mortar attack is meant as a show of force. Some pin or another was pulled from the shell, so it wasn't going to explode in any case. Headquarters believes the attack is somehow attached to the death of some famous IRA man."

"Dan O'Toole?"

"Yeah, he's the one. He's dead." Sylvia allowed her seat to recline. She slid back and cast one of her playful glances. "Looks like you get to sleep with the black girl after all," she laughed.

28

"...even saints are descended from Adam..."

The moment Captain Tony Greenwell recognized the Blackbird's recorded voice on the telephone, his stomach and throat twisted like the two ends of a towel being wrung to the point of breaking. His tension persisted as he strode in a blue business suit across the plush lobby of Belfast's Wellington Hotel, located well out of harm's way of IRA Catholic neighborhoods. Thank God for small favors, he thought, remembering how the Blackbird had previously dragged him into Republican no man's land. Tony enjoyed his clandestine role in fighting the Irish scum. He just didn't care for doing it as a clay pigeon.

Arriving at a public phone that was already ringing, he listened to a scratchiness that he guessed to be an aged recording. A chair scraped across a wood floor. Footsteps faded in and out of range. Someone said, "Do you know why you're here, Lieutenant Drummond?"

"I suppose it's because I let my best friend die in a Provisional IRA ambush and you're going to tell me that my feelings are normal."

"Would you like to lie down?"

"Is that what all the soldiers do who've let their best friends die in a Provo ambush? Lie down? I'll stand, thank you."

The conversation stalled, allowing Tony to hear his commanding officer's feet resume their hesitant scraping over the hard floor. It was difficult for him to think of Bartley Drummond as having ever been hesitant at anything.

"You want me to talk this whole thing out and I'll come to the realization that, 'Oh, Bartley, you can't beat yourself up because you're alive and your best mate is not.' Maybe you'll toke me up full of tablets, until I forget the sorrows I'm trying to drown in buckets of beer. Fine. If it gets me out of here and back to the war, I'll tell you. I'll tell you about every drop of the river of my best friend's blood I caused to run into a Belfast sewer."

Tony visualized a bare room with an olive-colored metal desk. He saw a blank-faced army psychiatrist with hands folded and thumbs tapping unconsciously. Tony's commanding officer wandered the room as he considered his words carefully.

"I'm the leader of the patrol: four combat soldiers supporting an armored car entering the Lower Falls section of Belfast. Shadows from the twin spires of St. Peter's Cathedral cut the street into strips of light and dark, which I find annoyingly distracting. And despite the fine weather, I see that every window in the line of red brick row houses is shut, every lace curtain drawn closed. Belfast neighborhoods are like brick mazes. The homes press down on you. Fifty metres ahead, a toppled double-decker bus is the centerpiece of a barricade sealing off the road.

Understand that the nationalists erect these barricades to create 'no-go' areas. They claim they are 'liberating' their neighborhood from us British. Our mission is to reopen the street.

"So, as we're moving in—we're flanking the four corners of the armored car—and I'm thinking, when had things changed? Understand that when you're on patrol and you know that each step you take is potentially your last, every fiber of your being is on full alert. You feel the wind in your nose, a pebble beneath your foot. Your eye catches the leaf twitching on a tree. It's like you're living your life on a giant film screen and you're one of the main characters. So, what I'm thinking as we entered the street is, when had things changed?"

"Could you explain what you mean by that? When had things changed?"

"Is it important?"

"Could be. You've repeated yourself a couple of times."

"Right then. When the British Army first arrived in Ulster six months ago, we came as a peace-keeping force to keep the Catholics and Protestants from slaughtering one another. Catholics actually thanked us for protecting them. We were heroes. The graffiti scrawled on Belfast walls read IRA = I Ran Away. The fact was, there was no IRA, outside of a band of old boys drinking in the bar and telling stories about fighting the Black and Tans or some such. So in a matter of months, I go from hero to stepping through the Lower Falls Road district of Belfast in full riot gear. Now I'm thinking this Belfast street is no different from the bush, and I'm facing a horde of mad Mau Mau, when I feel movement in a doorway to my right. I turn, presenting my weapon, and stare straight into the face of hate in the form of an old woman with straggled white hair. 'Murderers! Murderers,' she cries. I give the command for the formation to turn, but a corner of my brain has surrendered to the image of the old woman. I'd met her only a month ago. She'd given me a cup of tea and showered me with Irish blessings. That's what I mean when I say, 'When had things changed?'"

There was another pause. Tony now felt channeled into Bartley's mind and awaited the psychiatrist's comment. Only the silence persisted. There was a clicking noise, followed by a heavy exhaling of breath. The brigadier general smoked?

"Our patrol advances. The women banging the garbage bin lids retreat steadily, like bloody carrots on the end of strings pulling us into the barricade, which is positioned just beyond a T-cross in the road. Anything on the intersecting road was out of our line of vision, but it hardly matters; we never make it that far. We're already caught in the snare of hate. My eyes are sweeping over doorways and windows, but my mind is stuck on the women's sneering lips and wide, expectant eyes. I want to abort the mission. My mate senses this. He whispers, 'Let's clear the garbage and go for a drink. It's my round.'

"He's right. To pull out would give the nationalists a victory they could feed on for weeks, even longer. We'd end up the butt of a joke in some bloody rebel song that's sung for all eternity. The morale of the whole army would suffer. We press on.

"The bin ladies suddenly stop their pounding. The uneasy silence is the signal for a horde of kids to leap from behind the barricade and start throwing stones and screeching, 'Brits out!' Believe me, at that moment I wanted fucking Brits out, too. But what am I supposed to do? Shoot women and children? I radio for riot support. 'We're under attack. It's raining rocks,' I say. The radio communication ends when a petrol bomb sets my arm on fire, separating me from my weapon. I'm rolling over rocks and shards of glass, trying to save my burning arm and I hear their cheers, like I'm some felled beast.

"The patrol drags me into the doorway of Carson's Newsagents, where we huddle behind our riot shields. The armored car lumbers on toward the barricade. We hear the sirens wailing and we're counting the seconds until riot support disbands the horde with rubber bullets. A boy, about twelve years of age, breaks from behind the barricade and runs toward the armored car holding a petrol bomb. He's fair-faced and dark-haired. I can see the blue of his eyes from twenty meters. I'm thinking, *we can't shoot women and children*. In the armored car, there is a narrow slit for the driver to see out. The boy tosses the petrol bomb right through that opening. Above the approaching sirens, above the nationalist's battle cries, we hear horribly chilling cries, followed by a brief whimpering, like sobbing children, then...nothing. The armored car drifts to a stop just a few feet shy of the barricade.

"We receive sniper fire from an upstairs window across the street and it's actually a relief, because now we can use our weapons. Then for some godknowswhy reason, my mate decides he's going to save us all. 'Cover me,' he says as he breaks into the street, firing toward the sniper's window. Bullets dance on the road around him, but never hit him. Then his throat springs a gaping red hole and he spins on his heels and topples head first onto the street. His eyes fixate on mine. And I'm so happy to be alive that I don't even fire on the IRA snipers fleeing the building. My mate is smiling, too. Only he's dead and I'm thrilled beyond words and action."

There's a guttural clearing of a throat, followed by the psychiatrist speaking in flat, hurried tones, as if from rote memory.

"You are correct, Lieutenant. I am going to tell you that your feeling of relief was normal. Survival is a primal instinct. And so, too, is your sense of guilt normal for not feeling instant remorse upon your friend's tragic death. Survival is among our strongest primal instincts, exceeding even love. Typically, the next feeling that often descends, especially for leaders, is the anxiety of second-guessing. What more could I have done? Should I have done x or y? The feeling becomes acutely compounded when you add in resentment within the unit for what might be perceived as the lack of effective combat leadership. Then there is the questioning of why are we here in the first place. Why are we dying for the sake of the Irish, on either side of the religious divide?"

"Doctor, do you understand the role that true hate plays in war? Have you seen hate so close-up, so black and hard, that you can taste its burning bitterness, like shite on fire being shoved down your throat? It's hard to believe that this kind of evil can exist inside human beings until you see it firsthand, but hate has swallowed the Irish whole. But you know what I say, Doctor? I say that even saints are descended from Adam, the original sinner."

"You never spoke of your mate by name, why?" the psychiatrist asked.

"Because I will not utter the name of that brave soldier until the day his death is avenged. And I will remain in the Queen's army until that mission is accomplished."

The recording ended. The Blackbird's communiqué was finished. Captain Tony Greenwell stepped out of the hotel and hailed a taxi. During the ride back to barracks, he repeated the name his commanding officer dared not yet utter—Private Thomas Durrow, H.M.A.

29

"I don't see anything. You told me to close my eyes."

With nothing to look at for three days except a wafer of blue sky by day and sprinkling of stars at night, Mattie Joe Treacy quickly grew dreadfully lonely inside the roofless round tower. The old monk hideaway was sufficiently equipped. There was a refrigerator full of food, loads of blankets, and a toilet. The Blackbird had even supplied a microwave so Mattie Joe could heat his tea. Only there was not a drop of drink to be found, which made the loneliness crawling through him even worse. How the monks had managed to stay holed up in a round tower for days on end without going totally mad was a complete mystery to him. He was dead certain that the holy men hadn't survived on prayer alone.

There was a phone in the round tower, which only took incoming calls. The phone was both a good thing and a bad thing.

It was a good thing when each evening Mick Mulvihill called from the stage where he was performing. Rock 'n Nua had given Mick's career a much needed shot in the arm. Hearing the foot stomping and applause, Mattie Joe felt like he was in the front row of a jam-packed hall, where people once again were mad for Mick Mulvihill and the old songs. The folk singer must have known that he was isolated somewhere, because he found ways to slip in the news of the day while talking to the audience.

According to Mick, polls showed support for the Eire Nua referendum was slipping by an alarming five points a day—"thanks to the Rag Man," he'd cry out, and the audience would cheer mightily. "The Rag Man's quest had given Ireland cause for a national examination of conscience," Mick said. "The Rag Man is rebuilding the soul of Ireland." Then, in the middle of it all, Mick would switch to talking about Liam Riordon escaping from prison hospital, and there would be still more cheering. As much as Mattie Joe thoroughly enjoyed the phone conversations with Mick, sometimes he hadn't a clue what the folk singer was talking about. Such was the case with last night's conversation.

"You're very Homeric, Mattie Joe," Mick had said.

"Just because I'm after spending years wandering and risking my life, by dodging bullets and all classes of police and soldiers in hopes of finding my father, doesn't make me Homeric."

"Actually, it does. You're a modern day Odysseus, you are."

"Odysseus certainly sounds like a Homeric name. But there's a rake of women in Kilkenny who can testify that I'm not Homeric."

"I'm not sure we're on the same page here, Mattie Joe. Odysseus is another name for Ulysses. You've heard of him, sure?"

"I have, of course. "Tales of Brave Ulysses." Cream did that song on their Disraeli Gears record. Eric Clapton on guitar." Mattie Joe slipped in the bit about Eric Clapton for Brian. The pooka was a big fan. He might be listening.

"Well, we might not be on the same page, but we're in the same book, anyway. *The Odyssey* was written before the birth of Christ. Homer is the author. The very name Odyssey has come to mean quest on account of that story. All I'm saying is that you're on a quest."

"Odyssey? Is that the story where soldiers are after climbing into the belly of a wooden horse? I think I was sick that day from school."

"That was another Homer story. *The Odyssey* would have taken up a far sight longer time in school than a day. You could spend a month or more on that."

"I could have missed a month, I dunno. Anyway, Mick, you're dead on correct that I'm on a quest and have been for a long time. I'd like to say that to the people of Ireland that I'm powerful grateful for all their well wishes and their prayers. Please God, this will all be over soon and I'll be reunited with my father."

"Please God," Mick agreed. Then as he had the previous nights, he asked Mattie Joe if he had any requests. But before Mattie Joe could answer, the folksinger went ahead and sang "The Last Rose of Summer." Truth was, Mattie Joe would have requested "Tales of Brave Ulysses" or some other classic rock song and he would have dedicated it to Brian. Maybe then the pooka would let bygones be bygones and come back.

By now, Mick Mulvihill's audiences knew every word to "The Last Rose of Summer," and they sang along loud and proud. Yet hearing strangers sing his father's party piece only caused the loneliness to seep back into Mattie Joe. He figured that his feelings were such on account of being trapped in a round tower without a drop to drink and too much time to think. As soon as he put a pint in his belly, the world would look better and he'd probably be thrilled to hear the crowds sing the old song. At the finish of "The Last Rose of Summer," Mick straight away strummed the *thump-thump* of the Eire Nua Song. He'd get a verse of it sung before the gardai hauled him away. The audience kept up roaring, "Rag Tree! Rag Tree!" Then the phone line would go dead and Mattie Joe would be alone again—until the Blackbird called, which was what made having the phone a bad thing.

The Blackbird was even more difficult to understand than Mick Mulvihill. Mattie Joe didn't appreciate the way he spoke in a spooky voice, all low and breathy, like he was conducting a séance or something.

"I want you to get into a comfortable position, Mattie Joe. Close your eyes and try to breathe nice and steady. Let your breath become one with the wind through the trees. Let the peace envelop you. Now, contemplate on nothing but the moment. What you hear and what you see."

"I don't see anything. You told me to close my eyes."

The Blackbird gave a frustrated sigh. "I'm speaking of what you see in your mind's eye."

"It doesn't matter if it's my mind's eye or my real eye, it's bloody dark in here and I can't see a thing, only the moon and the stars. And there's no wind either for my breath to be one with."

"The moon and the stars are good. In fact, they're perfect," the Blackbird said, reverting to his spooky monotone. "Why don't you pick out three stars, one for your early childhood, one for your teenage years, and one for today. If you like, give the stars names. Make them as real as you can. Because they are real. These stars are your memories. And all the other stars are linked to them. I'll call you tomorrow and we'll talk more about the stars. In the meantime, breathe, look, and reflect. Trace your life through the stars. Breathe, look, reflect. See not just with your eyes, but with your heart. Breathe, look, reflect." *Click.*

The Blackbird hung up before Mattie Joe could tell him that he'd already picked three stars and given them names: Thirsty, Lonely, and Angry. And the more he looked at each star, the more real each of them became, especially Lonely. It occurred to him that, in his whole life, he'd seldom been completely alone. He'd always had Brian. He stopped looking at the moon and the stars. Instead, he searched for birds. One bird alighted in a nest that was built into a nook in the round tower's wall. "Brian?" he called up to the nest. When no bird answered, he went back to watching Thirsty, Lonely, and Angry.

30

"...The 'No' forces are swarming like the migids in June right now."

Detective Kevin O'Felan arrived in Dublin Airport feeling every bit like a load of cow pies stuffed into a wrinkled blue suit. He'd spent the night waiting out the Heathrow Airport traffic jam, curled in the back seat of Sylvia Hickey's car, unable to sleep.

He'd called ahead and asked Finbar Lawlor to give him a lift from the airport down to Kilkenny, where he was to meet up with Peter Doyle. Kevin found Finbar's hoot owl face tucked into the crowd bustling through Arrivals. It seemed like months instead of days since he'd seen his psychologist friend. Though still fat as a hog in slop, Finbar looked just as happy, and maybe even a bit healthier. His typically unruly grey hair was newly cut and brushed. His beard was freshly trimmed, giving him a sort of plumper Sigmund Freud look. Kevin handed over his car keys, even though his friend had lost his driver's license for the same reason he'd lost his psychologist practice. "Have we time for a jar?" Finbar asked. "You do look shattered. I'll buy."

Kevin briefly considered the offer of a drink, but only because the perpetually penniless round man had offered to buy. This was a first. He declined, explaining that he was to meet Peter Doyle in Kilkenny by noon.

Finbar lifted the brown leather travel bag off Kevin's shoulder and strapped it over his own. "You've talked to your partner then?"

"Briefly. Reception was bad. He filled me in about Skinny Farrell being killed by the fire rockets, Riordon escaping from hospital, and Dan O'Toole dying. He said that the rest could wait until later. You have any clues as to what "the rest" might include?"

"I took my tea at O'Shea's on Merchant Quay an hour ago. I've news that will fill up most of the drive. Some of it's good."

Kevin closed his eyes to the heavy Dublin traffic for what he thought would be just a moment. He awoke to the hum of a song and a vision of his Siobhán as a little girl smiling at him. His daughter's smile faded into the sun drenched Wicklow Mountains. The hum of her song had been the car's tyres moving over the open road. They'd already passed Naas. He'd been asleep for nearly an hour. He wiped a stream of cold drool from his chin and cracked a window. The smoky sweet breath of Ireland poured over him. Kevin rolled the stiffness out of his shoulders. "Start with the Rag Man's mother, Finbar. I'm told she's in hospital. What is psychogenic shock, anyway?"

"Simply put, her whole emotional system is shut off as if a plug were pulled. To start, she's diabetic and the heart isn't in the grandest of conditions. She could come out of it at any time, or it could put an end to her. Terrible what we put our parents through, no? Your man, Dessie, is under a bit of pressure," Finbar said, changing the subject.

"He's not my man. What pressure?"

"There's evidence of a hassle in the castle. The word at O'Shea's was that his bird has flown the coop. She was seen stalking out of the home last night, weighted down with suitcases. My sources tell me she's bound for France. If the amount of luggage is any indication, it isn't going to be a short stay."

"Dessie probably could use the break from Mairead. Maybe she's going off for the twenty-eight day dry out. Anything else strange?"

"Indeed. More storm clouds gathering around our Taoiseach. We're hearing whisperings of gun running to the north back in the '70s. Speculation is the 'No' forces have long known of Dessie's involvement with the guns and have been holding onto that card until just the right moment to derail the referendum. The moment seems to have arrived."

They descended down a long hill into the town of Kilcullen, past a few restaurants that made Kevin's stomach growl for its breakfast, and then back up a hill and out again on the two-lane open road lined thick with trees. Finbar must have seen him eyeing the restaurants because he asked, "We could stop for a meal. I'll buy."

Kevin waved a hand onward. "I've never known Dessie to leave any bones in the closet that would harm his political career. He's been calculating from the start. Besides, it would take some class of bomb to blow up that referendum now. I don't see it happening."

As they approached Carlow, the telephone poles were all dressed with strips of cloth. Only when he saw the word

"No" spray-painted in white on one pole did Kevin realize the significance of the strips of tweed.

"These scraps of cloth wrapped around the telephone polls, are they—"

"Rags," Finbar interrupted. "In support of the Rag Man. Wood Quay was completely dressed in rags this morning. As was the Ha'Penny Bridge. The 'No' forces are swarming like the midgids in June right now."

Soon, the "No" graffiti appeared on every telephone pole. Many of the Carlow shop windows held "No" placards. When traffic stalled, Kevin looked out at a newsagent's shop and scanned the headlines on the day's papers, displayed on a vertical rack. *Irish Press*: ROCK'N DISASTER. *Irish Independent*: IRA SAYS O'TOOLE DEAD." *Irish Times*: RIORDON ON THE RUN. *Daily Mirror*: HENNESSY, RAG MAN, AND DETECTIVE LOVE TRIANGLE.

"Hennessy, Rag Man, and what detective? Jasus! You get trapped in an airport traffic jam for a night and the world goes upside down," Kevin said, speaking only half his mind. Had he spoken his full mind, then he would have asserted his being trapped on the Heathrow access road was no accident. Just like his being exiled to England was no accident. Someone wanted to keep him out of the real action by having him chase after moonbeams. Of course, if he dared to say all this aloud, then the psychologist would accuse him of being paranoid, or dangerously self-absorbed, to the point that he actually believed the IRA considered him important enough to bomb an airport, so as to obstruct his swift return to Ireland.

"You really hadn't much time to talk to Peter, had you?" Finbar asked. His eyes retained a worried look.

Traffic crawled forward. Kevin tried to absorb Finbar's explanation that Peter Doyle's old flame, Kitty McGrath—Dan O'Toole's daughter long thought deceased—apparently had gone to America and returned to Ireland as the ghostwriter for the syndicated columnist, Thomas Hennessy. The American journalist presently was cooling his heels in the Kilkenny gaol with half his face battered in. Kevin would have bet even money that his partner still carried a torch for Kitty McGrath, but as short as their earlier conversation had been, there had been no edge to Peter's voice. If anything, Peter had sounded uncharacteristically pleasant. Seems like everyone had gone out of character in his absence, Kevin thought, again marveling at Finbar's upgraded grooming.

Creating the traffic jam were two teenagers standing in the middle of the road and crying "No...No...No..." They held up placards reading *"Rag Tree Song/Last Rose of Summer: 5 pounds."* From what Kevin could tell, everyone was stopping to buy a CD.

"Dessie banned Mulvihill's songs," Finbar said. "Doesn't take long to get the old bootleg tapes and cds out, does it? You have to give the "No" people credit for seizing the opportunity." Finbar added.

"I can understand banning that 'Eire Nua' song, but surely he's not banning 'The Last Rose of Summer'? He can't do that. The song is hundreds of years old."

Finbar nodded. "Banned them both before he went to bed last night. Obviously, he doesn't want the songs inflaming people's passions. From my professional point of view, though, someone knows Dessie's Achilles heel and is whacking away at it now. Music can be a very powerful psychological weapon. Revolutionaries have long sewn their seeds with rhythm and rhetoric. Here, give it a listen," Finbar said, pulling a CD from the breast pocket of his trench coat. "It's quite good, really."

Mulvihill's crooning voice was low and haunting. Kevin could almost see each word oozing from the depths of the singer's angry soul. He understood why the Taoiseach would not risk something so beautiful and lonesome tugging at Irish hearts. The last thing Des the Decent needed was for the Irish people to become reflective to the point that they might change their minds about the referendum. Mulvihill's guitar burst into a thumping, percussive attack and Finbar unconsciously bobbed his head in rhythm with the song. "...Rag Tree...you help the lame man walk...Rag Tree...you help the dumb man talk...Rag Tree..."

When Kevin heard the explosion of fireworks, he pushed the eject button. He didn't want to reflect on Skinny Farrell being cooked by fire rockets. What was he doing up in a tree, anyway? He wondered.

Kilkenny City resembled a massive outdoor laundry. From every window and door, scraps of cloth hung. On John Street, parading bands of young people wore tie-dye rags around their heads. Around the bronze cupola hovering seventy-five feet atop the grey stone Town Hall on High Street hung a broad white sheet with green paint proclaiming, "You are now entering NO country." The Rag Tree song blared from so many shops and street corner stalls that it wasn't until Kevin and Finbar were halfway up Patrick Street and well out of city center that the song's jungle beat finally faded.

"Placing guards on the streets would be like putting a match to a can of petrol," Kevin said, noting the lack of police presence. "Kilkenny is ready to blow."

They drove out of Kilkenny City and onto a two-lane road curling through billiard table farmlands, framed by freshly cut hedgerows. Rags aside, all Kilkenny seemed newly manicured, just like his psychologist friend, Kevin thought. Anyone who did not know Finbar would not give his grooming a second look, but to a friend, the change was astounding. It was at that moment, Kevin felt the itch in his brain getting its much-needed scratch. Finbar wasn't one to spend good drinking money on a haircut and trim, or to offering to pay for meals, for that matter, Kevin thought.

"If I were to call O'Shea's and ask if you were there this morning, I'd be told 'no,' wouldn't I?"

Finbar's knuckles turned white on the steering wheel as driving seemed suddenly difficult for him. "I...I...Kevin, why are you asking me this?" The road twisted sharply left. Finbar almost put the car in the ditch before steering out of the curve.

Kevin felt the blood rush to his face. "You're on the 'No' payroll, aren't you?"

"Kevin, please stop. You're tired. You're not thinking straight. I'm afraid you're suffering from paranoia. I can help you. There's tablets that—"

"Paranoid? I'm a detective. It's my goddamn job to be paranoid, especially when being lied to. You weren't at O'Shea's this morning. Everything you've told me is information given to you by the 'No' forces. They're the ones paying for your haircuts and travel expenses to Belfast to attend funerals. The Rag Man didn't leave that newspaper at Bruxelles' Café. You brought it with you. And you tore out the picture because you were in it. Pull over before you kill us both."

Finbar pulled his foot off the clutch too quickly and the car shuttered to a stop against the ditch. He turned to Kevin, his fat head shivering with desperation. "I don't know if it's the 'No' forces, or who it is. But he promised me my psychologist license back. I'm reinstated, Kevin. Driving privileges, too. I couldn't turn those down. I wasn't actually trying to harm—"

"Harm anyone? Paddy Burke is dead. So are Skinny Farrell and the bin lorry man. People are getting real goddamned harmed. Now who's paying you?"

Finbar was weeping about a man calling himself the Blackbird, when a succession of police squad cars sped past with blue lights flashing. Moving the distraught Finbar from the driver's seat, Kevin followed until coming upon a half dozen police dressed in full riot gear and cocking their batons in the face of an angry horde. Separating the two factions and standing guard against the Rag Tree was Peter Doyle.

The air was already thick with yelling and the scream of approaching sirens when there came a thunderous bang accompanied by a surge of black smoke. A Molotov cocktail had been hurled at the police. Peter Doyle fled the Rag Tree and flopped breathlessly over the car's bonnet. Kevin pulled an uzi out from under the passenger seat, then walked down the middle of the road, holding his badge aloft in one hand and the weapon in the other. Firing several bursts into the air, he dispersed the angry farmers to their homes, and then checked on the injured Peter Doyle.

"The locals have gone mad and it's all Dessie's fault," Peter growled. "He ordered the guards to remove all the rags from the Rag Tree." Kevin's partner was rubbing a spot where blood oozed from the knee of his trousers, when the grimace on his face fled in favor of a bemused grin. "What the divil happened to your hair?" he asked.

∽

The door was ajar just enough for Father Brendan Sheils to peer through at the silhouette of his niece, Angeline O'Toole, lingering by her father's closed coffin. She was tall and majestic with determined eyes. Thankfully she'd cut her hair back to shoulder length, relaxed the curls and restored it near to her natural deep brown color that Brendan loved. Angeline wore a sleeveless black dress. Candlelight sprinkled over the porcelain shoulders taut with anger. She wasn't ready, he thought. He pondered a funeral Mass that might have to start without the priest or a body.

From a table beside the flag-covered coffin, Angeline removed a candle and held it near a placard of photographs that rested on an armchair. For several moments, the candlelight flickered back and forth between the photographs, finally settling over the one Brendan had added just that morning. He held his breath. The flame fell to the floor. Angeline lurched at the coffin, opening it. She banged a fist three times on the tri-color flag, before racing angrily over to a window and ripping open the curtains.

"Brendan!"

Father Brendan sighed, "She's ready."

31

With trembling hand she opened the coffin.

From shadowed walls, the Sacred Heart of Jesus and Padraig Pearse looked down upon the placard of photographs chronicling the first twenty-five years of her father's life. A thread of silver light slipped past the drawn curtains. "To keep the faeries down," said the old ones at last night's wake, justifying the darkness. Truth was, the blackout was to hide from the British Army, lest they raid the house in Belfast's Twinbrook Estates and steal the body. Cait McGrath (no matter how many times Brendan tried to explain that he'd changed her name for her own safety, she wasn't changing it back) danced two fingers over the tri-color draping the closed coffin, wondering whom her father had served more, a leader of Irish rebellion, or the Son of Man.

Father Brendan Sheils, his protruding belly nudging against her at the coffin, murmured a gospel reading.

273

"Jesus stood still and ordered the man to be brought to him and when he came near, he asked him, 'What do you want me to do for you?' He said, 'Lord, let me see again.' Jesus said to him, 'Receive your sight, your faith has saved you.'" Brendan closed the book. "The funeral Mass starts at half-eleven," the priest said, softly. "If you want to have a last look, now would be the time." He tried wrapping a persuading arm around her, so Cait cracked him a good one with a swift snap of her right hand.

"When did I have a first look, Brendan? You stole that from me," Cait replied, tersely. It was the first she'd spoken to him since arriving in Belfast. Brendan sighed heavily before waddling away. The truth was, she felt unsafe without him. But calling him back meant forfeiting her anger, which, at the moment, was her sole possession.

She felt as if she were living inside a black dream that tossed her back and forth between her disjointed past and an utterly uncertain future. The black dream swept back to last night's wake where her father's old friends sprinkled the words "hero" and "soldier" and "sacrifice," as they pointed at the photographs of him. The black dream then stole her back to America, to a street cafe where she and boozy-eyed Thomas Hennessy laughed over cups of strong coffee. Together, they were going to make a bundle and, better still, pull the wool over the eyes of the editors at *The Washington Post*. And the black dream put her inside a milking parlor where she pinched her nose against the smell of shite on her boyfriend's Wellingtons. Given the chance now, she'd swim through shite to be back with Mattie Joe.

The photographs were assembled chronologically. By the time of his First Communion, he had stretched out to all legs and smile, the same smile he'd had as an infant, she now noticed. By Confirmation, he was tall, sinewy and well on his way to becoming a very handsome man, yet retaining the look of a boy who found joy in all he witnessed. That's the way he looked in the wedding photograph as he beamed at Cait's mother. Tall and elegant, she wore a measured grin that clung to her face like a satin veneer, as if she already knew there wouldn't be time for many more photographs. Cait looked with curiosity at the handsome man and his pretty bride, but felt no more connection than one would for strangers in a magazine. They had never belonged to her.

Cait then searched the lower right hand corner of the placard, finding a photograph she must have lost in the darkness. It was a family birthday party. Mother, father, toddler, and cake. Unlike the wedding photograph, Cait's mother seemed not contained by self-awareness. Rather, she snuggled, happy cheek to happy cheek, with a curly-haired girl of about two years of age, squeezing her mightily.

"Oh no..." Cait muttered aloud. The stunning realization that, once upon a time, she had been deeply loved sent tears streaming over her cheeks. She pressed the birthday photograph to her chest and looked upon the closed coffin with new eyes. She now wanted to see the man who once had smiled upon her. With trembling hand she opened the coffin. It was empty!

She found herself by the window and ripping wide the curtains to escape the darkness. Through the fog building in her head, came a disembodied voice screaming over and again for Brendan. When the fat priest came through the parlor door pushing a man in a wheelchair, Cait clung to the curtains to keep from falling.

The grey light of a rainy day cut across the parlor and landed upon his gleaming white hair combed straight back. Hands like gnarled twigs protruded from the cuffs of a pressed white shirt, the collar of which swallowed his shrunken neck. The wheelchair moved slowly forward. His eyes settled. And Angeline O'Toole was wrapped in the broad, joyous smile of her father.

He reached for her by holding out quivering hands she thought might snap. She recoiled, causing his eyes to blink knowingly and his arms to fall limply against the wheelchair. He spoke to her in a croaking whisper. "I stole your childhood. I sent your mother to an early grave. I gave away my own life. But I never...stopped loving you. Never stopped dreaming about you. I am so sorry, Angeline."

"Why?" she demanded. She needed for him to keep reaching.

∽

A rowboat swept Donal Mór over the sun-drenched lake as silent and smooth as a swan, even though the wind was blowing in loud, steady gusts. He rested his head against the stern and savored a pleasant stupor somewhere just shy of consciousness. He was wondering if this is what heaven would be like when the wind suddenly stopped.

"Donal," a voice called. "Donal, wake up."

Opening his eyes, he found himself strapped into a wheelchair and rolling into a glaring light. A plastic tube dripped fluid into his right forearm, another one pumped air into his nostrils. It was the sound of his belabored breathing and the pain tearing through his brittle chest that assured him he was still alive. Yet, despite the physical suffering, he found it difficult to stay awake. The rowboat wanted to take him away again. Then someone drew the curtain closed. The glare descended. Walking on water right toward his rowboat was the most beautiful woman he'd ever seen.

I've fought all my life for freedom. And I'd give my life just one day to be free.

Donal Mór made no attempt to evade his daughter's daring stare. In fact, he admired the way she held her chin firm, like an O'Toole. "For Ireland," he answered in a tone dressed in neither pride nor shame, but only in a naked truth. It was all he had to offer.

Angeline studied him for a long time before her red lips began trembling and she said, "But I wanted to love you back."

"Yes, but if you can love what is left of me, we can still love forever."

He wasn't sure if his words could crack his daughter's anger, but they sure worked on Brendan. When the poor fat divil broke down, sobbing, Angeline ordered him out of the parlor. Then without speaking, she began rolling Donal slowly around the room until she brought him to the window where he looked out over his beloved Belfast and to the green, velvet Hill of Key looming in the distance. She surprised him by kneeling down alongside him and clutching his hand. He stroked her satin hair. When he tried to speak, she raised her ice blue eyes to him and placed a finger to his lips. "No more apologies. We have both lived the only way we knew how." Then she added, "We *will* love forever...Dad."

He watched the rowboat drift toward him from the knobby peak of the Hill of Key. It was moving swifter than before. He pressed his lips against Angeline's ear. Whispering to her, he felt Ireland's war flowing out of him. It was no longer his to fight. The rowboat was just outside the window, floating on a sea of light.

When he awoke again, it was to the sound of Angeline's voice. Her soft hand lay on his shoulder.

"Only because my father asked if I would give the eulogy."

"Do you know what you're going to say?" Brendan said.

"I do. My father told me what to say. I'm going to tell the world where he's hidden the guns."

32

"…Mattie Joe, you're the most popular man in all of Ireland…"

By the third day of his captivity inside the round tower, Mattie Joe Treacy had done all the breathing, looking, and reflecting that he cared to do—and he was going to tell the Blackbird as much the next time the gloomy bastard called. The truth of it was, it was dripping rain out and Thirsty, Lonely, and Angry stayed hidden behind a blanket of clouds, making the inside of the round tower a cylinder of darkness, so black that Mattie Joe could not see his own hand when he held it front of his nose. With no sky to stare into and no phone calls today from Mick Mulvihill or the Blackbird, there was nothing for him to do *but* to breathe and reflect. And as had been the case for most of the three days, many of his reflections were not pleasant ones.

He'd convinced himself that, though it might take a while, he and Cait would eventually be reunited. What haunted him most was how Brian had abandoned him. At first, he thought the pooka had just gone on a prolonged piss-up and that, once he'd sobered, he'd come around again. But with each passing day, it seemed more likely that the temperamental pooka would not return. And the more he thought about that, the more he wondered if his father had not abandoned him, too. This was a notion so frightening that in the past he'd always put it out of his head immediately.

At last the phone rang. "Hello, Mattie Joe," the Blackbird breathed.

"Hello yourself, you eegit. Where the hell have you been? I want out of here, understand?"

"Patience, Mattie Joe. In due time. Understand that everything has a purpose that must be fulfilled. Right now, your purpose is to stay hidden, safe, and well. Everything is working out just as I planned. I couldn't be more pleased."

The Blackbird did sound a bit chirpy, which Mattie Joe found to be totally out of character.

"Forgive me for not sharing in your joy. But I've been stuck in this black hole for the last three days, and I don't know fuckall of what you're after talking about."

"Fair enough, Mattie Joe. I suppose you deserve to know, since you have been the spark that's lit a wonderful flame. Today, your friend, Cait, gave the eulogy at her father's funeral. But before the old rebel died, he told his daughter where he had hidden the guns. There's a real chance for peace! By the way, there's already mention of Angeline— Cait—becoming a candidate for a government post. We've done it, Mattie Joe. Eire Nua is crumbling. We've saved the soul of Ireland!"

"Cait got to meet her father? She didn't even know she had a father." Mattie Joe supposed he should be happy for Cait, but he couldn't help but feel even sorrier for himself.

The Blackbird chirped on as if he hadn't heard Mattie Joe at all. "Tomorrow, Des O'Hanrahan will admit to being involved in a '70s gun-running operation. The Coalition government will abandon him. He'll be finished as a Taoiseach in a fortnight, and he'll take Eire Nua with him."

"But what about me? What about my father?"

"You? Mattie Joe, you're the most popular man in all of Ireland. Why at the funeral today, there was a rag in every fist. There would be no saving the soul of Ireland without you, Mattie Joe. Understand that my plan depended upon someone whose love knew no bounds. Someone who would go to any lengths to get something he held dearer than life itself. You possess that passion, Mattie Joe. I simply held it up for the people of Ireland to see."

The Blackbird was excited. He had to stop to take a breath before continuing.

"You'll be found innocent of the murders and do a bit of time in prison. Easy time, most of it in hospital getting well. You'll come out of this whole caper an enormous celebrity. I've already arranged for *The Sunday World* to buy your story for five hundred thousand quid. You'll never milk another cow, Mattie Joe. Trust me; you'll step out of that round tower and be embraced by a grateful nation."

The Blackbird finally stopped running at the mouth, though in Mattie Joe's view, there was more to run on about.

"There was never a mention about prison. You ramble on about love of Ireland and such, but I didn't become the Rag Man for the love of Ireland. Where is my father? You haven't mentioned him."

There was a pause before the Blackbird spoke. Mattie Joe didn't like the sound of that pause a'tall.

"Mattie Joe, when your father went to England fifteen years ago, he was arrested and held under the Special

Powers Act. There was a lot of IRA bombing activity in Britain at the time. The British government panicked. I'm sure your father's only crime was being Irish, in the wrong place and at the wrong time. There was a fire at Dartmoor Prison, south of London. Not everyone made it out alive, Mattie Joe."

Mattie Joe grunted. "The curse of the O'Neills would have protected my father—the eldest son will not survive the father, remember? Have you tracked down his whereabouts since? If he's still in prison, let's go get him. I've got this escape stuff down now. It shouldn't be a problem a 'tall."

"You're not listening, Mattie Joe. There will be no more prison escapes. Your father is gone. He didn't make it out of the fire. I'm very sorry for your loss."

"You're saying he's dead? He can't be dead. The family curse—"

"For the love of God, there is no curse. There are no faeries. Your mother has pounded that bullshit into your head, and the fact that you can't discern this for yourself is a sign of arrested development, perhaps even schizophrenia. More than likely, it's the cause for your alcoholism."

"A moment ago, I possessed a passion that awakened four million Irish hearts, and now I'm a boozed lunatic? You know who I think is full of bullshit? You! You feed people a pack of lies and throw buckets of money around—which, by the way, I haven't gotten, fuckall. You're after telling me to stop believing in the curse, but you've used that curse to ignite the passions of a nation. You're a dishonest fucker. From here on out, I'll find my father without your help. Just let me out of this damned round tower."

The Blackbird only chuckled. "Be serious, Mattie Joe. There is no real Rag Man, only an imaginary one I created to save the soul of Ireland. All along, the Rag Man was watched over every step of the way by soldiers, Gardai detectives, and more. Every door was left open for you. It's taken dozens of people and a small fortune to create the illusion of a single Rag Man." The Blackbird then reverted to his customary stern tone. "And you best mind yourself, boyo, because I can have the electricity turned off in that tower and you could rot in there for all time. I'm in control, not you."

Just then, the clouds broke and Mattie Joe looked up to see the fiery smiles of his three stars, Thirsty, Lonely, and Angry. "Tell me more about Cait. Why did she have to be involved?" He figured that he could keep the Blackbird on the phone by giving him the opportunity to crow some more about the genius of his plan. Meanwhile, Mattie Joe had a plan of his own, thanks to Thirsty, Lonely, and Angry. With the phone cradled under his chin, he climbed the ladder to the top level and, using his cigarette lighter, set the mattress on fire. Flames soon climbed the tower's walls.

"You see, Mattie Joe, if Ireland is ever to be truly at peace, we have to get the guns out of everyone's hands. Donal Mór O'Toole was the key to the IRA's weapons caches. And the only key to Donal Mór was reuniting him with his long, lost daughter. That would be your friend, Cait. Do I hear something crackling?"

"Only the fire from the bed. I'm after putting a match to it. The flames are shooting out of the round tower like a giant torch. It shouldn't be long now before someone comes to save the most popular man in Ireland. Maybe I can be the Rag Man all on my own, after all. You lying bastard!"

Mattie Joe had just outsmarted the Blackbird. His spirit soared. As he admired the smoke twisting off the mattress in a rising black stream, he felt his anger and fatigue floating off, too. He was so happy that he could not help singing, "'Tis the last ro-ose of summer, left bloo-ooming all alone…"

He'd been singing for half an hour when the first car came grinding up the mountain. Before long, the sound grew into a long churning hum punctuated by the slamming of doors. Voice after voice joined in singing his father's party piece, until the chorus nearly drowned out the crackling fire, which had begun biting into the plywood floor. Mattie Joe did not contemplate the fire for long, though. He was busy considering how at any moment the tower door would burst open and hundreds would greet him as the most popular man in Ireland. He only wished that Brian were here to see it.

33

...an elaborate formation of dominoes...

Feeling protected in a dark room, the Blackbird cradled a phone against an ear while marching his fingers over a tabletop to the sound of a martial band playing in his head. He loved the boom of the bass drum and the rat-a-tat-tat of the snare. Fife and drums were his favorite. He preferred sprite marches like the Garryowen, though tonight the band inside his head played the dark "O'Neill's March," which spun round and round, bundling tension without hope of resolution. Over the phone, he heard fire raging through the round tower, like the sound of the wind ripping through tall trees and he considered a humbling notion: could the one pure heart that he'd employed to save the soul of Ireland now wreck him?

Calling out several times for Mattie Joe, he had to endure long, breathless moments before at last a loud, echoing voice cried out, "Oh God. Oh God, save me! It's so hot..." He then screamed so horribly that the Blackbird's stomach leapt into his throat.

"Mattie Joe! Mattie Joe, can you hear me?"

Low groans trailed off into ominous silence. The Blackbird closed his eyes against the vision of Mattie Joe's charred and curling body. "O'Neill's March" played on. The Blackbird's fingers picked up the pace.

"Aye, I'm still here," Mattie Joe chirped. "I'm not cooked as yet, though I just might be soon. Aaaaaahhhhh," he screamed, then broke into a fit of laughter. The fire is shooting out of here like a Roman candle. It's fuckin' brilliant, man.

"By the way, Blackbird. There's one question I've been meaning to ask you and I'd like to know the answer before I die in here. What is that tap-tapping I hear every time you call me?"

"Just my fingers moving across a tabletop. It's a habit. It soothes my nerves."

"Oh, but there's a long stretch of taps, too. It couldn't be just your fingers."

"It *is* my fingers and now listen to me, Mattie Joe," he insisted. "I can get you out of the tower. But you have to cooperate."

"I'll get my own self out of the bloody round tower. I'm through listening to you. It was your lies that put me in here," he said, then resumed singing. "'Tis the last ro-ose of su-u-ummer, left bloo-oo-ming a-all alone...C'mon, from the top. 'Tis the last ro-ose of su-u-ummer, left bloo-oo-ming a-all alone..."

"Be rational, Mattie Joe. I'm not God. I can't raise your father like Lazarus from the dead. Mattie Joe?"

To the Blackbird's utter disbelief, Mattie Joe Treacy had hung up on him. He considered for a moment that, maybe it *was* only the wind through the trees he'd heard and there was no fire. He considered, too, the minimal risk if Mattie Joe were to cook to death. The body might never be discovered. Obstacles? Peter Doyle was a possibility, though he instantly dismissed the notion. The chances of Peter Doyle suddenly developing a conscience and implicating himself were more remote even than a body being found inside the long forgotten tower.

The bigger issue for the Blackbird was, could he justify Mattie Joe's death as a casualty of a just war? Had he placed Mattie Joe's life in imminent danger? Or had Mattie Joe done this to himself? Could a general be blamed for a soldier placing himself in peril by ignoring orders? At the end of the day, was he responsible for a fool acting like a fool? The answer was as simple as it was undeniable: Yes, he was responsible, because he had the capacity and opportunity to save his soldier. The only ethical thing to do was to save Mattie Joe, even if it meant risking exposing himself.

Racking his brain for some alternative, he concluded with dismay that, given the dire hurry, his lone option was to contact the one man he'd long avoided. It would not be an easy phone call. Things had ended badly between them. Besides, he didn't have the man's mobile number handy and it wasn't as if he could ring him at home and say, *"How have ye been since?"* No, the contact must fit neatly within the plan that had been impermeable—until an amadán decided to start a fire. The Blackbird's anger began to surge when he considered how much easier things could have been if, for only once, the man would sacrifice his die-hard principles and act out of reason: do what was best for everyone; do what was best for Ireland!

He took a chance and dialed Finbar Lawlor. *"The mobile phone you are calling is either turned off or out of—"*

The tempo of "O'Neill's March" became dirge-like. His fingers slowed to a crawl, moving hesitantly toward an elaborate formation of dominoes assembled across the full length and breadth of a polished dining room table that glimmered in the low luster of the light passing beneath an adjacent door. He picked up a solitary domino and considered it thoroughly. He then punched another number into the phone. After several rings, a groggy voice—female and British—answered. "Hello?"

"Sylvia," the Blackbird said.

"Who? Oh. Why are you calling me? I did my job. I'm finished." By the end of her statement, she sounded more annoyed than sleepy.

"I need Kevin O'Felan's mobile phone number."

"What? You want him now? You paid me to keep him preoccupied, which, thanks to you, almost included going to bed with him. Besides, you've won. I heard the news. Dan O'Toole's daughter told where the guns are hidden. Why would I turn Kevin over to you?" she added.

"No one who has cooperated with me has gotten hurt, Sylvia. At the moment, you're not cooperating." He paused to give the weight of his threat full effect, and then added in a conciliatory tone, "Sylvia, a man's life is in imminent danger. All that has been gained stands to be lost. Kevin O'Felan is the only one who can salvage the situation. Not giving me his number will cost one man's life surely, and ultimately hundreds more, when the new peace comes ripped apart at the seams. Do you really think I can't find Kevin? For goddsakes, the clock is ticking. The Rag Man is about to burn to death."

"Why? Did he not cooperate with you? Blackguard," she added.

For the second time in a matter of minutes, the Blackbird found himself reprimanded by a subordinate. What was he guilty of? Treating foot soldiers like foot soldiers? When did people begin to think they were in position to insult their superiors? His knuckles hurt from squeezing the phone too hard.

"What are you going to do to restore the dignity you took from him?" Sylvia said in a tone that indicated that she might have been asking as much for herself as for Kevin O'Felan.

"Sylvia, I'm sorry I put you in a compromising position with Kevin. Maybe I was insensitive to that. But this has been a very complicated operation, and a very successful one, mind you."

"You're missing the point," Sylvia interrupted. "I played the role and took your money. But the show's over for me now. I'll be back putting on the makeup and walking the catwalk on Monday. But where's Kevin's piece? You haven't paid him fifty thousand quid to stay out of the way. It seems to me that your whole *masterful* plan hinged on him, really. By the way, I didn't sleep with him."

The Blackbird twisted the single domino between his fingers as Sylvia ranted the truth. She concluded with, "I don't know who you are, but I can guarantee that Kevin does, or soon will."

The Blackbird sighed heavily. "**Estée Lauder** is diversifying and is looking for just the right woman to extend its marketing."

After a very long pause, Sylvia Hickey asked, "What about Liz? Is she out?"

"No, Liz is not out, yet. She's not getting any younger, y'know. But the company wants a comparable ebony image. Marketing will start with some products bearing the faces of both women. I can only think that whoever joins Liz on the cosmetic adverts will be the next Iman, the most recognizable woman of color in the world. I need the phone number now, Sylvia."

Sylvia gave him the phone number, as he knew she would. The Blackbird rose from his chair and walked to the middle of the table. Again, he considered the final domino, the one he'd reserved for Kevin O'Felan. He placed it in the center of the domino formation. With a flick of his finger the whole labyrinth tumbled.

34

…there is a new face for Ireland…

The Daughter stands outside Saint Agnes Catholic Church waiting for the slow march to Milltown Cemetery, hugging herself against a cold morning rain, dripping its last teardrops through a veil of fog hovering stubbornly over Belfast. Inside the church, the organ hums a languid "Faith of Our Fathers," even though the funeral Mass ended a quarter of an hour ago. Her uncle, a rotund Catholic priest, from whom she is estranged, brushes past her, whispering, "It's your father's favorite hymn." She dodges his attempt to embrace her. Later, she'll confess that she needed that hug and a million more besides.

Angeline O'Toole remembered once hearing that a person in the midst of intense personal turmoil reverts to her most primal instincts, as a means of self-preservation. Personality affectations fall away like molted skin. Only the raw animal remains to protect itself. As the old saying went, "Even a rat will bite if trapped in a corner." It was a sad premise for her at the moment, but a true one nevertheless. She did feel trapped, and, yes, a bit like a rat. Throughout the funeral Mass, she had tried mightily to play her role as the grieving daughter. She *wanted* to be the grieving daughter. More that anything she would have liked to return to Twinbrook Estates and cuddle with a smiling, dying man. But she hadn't been a daughter long enough and her weary mind was giving way to her journalist's instincts. Even as she tried organizing her father's eulogy, in her mind she was keeping a journalist's account of the funeral.

The cortege is reported to be the largest in the history of the Six Counties. An estimated two hundred thousand people jostle back and forth on the Falls Road like nervous racehorses at the starting gate. Lying before them is an asphalt no man's land, lined with scaffolds occupied by television news teams. A French newswoman reporting from curbside breathes into a microphone, "La mort de dernier de l'Irlande." The death of Ireland's last rebel.

The sun suddenly pokes though a round gap in the rolling charcoal clouds, prompting the priest to look skyward. The Daughter now realizes that the fog was the cause for the delay. If it didn't lift soon, primetime America would miss the chance to gawk at the freak show of an IRA funeral.

Standing solemnly alongside the flag-draped coffin and just in front of the Daughter, are four grey-haired men in their fifties— or older. They are the pallbearers. The priest whispers to each of them as though telling secrets, then clasps their hands in turn. They each peep shyly at the Daughter, but quickly turn their heads to avoid catching her eye. She wonders: Are the old boys up to the long walk?

The organ sighs with finality. The flutter of a hovering helicopter is heard, but only briefly before a trio of bagpipes begins honking and squawking. The Daughter loathes the bagpipes.

Bagpipes grate on her ears worse than fingernails scraping across a blackboard. Fingernails can be trimmed. Bagpipes need to be burned. Yet today she must tolerate the bagpipes, because she is, after all, the Daughter.

But when the bagpipes begin a sprite, martial rendition of "The Minstrel Boy," her blood stirs fast and warms all the way from her chest down to her cold feet, now eager to march. Too much has happened over the past month. Nothing much surprises her anymore. An hour from now, she will have delivered the eulogy. The international press will push her for answers. She'll nervously brush a lock of hair from her eyes, but not expand on her feelings. To do so would take her too close to the flame of her sorrow. If she does happen to break down, most will believe it is because of the loss of her father. Some will suspect it's because of the loss of her lover. Only she knows it will be because, in order to find herself, she had to lose everything all over again. Only the raw animal remains.

"...The minstrel boy to the war has gone. In the ranks of death you will find him..."

The Daughter closes her eyes and searches for her father's smiling face, but sees her lover's instead. She now understands how a song could be more than melody and rhythm, but a transcendent that wraps you in its warm embrace and carries you to another time and place. Opening her eyes, she watches the four grey-haired men hoist her father's coffin onto their shoulders. Do they know that it is empty?

Tied to one of the brass handles is the tweed rag her lover gave to her father. The rag transfixes her. (Were both she and Mattie Joe rats? Trapped together, now running? She wants him back. But she wants him free. It can't be both ways.) She is still contemplating the rag when, stepping suddenly out of the fog, come six men dressed completely in black. They surround her father's coffin. Out of two hundred thousand people, only the Daughter *seems startled. This is Belfast. People long ago traded being startled for being angry.*

The six men look like black mummies. Dressed in black berets, black gloves, and snug black turtleneck sweaters, they are tall and fit. Muscles bulge from their arms and chests. White belts cut them in half at their narrow waists. Only the slits of pinks peering out of the eyeholes of their black ski masks keep them from appearing utterly robotic. The procession lurches forward. The Daughter now knows the fog had not been the cause of the delay, after all. They had been waiting on the IRA.

Throughout the slow march toward the cemetery, she observes the clenched jaws and frozen eyes of those around her. She wonders why it is that the hard face comes so easily to the Irish. It is a brief pondering, though, because the answer is all around her in the forms of the large, ornate murals, looming on the sides of Falls Road buildings. There are paintings of dead hungerstrikers smiling beatifically, like some sort of Nationalists' guardian angels. There are paintings of masked gunman captioned with the words "The spirit of freedom. Tiocfaidh ár lá. Our day will come." The murals are testimony to wounds that are open and flowing. They are the ubiquitous reminders of a ubiquitous pain.

On the side of a building, in man-sized white lettering, are the words "While Ireland holds these graves, Ireland unfree shall never be at peace." The Daughter knows the quote, of course, as belonging to the patriot Padraig Pearse. The quote became a battle cry that refuses to go away, just like the open wounds and the ubiquitous pain. Looking at the murals the Daughter realizes that the Irish pain has been a line unbroken, coursing straight through the centuries like railroad tracks, connecting rebellion and famine and genocide. The tracks never end. Today, they are passing through her father's funeral and the stone faces around her. She has seen the stone countenance too many times before, in the mirror, and realizes now that she had been looking at the face of her mother. Do Irish wounds ever heal?

The cemetery gates are in view when a thin man holding a camera nearly as large as his head comes skipping alongside the Daughter. An inspiration whispers to her (Is it her father's voice?) that the world had seen enough of wounded Irish faces turned cold and hard, and hidden behind black masks. The voice tells her that she is the chosen one to reveal the new face of Ireland. The new face shines with the light of resilient Irish soul burning within. The soul is immortal. It embodies hope, love, faith, and warmth. "Show them the rag," the voice tells her.

Reaching up between the panting pallbearers, she unties the tweed rag from the brass handle. She gives her lips a quick lick and sweeps a hand through her hair—because a girl has to look good, after all. The photographer, striding steadily five feet parallel to her grins knowingly, then ducks behind the lens. The Daughter holds the rag out inches off her chin, offering it as a priest would Communion. Peering into the lens, she thinks of her father's smile. She listens to Mattie Joe's laugh. She has a vision of her second birthday party and her mother's unbridled joy. Behind the hurt, beyond the loss and sorrow, there is a new face for Ireland: the joyful face of a prodigal daughter returned home. The camera emits a stream of clicks. The photographer looks up and, as he falls into the wake of the marching cortege, his mouth forms the word "Wow."

The pipers abruptly stop playing at the gates of Milltown Cemetery. The soothing drone of marching feet dissipates into a haunting crunch as the cortege treads the final steps over a cinder path winding toward a conglomerate of massive boulders—one for each of the Six Counties. The Daughter ascends the largest boulder and stands behind a curtain of microphones. She watches the cortege pour across a sloping landscape, dotted with stone angels and Celtic crosses. The voice returns, telling her, "All of Ireland is here, the living and the dead. You must tell them." The Daughter nods in agreement with the voice. The hole in the clouds opens wider and she stands in the spotlight of the sun's warming rays.

The coffin is lowered onto a ground strewn with flowers. The six IRA men stand rigidly on guard. There is a minor disturbance as a gaggle of small children wiggle their way past the IRA as nonchalantly as if shifting through trees, then gather round the pallbearers, hugging them at the knees. The children, all well dressed in their Sunday clothes, are appropriately solemn, save for one little moon-faced boy with black hair, cut in a bowl just shy of his merry, blue eyes. He is absolutely delighted to be at such a big party. He couldn't be more than four years of age and he giggles loudly as he slides around and through the legs of one of the pallbearers. The older children vainly try to shoosh him. His grandfather lifts him onto his hip. The little boy looks toward the large boulder, his blue eyes wide with excitement.

And in the millisecond between when the little boy smiled broadly and his grandfather put a finger against his lips and said, "Shoosh, Donal," Angeline understood that she had never truly stood alone—only apart. There at the graveside were dozens of men and women who now gazed upon her with her father's smile.

The little boy slid free of his grandfather. "Auntie Angeline!" he cried, as he scooted through the IRA and up onto the boulder. He leapt into Angeline's arms. She could feel his tiny heart beating fast against her chest. He had a large wad of snot in his left nostril. He was absolutely gorgeous.

"Well, hello to you," Angeline said, her voice ringing through the loudspeakers. "And what might your name be?"

The little boy turned suddenly shy. He whispered in Angeline's ear.

"Oh, that's a very good name. Who else has that name?"

With one hand in his mouth, the boy held a tiny arm out toward the coffin.

"That's right. Now take your fingers out of your mouth and tell everybody what your name is."

"Donal O'Toole!" the little boy blurted into the microphone.

A man and a woman anxiously approached the boulder. They would be the boy's parents. The father had the proud O'Toole chin and premature grey hair.

"Is it all right if I keep him for a moment?" Angeline asked. The parents nodded, wide-eyed.

"Well, Donal, I'm going to tell you a story. Would that be all right?

"When I was a wee girl—not as big as you, mind you—before I went to sleep at night, I'd play a game with God. Looking out my bedroom window, I'd stare up at the sky and count the stars. If I could count them all, then God would bring Mommy and Daddy back to me. That was the game. Many's the night my eyes tip-toed all over the universe. I just *knew* that Mommy and Daddy were there somewhere, waiting for me. And the whole while I counted, I believed that my parents were counting stars, too, trying to find their way back to me. There were a lot of stars and lots of one-way conversations, but I never gave up hope that my parents were somewhere up in that sky and talking back to me."

Angeline addressed the cortege. "Take a good look at his face. A face not yet wounded by injustice and burnished in the kiln of hate. It is the face of his father, my father, and generations of fathers before, a face that has for centuries been too easily lost to the Irish." Angeline paused to allow wee Donal to slide down and scurry over to the waiting arms of his proud father.

She continued. "Today, the star counting is over. The universe no longer separates me from my father. It connects us now more than ever. So, knowing that my father is listening, I'm going to speak to him now.

"Daddy, you were born here in Belfast, and for too brief a time you were wee Danny boy, your parent's pride and joy. There were no toy guns for you, no playing cowboy and Indians. Too soon, Daddy, your gun was real. Too soon, you became Donal Mór, Big Dan. Too soon, you became a hero…"

35

His Army of Five was now in position.

Brigadier General Bartley Drummond studied the television monitors showing the scaffolds along the Falls Road one by one emptying themselves of news teams, which then chased after the funeral cortege. Once Falls Road became barren, Bartley whispered to himself, "Ranger move into position." A figure slipped from behind a television camera and climbed down the scaffold. Tony Greenwell started to say something, but Bartley stopped him with a terse wave of his hand. Tony's pacing and sighing was wearing on Bartley's nerves. Earlier, he had tried to obscure the annoyance by mindlessly whistling. Now, he needed to hear Angeline O'Toole's voice sounding though the speakerphone in the Falls Road Police Station surveillance room.

"Daddy, I know you will agree that I must give tribute to my mother and to women everywhere who marry men sacrificed to a cause. In their hearts they must know that love will be short, but they love nonetheless, unconditionally. Mother, too, loved for too short a time. The only thing she loved more than Ireland was you."

Bartley murmured, "Lawrence Olivier, move into position." Holding his breath almost to the point of dizziness, he watched the second member of his Army of Five ascend the police station watchtower and convince the two watchmen that they were relieved of duty.

"Daddy, you spent most of your life living either in shadows or trapped in the cages of Long Kesh. You were among us for such a very short time. So how is it that we come here today in thousands upon thousands? Part of why we are here is because of your legend. You were the great Irish warrior-savior incarnate, the Chuchulainn of our times. We will cherish your memory always, because it, like the echoes of rebel songs in the night, is an ember of our dream of an Ireland united, Gaelic and free. And today your ember is ignited anew. *Tiocfaidh ár lá.*

Daddy, what makes your death so hard to bear is knowing that you could have saved yourself by accepting medical treatment. But you refused that medical treatment because you would not risk the loss of our dream. You believed that by your suffering *you* could redeem Ireland. And so it will be..."

Tony Greenwell blurted, "What the hell is she talking about? Let's get on with it."

"Quiet!" Bartley commanded.

"So, today, we come to bury a hero, my father. As God has taken his immortal soul, we now plant into sacred soil his mortal remains, as Ireland has for hundreds of years planted the remains of her heroes. But while we bury his body, he has new life, eternal life, with God and forever here on Irish soil."

Across a television screen moved a tiny speck so small that only Bartley could have known it was an automobile. Graham Hill had arrived. His Army of Five was now in position.

"For what kept my father alive all those hard years inside Long Kesh were two things: a secret and a dream. His dream was to be the last Irish hero to go to an early grave. His dream was that Ireland would no longer plant its heroes in the ground, like seeds to germinate and become flowering reminders for future generations of martyrs. Nor did my father believe that Ireland's struggle could ever end if it were to surrender its weapons, as he was repeatedly asked to do, right up to the end. Surrender was *never* an option. But he also knew that an Ireland bearing arms would also continue to bury its heroes. And so it was that with his final words, in a voice choked in pain, he passed to me, his own flesh and blood, his secret. He chose to paraphrase those immortal words of Padraig Pearse at the graveside of the great Fenian O'Donovan Rossa. I think he chose these particular words so that the circle would be completed for Ireland's long suffering. He said, 'While Ireland holds these graves, Ireland *free* shall *forever* be at peace.'

"My father told me that the weapons are buried in the graves of Irish patriots throughout Ireland. The weapons lie with Michael Collins and Padraig Pearse, with Wolfe Tone and Kevin Barry, and with scores of others for whom the flame of Irish passion burns eternal. Surrender our weapons? Never. But, yes, the weapons are now 'put beyond use,' in the protection of those who gave the ultimate sacrifice for Ireland. So, to our brothers and sisters in the Republic of Ireland, I say that on this day, having for so long shared in Christ's crucifixion, the people of the North of Ireland now joyously begin to share with you in His resurrection. And now that *our* day *has* come, we implore you not to inadvertently give it away. You must honor our patriot graves, honor the resurrection. You must vote 'No' on the referendum, because the true New Ireland is coming."

Drummond listened for a moment to the roar from the cemetery, then clapped his hands vigorously. "It's over. *Over!*"

His attaché took a step toward the rack of televisions, as if a closer look might change what he saw. "I don't understand. What about killing the Irish beast entirely? Tommy Durrow? The Army of Five?"

Bartley allowed a moment's silence so Tony could fully choke on his guffaw. Chants of *"Tiocfaidh ár lá"* could be heard coming over the speakerphone. Tony's eyes widened with a dawning realization.

"Army of Five? Tommy Durrow? I don't remember discussing either with you, Captain. Tommy Durrow, you knew by these, of course," Bartley said, twirling the dog tags and chain around an index finger. "But no matter, I knew that the Army of Five would intrigue you. A well disguised drunken comment, no?" He turned toward the televisions. "My Army of Five is in position now. See, there's Ranger," he said, pointing to a man lurking outside the Milltown Cemetery gates. "Fast as bloody lightning. He'll join the Glasgow football club tomorrow. A tryout, that's all he's asked for. And his fifty thousand quid from the Blackbird, naturally." Bartley moved his hand over to the television showing the watchtower. "Up here is a fellow I call Lawrence Olivier. An aspiring actor, he could talk his way into the Queen's knickers, he's that good. The only thing he does better than act is handle a long-range firearm. And third, is this little speck here. That's a car. I call the driver Graham Hill." Bartley turned and faced Tony. Ugly lines of confusion grew across the captain's face. The poor fellow hadn't a clue that a snare existed, let alone the fact that he had stepped fully into it, Bartley thought. "I've always been a Formula One racing enthusiast, did you know that, Tony? No, you didn't, did you? No more than you understand the mission of the Army of Five, or that the beast *has* been killed entirely.

"You see, Tony, the beast is not the Irish themselves, as you would believe. Rather the beast is their living dead. Oh, I might be accused of sparing the beast by letting the Irish believe they have won the battle, but what's the harm in that? Have they not given up their arms? What's more important is that they did not have to give up their *integrity*." Bartley raised his voice and pounded his heart for emphasis. He knew he was lecturing to an unwilling pupil, but that mattered little. Hearing his greatest victory put to words made him feel magnificently alive. "That is why, this time, the war is truly over. With no more martyrs come no more mourners. And with no more mourners, the living dead have no rebellious blood to stir. Imagine, Tony, for the first time in nine centuries, Irish cemeteries are a place to truly rest in peace. There will be no more ghosts to haunt and murder."

He paused and placed a thoughtful finger alongside his temple. Closing his eyes, he summoned carefully chosen words from deep within his heart.

"It is only through the rise of humanity that war truly can be conquered. And true humanity can only exist where justice also exists. *Jus In Bello.* Justice in War. Is there justice using vastly superior military might for nine centuries, when all we have managed to do is to contain the Irish? The proportionality between the destruction wrought and what has become a nebulous objective, at best, has become utterly skewed. We long ago wrung the last droplets of economic value out of Ulster, yet we have remained at war here out of an adherence to honor."

Tony turned on the light switch with an angry swat of his hand. "No, I don't understand dwelling on humanity when in reality what you're talking about is ultimately giving away Ulster to the murdering Irish scum."

"Have I given away Ulster? I don't think so. Democracy is still being served. Oh, perhaps someday at the polls it will change hands. But that is not the soldier's concern. The soldier's concern is to maintain life by conquering that which threatens it. Today, *we* have achieved that. Our job is done."

"But what about Tommy Durrow? He saved your life, for goddsakes! He sacrificed himself to the IRA butchers so you and the others could survive. If you're saying there's justice in Tommy Durrow giving his life for nothing, then I don't understand a just war, and I'll be damned if I'll be included in this *we*. Forgive my direct language to the commanding officer, Sir!"

"I'll answer your question first by posing another. Can a soldier truly love his enemy? Can he love his enemy and still kill him, under the pretext that doing so will save lives? The just war says that this is possible. *I* say it is possible. That is how I can live with myself for having killed Tommy Durrow."

"What?"

"That's right. The IRA did not shoot Tommy Durrow, I did. I shot him down in Gregory Street because he was an informer who gave up our patrol. While the IRA sniper fire rained on us, none of it fell on Tommy Durrow. I knew at once who had betrayed our mission. I turned my weapon on him. He tried to flee across Gregory Street to safety when I killed him." Bartley paused, digging his eyes into the captain's. "And I'd kill him again.

"Understand, Tony, I learned an important lesson from Tommy Durrow that day. I learned that, as much as they are despised, traitors are a fundamental component of war. A battle plan that precludes their existence is doomed to failure. I vowed never to make that mistake again. The upshot of it is, I took the next step by *including* the traitor in my battle plan. This would be you. You, Tony, are...the fourth member of my Army of Five. Six months ago, when you signed on to continue as my aid, your papers in reality were filed for discharge. De facto, you do not exist in the Queen's army. The Blackbird gave you an opportunity to be part of history, but your own hate consumed you. You went rogue."

Tony's mouth hung open. His eyes slowly shifted toward the door, then back to Bartley. The funeral ceremony had become quiet as a priest directed prayers over the grave.

"You're the Blackbird," Tony uttered. "All this talk of just war and humanity, you're *him*. You used me all along."

"No and yes. No, I am not the Blackbird. Nor do I know who he is. I have spoken to him. His motivation remains unknown to me. But he offered me the opportunity to end an interminable cycle of death, which, I'm afraid, includes eliminating the one person in the cabal who went rogue. My conscience is clear."

"If you're not the Blackbird, then you have no proof of any wrongdoing on my part. I can make counter accusations. You'll be disgraced."

"Oh, I have proof. He's right there." Bartley pointed to the television screen showing the fat priest praying at the graveside. "You've been wondering, of course, who is the fifth soldier in my Army of Five?"

"Chubby," Tony said, barely audible.

"Father Chubby, to be precise. I wish I'd another name for him, something more respectful but, yes, it

D. P. COSTELLO

was Chubby who tracked you to Dublin. He was in the restaurant when you shot the Irish detective. The bullet pulled from the detective's skull matches the one that killed the bin lorry man, and the poor cat, for that matter. All fired from your weapon. You are a murderer, and a traitor, Captain. And, unfortunately, you do know too much to be left unaccounted for."

Bartley reached for the desk drawer where he kept the Drambouie.

Tony shook his head. "None for me, really. I can't celebrate this...this travesty, this betrayal of all the Brit soldiers who have died for the crown in this pope-infested country. I'm utterly—" The captain stopped short when he saw the pistol in Bartley's hand pointed at his chest.

Bartley laid the gun atop the desk. "The pistol is here for you, should you choose to use it," he said, softly. Your mother will be told that you died in an automobile accident. She'll receive a compensatory pension. You'll be buried with full military honors." Bartley paused, then added, "You could make a run for it, of course. But if you do, know that you will be shot down in the street—just like Tommy Durrow. Now, if you'll excuse me, there's something I must do. May God have mercy on your soul."

On the floor by the desk was a blue athletic gym bag emblazoned with the Union Jack. Bartley picked it up and left the building.

Outside, the piper's lament, "The Last Post," carried over on a chill breeze from the cemetery. Bartley strode purposefully toward the watchtower. When he heard no gun shot, he knew Tony Greenwell was going to make a run for it.

Moments later, Tony raced past and headed up the deserted Falls Road. While ascending the watchtower ladder, Bartley watched Ranger give chase, staying a comfortable

306

fifteen meters behind. Joining Lawrence Olivier, he took a pair of binoculars from the gym bag. The piper's lament ended. The IRA honor guard in unison snapped handguns into the air. Olivier crouched behind his weapon. "Now!" Bartley said. At the same moment the IRA gun salute sounded, Olivier fired a single shot. Captain Anthony Greenwell's body jackknifed, then tossed face down in the street, the back of his head gone. Ranger swiftly scooped the body and loaded it into the boot of the car. Graham Hill sped away. Olivier dismantled the firearm and placed it in Bartley's gym bag.

Bartley said, "Help me with this, please." From the gym bag, he had taken a white sheet.

∽

After Father Brendan Sheils concluded the prayers at the graveside, he stood off and watched Angeline being wrapped in a rugby scrum of O'Toole cousins and aunts and uncles, her face radiating with joy. Brendan breathed in an immense bellyful of air in an effort to stave off the surge of tears he felt building inside. It would be inappropriate now for him to weep, to spoil the family reunion. The media crowded in and cameras flashed over the child of war, to whom Brendan long ago had surrendered his heart. Reporters shouted to her. "Would she enter politics? Would she write a book?" The questions took his niece off guard. Her blue eyes widened with a startled innocence. Her lips formed a little oh-my-gosh letter "O," and Brendan again fought back tears. "Ah, Bridgid, I knew you'd come," he softly whispered. His eyes clung to the vision of his sister until she slipped away again to heaven, gone now forever. Soon, maybe even before the day was out, she would be joined by her husband, Brendan's best friend.

He walked alone amid the thousands inching back toward the cemetery gates and the Falls Road. Gazing up at the police station watchtower, he saw tied round it a massive white rag. A soft smile lifted his heavy jowls. The signal was given: the war was now truly over. Long had he prayed for this day.

Ireland's struggle now would go on in a different way. Census studies predicted that in twenty years the Catholics in the North of Ireland would outnumber the Protestants. God willing, he'd live long enough to see that happen. The thought brought another small smile to his face. Today marked his last as a soldier for *Oglaigh na hEireann*. He now would quietly return to being a full-time man of God; no more would he have to live the paradox of priest-warrior.

He carried his heavy feelings outside the cemetery gates to where a string of black taxis cued along the curbside. The taxis would transport the O'Toole family to a private reception. He could go, of course, but he wouldn't. Let her have her time, he thought. She had a lot of catching up to do. Besides, he'd had enough good-byes for one day. He couldn't sustain another.

The mere thought of saying good-bye to Angeline caused him to weep. Passing by the last of the black taxis, he wiped away stinging tears that saturated his cheeks and lips. Maybe he'd drive back to Derry, sit by Bridgid's grave, and stare out at the majestic hills of Donegal. Maybe he'd even bring along a bottle and take a drink with his sister. Yes, that is what he'd do. He'd share a drink with his sister and talk about the day. They would talk about all that Ireland had won and all that they had lost.

36

Kevin at last found his missing color.

Detective Kevin O'Felan sat with Finbar Lawlor inside a Kilkenny restaurant, looking out on the streams of pub-hoppers crisscrossing up and down a lamp-lit street. As far as Kevin could see, the new chic mode of dress was having rags hanging from arms and legs until a body resembled a scarecrow. Several of the parading young pretties wore the new Rag Man T-shirts pulled so tight over their breasts that Mattie Joe Treacy looked as if he had a bad case of the mumps. Fat cheeks or no, the Rag Man was the sexiest man in Ireland. The T-shirts said so. Since Rock 'n Nua, the Rag Man had become the Lone Ranger and Don Juan rolled into one. Lying next to a cup of tea that had long since gone cold was a glossy magazine that Kevin had wrung into a baton, only to unroll it every few minutes and gaze upon a photograph reminding him that he could trust no one.

He no longer trusted Finbar, who intermittently lifted his bearded face out of a pile of mashed potatoes and gravy, to comment on the RTE news being shown on a television hanging from the ceiling.

"Well, Dan O'Toole's daughter has told us where the guns are, Kevin. A fine looking woman, she. They're calling her the new queen of Ireland. I'd say there's an opening for that job, what with Des's missus being caught in a romp. Poor man. I bet he wishes he could go back to bed and start this day all over again."

On the television appeared Angeline O'Toole looking as beguiling as Kevin remembered her being when she was Peter Doyle's winsome and somewhat headstrong girlfriend, then known as Kitty McGrath. She was holding forth a strip of cloth as a priest would offer Holy Communion. Kevin considered how something nondescript as a scrap of cloth took on a whole new identity, when placed next to a pretty face.

The television image switched to a moderately close range photograph of a topless woman sunning herself on a beach in the Riviera. It was Mairead O'Hanrahan—with another man.

"Another fine looking Irish woman. It's good to see our generation can still turn a few heads." Finbar chuckled. "The photographer only did half his job, though. You can't tell who the lucky lad is. He had sense enough to keep his face behind the dark glasses."

The television cut to an image of Desmond O'Hanrahan looking hung over and beat up. The bags below his eyes sagged with the weight of his worry. Heavy block letters spelling GUN SCANDAL pressed down on his curly grey head. Finbar pulled the fork from his mouth and placed it down on his plate. The news report included the words INDEPENDENT TRIBUNAL and RESIGNATION.

"Poor Des," Finbar finally uttered. "For all he's done for Ireland, it's come to this. No words of support from Washington or London. The Eire Nua Des worked so hard to achieve is dead in the water." Finbar consoled himself with a forkful of potatoes studded with green peas. "And you know what the pity of it is, Kevin?" he said with his mouth full. "While it's the gun scandal that is bringing Des down, people are angrier with him for being a cuckold. She's his downfall, not the guns. But I guess you feel vindicated, Kevin. You've never been his biggest fan."

Kevin tapped the rolled magazine on the table and bit down hard on the words he would lash Finbar with, *if* he was talking to him. *"No, I haven't been his biggest fan. Nor do I feel vindicated. Not yet. But soon."*

Finbar wiped his grey beard clean with a napkin. "Well, I, for one, feel compassion for a poor man who has so many problems, at the moment, that the television news hasn't the time to report them all. Did you notice how there was no mention at all of the escaped IRA man, Liam Riordon? He's yesterday's news now. Poor Des. Job himself wasn't such a victim of a coalescence of bad fortune. No matter how much I might agree or disagree with his policies, I prefer to look at the whole situation with a sense of humanity. That's a quality I had always admired in you, Kevin," he added.

Ouch. Finbar's backhanded compliment slipped beneath Kevin's passive-aggressive guard, catching him square in the gut. But before his friend's glare could completely crumble the fortress of anger he'd built around himself, Kevin unfurled the magazine to a glossy advert of a sleek, nude ebony woman, barely distinguishable in the dark of night. A long leg and slender arm crooked at just the right angles hid the intimate body parts. Diamond earrings shimmered against Sylvia Hickey's black satin cheek. The advert read, "Seize the night." Kevin could smell the sweet scent of her hair and feel a buttery hand slip over his thigh. His nose had nearly touched where the diamond earring shimmered. Remembering how easily Sylvia had led that nose all through the England investigation made his stomach turn. Add Sylvia Hickey to the list of people he didn't trust.

And add to the list Roy Atheridge and Graham Potter, with whom he'd met in the English countryside cottage and now suspected were not Scotland Yard men at all, but players in the magnificent plot, like Sylvia. Add Skinny Farrell. Add everyone who Kevin had worked with on the Rag Man case, because he trusted no one—most especially the Blackbird. He was the puppeteer pulling all the strings. What piqued Kevin most was how he'd let himself get yanked around without realizing it.

Fixing his eyes on the magazine, Kevin painted another color into his big Rag Man picture. It was black. Black as Sylvia's skin. Black as Skinny's charred body. Black as the left eye of Thomas Hennessy, whose battered face now appeared on the television alongside the word DEPORTED. Black as the darkness that had been growing like a slow fungus over Kevin's heart.

Next to appear on the television screen was a roguishly grinning Cathal Slattery. Whatever the RTE newscaster said in the next few seconds would be the most predominant color yet in the whole Rag Man picture, Kevin thought. Cathal Slattery was never small news.

The young RTE newscaster moved his head in robotic twitches when he spoke. "Cathal Slattery, CEO of Bounty-Co., one of the world's largest food manufacturing companies, announced that he is going ahead with the planned Bounty-Co. processing plant in County Monaghan. The Bounty-Co. decision is expected to allay fears that the many foreign businesses currently operating in Ireland would abandon the country in the wake of what appears to be a looming defeat of the Eire Nua referendum. Said Slattery, 'Bounty-Co. still believes overwhelmingly that Ireland is the optimum location to expand its position in the European marketplace.' Repeating breaking news, Cathal Slattery says the Bounty-Co. processing plant a go for Monaghan."

Kevin sipped the tepid tea. His mobile phone rang. "I've been waiting. Calling to gloat?" he asked.

There was a long pause. "Kevin, at some point I will explain it all to you," a heavy voice said. "But right now I need your immediate help. Are you somewhere where you can speak freely?"

Kevin lowered his voice to a strangled whisper. "Can I speak freely? Hmmm. Let me see. I'm sitting with Finbar Lawlor, who, all of a sudden, has a driver's license and a psychiatrist's license. I've a photograph of Sylvia Hickey, who, it seems, is some class of model or actress. I saw Peter Doyle today, so love struck that he's stumbling about like a sedated cow. The new woman already has him shaving away his moustache and cutting his hair. I'm quite sure she didn't just fall out of a tree—like poor Skinny Farrell. All of them are on your payroll, I'm sure. Yes, I'd say I'm pretty free to speak openly right where I am."

"You can give out to me all you want later, Kevin. I *need you now.* Mattie Joe Treacy is in danger. I've locked him away in an old round tower for safekeeping, but...oh, christalmighty it's a long story. The thing is, if we don't move, he'll burn to death, just like...just like his father."

Ouch again. Another blow slipped Kevin's wall of anger. As much as he wanted to reach through the phone and grab the Blackbird by his pompous fucking throat, he wasn't prepared for Mattie Joe being in trouble. In Kevin's mind, bringing the Rag Man to justice was one thing, but poor, simple Mattie Joe Treacy dead was quite another. At the end of the day, he was nothing more than another Blackbird puppet being pulled hither and yon. Only the boy made of wood was about to burn.

Kevin listened as the Blackbird snorted a few times, and then erupted. "For the love of God, Kevin, the soul of Ireland is saved! Isn't that what you'd want? The north will be ours; it's only a matter of time. The Eire Nua referendum is finished. There will be no Yank or Euro warships in Cork Harbor. No Irish lads marching off to slaughter, in the name of some grand European defense force. If the only way I could accomplish this was manipulating you out of the picture, then, yes, the ends do justify the means. You would have wrecked everything by apprehending the Rag Man from the outset. Eire Nua would have passed and the Ireland we both hold dear would be lost forever—because you're the most stubborn man God *ever* put on this earth. Now, can you put all that aside and go save a man's life?"

"You had planned to call me all along, hadn't you? You knew that eventually I'd do whatever you asked, just like everyone else. Just like I did thirty years ago." Kevin concentrated on a growing sickness in his belly, because he didn't want to believe the Blackbird anymore. He didn't want to like him. Like he used to adore him.

"I'd prefer that you think of it in the same terms I do, which is that I knew I could count on you. I knew *Ireland* could count on you. Kevin?" the Blackbird added. "You knew I was behind all this. When? Why?"

The Blackbird's voice wrinkled with desperation that Kevin would have thought he could savor for hours. But actually hearing the almighty beg was somehow chillingly disturbing, as if some natural order had gone horribly awry. "The photographs of Mairead sealed it for me. You'd stop at nothing to bring him down. And you don't mind who goes down with him, as long as it serves your grand plan. You act like God."

"For Ireland, Kevin. For *Ireland*."

Kevin pressed as strongly as he could while still speaking in a whisper. "What if we get Mattie Joe out? What chance has he to walk away clean?"

"Slim and getting slimmer by the moment. There's something else in that tower along with Mattie Joe."

"Please tell me this isn't the tower in the Blackstairs Mountains? You've cleaned that out in the past thirty years, surely?"

The ensuing moment of silence answered the question, and not in the way Kevin wanted. It *was* the tower atop the Blackstairs Mountains. The Blackbird told him the key code to the lock.

"Very symbolic combination," Kevin said. "Twenty-six counties, plus six counties, equal one Ireland free. Or is it one massive problem gone off the Blackbird's plate? Maybe the whole place blows apart the instant I punch in the combination, taking me out, along with Mattie Joe."

"Kevin, I wouldn't—"

"Save it. Call Sylvia Hickey and tell her to get back to Surrey Manor. She should arrive there about the same time I reach the tower. If she doesn't call me, I don't go in after Mattie Joe. Understand?" He hung up on the Blackbird, thinking how really sad it was that such a small personal victory would give him so much joy.

The car tyres whined as they worked to hug the country road, twisting toward the Blackstairs Mountains. The windscreen wipers pawed hypnotically at the soft rain. Spectral wisps of grey-white fog leapt out of the glens to steal the road, leaving Kevin with the not unfamiliar feeling of being at a loss of control. *Control.* Therein lies the big joke, he thought. When had he ever had control over his life? The Blackbird had taken that away thirty years ago. All Kevin knew at the moment was that the dark side of his soul, the place where he'd hidden all the distrusts that he'd dwelt on when he was alone, was welcoming him back to the road where it had all began. The road hadn't changed an inch during the three decades.

He was seventeen years of age then, and pumped up on blood so hot that it routinely boiled over and burned up whatever two ounces of common sense he might have possessed on any given day. Those two ounces of common sense had already well turned to cold ash on the day his boyhood hero, with tearing eyes and shaking fist, asked *"Will you not join me so Ireland can free itself from the shackles of eight hundred years of British oppression?"* He realized now that, more so than the gobs of money, or the legions of followers, that the most powerful weapon in the Blackbird's considerable arsenal was his gift of fiery speech. He remembered being only ten years of age when the Blackbird described to him a sunrise in such vivid detail as to make it sound like the event was nothing short of pure magic. That very night, the bedroom windowsill was Kevin's pillow. He nodded and dozed but awoke in time to witness that summer red sunrise, starting out as a flaming match head and slowing growing into a glowing ball. That image was etched in his memory as indelibly as his mother's smile. That's how controlling the Blackbird could be.

The windscreen wipers scraped away. Each oscillation left in its wake a new universe of clear droplets, one each for all the sleepless nights and involuntary sunrise sightings that Kevin had known since the Blackbird had implanted his voice into the dark side of his soul.

"Just imagine, Kevin, if ours is the lorry load of guns that brings Ireland her freedom," the Blackbird had exclaimed.

His face glowed red like the sunrise and he seemed no less magic. His eyes danced crazily round like a mad man's. *"The men of the north are mobilized, Kevin. There's going to be a massive battle. It's going to be 1916 all over again. Only this time there's television. And Ireland's struggle will be seen in homes around the world. Nations' leaders will start asking questions. England's human rights violations against the Irish will be front-page news. England will be forced to leave Ireland—forever."* As the Blackbird spoke of the plan in detail, he had used cool military words like "rendezvous" and "stealth."

As a teenager, Kevin had wanted a red face and mad man eyes. So, of course, he had agreed to drive through the rain and fog with the headlamps switched off—that was the stealth part. And since the plan had changed "only slightly," the Blackbird would not accompany Kevin in the lorry, but would *rendezvous* on the side of a forgotten mountain, where once hermit monks lived cloistered in the woods. Together they'd hide *their* guns away into an old round tower. The IRA would smuggle them north for the decisive battle.

The notion that the guns—his and the Blackbird's guns—would be the ones to bring down the army of the wretched Crown, sent chills through the teenage Kevin. There would be a rebel song written about him. If, God forbid, he died while serving Ireland's cause, the song would be called "Bold Kevin O'Felan." Please God, he would live, though, and instead be forever immortalized as "The Blackstairs Mountain Boy." He'd even composed a verse of the song himself and had sung it to calm his nerves, while the lorry's grinding gears shouted his presence throughout the Blackstairs Mountain glens.

> *On a rain drenched night he joined the fight*
> *To free his native land*
> *On a mountain side where saints did hide*
> *Old Ireland would make its stand*

To England's alarm, the rebels were armed
Their enemies they'd destroy
And freedom was won thanks to Ireland's son
The Blackstairs Mountain Boy

The windscreen wipers slapped in waltz time and Kevin found himself humming the silly song for the first time in years. The Blackstairs Mountain Boy now was forty-seven years of age and so lost in the pain and anger of a re-opened wound that he couldn't recall driving through the villages of Thomastown or Inistoige, or any of the hippity-hop roads in between. He wound down a window in hopes that the cold, wet hand of reality would slap him to his senses and make him turn around and go home to his family. Instead, he was grabbed again by unanswered questions of the past.

Why do teenagers only learn lessons the hard way? Why did the Blackbird have to lie to him and not rendezvous? And never once, in the thirty years since, explain himself or apologize? The overriding question, however, was why was he once again rushing through the dark of night to follow the Blackbird's bidding. To find another sunrise?

Having passed through the pub-lit village of Graiguenmanagh, he pulled to the side of the road and, with headlamps turned off, searched through the fog for the Blackstairs Mountains. He found nothing there. The mountains were cloaked within the abyss of the starless night, a massive expanse of nothingness that Kevin thought very much resembled the canvas that he'd been painting for himself these past thirty years. Upon that canvas, he'd painted millions of brush strokes in hopes of understanding why his coming of age revelation had not been about sex and love, but about the lack of trust in the world. But all his colors soon faded and the canvas revealed only darkness. What troubled him most was that he didn't know if the dark canvas wasn't a picture of his own unforgiving heart.

Then a small light interrupted the abyss. No larger than a pinhead, it was a speck of translucence hanging so all alone in the middle of the black sky that it reminded Kevin of that first enthralling and fragile peek of sunrise. With each passing instant, his eyes cut away at the darkness, until the match head sized fire burned away the darkness and all there was, was light. The clear image was there for him to fill with a life-defining color of his choosing.

There flickered a second speck of light, followed by a third, a fourth, then a fifth. Soon, small round crystal balls of light cascaded down the mountainside like a single strand of lights on a Christmas tree. And within that sparkling band, Kevin at last found his missing color. It was clarity— the color of faith. If only he allowed himself to believe—as the Rag Man believed—then the darkness might just, bit by bit, disappear. Staring at the biggest and brightest light at the top of the strand, Kevin allowed himself a small wry grin as he thought of a man who, possessing only faith, had lit the flame for Ireland. "Yes, Mattie Joe, I understand the haunting," he murmured as he turned the ignition. The engine roared in the still night. "Now let's burn it away forever."

Through the open car window gushed a sour-sweet pine breeze, carrying with it ethereal echoes of a chorusing voices singing "The Last Rose of Summer." At the base of the mountain, Kevin found the long strand of lights to be a queue of idling cars illuminating a snaking path leading to the round tower. White light bleached the sweat-slick features of men, women, and children conveying buckets of water taken from a stream up the mountainside. So engrossed were they in their mission and song that none seemed to notice Kevin striding past with his uzi held high in his right hand. The fog-moist mountain air poured like fuel into his lungs, making his breathing surprisingly strong and steady. There was no belly flopping over his belt. His knees felt pain-free and his legs spry as…as a teenager's. A distant siren sliced through the chorus of voices. The fire brigade was on its way. The local Gardai would follow. Within the hour, Mattie Joe Treacy would be dead or captured, Kevin thought.

The round tower stood inside a clearing the size and shape of a traffic roundabout. Where once generations of monks had circled the tower, for long hours of meditative prayer, women now knelt with heads bowed mumbling the rosary for Mattie Joe. Soft rain pushed smoke down on them in an ashen veil. Kevin pressed an arm across his mouth to keep from choking. From a tall pine, a man tossed the buckets of water into the burning tower. Another man stood atop a ladder and hammered away at the tower's steel reinforced door. The droning incantations to Jesus' mother grew louder. They're praying for a miracle, Kevin thought, as he raised his weapon above his head. He lowered it when his mobile phone rang.

"Sylvia? No, listen. I know all about you and the Blackbird. It's your turn to apologize later. Are you at Surrey Manor? Good. What I need for you to do now is to get old Bernie Tolleson to sing a song. Now tell me, is there anyone about that can play the piano?" He heard Sylvia asking if any of the night staff could play the piano. A long silence followed her question and Kevin could see in his mind's eye a confused night staff looking first at one another, then at the poor old creature with the half mutilated face rocking away in a wheelchair. "What about you, Sylvia? Can you not play a piano at all? One finger will have to be enough. What do you mean you don't know "The Last Rose of Summer?" All right, so you never paid attention to the melody. Well pay attention now!"

A crack of gunfire paralyzed those on the mountainside. Kevin shouted, "Special Detective, International division. Everyone move away from the tower now. It's full of explosives. Move!"

The fog thinned and Kevin could see the line of people marching toward the flashing red light of the fire engine, trapped behind the serpentine queue of cars. The Rag Man was his to save or let die. He found himself recalling Finbar Lawlor telling him how an emotionally healthy man sought reconciliation with his past, while the haunted man was driven by the need for a reckoning. Healthy or not, the reckoning was here, Kevin thought. Ascending the wobbling ladder to the tower door, he pressed his lips against the mobile phone and began singing "The Last Rose of Summer." His singing voice was so bad that it would be a miracle if Sylvia Hickey were able to turn his croaking into some sort of recognizable melody. Of course, a miracle was exactly what he was counting on. A miracle in the form of a familiar melody that would unlock a sick old man's long lost memory.

37

Come away, O human child!
To the waters and the wild
With a faery, hand in hand,
For the world's more full of weeping than you
can understand.
W.B. Yeats "The Stolen Child"

When Mattie Joe Treacy found himself swatting away at a steady drizzle of blistering yellow embers, he suspected that igniting a fire inside the round tower wasn't such a smart thing to do, after all. Above him, orange flames clawed at the night sky. Outside, the lads smashing at the tower door hadn't managed to put even a crack in it. The singing was losing its fervor and rising in its wake were voices praying the rosary, letting Mattie Joe know that his situation was dire, since people wouldn't be bothered to pray aloud for any petty petition. In his view, this was all Brian's fault.

If only the pooka hadn't dispensed so many warnings and made each one sound like it would bring on the end of the world, then, maybe, Mattie Joe could have known which advice to follow and which to ignore. If only some of the advice had been constructive instead of being so critical all the time, then, maybe, he wouldn't be stuck inside a stone oven, he thought.

Descending the ladder to the last refuge on the bottom floor, he slumped against the tower wall, letting the cool stone sooth his burning cheeks. The floor above him was, for the moment, intact, leaving only patchy firelight glowing like a child's night-light near the ladder opening. At the fire's present rate, Mattie Joe figured he had thirty minutes, no more.

With a sense of temporary safety also came a weariness that opened his heart and let the anger and fear that had fueled him for the past three days fast drain away. In its place came a pleasant semi-conscious stupor, like the feeling he got when taking a nap after an afternoon drinking session. Closing his eyes to the fire, he heard the peace of his steady breathing, just like the Blackbird had taught him. Below the floorboards where he sat, a generator hummed lowly, like the sound of tractors pulling through faraway meadows at dusk.

The yellow platter sun seeped low into hayfields where Daddy drove the tractor back in a wide circle. Mam chatted with Biddie Tynan across the bracken hedgerow separating their two dairy farms. Mattie Joe could see everyone, but no one could see him. The hay at cutting time was nearly as tall as he, so it was easy for him to spy from below the blanket of stalky green grass. Whenever Mattie Joe wanted to get his mother's attention, all he had to do was start wandering toward the Rag Tree and Mam would come running. He was thinking about wandering over to the Rag Tree now, so Biddie Tynan would have to shut up.

But Mattie Joe was too tired to go to the Rag Tree tonight. Instead, he decided to just lie down for a while until Daddy finished cutting the hay. Mommies were always near. Daddies were always just beyond near. Mommies put you to sleep with a tuck-in song.

"This little light of mine, I'm going to let it shine. This little light of mine I'm going to let it shine..."

Soon, he heard other voices join his mother's, little giggly voices that did not sing the words to his tuck-in song. Turning round and round in the hayfield, he called out over and over, "Mam? Mam?" He found her at the Rag Tree and dancing ring-around-the-rosy atop the knoll, with four very little girls in pink dresses. Mattie Joe had never before seen these curly haired little girls, so he ran through the hay to get a closer look. Daddy's tractor kept roaring and purring. Purring and roaring. Mam kept singing his tuck-in song.

"This little light of mine, I'm going to let it shine. This little light..."

The girls' happy giggles grew louder and louder, but the tractor only purred faintly. Daddy had gone to a faraway field. Mam danced round and round and looked down at her four little girls, all the while, wearing a smile so big it made her eyes disappear.

"These arms of mine, they are burning, bu-urning from wanting you. Thee-eese a-arms of mi-aye-aye-ine, they are wanting, wanting to ho-old you...Sorry for the poor choice of words. Otis Redding, brilliant singer altogether. He burned up, too. But not in a round tower, so. He died in a plane crash in 1968. Before your time, Mattie Joe. By the way, is there any drink about?"

Mattie Joe awoke from his stupor with drool streaming cold over his chin. The image of his mother and the four little girls was still hazy in his brain. A raven emerged from out of the flames, flapping his wide wings three times before finally settling on the ladder. Mam and the four little girls faded into a mist.

"Brian! Thank God you're here. You've been quite the stranger lately," Mattie Joe said, his head clearing of sleep.

"Stranger is it? I seem to remember a certain conversation in the milking parlor where ye told me to get lost. Any drink about, Mattie Joe?" he asked again.

"Jasus, I've told you to get lost loads of times. Why did you have to pick now to listen to me? I'm near burned to death. And, no, there's nary a drop here to comfort a man. It's a harsh environment altogether." He put his cheek back against the stone wall, soaking up the last of the damp coolness.

"Three days sobriety hasn't hurt ye, I'd say. Ye look better for it. Pity ye couldn't stay locked up here for a month." The raven poked his head in and out, then muttered as if thinking aloud. *"Still, it's hard to have a proper farewell without the parting glass. What's that humming I hear?"*

"I think there's a generator powering this kip. It never stops humming. What's this about a parting? Are you going somewhere? You just got here."

Brian did not answer. Instead, he hopped from rung to rung, first down, then up, and then he flapped his wings and alighted on Mattie Joe's right foot.

"A generator? A generator runs on petrol. Ye haven't seen anyone come to fill up a tank, have ye? There's an electric line running in here, somewhere."

"I suppose you're right. Now, what about this parting business?" Mattie Joe pulled his knees into his chest, bringing him eyeball to beak with Brian. There was anger in the pooka's black pellet eyes.

"*That's the problem, Mattie Joe. There's been too many times when ye only supposed I was right. Of course, I'm right. The Daoine Maithe are always right. As for the other matter, well, there's no good way to part, really,*" Brian said, softening his tone. "*It's either slow and heart wrenching, or too sudden, no time to adjust. Either way, we go with our arms outstretched, reaching for what has become just beyond our grasp. Most people eventually do let go and accept the reality of their fates. Most people can only survive a short time hugging shadows and kissing memories. In fact, it's the cause of your troubles, really. Your dreams are far too real. Ye are able to feel the shadows. That's been your real curse.*"

Mattie Joe placed his other cheek against the tower wall. "What are you saying, Brian? And why are you calling me Mattie Joe? You never call me Mattie Joe. You call me "*boyo.*"

"*Lemme see. How can I best put this? Ye remember, of course, how we used to talk about poor Icarus?*"

"Could I ever forget you harping on and on about an eegit who flew too close to the sun? But that's never really been too much a worry of mine. I've got you to protect me. So start protecting, and get me out of this oven before I'm cooked. We can chat later about parting with Icarus."

"*I can't believe I have to do this without the benefit of a drink,*" Brian whined. "*Mattie Joe, I lost that job of protecting ye. The good news is the curse is broken. Ye no longer have to die before your father. Ye can live a long and happy life, and ye can thank your dear mother for that. She broke the curse. She up and walked onto the faery rath by the Rag Tree of Bamford Cross. Pity her timing wasn't better, though, what with ye being stuck here in the round tower and all. What I'm saying, Mattie Joe, is I'm afraid ye have flown too close to the sun this time. I've no powers to get ye* out of this burning tower alive. By the way, it's goddawful warm in here. Ye might think of pulling up that floorboard leading to where that humming sound is coming from. Ye could buy yourself a bit of time, anyway. I'm going to have to leave soon."

Though Mattie Joe wasn't at all pleased with Brian's attitude, he had no other option but to do as the pooka instructed. Slipping his fingers into a gap between the tower wall and the floorboard, he pulled at the inch thick sheet. The nails groaned as the floorboard held fast to the beams. Mattie Joe panted for air.

"It's probably a good time to take stock of what ye have done with your life, Mattie Joe. It appears ye will be answering that question to St. Peter himself soon enough."

Mattie Joe kicked a heel into a second floorboard, stinging his foot, but not putting as much as a dent into the hard wood. "Which would you have me do, pull up the floorboard or take stock of my life? I'll tell you what I've done." His lips quivered and the words caught in his throat. The dam of tears building inside him broke and ran in stinging rivulets over his baked cheeks. "I've never given up, that's what I've done," he cried. He jerked violently at the floorboard, but it only opened a fraction more, still far too small for him to pass through.

"Never given up, ye say? I think ye have given up a lot, Mattie Joe. By the way, there is another side to that floorboard, y'know. Would ye not think about giving the other end of it a pull? Or are ye going to keep fighting with that end until the fire comes?

"Now, where was I? Oh yes, ye don't ever quit. Seems like you quit on a nice girlfriend, no? She could have made ye happy for the rest of your days. She's no time now to cry for any Rag Man. And ye gave up on your loving mother. Ye were calling out to her in your sleep when I flew in. When all is said and done, it's the mothers that we all turn to in our hour of need.

"She was smiling, wasn't she, Mattie Joe? I wonder why is it that the moment someone leaves us, the image we keep is the smile on his or her face. No matter how stern or how much of an old curmudgeon a body is during their lifetime, all that goes away the moment they leave us. And what do we remember? The smile. The good part of people. Only your mother is smiling because she's dancing with her dead baby girls, all lost to miscarriages. All these years she's been missing her dead baby girls. And what did she get from ye, in return, but a life of heartache?"

The pooka flapped up to the top wrung of the ladder.

"Oh, listen to all your fans outside, Mattie Joe. They've already tired of singing that moldy old song of your father's. They'll all be gone before your cold ashes are carted away in a bag. And even the Rag Man will be forgotten before the obituary page yellows and is used to swat flies in the kitchen. Go on and cry, Mattie Joe. Cry hard, because it's the sad truth that tears too often are the prism through which we are able to see how things really are, instead of how we want them to be. So what if ye never gave up? Seems as if that's a family trait. Since your mother never gave up on ye, even though she's long carried the burden of making excuses for a child, who, in her heart of hearts, she knew would never make good in this world. She should have gone to her dead babies, long ago."

"That's not true!" Mattie Joe screamed. Only because the raven had flown out of striking distance, did Mattie Joe pour his fury into ripping at the floorboard. The nails yelped and a sheet of plywood split in half with a loud crack. Mattie Joe, stunned and gasping for air, stared into the hole backlit by the yellow flames shining in from above. Brian returned and landed on his shoulder.

From outside a voice cried, "Special Detective, International division. Everyone move away from the tower now. It's full of explosives and it's going to blow. Move!"

D. P. COSTELLO

Minutes passed. There followed a rustling at the door. The same voice began to sing "The Last Rose of Summer." Whoever it was had a terrible singing voice. By this time, Mattie Joe knew that the tower door would never open.

"Well, would ye look at that? Someone's been hiding something here other than ye, boyo," the raven said.

Brian flew down into the ten-foot hole ahead of Mattie Joe and began pecking his beak against a stack of wood crates visible in the flickering firelight. Mattie Joe followed by dropping onto a hard dirt floor.

There were nine crates stacked three high and three across. Brian pecked away at one of the crates as if his beak were going to bore holes through the lid. Whatever was in the crates was very heavy, because it was all Mattie Joe could do to push the crates away from the third tier, even though his strength had returned, along with renewed hope for survival. Brian flapped his way clear as one of the crates tumbled and broke open. Rifles and bullets spilled out onto the hard earth.

Brian flew in circle round the tower wall, singing merrily, *"Armored cars and tanks and guns, came to take away our sons. And every man must stand behind the men behind the wire...Those guns weren't put here yesterday, boyo. Those are Armelites. There were loads of them smuggled into Ireland during the '70s—the hay days of the Troubles. God! How I loved the '70s! If I had the time, oh the stories I could tell ye about those days...Open another one."*

Mattie Joe opened one crate after another, finding each containing a similar collection of rifles and ammunition. There didn't seem to be anything in the crates to help him, unless he wanted to shoot himself, and Brian.

"Jasus, there's enough gunpowder here to send this tower up like a rocket ship, and ye all the way to Tipperary. Pity all these

*explosives aren't on the next floor up. An explosion there would
split the tower in half and ye could skip away, unless the falling
stone crushed ye first, of course. Look in that last big crate, boyo.
Maybe there's something in there of use to us."*

Mattie Joe moved to open the last crate. It was the
source of all the humming he'd been hearing. He opened
the crate and had the tower wall not been there to brace
him, Mattie Joe would have fallen flat on his back, because
the final crate proved to be no crate at all, but a refrigerator
containing the body of a dead man.

Brian hopped around on the face of a dead man frozen
to a dull grey, like the color of a bad tooth. He had one eye
closed, but the other was wide and glistened in the light
like blue marble. Lips, like two purple worms, twisted
around his toothless gums, coated with crusted brown
blood. Despite the corpse's ghastly appearance, there was
evidence that someone had tried to dignify the body before
stuffing him into a cold box. His black hair had been neatly
brushed straight back and his stiff hands were folded over
black rosary beads, which rested atop a blue hospital gown.
Tucked neatly into the crook of his frozen arm was a bottle
of John Powers whiskey.

*"Hooray, hooray. Let the hooley begin. I knew there'd be some
drink somewhere. It's even cold. Open that bottle, boyo, and pour
us a drop of the old cure."*

"It's Liam Riordon," Mattie Joe said, his shaking hand
running a hasty sign of the cross against his forehead and
chest and shoulders.

*"Well, I guess he didn't escape hospital for too long. He didn't
even have time to put on a decent set of clothes, or shoes. Where's
his teeth?"*

Mattie Joe saw now that poor Riordon, as well as being
blue-grey, leathery, and toothless, was barefoot. He turned

331

his eyes away from the sickly, yellow toenails and suspended a wavering hand over the corpse before closing Riordon's frigid eyelid.

"This man didn't escape from anywhere. He died in hospital, the poor divil. Only someone didn't want that known. No doubt, it is the same someone who locked me away in this tower. No time for embalming or anything. His teeth were taken so the body could not be identified after decomposition."

A man with his teeth ripped out was nothing to stare at for too long, but it was the rotting toenails that most sickened Mattie Joe. He removed his own blue jumper and draped it over the stone hard feet of the deceased. Riordon looked a bit better now.

"That's powerful profound, boyo. Ye could have been an undertaker, so. Ye mean to say that the cold bomb maker here didn't scarper out of hospital and run here to hide in the tower? Ye think maybe it serves someone's purpose that all of Ireland believes there's an IRA fugitive running around barefoot and sucking his gums? Maybe he left his dentures outside?" Brian hopped onto the bottle of whiskey and began pecking at the glass. *"Listen, why don't ye open this found treasure? Ye said yourself ye were aching for a drink. We can have our proper farewell."*

Mattie Joe took a measured look first at Riordon's rigid features, and then slammed the refrigerator door, clipping off a tuft of Brian's blue-black feathers as the startled bird flew hastily back to the ladder.

"You're a nasty, selfish little fucker, Brian. That's Riordon's bottle. We've no rights to it." He took another measured look at the door, then at the wood crates laden with bullets.

"No rights to the whiskey? And since when did Matthew Joseph Treacy become too high and mighty to be drinking someone

else's gargle? B'god, all ye have ever drunk is what someone else was willing to pour down your sorrowful, lousy gullet. Ye were born with your hands in your pockets and they haven't come out with as much as a tuppence since. Now open that cold box and pour us a drink."

"I'm done with drinking. And I've things to do. It's time for you to be flying out of here. Goodbye, Brian."

"Done with drinking, are ye? Take a look around ye, boyo. Ye are done, period. The moment I fly away, ye are on your own now and forever. The great beyond awaits ye in a matter of minutes. Ye think walking up to the Pearly Gates sober is going to make a difference now? I would think a last act of kindness would serve ye better."

The ball of fear and anger that had been growing in Mattie Joe's gut slipped up into his throat as he watched as the raven made a good show of flapping angrily up and around the cramped confines of the tower. Theirs had been a long and twisted journey. The truth of it was, he had lived more of his life with Brian than he had with his own father. If it weren't for the cantankerous bird, Mattie Joe wouldn't be alive today. But it was time to move on. There would be no parting glass.

Mattie Joe put his hand to his forehead and saluted. "Safe journey, Brian. I appreciate you putting out the effort for me."

With that, the raven flew away without another word.

Mattie Joe, his hope and strength renewed, stripped and then dressed himself with Riordon's blue hospital gown. Transferring his own clothes—except for his shoes—onto a stone-cold dead man proved to be a difficult task, since none of the body parts moved. Neither did Riordon cooperate when Mattie Joe tried pulling him from the refrigerator. It was like lifting a felled tree. He then began tossing box after

333

box of bullets onto the floor above until his back ached and weary arms hung limply at his sides. Now fully lathered in sweat, he extended one leg into the refrigerator, as someone might test the temperature of the sea. The frigid air swiped across his burning skin and Mattie Joe wondered would he catch his death of cold. Then, in what he thought would be his last act before entombing himself, he called up through the hole in the floor. "Whoever you are, get away from that door now. This kip is going to blow any moment."

The voice answered. "Mattie Joe Treacy, come to the door. Your father is on the phone."

38

Then there came a blast.

Detective Kevin O'Felan stood on a ladder punching an index finger against the lock's digital pad. He could see the red numbers illuminate and hear the lock tumblers click, but the deadbolt had been so damaged from hammering that it was hopelessly impacted inside the stone wall. Over the mobile phone, Kevin could hear an old man's labored breathing. In the background, Sylvia Hickey was plunking out halting notes belonging to "The Last Rose of Summer." From the top of the tower, flaming yellow and red tongues lurched and licked the pine needles on nearby high hanging branches. Kevin's feet ached from the standing on the ladder so long.

From inside the tower came muffled voices. As in more than one. Either Mattie Joe Treacy was speaking in tongues, or someone else had made it inside the tower, Kevin thought. But how was that possible? If someone had been able to unlock the door, then why wouldn't Mattie Joe have escaped? Looking into the fire-lit sky, Kevin saw a small arched opening fifteen feet below the top of the hundred-foot tower that only a bird could get through. "No way," he muttered aloud. The supposition presently teasing his sense of reason was sheer lunacy. Wasn't it?

Putting an ear to the fire-heated steel door was like laying his head next to a frying pan. Each time he tried he captured only snippets of an argument before having to pull his head away.

"Cry hard...Never give up..."

"Guns...Liam Riordon...Rag Man..."

"Hooray...Let's drink..."

There was pitiful crying mixed with angry screams followed by prolonged silence, but there were never quite enough words strung together for Kevin to make sense of any of it, except for the mention of the guns, for which he needed no elaboration. At last, he clearly heard Mattie Joe say, "Good-bye, Brian." At that moment, Kevin wished a grey sheet of fog would sweep across the tower and protect him from having to accept that he ever saw a raven named Brian soaring from the tower window and flying in an S-shaped pattern above the spouting flames. From inside the tower came the CRACK, then PING of a bullet exploding in the fire. Kevin's legs instinctively headed down the ladder. He had to move before what had now become a steady stream of CRACKS and PINGS became one big BOOM!

Then a voice called from within the tower. "Whoever you are, get away from that door now. This kip is going to blow any moment."

Kevin halted his descent down the ladder and cried, "Mattie Joe Treacy, come to the door. I've got your father on the phone."

The trees' heated sap snapped like high-pitched gunfire and Kevin instinctively jerked away his head and shoulders, causing the unsteady ladder to lose its footing.

Falling away from the tower was like being attached to a string that gave way a begrudging inch at a time, like the drag on a fishing line during a big catch. Kevin felt his hands break free from the ladder and his arms spread from his shoulders like wings. His mobile phone floated gracefully next to him. A large black bird moved out of the small arched window and sailed through the misty grey sheets of ash and fog. The blackness in Kevin's life was gone. All was light. The raven caught the mobile phone in his beak and held it close to his ear. The piano was sweet and light. Single drops of melody dripped like dewdrops from heaven, and mingled with low raspy whispers that echoed with joy. Kevin had found Mattie Joe Treacy's father.

"'Tis the last rose of summer, left blooming all alone. All her lovely companions are faded and gone..."

Kevin collided with the earth. He felt his spine breaking through his chest and the worst pain he'd ever experienced cut through his entire body. His legs would not move.

Then there came a blast.

"...Since the lovely are sleeping, go sleep now with them..."

He watched the tower falling toward him.

"...And freedom was won thanks to Ireland's son...The Blackstairs Mountain Boy..."

337

39

He was an old pooka now...

The first explosion to rip through the Blackstairs Mountains that night blew the door off the round tower like a cork from a pop gun. After a loud POP, a hole appeared in the tower's gut and the old stone sanctuary wobbled at the waist. The top half of the tower was still pitching unsteadily when a booming blast severed it at the ground. Blocks of stone rolled over the mountain like pebbles tossed from a giant's hand. The explosion caused the crowd of people gathered at the base of the mountain to cease their praying and fall to their knees in fear. The ensuing fire charred a black scar into the forest. Brian kept watch on the fiery round tower while hovering safely above.

He was an old pooka now and he'd seen Ireland burn many times before, though it had been a long time since he'd seen something as sorrowful as the holy tower crumbling to the ground. At daybreak, curls of white smoke still wafted from the earth, like steam out of something just taken from an oven. Brian sat perched on the naked branch of a charred pine tree, looking down through a soft rain at the sad black hole in the side of the mountain. The crime scene investigators had wrapped yellow tape around the old tower clearing. Half a dozen men dressed in boots and rubber gloves meticulously picked through the rubble of stone and ash. They were just starting the job and had not yet come upon the freezer—or a body.

Peering into the crater where the round tower had stood were two somber figures wearing tan trenchcoats. When Brian quietly flew down to the ground to get a closer look, he saw that one was the big cop who'd dragged Mattie Joe into becoming the Rag Man. The other was his pretty detective girlfriend. Raindrops gathered over Doyle's brow and dripped off the tips of the woman's long dark lashes. It was hard to differentiate between rain and tears. Sometimes Brian thought there wasn't much of a difference anyway. In Ireland, the sky was often crying over sorrow-drenched faces like Peter Doyle's. Sometimes the tears flowed hard, but most times they were soft and steady, like today. The girlfriend rubbed the small of Doyle's back with one hand, while holding a folded newspaper against her hip in the other.

Brian didn't care a'tall about the big man's tears. What worried him was the newspaper getting wet before he had a chance to read it. He was dying to know what the journalists had to say about last night's big events, and if people had finally figured out what he had known all along. If there were any justice in it a'tall, he would get a mention in the paper, seeing as how it was he who had looked after Mattie Joe all these years. Hopping closer, he saw that the portion of the newspaper showing was the front page below the fold. On it were two color photographs. One showed a young man, handsome and smiling. The other was of an old man whose face was badly scarred. The headline below the fold read "Rag Man Dad Found?" Brian couldn't read the small print, but then again he didn't have to. It had been donkey years since he'd laid eyes on Tim Treacy, but if he lived to be a hundred and a day, he would recognize that the young man with the twinkling eyes and easy grin and the poor old soul with the ravaged face were one in the same person.

He was quite sure Mattie Joe got the day's headline. But the woman never came near enough for Brian to read the paper. She was too busy consoling the big cop by squeezing his hand and saying, "Kevin will pull through. He's strong." Her words only served to make her boyfriend weep even larger tears. Because he had neither the patience nor the energy to watch a big man cry, Brian flapped over to where two of the inspectors were poking through the stones. He wished, though, they would just get on with it and go over the refrigerator turned on its side.

What used to be a white steel box was now charred grey and black and didn't look too much different than the tower's stone blocks surrounding it. Brian flew over and alighted on the battered appliance. He cawed and flapped his wings, but the inspectors kept their heads rooted along the ground. Every few moments, they picked up pieces of old rifles with their gloved hands and examined them. They chatted idly as they worked.

"Last word was he resigns at noon today, on the condition that the tribunal on the gun charges is called quits," said one inspector. He looked through the upper half of a pair of bifocals at the butt of a rifle while holding it at arms length. "This is the end of Desmond O'Hanrahan," he added.

Brian gave up on the two inspectors and turned his attention squarely on Peter Doyle. He squawked until the large cop had no choice but to turn his sullen eyes toward the commotion. There was a second's confusion, and then the recognition that made the big man tremble. For a moment, Brian thought he might see a second tower tumble. The girlfriend grabbed Doyle by the elbow, supporting him. "What is it," she asked. But Doyle was already pulling away and moving toward the ice box.

"Turn it over and look inside," Brian said. And he could tell by Doyle's glassy stare that he had heard him. In the months ahead, Doyle would hear and see a number of things that he had been blind and deaf to until now. Being scared within an inch of one's life will do that to a person, Brian knew.

Doyle was a strong man, and to Brian's delight, he had no problem turning the bulky appliance over with a single push.

"Open it. Hurry," Brian said.

Doyle opened the refrigerator door.

"It's a foot," one of the inspectors called, interrupting Doyle. The inspector held up in his rubber gloves what looked like piece of coal with toes. "The bugger wasn't wearing any shoes. Oh, oh, here's a hand," he said after walking another five meters and digging under a stone. He put the body parts into a plastic bag, and then said to Doyle. "We're likely to be finding pieces of him for hours."

Doyle reached into the refrigerator. His hand emerged clutching a bottle of whiskey. "Where is he?" the big cop shouted. "I'm talking to you, Brian. Did he get away? Goddamnit, answer me!"

Brian flew in a low circle around the tower clearing and cawed as loud and shrill as he could while Peter Doyle ranted at him. Brian wasn't about to answer. He'd let Doyle wonder until his grave whether or not he had indeed heard a pooka speak. Besides, Brian wasn't about to give up Mattie Joe that easily, even though at the moment he was sorely peeved at him. One look at the half full whiskey bottle was all he needed to see that blackguard Mattie Joe hadn't given up drinking a 'tall.

After circling the clearing a few more times just to torment the outraged Doyle, it was time to fly home and take the rest that he more than well deserved.

He glided over the quilted farmlands, flapping his wings only when necessary. The rain was heavy on his feathers and he was oh so weary now. Mattie Joe had been tough duty for an old pooka, but to be honest, he'd do it all over again if given the chance. Still, as he sailed back for Bamford Cross, he looked down on the lazy cows below and thought how nice it might be to finish his days as one of those lumbering beasts, just eating and sleeping without a care in the world. Wherever he was, he wouldn't have far to go. He sure as hell wouldn't have to fly the thirty-two counties chasing after eegits with a dream.

He landed with a sigh on a high and comfortable branch of the Rag Tree and was looking forward to a long nap when he saw a solitary figure trudging up the lane. It was the Daoine Maithe's old nemesis, Biddie Tynan, coming to spoil his peaceful homecoming.

Biddie was dressed in Wellington boots and a drab coverall coat that stopped just short of an old blue dress that Brian hadn't seen her wear since her cow-milking days. Her dyed hair was tousled; white roots ran in a row down the center of her scalp. Her face was wan with grief. Gone was the rouge on her cheeks and mischievous twinkle in her eyes. Gone were the riding boots and hip hugger blue jeans. Gone was the other pea in the pod. As she drew closer, Brian could see that her small eyes were red and swollen—more tears for Ireland, he thought.

Biddie gave the red kitchen door one aching glance and then turned and marched, with purpose, toward the Rag Tree. Biddie had never before come to the Rag Tree. She'd always been a non-believer and, in Brian's view, a spineless sort as well. The better part of Biddie's spine was in hospital, along with the other pea in the pod. But the talkative little woman must have grown a new backbone, now that she was on her own. Biddie held her hands deep in the pockets of the old coverall. From one pocket, she pulled a scrap of cloth, dabbed at a tear, and then slowly tied it to a branch, loosely, so it had a better chance of falling off. He watched her dab away the last of her tears with a bare finger, then wag that same finger at the rag she'd just tied to the tree. "Don't you be staying on there long," she said with a wink. Then she headed to the milking parlor to milk her best friend's cows.

Sooner or later, they all come around, Brian thought. Even after the tears are dry, the hope endures. And at the end of the day, people will believe in anything, if there's a need to.

Epilogue

Mr. and Mrs. Kevin Joseph O'Felan
Cordially invite you to the
Marriage of their daughter,
Siobhán Marie
to
Liam Michael Kehoe
In St. Patrick's Church
2:30 in the afternoon
Saturday 21 July
Reception to follow in the Great Room of
Clontarf Castle
Howth Road, Dublin

Any father wonders how he will react on the day Daddy's little girl leaves him to become another man's wife. Will I smile? Will I cry? Will I lock my jaw with a rigid teeth-grinding grin, for her sake, every time I greet the unworthy creature stealing away a piece of my heart? Kevin O'Felan had privately fretted for years about his eldest daughter's wedding day, but now that he was living the moment, his heart swelled with a joy the likes of which he had never known.

His brothers, Pat and James, each took a hand as they cautiously lifted him out of the wheelchair like a plank of wood rotating on its end. They then placed him into the waiting arms of his precious Siobhán. Though the back brace holding together his damaged vertebrae allowed just enough mobility for him to gently rock back and forth, he felt as if the love burning in his daughter's brown eyes could hold him upright long enough for him to grow wings to fly. This would be his only dance. Mary stood close by clutching the wheelchair; she would swoop in and catch him the moment the song was over.

The wedding singer crooned, "You are my sunshine, my only sunshine. You make me happy when skies are grey. You never know dear how much I love you. Please don't take my sunshine away..."

There were three hundred guests inside the great room of the lavishly restored tenth century castle, yet only two sets of dry eyes. Kevin allowed himself a gratifying look around the reception hall. "Is it everything you've ever dreamed of, Siobhán?" he asked, thinking how far the occasion was succeeding beyond his own wildest dreams.

"I'm looking at everything I ever dreamed of," his daughter asserted.

Now there was only one pair of dry eyes. Siobhán wiped a finger across his cheek and held him fast with her smile.

The song ended to enthusiastic applause and Mary wheeled him back to a round table, where, for the moment, they sat alone. The five-piece band pounded out hard driving '60s Soul music that filled the dance floor.

If it was only love that could impress his daughter, at least his wife was moonstruck by the castle's grandeur.

Mary wore a yellow chiffon dress off the shoulder. Her flaming red hair clung in ringlets to the nape of her neck. All afternoon, her eyes had been racing around the beautiful castle. She'd clutched her chest so many times that Kevin wondered should he have brought a paper bag.

"You were magnificent," she cooed into his ear.

"Was I? I don't think I've heard those words from you since *our* wedding day. Or was it the wedding night?"

Mary slapped him on the wrist. "Have you spoken to your second cousin yet?" Have you thanked him for getting us this castle?" She leaned close and whispered, "People are saying that a reception here goes for fifty thousand and then some. Everyone is wondering how you managed it. I say, let them wonder."

"It's 'and then some,' and then some more. And, no, I haven't spoken to him. I'm slow making the rounds at the moment." Kevin slapped the handles of the wheelchair. "Besides, I'm the father of the bride. It's his duty to call on me. Any more of those barbecued prawn starters stuck on the skewers with the pineapple?"

He lifted a pint of ale to his lips. Mary frowned.

"The prawns are long gone," she said "But there's plenty of potato soup left, if you're still hungry. How's the medication holding up? You have to stay ahead of the pain, y'know. And not by drinking. How many have you had? You will tell me when it's time to go back to hospital?"

While there was concern in Mary's eyes, Kevin knew that the last thing she would want him to do was to leave this dream early. He'd been in hospital for a month and had to report back that evening to be restrung in traction for another week. Nor for an instant did he think that Mary really minded him taking a drink. She was only protesting out of a sense of duty.

As it was his duty to defend himself.

"Woman, I'm here on loan from hospital. Could you not spare me a couple of drinks on our daughter's wedding day? This is my second," he said, holding up a half-full glass of brown ale. Mary would know that he was lying by one pint, at least.

Finbar Lawlor interrupted the debate when he came twisting past shouting, "R-E-S-P-E-C-T. That's what my baby means to me..." The psychologist's big rump nearly knocked the drink out of Kevin's hand.

"Mind that caboose, Finbar. The chief inspector here is counting dropped drink against my ration."

Finbar laughed. So did Mary. And Kevin pondered how wonderful it was that among the many things for him to be grateful for on this day, his heart still fluttered at seeing his own bride so happy.

Love had changed for them since they were Siobhán's age. Love was more often endurance than it was kisses. Love was putting dreams on hold for so long that, one day, those dreams were gone and you had new ones. At least today he was able to give Mary a dream wedding for their eldest daughter. He surprised his wife when suddenly he took her hands and held them to his chest. "Have you ever thought that God gives us moments like these so we will have a small glimpse at the perfect happiness of heaven?"

"That is a very nice thought. But don't be thinking too much about heaven. I nearly lost you to heaven a month ago. I'm not ready for you to go."

A body can only contain so much emotion before it starts spilling out somewhere, Kevin thought. Mary was on the verge of weeping a month's worth, when Peter Doyle and the stunning new girlfriend stepped in to say hello. Mary somehow gathered her emotions in time to make a quick study of the tall woman with the matching sky blue dress and eyes. Kevin raised his glass and sang, "I have often heard it said by me mother and me father, that going to a wedding is the making of another…"

It was fun seeing big Peter blush. Mary slapped Kevin's hand, again. "Hush," she said.

Peter presented the slender, black-haired beauty. "Róisín Tiernan, I'd like you to meet the parents of the bride. This is Mary. And this…this is my…" He stopped, choking on his words.

Kevin extended a hand. "I was his partner. Retired now. Full disability. Even though the doctors say I'll be jogging again within a year." He smiled and gave the wheelchair another slap.

Peter Doyle gathered himself while shaking his head. "More than a partner. My mentor. The most honest and decent man ever to serve in the Special Detectives."

Mary broke in to keep things from becoming a sentimental slobber-fest. "She's lovely, Peter. And a lucky girl, I'll add."

Kevin clasped Doyle by the sleeve and pulled him down to where he could whisper in his ear. "Peter, would you not do me a favor and ask Mary out for a dance? I hate to see her stuck with me at the table. And have young Kevin bring me another pint."

"I will, of course, Peter Doyle said."

At that moment, Mary gasped, "Here he comes, Kevin's second cousin. Have you met him?" she asked Róisín. "Their mothers are first cousins," she added.

As the recently resigned Taoiseach of Ireland kissed Mary on her blushing cheek, Kevin fidgeted in the wheelchair. The air around him suddenly became as stiff and heavy as the back brace squeezing him. An animated Des O'Hanrahan—his second cousin—showered compliments on everyone, and then released Mary to dance with his godson. Des settled into a chair next to Kevin, pulling it close to keep their conversation private.

"I didn't know if I'd ever see you again, let alone here today. I'm honored by the invitation. Siobhán is ravishing. Reminds me of her mother on her wedding day. You're looking well, all things considered," Des said.

"Not too bad, thanks. A month in traction has stretched me out so much that I'm finally over the Gardai height requirements. You've had a few bumps yourself, lately, of a different kind. The Eire Nua referendum got cut off at the knees, but you look as if you're still on your feet. The television makes you look older."

"Aye. It's been a rapid fall from grace, to be sure, but the landing has been soft enough. Between you and me, I'm happier for it. Mind you, I would have preferred to step down on my own volition and with my legacy intact, but… sure time cures all, they say." Des shrugged his shoulders and his tiny eyes bounced like grey marbles inside his round, cherub face. It was the happy face that Kevin remembered once belonging to Citizen O'Hanrahan, before he became the iconic stranger called "Des the Decent."

"To be honest, you do look better for it. The layers of worry are gone from your face. You look younger, like someone…" Kevin stopped just short of saying, *"Someone I knew long ago."*

Des rescued an awkward silence, saying, "Any man would look younger being rid of that job. Being a single man for the past month hasn't hurt me either. I wonder do all bachelors sleep well?"

Young Kevin slipped in and conspiratorially pulled a pint of ale from inside the jacket of a black tuxedo identical to his dad's, except for the ravaged white rose boutonniere drooping from his lapel. "Peter told me not to get caught by Ma," he announced proudly. "Hello, Des. Sorry about you not being the Taoiseach anymore. It's unfair."

"You've gotten tall, young Kevin. Past your father already, I'm sure."

Kevin pointed a finger at Des. "What are you drinking? Still Jameson's neat, is it? Kevin, go fill Des's glass. And keep a look out on your mother," he said. Once young Kevin was out of earshot, he added, "You mentioned Mairead, in a roundabout way. How is she?"

Des chuckled and then shrugged dismissively. "That woman is up the loo at the moment. Her secret admirer is out of the picture—literally and figuratively. Neither of them can show their faces in Ireland, on account of the naked photographs. Besides, there's no home for her to come back to. I've put the house up for sale. And with me being gone from office, she's no job either. She's stuck on the Riviera without a paddle, you might say." Des chuckled again. "Maybe the sun will help dry her out. I'll bring her home when her head is back in order."

"Bad luck for her that there was an Irish photographer on the beach that recognized her. The detective in me would wonder was someone paid to get the incriminating photographs?"

"And we all know what a good detective you are," was Des's way of answering the question. "Big funeral," he said, changing the subject. "Bigger even than Dan O'Toole's. And what about the irony of him being laid in the same grave that all these years was thought to be his father's? Now the father is found to be alive and the Rag Man is gone." He heaved a heavy sigh, then smiled at the dancers whipping past. "A piece of me would have liked to have attended that funeral, but it would have been massively inappropriate. Of course, some like to claim that the Rag Man himself wasn't in attendance."

"Forensics and medical reports disagree with those claims."

"Forensics and medical reports can be changed as easily as hiring someone to take incriminating photographs. Would the detective in you not want to find out why there's been neither sight nor sound of Liam Riordon this past month?"

"The detective is on the pension, remember?" It was Kevin's way of saying, "No."

Des nodded. "Ah, but at the end of the day, people love a mystery, so. And now they've got a good one to chew on for some time. In the years to come, I suppose we'll be hearing about Rag Man sightings, just like we do about Elvis, the poor 'ol divil."

Kevin stifled a laugh when he saw a reflective look veil his cousin's face. Young Kevin returned with the Jamesons. The band kept Mary on the dance floor by playing an old time Irish waltz called "The Galway Shawl." Ireland's deposed leader twirled the glass in his hand and stared at the clinking ice cubes. His head jerked instinctively at the sound of a fiddle.

"At the end of the day, we're all the sum of our experiences, wouldn't you say, Kevin? The decisions we make, the things that happen to us, it all goes into forming the persons we become. I think the secret is, do we embrace our experiences and use them to build ourselves into becoming something better, or do we let them slowly eat away at us, like a cancer?" He sipped at the whiskey. "The past few months have presented me with many experiences. I plan to use them to make a better Desmond O'Hanrahan."

More than his words, it was the tone Des used that spooked Kevin most. Not the voice of the vainglorious speechifying politician, who lived upon a pedestal above an adoring nation, but the raw honesty of the second cousin whose shadow he had chased since leaving the cradle. "You have plans?" Kevin asked, grasping for words, then immediately regretting the ones he chose.

Des's chest puffed up and the grey marbles again began spinning inside his head. The moment of humility was gone.

"I do. I've set up my own consulting operation. It's quietly been in the works for some time, really. Years, only I couldn't tell a soul. I'll be helping governments of emerging nations to attract foreign companies to set up operations in their countries. I've got all the business contacts. And two contracts already. It's big money, Kevin. *Big money.* A man could retire for what I'm being paid by one country alone."

Kevin listened, nodded, grinned, and then stuck his face inside the pint glass. He did everything he could to disguise a feeling of being punched in the gut. He could only conclude that, at the end of the day, some people were born with all the luck. Sure, he had been lucky to survive the fall from the ladder, but Desmond O'Hanrahan had fallen so much farther than he, only to be caught in the soft and promising hands of opportunity.

Kevin, feeling he needed more space to harbor his resentment, wheeled his chair back a couple of paces. But Des pulled his chair in until their knees met.

"It's a big job, Kevin. I need help. Honestly, I was hoping to get *your* help. If you could see yourself working with me, that is. Security is a compulsory component to the consulting services. These countries need to know how to assure the corporate bosses that there are no civil issues that would harm their investments. Who better for such a job than a top man from the International Cooperation Unit?"

At that moment, Kevin considered it fortuitous to be stuck in a wheelchair, because if he had been standing the breeze from the passing dancers would have been enough to blow him over. "That's why you had me transferred into the ICU. It's why I was sent to England."

Des nodded. "You've got the résumé. I need a partner."

"Partner? As in fifty-fifty?"

"More like forty-forty-twenty. Like I said, it's a big job. I think we need some younger legs to join us. We'll be better for it in the long run."

"Peter Doyle, of course," Kevin said, his ears still ringing. *"A man could retire for what I'm being paid by one country alone!"*

Des screwed his face as if he'd just bit into a lemon. He shook his head. "No, Peter was born with a silver spoon in his mouth; he doesn't need the knife and fork given to him as well. Besides, he's plans of his own, so. He and the new bird have resigned from the Gardai Síochána. Something he saw up on that mountainside spooked the b'jasus out of him. Anyway, he's convinced his father to build a golf course at Doyle Manor and he's going to open a golf camp for children from the north. Mixed teams, Catholic and Protestants. Walk eighteen holes with someone and you get to know them pretty well. It's a good idea. And to tell you the truth, I'm proud of him. He was never the sort to look much further than a mirror. Like I said, something up on that mountainside spooked the hell out of him. Róisín will be his partner, and his wife, too, if he doesn't fuck it up." He paused and searched the dance floor until he found who he wanted. "No, I had someone else in mind for the third man. Someone good with numbers. Isn't your new son-in-law an accountant?"

The waltz ended. Mary was heading back to the table. The band member playing the fiddle now held the instrument over his head and began chanting into the microphone, "Des...Des...Des..." The guests picked up the cue and clapped their hands in rhythm with their cries of, "Des...Des...Des..." Siobhán stood nearby with her hands folded against her chest. She mouthed the word, *"Please."*

Des stood up. "Can't refuse the bride, now can I? We'll save telling Liam until after the honeymoon," he said, and walked toward the bandstand as he played to the crowd by pumping an arm in the air to their cheers.

"Save what?" Mary asked, sitting down. "Save what?"

But Kevin wouldn't speak...couldn't speak. His eyes were locked on his cousin Des tucking the fiddle under his chin, as naturally as a father would tuck a child against his shoulder. He gave the bow a few quick test pulls over the strings, and then played a sprite hornpipe that brought the guests rushing back to the dance floor. Some of them knew how to do the proper "Stack of Barley" dance, but others did jigs or reels or just jumped up and down.

The tears were now welling heavy in Kevin's eyes and he would make no effort to stop them.

Mary saw his tears, too, and smiled. "Oh, I know how much it means to you to have the real Irish music at the wedding. And it's just wonderful to hear him play again. I've always loved this tune. It's so bouncy and...well it just makes people happy. Do you know the name of it, dear?"

Yes, he knew the name of it. But, at the moment, he was seeing in his glistening eyes the sparkle of a new sunrise. He swallowed, and then squeezed his wife's hand. "The name of that tune is "The Blackbird.""

The End

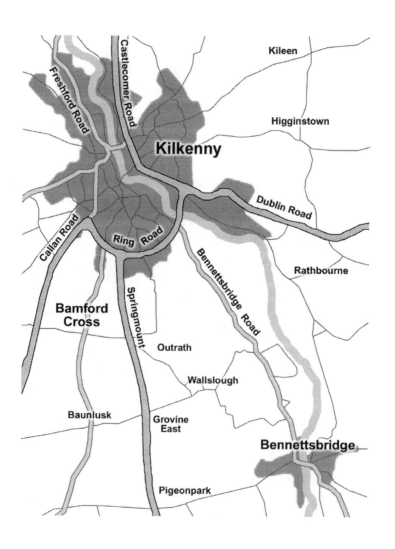

Kileen

Higginstown

Castlecomer Road

Freshford Road

Kilkenny

Dublin Road

Callan Road

Ring Road

Rathbourne

Bennettsbridge Road

Bamford Cross

Springmount

Outrath

Wallslough

Baunlusk

Grovine East

Bennettsbridge

Pigeonpark

Acknowledgements

I really can't remember when I began writing *The Rag Tree*, but it was sometime in the 1980s. The story, in its finished form, bears little resemblance to what I wrote in the early goings, though it is without question the culmination of a long (very long) singular effort. I've come to think of it as being like the bay at the mouth of a long and winding (especially winding) river.

Ireland was very much different back then. An ancient culture, but only sixty years a nation, it remained rooted in a struggling agricultural economy, suffering from the continuous loss of its young people through the slow bloodletting of emigration, and the "troubles"—the eight hundred year plus struggle for independence from England— were in the midst of one of the most volatile periods in generations. As for me, in my footloose twenties at the time, I admit to having been infatuated by it all: the romance of its history, the wit and wisdom of its literature, the beauty and passion of its music, and the magic contained within a certain black beer. The enchanted land and noble people I had heard about since the cradle had become manifest.

The new millennium has brought Ireland its "Celtic Tiger" boom economy and unprecedented prosperity. The troubles in the north have abated, thanks to the historic 1999 Good Friday Peace Accord. I quip sometimes about the length of time it has taken to write *The Rag Tree* by saying, I started to write a book about war and then peace broke out. But what I've come to understand about *The Rag Tree* was that it required every day it took to write (and rewrite), because through the journey of the story's own growing pains, it became a story of a country and its people amid a historic transition.

To say the very least, my long and winding journey was not without its ports of call and safe harbors, these being the many friends who provided support and guidance without which I would not have been able to ever finish. They include:

From the earliest days...

Ginny Howard, Joe Ranalli, Jimmy Nalls, Tom Guay, Joe Viola, and Ted Skowron, all of who were willing to listen (and listen) to my ever-formulating ideas.

John Moore for arranging a certain clandestine meeting that provided background information essential to creating the Maze Prison scene.

For the writers who have mentored me:

Alice McDermott, Jack O'Connell, Denis Collins, Michael Farquhar, Michael Dolan, Chiquita Mullins Lee, Brody Mullins.

John Deegan for his ongoing support and especially for printing draft copies of the book from which I was able to obtain vital feedback.

Lisa Monias for designing the book jacket

For the faculty of Gonzaga College High School, past and present, especially Andrew Battaile, Helen Free and Rick Cannon, for their encouragement and guidance.

Molly and Larry Goldberg for providing me the use of their beach house for "writer's escape."

Anne Mitchell, my friend from Belfast who gave *The Rag Tree*, and me, a boost when I needed it most.

Edie Mulholland, the unsinkable one. She never let me quit. I miss her.

Michelle Mulholland France, for being a marvelous editor and an even more marvelous friend.

Priscilla Flynn, for keeping the PR machine running

Pindar Van Arman, for the gift of his artistry

Father Bill Sampson, S.J., for convincing me that I should write.

And to the people in Ireland who through the years have time and again opened for me the doors of their homes and their hearts, including:

My Irish cousins, the Costellos and Folans from the village of Cornarone in County Galway, and the Boyles of Castleisland and Castlemaine, County Kerry.

Gemma Langton Loli, my friend and band mate with the Fabulous Potato Heads, who first told me of the legend of the Rag Tree of Bamford Cross.

My best friend, Michael Hickey of Kilree, County Kilkenny. For thirty years he has been the giving hand that never falters.

My Irish great-aunts Nora and Kate, who long ago planted the seeds for this book by making Ireland real for our family.

And most of all...

For the love of my wife and best friend, Chris, who was with me on this journey from the start, and for our children, Sean, Cara, and Christie, all of whom joined along the way. We did it, Gang.

Glossary of Terms

Barry, Kevin – Eighteen year old medical student hung by the British in 1920.

Birmingham Six – Initially found guilty of carrying out a 1970s IRA bombing mission in England, the group's convictions were subsequently overturned after having served several years in prison.

blackguard – scoundrel

blackthorn – a type of bush common to Irish hedgerows

Bord Failte – Irish Tourist Board

cé n scael – what's the story?

chockablock – crowded, full

Collins, Michael – Irish leader in 1916 rebellion and War of Independence, subsequently killed by anti-Treaty sympathizers in 1922.

cueness – attention

Daoine Maithe – good folk, faeries

eegit – idiot

Emmet, Robert – Led ill-fated rebellion in 1803 and was subsequently executed

Fenian – A group founded in the 19th century term to establish Irish independence, the term is commonly used to describe association with Irish nationalism.

gaol – jail

Guilford Four – Initially found guilty of carrying out a 1970s IRA bombing mission in England, the group's convictions were subsequently overturned after having served several years in prison.

loose chippings - gravel

Hunger strikers – Hunger strike had been used as a form of political protest in Ireland several times during the Twentieth Century. The most notable of these hunger strike protests occurred in 1981 when ten men died of starvation while protesting prisoners' rights.

Oglaigh na hEireann – Army of Ireland

Pearse, Padraig – 1916 Rebellion leader, subsequently executed

Penal Times – A period beginning in 1695 and lasting until 1829 during which harsh colonization policies known as the Penal Codes were enacted for the purpose of eradicating Catholicism in Ireland.

Provisionals (Provos) – Provisionals is the name adopted by the Irish Republican Army (IRA) in the 1969 to distinguish itself from the "Official" IRA, which at the time was not engaged in armed aggression against the British.

quid –slang for the Irish or British pound

Red Hand of Ulster – symbol used (as on a flag) to denote the province of Ulster

RTE – Radio Television Ireland

Sands, Bobby – Died in 1981 after sixty-six days on hunger strike

scarper – escape

screw – prison guard

shite – expletive

Special Powers Act – A controversial act of security legislation viewed by Irish nationalists as tool of oppression.

Taoiseach – the Irish equivalent of Prime Minister

tíg – house

Troubles – periods of open armed conflict against the British

Twenty-six counties – the Republic of Ireland

Ulster – Commonly used as a synonym for Northern Ireland, Uster is one of the historic four provinces of Ireland. Ulster contains the "Six Counties" under British rule and three counties which are part of the Republic of Ireland.

Wellingtons – rubber boots

Wolfe Tone, Theobald – Regarded as the "Father of Irish Republican Movement", he was a leader in the 1798 Rebellion.

The Rag Tree at Bamford Cross, County Kilkenny